WARNING TRACK

WARNING TRACK

A BASEBALL NOVEL

Jack Corrigan

PEAKVIEW PRESS

2005

Warning Track
Copyright © 2005 by Jack Corrigan
Published by Peakview Press

All rights reserved. No part of this book may be reproduced
(except for inclusion in reviews), disseminated or utilized in any form
or by any means, electronic or mechanical, including photocopying,
recording, or in any information storage and retrieval system,
or the Internet/World Wide Web without written permission
from the author or publisher.

Book design by The Floating Gallery
www.thefloatinggallery.com

Printed in the United States of America

Library of Congress Control Number 2005901674
ISBN 0-9766615-0-0

To My Parents

*They taught me everything
that was important about Life.*

ACKNOWLEDGEMENTS

It was a wonderful experience making this story come to life, and I owe numerous people my deepest appreciation for their knowledge and support in making this happen. As a neophyte in this business, I am grateful to the people who provided insight and instruction. My good friend, Chuck Kyle, an outstanding teacher and coach, provided much of the early direction as I tried to bring this story together. Jim Neff, a high school classmate and a terrific writer himself, pointed me in the right way at a time when the project stalled. Thanks to Larry Leichman and Joel Hochman of The Floating Gallery for their guidance, and special kudos to my editor, Jerine Watson, who added so much to *Warning Track*'s final flavor.

I must acknowledge some special people. Jeff Kingery and Tom Hamilton are wonderful broadcasters, but they are even better friends. Mike Fucci and Bill Applebee have believed in this project for a long time, and their overwhelming friendship and support allowed it to become a reality. Most of all, I owe so much to George Soos. He was the one who convinced me that I could write this story, and he made certain that it came together. To just call him a friend seems so inadequate, but I am certain he knows how much he means to me.

Finally, I cannot ever thank enough my wife, Lisa, and my children, Megan and Mike, for their patience. They probably thought I had lost it when I informed them of my intention to write a novel, but with their love and understanding throughout the process, I was able to make it.

I have been so blessed by my family; they make everything worthwhile. Likewise for my parents and my siblings, who have always supported everything I have attempted. Dad was not able to see this book in print, but I know his guiding hand was still there as we went through the final stages of publication.

· ONE ·

THE RUNNERS MOVED impatiently on and off the bases, occasionally clapping, daring the pitcher, encouraging the batter at the plate. The opposing infielders readied themselves for the wind-up, shifting behind the runners; the outfielders eyes were glued on the hitter. In the dugouts, teammates paced, clapped, yelled and spat.

It started out as just another game on just another unbearable central Florida night, temperature nearly ninety with enough humidity to keep the threat of rain constant and the perspiration draining down backs and brows, stinging every eye squinting to keep track of the game out on the stark floodlit field.

The Castle, the new ballpark for the Orlando Jesters, should have been packed for this late season match-up with fellow National Conference playoff contender, the Phoenix Diablos, but the recently ended players' strike coupled with an anti-player antipathy whipped up by sports reporters and columnists had created an antagonistic atmosphere which left many fans disappointed and dismayed. Add to that anger over a strike-shortened season and frustration with higher ticket prices causing many fans to stay away. The apathy was a growing concern for team owners, who were at a loss as to how to stimulate more interest.

It was a little after nine and the Jesters were behind. This was the best chance the home team had had all night. Some people had already left the park. Rain threatened, but just like the attitude of the fans toward the ball game, nobody in the stands expected anything to happen.

Overhead, lightning flashed, thunder rumbled, but nobody paid the least bit of attention. Veteran spectators fanned themselves with programs, mothers fussed with restless children, and even the vendors were listless, resting their heavy trays on the steel pipe barricades, too beat to care whether they sold much or not. The smells of boiled franks, roasted peanuts and sour beer mingled while the play-by-play from portable radios and the speakers scattered around the half-filled ballpark cut through the damp, still air.

Out in centerfield, Diablos centerfielder, Omar Sandoval, a young Colombian who was one of the game's bright new stars was feeling pumped. He was hoping for a fly ball to end the inning. The hitter was a cinch for flying out and Sandoval was certain their closer could get the team out of the jam.

The player at the plate backed out of the box, swung his bat experimentally, tugged at his batting gloves, stepped back in, raised the bat to his shoulder and waited. Some in the crowd leaned forward in hopeful expectation.

"Orlando down a pair . . . two on and two out, bottom of the eighth . . . one-one the count on Mark Mutryn . . ."

The commentary came out in halting bursts. The announcer didn't have any more energy than the rest of the people in the ballpark. Strangely, there seemed to be more crowd noise coming from portable radios than was actually emanating from the spectators.

"Kellog has the sign and straightens on the mound . . . checks the runners . . . takes a deep breath . . . checks the runners again . . . and here's the pitch. There's a drive to left center . . . this ball is really smoked!"

It was a gift, totally unexpected. The hometown fans stirred, a frisson of excitement racing through the stadium. Many stood up, rising in sync with the lofting arc of the ball, anticipating a big play, their eyes following the ball flying out to center field as the runners started to tear around the bases.

Out in center field, Omar Sandoval charged back toward the wall, cursing himself for playing too shallow. The ball had been hit harder than he had anticipated and now he had to race backward to make the play. But with each stride, he wasn't sure he could. An easy out had turned into a possible score, maybe a game-winner. Sandoval was not about to let that happen. He put on the afterburners, his strong legs churning beneath his hips as he charged for the end of the ball's trajectory, concentrating solely on the baseball to the exclusion of everything else.

"Sandoval on the run . . . to the track, to the wall . . . it's off his glove . . . Sandoval is down and the ball is rolling away from him. Two runs are in, and now here comes Mutryn . . . he's going to score . . . the Jesters have taken the lead."

The crowd erupted with shouts and applause — trying to ignore Sandoval down on the ground. They focused instead on the thrill of three runs charging home and going ahead. Strangers in the stands were now best buddies, sharing smiles and yelling out their approval, slapping each other's backs and arms. Jester runners high-fived themselves at home plate and then again back at the dugout. But a few eyes strayed to the prostrate body out on the field.

"Sandoval is still down on the warning track in left center . . . he looks hurt."

The noise in the stadium quieted to a murmur as heads turned to check-out the fallen player. He lay sprawled across the warning track that separated the outfield grass from the concrete wall by a ten or fifteen feet.

No two ballparks are alike and on this night the visiting team fell victim to that baseball reality. Each stadium has its own quirks, its architecture giving the place its particular character. For The Castle it was a serpentine outfield wall filled with nooks and crannies unseen by most fans sitting hundreds of feet away. Visiting players had a decided disadvantage in not knowing the nuances of that barrier. It was a factor that could sometimes make all the difference in a game. At times, it produced a fortunate bounce for the Jesters; other times, it could mean serious problems.

Omar Sandoval had taken off after the Mark Mutryn hit almost before the ball had left the bat. In the time it took the ball to travel nearly 400 feet at ninety miles per hour, Sandoval's brain processed a mountain of information as he ran at full tilt to position himself for the catch. He subconsciously analyzed the trajectory of the ball, the geometry of his position in relation to the back wall, the speed of the runners racing around the bases, where to throw the ball if he could not make the catch.

But what he could not input were the unique characteristics of this unknown field, the different distances from his own home field. And that miscalculation was going to cost him. Seconds later, Sandoval ran into the wall in a bone-crushing collision.

A world away in the infield, the runners' had rounded the bases which put the Jesters into the lead, but the focus of the now silent hometown crowd was on the motionless player. "Get out here! Get out here now!"

Calling frantically, the other Diablos' outfielders yelled for help, waving their arms and hovering protectively over Sandoval, whose neck was angled awkwardly down and away from his shoulders. Diablo players, team trainers, doctors umpires, EMS personnel, all hurried out to the injured player. A small crowd swelled around him. The medical experts examined Sandoval, preparing to administer aid. A few players stood frozen, their heads bowed. Someone from the Jesters' front office spoke into a walkie-talkie at the same time signaling with his arm and a moment later, an ambulance raced onto the field. Deftly, cautiously, the young ballplayer was lifted onto a stretcher, strapped securely into place, and then slowly, placed into the emergency vehicle.

"Jesters fans, let's hear it for Omar Sandoval," came the announcement from the public address system.

The crowd applauded as the ambulance drove away through an open gate in the wall, but their response seemed hollow and confused. The clapping died down, and the fans settled back into their plastic seats. The game resumed in a half-hearted fashion, and Orlando went on to post a four to three decision. But a game in the win column was not what was going to be remembered this night.

The worst fears became reality shortly following the game.

"Ladies and gentlemen, I have some terrible news."

Rich Nelson, the manager for the Diablos, was trembling as he addressed the gathering of reporters, television and radio crews, and fans outside the visitors' clubhouse. It was hot, sticky, and everyone wanted to go home but stuck around for last minute news.

"We have received word from the hospital that ... that Omar Sandoval has died from his injuries sustained in his accident on the field. I have just informed my players, and we are in the process of trying to contact his family."

Nelson, his expression grim, wiped his eyes before continuing.

"I hope you can understand we need some time right now to deal with this. I am certain more formal information will be available later. Thank you for your patience and support. Right now I need to go back and be with my team."

The late-night sports shows ran and re-ran the video of Sandoval's collision with the wall. Not since the early days of the game when the absence of batting helmets resulted in several deaths from beanballs had baseball experienced anything like this. Among the many interested viewers was Jayvee DellVecchio, the popular host of DBC's *Totally Baseball*.

"It doesn't make sense," said DellVecchio to no one in particular in one of the busy edit suites of the Digital Broadcasting Company. "He's the best center fielder in the game right now. No way he didn't know the wall was coming."

DellVecchio, the only child of the late baseball legend Mike Dell-Vecchio, had been in the spotlight since winning the Little World Series for Team USA at age twelve with a last inning grand slam against a team from Korea. Fourteen letters in high school in four different sports, three times an All-American and national Player of the Year honors at Cornell came next, but ultimately, no spot in professional baseball. The game was still not ready for a woman player. However, if she couldn't play the game, she was determined to be a part of it. Jayvee's knowledge of sports, and a funny, irreverent personality, made her popular in the field of broadcasting, eventually leading to a spot with the sports network. Why shouldn't she be a baseball expert? Sure she was Mike DellVecchio's kid, but she could stand in there with anyone when it came to knowing the inside story of the game she had always loved.

"Jayvee, what are you doing?" An associate interrupted DellVecchio's musings. "The show starts in less than a minute."

Reluctantly, DellVecchio scrambled to her feet, gave a quick glance in the nearby mirror as she ruffled her hair, jumped out the door and headed toward the studio. Further analysis would have to wait for a little while, she thought to herself, her brow furrowed. *There's something wrong there. I know it. Sandoval was too damned good to make a stupid — and deadly — mistake.*

Mike DellVecchio was one of baseball's greatest heroes. DellVecchio was an instant hit when he came to the big leagues with the Cleveland

Ironmen. His good looks and sweet charm would have endeared him to almost anybody, but the fact that he could hit a baseball a country mile and then go run it down didn't hurt his status either. The Ironmen had been perennial losers in the BBL until DellVecchio came along. His talent and leadership galvanized the underachieving team into a playoff winner for the first time in years, and Cleveland went on to a run of successes, with DellVecchio at the heart of it all. When he retired, Mike DellVecchio left a legacy future players could only hope to emulate.

Jayvee DellVecchio, always Jessica Victoria to Mike, was forever Daddy's Little Girl. Jayvee took to baseball almost from birth, and Mike loved her passion for his game. Wherever Mike DellVecchio went, it seemed his precious Jessica Victoria was at his side. Her mother worried she wasn't doing enough of the things little girls usually did, but Jayvee didn't care; all that mattered was her dad and baseball. Hitting, throwing, and catching came as natural to Jayvee as getting out of bed. If she wasn't with her father at the ballpark, Jayvee was playing baseball with the other kids in her West Park neighborhood of Cleveland.

When she was twelve, it was through baseball she got the name by which everyone knew her. Since girls playing baseball in organized youth leagues was still a new phenomenon at that time, Jessica Victoria DellVecchio was listed as J. V. DellVecchio on the roster of the West Park Wildcats of the Four Corners Little League.

"Wait a minute. You've got a girl over there. You can't have a girl on your team."

"Why not? There's nothing in the rules that says boys only."

The coach for the Wildcats pulled a rule book out of his pocket for further proof.

"Look, right here on page five. It says the league is open to any resident of the Four Corners area from the ages of eight to twelve."

He jabbed his pudgy finger on the page, and then waved the book at his counterpart for the Lakewood Eagles.

"As far as I'm concerned, Jessie can play. And if you want to be the one telling Mike DellVecchio his kid can't play baseball, you go right ahead."

The Eagles' coach wasn't happy, but he certainly wasn't going to be the one to get on the wrong side of Mike DellVecchio, not in Cleveland anyway. Jayvee DellVecchio was going to play, and the young men wearing green T-shirts with Eagles across the front were prepared to make her pay for invading their domain. They were merciless in their jeering.

"Hey, Forty-Seven, did you get lost on the way to the jump rope competition?"

"You have to have ice to figure skate, sweetheart. The rink doesn't open until November."

"What's the J stand for? Jack? You don't look like a Jack. More like a Juliet. Can I be your Romeo?"

Jayvee smiled and stuck her tongue out at the Eagles.

"Go ahead and tease me; Daddy's always talking about the players doing that. I can tell him we're doing the same thing." As she turned away from them to grab her glove off the bench, Jayvee's smile disappeared. "Calling me Jack, though; that isn't right. I'm a girl, even if I do like to play baseball. Where do they get off calling me Jack?"

The jabs from the Eagles were an effective distraction in the early innings of the game. Jayvee misplayed a routine fly ball at her centerfield position in the second inning, and then she popped out with the bases loaded in the fourth. As the Wildcats came up for their last at-bats in the bottom of the sixth trailing by two runs, the Eagles began another verbal assault.

"Nice team you've got there, Wildcats."

"Whaddya' expect? They've got a girl playing. Maybe I can get my sister to play first base for us next time."

"I wonder if they're going home to play house after the game."

"Yeah! Maybe bake some cookies, too."

With one out, the Wildcats got a runner on base when the first baseman couldn't handle a bunt. Then, after a second out, the next batter ripped a double to left center to put runners on second and third. A hit could tie up the game. Mike DellVecchio's little girl marched towards the batter's box, knowing exactly what she had to do.

"It's the ball game, guys," shouted the Eagles third baseman toward home plate. "Miss America is all they've got left. Come on, Miss J. V. DellVecchio, where's your crown?"

"When I joined this league," added the Eagles catcher, "I thought we were going to play the best players . . . you know, the Varsity. I guess we have to settle for beating up on the JV's."

His voice was loud enough to be heard throughout the sandlot, and he scraped the dirt behind home plate with his sneakers, sending a cloud of dust in Jayvee's direction. That Eagles catcher wouldn't know it, but the steely look he got in return was just like one that had been seen by many a BBL catcher when Mike DellVecchio stepped in to hit: it was a face a player didn't want to see.

The stream of abuse continued as the Eagles' pitcher's final fastball headed home. It ceased immediately when Jayvee launched the ball over the heads of the outfielders, deep into the woods surrounding the sandlot. From that moment on, the Wildcats' slugger would no longer be known as Jessica. Stepping on home plate, surrounded by her delirious teammates, DellVecchio turned to the Eagles' catcher and said:

"Not bad for J.V., huh?"

A sandlot legend was born, and to her parents' dismay, the nickname had stuck for Jayvee DellVecchio.

Following her show, Jayvee went back to the editing suites to further analyze the tragedy that had occurred hours earlier in Orlando. A young video editor replayed the footage of the Sandoval collision while Jayvee stood behind his chair. Since DBC was the principal broadcast partner for the Baseball Big Leagues, the sports giant had complete access, by way of satellite, to all the video from that night's game between the Diablos and the Jesters.

"What are you looking for, Jayvee?"

"I'm not sure, really. It's just that something's not right."

Mike DellVecchio had been considered the greatest defensive centerfielder ever to play the game, and he had passed on those talents to his daughter. He used to tell his friends that Jayvee could play the position better than anyone in the big leagues; she had an instinct for positioning and staying on the ball that couldn't be taught.

"Hold it! Back that one up."

The technician had video from each of the camera positions that had caught the action of the fateful play. He hit a button on his computer keyboard, rewinding the tape taken from a camera located near the left field foul pole.

"Right there!"

She squeezed his shoulder hard causing him to jerk away from the keyboard momentarily.

"What's he doing with his head? Why would he take his eyes off the ball if he wasn't checking to see where the wall was? Dad always said you watch the ball all the way, or you take a peek to see where you are."

The pair continued to review the video, looking for the answers to her questions. A news conference was set for the following afternoon in Orlando, and Jayvee DellVecchio was determined to be prepared.

The Baseball Big Leagues cancelled all of its games the next day out of respect for Omar Sandoval. An army of media had converged on The Castle in Orlando for a briefing from the medical personnel investigating the accident. It was a tight timetable for the team's doctors and the coroner's office from Orange County, but people were demanding immediate answers. Complicating matters, Sandoval's family wanted his body returned to Colombia as quickly as possible. They didn't care about the details of their son's death; they just wanted him home.

The medical panel was headed by Lou Wilder, the lead physician for the Jesters. Front office personnel from the club and the Diablos, as well as representatives from the Baseball Big Leagues, were also seated at the head table. The conference was taking place in a large meeting room in the lower level of The Castle, and more than one hundred reporters and camera personnel awaited information surrounding the player's death.

"Ladies and gentlemen," Doctor Wilder began, "we will entertain your questions after we detail what we know up to this point."

Wilder paused to shuffle through some of his notes. He was a tall, thin man with a professorial air about him. Reaching down to take a sip from his water glass, Wilder heard an impatient groan from the assembled. A small smile creased his face; he was going to savor his moment in the spotlight.

"Initial reports indicate the cause of death as a massive cranial fracture as well as multiple fractures of vertebrae."

Pointing to some x-rays that appeared on a large screen behind him, the doctor continued.

"The severity of these fractures and their locations indicate Mr. Sandoval was going too fast and was at an improper angle when he collided with the wall. It is my opinion the impact might have caused his immediate death."

Doctor Wilder went on to make several other medical points while reporters wrote feverishly in their notebooks and the video cameras transmitted images back to their respective broadcast outlets. Several neurological specialists added testimony, but for most of the media, it was medical jargon beyond their expertise. There were plenty of questions, however, for the baseball representatives.

"Was the outfield wall adequately padded?"

"Did the other outfielders for the Diablos try to warn Sandoval about the wall?"

"Is anything special planned as a result of this?"

"How long before the games resume?"

Despite her prominent position among the media, Jayvee DellVecchio sat toward the back of the conference room and listened intently while her cohorts peppered the experts with questions. Her expression didn't change but her body language indicated her high degree of tension. Just when it appeared the panel had satisfied the media's inquiries, she spoke.

"Doctor Wilder, can you tell me why Omar Sandoval's head dropped just as he reached the warning track?"

"I don't understand your question. To what are you referring?"

"I will ask you again, Doctor. Why would Omar Sandoval drop his head the way he did just before he collided with the wall? He was an outstanding defensive player. Why would he make such a fundamental error?"

Lou Wilder was caught off-guard by the direction of Jayvee's questioning. A murmur flowed through the crowd of reporters. The medical panel's focus had been on the head and neck injuries suffered by the Phoenix outfielder. The demand for information in such a short turnaround had directed their attention to the cause of death but perhaps not THE cause of death. Most seemed satisfied with labeling Omar Sandoval's death as a tragic accident. Not Jayvee DellVecchio.

"Ms. DellVecchio, we have compiled as much appropriate data as possible within the time frame available in order to present an accurate picture of exactly what took place last evening."

"Omar Sandoval suffered a massive fracture of the frontal bone of the cranium resulting in severe bruising of the brain. In addition, the whiplash effect from the impact caused fractures in the C-4 and C-5 areas of his vertebrae. It is our preliminary opinion that the violent nature of the collision resulted in the almost instant cessation of his life."

"I have no doubt about your information, Doctor. I'm sure your assessment of the fatal blow being caused by the collision is well-founded. The question remains, however, is what would cause one of the best defensive outfielders today to make such an uncharacteristic move, one that put his life in jeopardy?"

Jayvee DellVecchio had spent a good portion of her life being in the center of the action, so she did not even notice the attention of everyone in the room had riveted to her.

"Doctor Wilder, would you not agree it appears Sandoval made no attempt to slow down, or that he appeared to have no awareness he was about to crash into the wall?"

The Orlando team physician smiled, almost paternally, before answering.

"The video replays certainly seem to indicate that. But you have been around baseball your whole life, Ms. DellVecchio, and I know you have witnessed numerous occasions when players have collided with outfield barriers."

"Without a doubt, Doctor. But if I brought to this news conference video demonstrating those collisions, I am confident in each clip you would see the eyes of the outfielders glued to the path of the baseball. At that last moment, Omar Sandoval was not focused on the ball, and he was not looking for the wall. What happened when he stepped on that warning track?"

The room erupted as other reporters joined with Jayvee in a demand for answers — answers the panel did not have. The news conference was hastily concluded with the promise that a more detailed analysis would take place. A full blood work-up and a toxicology report would be done to gain additional information. To the disappointment of his family, Omar Sandoval's body would not be returning to Colombia as soon as they wanted.

Two days later, the media again gathered in Orlando for another briefing by Lou Wilder. A summer rainstorm fell from the cloudy skies in gray sheets but did nothing to lower the temperature. It was like a day in the tropics, steamy, damp and miserable. Speculation had run rampant over the preceding forty-eight hours, and the media horde eagerly awaited the latest update from the solemn doctor at the podium.

"Thank you for coming, ladies and gentlemen. As we did earlier this week, I will detail the results of our findings and then I will answer your questions . . .

"In cooperation with the Coroner's Office here in Orange County, we have performed a series of tests on Mr. Sandoval. Extensive blood and tissue samples were taken which were then sent to two different laboratories for independent verification. Both labs came up with similar findings."

The whirring motor noise made by the cameras of the photographers was the only other sound that could be heard in the auditorium.

"Our conclusions are that the impact endured by Mr. Sandoval and the injuries he sustained would have been sufficient to cause his death. However, analysis of cardiac tissue samples indicates the victim suffered severe trauma in that area, probably as the result of some type of cardiac arrest. Family histories — such as we have been able to discover — show no indication of heart trouble. Nevertheless, it seems quite clear some level of severe cardiac stress was a prime contributor to the eventual fatal incident for this young man."

The sea of reporters and camera people was rising with interest, just as it had done at the earlier conference when Jayvee DellVecchio's questions had given it life.

"Since there was no family history of heart problems, we set out to determine potential causes for the cardiac arrest. Our investigation eventually uncovered a significant amount of an anabolic steroid, Equipoise, in Mr. Sandoval's system. In addition, a substantial amount of Ephedrine, a stimulant drug, was also detected in the toxicology analysis."

Several reporters leapt to their feet, trying to interrupt the doctor's statement. Wilder ignored the hubbub and continued.

"These substances react in different ways depending on a number of factors. I cannot state with absolute certainty they were the direct cause of this fatal accident, but it is not a stretch to believe they were significant contributors to the chain of events resulting in this tragedy."

Doctor Wilder concluded his remarks with thank-yous for the various people who worked the investigation and condolences for the Sandoval family. The media pressed Wilder to commit, without equivocation, to the fact that steroids and supplements were the fatal ingredients for Omar Sandoval, but the veteran physician would not be coerced into making such a statement. It certainly appeared baseball had a problem with supplement abuse, and as the public's representatives, the media demanded to know what was going to be done about it.

· TWO ·

"A<small>IN'T NUTHIN' LIKE</small> that smell."

It was always that way for Ryan Hannegan. Like the aroma of Mom's cooking reminiscent of home, he felt this way every time he got near a ball field. New-mown grass, Georgia clay, pine tar, somebody dipping a little fresh chew, and a healthy dose of sweat might not seem like a fragrant combination, but to Ryan Hannegan it was the perfume of roses. Since his first day at Little League, one good whiff always got him going.

Baseball's scent may be heavenly, but something else was also in the air on this early spring morning in Florida. Baseball was enduring some tumultuous times, adding tension to an atmosphere already difficult enough for a veteran player trying to hold a roster spot. Spring training had always meant a challenge for Hannegan. He spent eight years in the minors with three different organizations; his Baseball Big Leagues career was more of the same, with equipment bags from four different teams in a closet back home. "I like you, Hannegan, but it's just that . . ." was an all-too-familiar refrain Ryan had heard throughout his career. He had all the tools; he could run, had a good glove and a decent eye at the plate — but unfortunately, he didn't seem to produce quite enough of the power expected from players at his position.

Ryan was well-respected by his teammates at each stop on his baseball odyssey and they loved the fact he always seemed to take the lead in organizing the latest card game, clubhouse pool, or team meeting at a local establishment.

"They should call me 'Super Glue'," Ryan once said. "This team would fall apart if it wasn't for me!"

Actually, Warning Track Power might be a better nickname for Hannegan, which was a baseball slur for a player whose actual achievements were just a little bit short. It was an apt description for Ryan's career. He could do it all, but never with enough oomph to keep him free from worry when the next spring training began. That was for another time, however, not at this moment when the Florida heat mingles with the anticipation of a new beginning. Nothing was going to discourage Ryan's hopeful spirit.

"Ain't nuthin' like that smell, Baby. This year's gonna to be different."

The crack when bat meets ball could be heard echoing in the hitting cages out beyond the right field wall. Ryan climbed the steps to the main clubhouse of the Boston Colonials' spring training complex. Strains of the latest pop music seeped through the cinder block walls as well as some raucous laughter, probably at the expense of an unsuspecting rookie. Ryan paused at the top and then reached for the handle of the large steel door that separated the players' domain from the rest of the world. Inhaling deeply, the sweet smell of baseball transformed the thirty-five year old into a kid again.

"Hey, Mom, I'm home. What's cooking?"

With that, he walked into the clubhouse. A new season had begun . . .

Baseball was going to be different this season as a result of a series of events that had taken place over the last twelve months. The sport was big business, a multi-billion dollar industry, yet somehow the fans and the media expected baseball to remain the game they remembered from their youth. Instead, many were finding it more difficult to separate the finances from the fielding. A series of players' strikes and lockouts by team owners over the past several decades had diminished baseball's popularity in the minds of the sporting public. A crisis threatened when another work stoppage occurred early the previous spring.

"Jayvee DellVecchio outside a conference room here at the corporate headquarters for DBC Television in New York City . . ." Identifying herself, the female reporter spoke into the camera which focused in a close-up on her intelligent but quizzical expression. Even in the heat, she appeared cool and collected, wearing a pale yellow silk Armani suit with a sheer navy blue polka dot blouse. Her long brunette hair moved slightly in the soft wind. She brushed her bangs to the side of her forehead with a sweep of her hand and never lost a beat in the cadence of her words.

"This recent baseball shutdown has raised questions as to how DBC might respond to this latest bump in its programming.

"Mr. Patrick J. Murray, chief executive for the Digital Broadcasting Company, has called the media here to discuss what's next for his company in its current situation with the Baseball Big Leagues. Let's go inside for Mr. Murray's announcement."

The camera followed a graciously smiling Jayvee into the interior where Murray, a distinguished, well-dressed gentleman, approached the podium at the front of the room and began to speak in a well-modulated voice.

"Thanks to all of you for coming. For those of us who love baseball, these are trying times. For the third time in the last ten years, we have seen the game come to a screeching halt."

Murray's words may have sounded altruistic, but baseball's labor troubles were hurting DBC's bottom line. Since DBC was the outlet for most of the baseball broadcasts in this country, a cancelled season, including the playoffs with its additional advertising revenue, would mean severe financial losses for the company.

"I have been asked by many of you what role DBC might play in bringing about some resolution to this crisis. Too often, we have been accused of choosing sides in this conflict and, perhaps, making matters worse as a result. That will not be our position this time."

Murray paused for dramatic effect, then inhaling deeply, continued. "Tomorrow morning we intend to file a breach of contract suit against both the Baseball Big Leagues and the Players Association. If these two sides cannot come to an agreement, then they will be punished for destroying the trust they've had from the American public."

The screen was once again filled with Jayvee's face as she signed off the special announcement. "Ladies and gentlemen, please stay tuned for further developments. Thank you for watching."

The network then resumed its regular broadcasting schedule.

It might be simply about the dollars and cents for DBC, but it was an emotional cost for the fans. They were mad as hell, and they intended to let everyone know. Demonstrations against both sides took place at a number of stadiums around the country. Several teams had massive debt service to contend with, the result of new facilities being built in the quest for additional money sources. There were potential legal entanglements with the local government groups stuck with their portions of the bills from the stadium construction boom. The answer in the boardrooms of the BBL was simple: "Get back to playing or shut the doors forever."

The season eventually resumed, but the death of Omar Sandoval blindsided the recovering sport. When the revelations of possible substance abuse came to light, the media and the politicians clamored for an official investigation. Even the President of the United States, whose grandfather had been an owner of the Atlanta Scarletts, joined in the demand that baseball make some changes. Baseball was at a crossroads in its existence; something dramatic needed to be done to ensure the sport's survival.

"Everybody having a good time?"

The attempt at humor by the owner of the Seattle Stevedores was met with glum faces from the other team owners. The annual baseball meetings were taking place in Palm Springs, California, but no one was enjoying the late November sunshine in the desert.

"We've got to get something done here and done now," complained the owner of the Chicago Blaze. "I can't afford any more negative publicity. My ticket sales are going to go down the toilet unless we do something positive."

The owners had gotten the players to agree to increased drug testing for the following season, but the public and the politicians remained skeptical. They had also received the resignation of the current commissioner, and they were trying to select his successor.

"It has to be someone people will rally around," commented the owner of the Chicago team.

"What about Rich Connor?" asked the owner of the Philadelphia Quakers. "He was a ten-time All Star and the fans liked him."

"I don't care how much the fans might have liked him. I am not having an ex-player as commissioner." The owner of the New York Gothams threw his pen across the table.

The discussion continued in this manner for the better part of the afternoon. Names with direct ties to the game were offered, only to be rejected for one reason or another. Finally, the owner of the Washington Federals made his suggestion.

"What about Hoppy Hopkins?"

Retired Brigadier General Michael Hopkins was a storybook character come to life. A country boy from Virginia, Hopkins was a graduate of West Point where he starred on both the football field and the baseball diamond. He began his military career on the front lines during the war in Viet Nam. Rising through the ranks, Hopkins became an assistant to the President for eight years, followed by more decorations for his leadership during the Gulf War. His military career had recently ended after serving as the commandant of the War College in Carlisle, Pennsylvania.

"I know the man loves baseball, and how can anyone object to a national hero?"

"But he's going to want to be in complete charge; that's the way his personality is." The Gothams' owner was skeptical. "Can we give him that kind of power?" Another owner expressed a fear of giving away too much influence to someone who wouldn't be equitable.

"Do we have any other choice?" The Washington Federals' owner was quietly firm and confident about his suggestion.

A revered national figure with a spotless record, and above all a baseball fan, Michael Hopkins seemed to be the best selection to lead the sport's turnaround. The lords of baseball decided he was their only choice.

Hopkins was delighted with the appointment and responded with the following quote appearing in the newspapers the following day. The public was hopeful he could restore the ethics of old-fashioned baseball to their favorite game.

"I have had the privilege of serving this country in a number of roles during my life, and it is a humbling responsibility to safeguard the trust people place in me. My decisions may not have always been the best choices and my orders may have been difficult for some people to handle. They were always made, however, with the maximum of integrity I could bring to the situation, and in the best interests of those people who entrusted me with their care."

It was a crisp December afternoon in upstate New York for Michael Hopkins' installation as baseball's commissioner and someone in the public relations department for the Baseball Big Leagues was going to get major kudos for staging the event on the steps of the Baseball Hall of Fame. Hopkins had a commanding presence anyway, but with his ramrod-straight posture and custom-tailored pinstriped wool suit against the backdrop of the Hall, he was an impressive figure.

He looked out over the crowd and smiled, full of confidence and pure All-American Apple Pie spirit. The people grew quiet and eagerly absorbed every word he had to say.

"Baseball is the greatest game in the world. I played all sports growing up. I had some success on the football field at West Point, but my favorite has always been baseball. It is a game for families, a love for the game passes from generation to generation. It has many special moments like a game of catch in the backyard or that first visit to the ballpark. It's the anguish when a favorite player gets traded away; the utter exhilaration when the home team pulls one out in the bottom of the ninth. Baseball is a shared joy.

"Growing up where I did in rural Virginia, I didn't have the luxury of having one of our big league teams right there. Nevertheless, my childhood was filled with many memorable moments listening to Federals' games on the radio with my parents on our front porch as night fell on the Chesapeake. Sometimes when the conditions were right, I could even pick up the Scarlett games from Atlanta as they boomed in after sunset. Baseball meant everything to me then, and it has remained a passion for me throughout my life."

Hopkins' voice was a rich baritone rumbling through the crowd assembled on the front lawn of baseball's hallowed place. The temperature was just cold enough to condense the general's breath as he spoke.

"The beauty of the game is that it can cross boundaries, and it can be a unifying force, a common ground. I saw that happen throughout my career, whether I was sitting in a rice paddy in Southeast Asia or in the desert in the Middle East. I had a shared connection with my men and that bond for so many of us was baseball.

"I realize today's realities do not always hold up to the dreams of our youth, but the game of baseball is still wonderful. I promise my best effort to recapture some of that childhood magic for the game today. The BBL is committed to making baseball the national pastime once again: to make the baseball I love — and that so many of us love — America's game once more."

A wall of noise greeted Ryan Hannegan as he made his way into the team's clubhouse. The Colonials' spring complex in Fort Myers, Florida, was not the most lavish of the BBL facilities in Florida, but it was large and had all the necessities players had come to expect.

"Hey, Blade!"

Ryan waved to Pete Hudec as he passed the trainer's room. He wondered to himself why a trainer would have a nickname like Blade. Hannegan was not sure he wanted to find out, but the Boston trainer seemed like a good guy who knew what he was doing. Heading toward the locker area, Hannegan heard a familiar voice above the cacophony of sound.

"You, worthless sack of shit! Any hope we had of ending this jinx died the moment we picked up your sorry ass."

The clubhouse for the major roster players had some fifty ample stalls aligned around its perimeter, and Hannegan made his way across the room toward the bare-chested figure jabbering at him. A big screen TV blared in one corner and the latest stereo gear was blasting away in another.

"Doc, how in the hell do people keep from tossing their cookies looking at that ugly mug of yours ... and that poor excuse for a body." Hannegan grinned at his teammate.

Doc, named in tribute to the longtime children's author Doctor Seuss, was Boston third baseman, Dennis Soos. Losing with his hairline and gaining ground around his waist did not make Soos the typical-looking athlete, but he carried himself with dignity. Rising from his stool, Doc made a sweeping bow like an actor at a curtain call, adding a side profile and a belly rub for Hannegan's benefit. The pair had been teammates in high school and college, and finally re-connected when Ryan was acquired in a late season pennant drive deal last August. He was the best friend Hannegan had ever had.

"It figures you'd get your locker right by the spread. I'm surprised that there's anything left."

Hannegan gestured towards a large table filled with enough boxes of cereal, fruit and assorted pastries to impress any breakfast buffet aficionado. When the players returned from their morning workouts, a stack of cold cuts and loaves of bread, more fruit, and a large, steamy kettle of today's soup would replace the breakfast layout. Baseball players may have contracts far more lucrative than the men who played in the game's early days, but the tradition of food in the clubhouse has remained.

"Hey, everybody has their own way of getting ready for the season. I have learned from my many years in the game what I need to do to prepare," Soos answered with another rub of his ample midsection. "This engine needs fuel, and I have to be ready to fill it up."

With a laugh, Hannegan grabbed a doughnut from the spread and bounced it off his friend's stomach. Snickering, Soos picked it up off the floor and shoved it into his mouth, leaving a ring of powdered frosting around his lips.

"You know, Ryno, there'll probably be more guys looking like me this season." Bits of donut spewed out as Soos spoke.

"No kidding. The general sounded like he meant business when he talked about the drug-testing program. It's going to be different for all of us."

Given the freedom to do almost anything he felt was necessary, Hoppy Hopkins fell back on his military training. Discipline would be the foundation of the Hopkins' recovery plan for baseball. The sport would have a drug testing policy for all of its employees and it would be the most stringent of any of the professional leagues. Using the latest models from the Olympics, baseball would be prepared to remove chemical enhancement from the sport. In addition to mandatory tests at the start of spring training, everyone in the BBL would be subject to random tests throughout the season.

"We've all started looking like freakin' Schwarzeneggers the last couple of years. But I don't know if it made us better ballplayers," said Hannegan grinning at Doc Soos as he removed his jeans and hung them on a hook in his locker.

Soos and Hannegan were like most of the players in the big leagues. They had seen the physical changes in others around the game. Now, nearly every player engaged in a year-round conditioning program as they followed the mantra of today's athlete: bigger, stronger, faster. For a few, that meant cutting corners to achieve those goals. The risks were obvious, but the resulting success could be worth the potential danger.

"It sure made the line longer to see The Blade. Everybody and their brother seemed to be pulling this or straining that, and the shit's supposed to do that to you. It got so a man couldn't find a decent place to sleep around here anymore."

"Doc," Ryan glanced up at his friend. "I thought you only used the trainer's room to duck the media after a game when you left 'em loaded or clanged one with those stone hands of yours."

"Bite me, Ryno."

Soos reached up into Hannegan's locker and grabbed an object that he flipped in Ryan's direction.

"Here."

"What's this?"

"It's your new best friend, courtesy of the BBL. Don't leave home without it."

Ryan spun the small, plastic jar around in his hands to read the label on the other side: Ryan Hannegan, Boston Colonials, Urinalysis Test. He felt a slight shiver run down his spine as he placed the specimen bottle back in his locker.

"Doc, you ever think about juicing?"

"Not me, man. I couldn't handle the needles even if I wanted to. I tried some creatine a couple years ago, but that's been about it. How 'bout you?"

Hannegan briefly flinched before answering his friend's question.

"I'm like you, Doc. The needles do me in. I couldn't even do andro. It might make you look great, but I worried that too much of my stuff would end up on the warning track anyway."

Soos laughed.

"They should name that thing the Hannegan track. Nobody leaves them there like you, Ryan."

Hannegan smiled at the jab, watching Doc's reaction to his answer. If Doc bought his story, then everything was okay. If he didn't believe Ryan was clean, how was it going to be with other people?

Creatine and androstenedione were two of the supplements athletes had been using in recent years to improve strength and stamina. Unlike steroids, these products did not need to be injected, and they were not on the banned substance list for a number of sports. Baseball is more of a hand-to-eye coordination sport than one of brute strength and raw speed, but it is a game of power. Players of all sizes saw an opportunity to cash in with a new and improved physique. In time, the lure to accelerate muscle development with chemical help was too much for some to ignore. It was a fatal attraction for Omar Sandoval.

Sandoval's steroid use alone did not cause his accident, although it certainly contributed to its probability along with the energy drink he frequently used. It was a typically steamy August night in Florida when the Orlando Jesters and Phoenix Diablos had met in that late season battle. The potential damage done by the steroids, the ephedrine-laced energy drink, the humid conditions and the lack of enough hydration, had placed Omar Sandoval in the downward slide into danger.

Additional testing had revealed Sandoval suffered a massive coronary — total cardiac arrest — as he chased Mutryn's drive onto the warning track. His head dropped away from the flight of the ball, as Jayvee DellVecchio's investigation had discovered, because he was, literally, a dead man running when he smashed full force into the outfield wall. The head and neck damage would have been fatal, but on that night in Orlando, it did not make any difference.

"You okay, Ryno? You look a little funny."

"Yeah, I'm fine, Doc. It's just this whole testing thing is going to turn into a royal pain in the ass."

"What are you worried about? They're just going to worry about superstars like me."

Soos flexed his right arm and pointed to his bicep. He was not going to win any body-building competitions.

"You keep thinking that, Butch. That's what you're good at . . . thinking."

Hannegan continued pulling on his gear, smiling about calling his friend 'Butch' just as he had when they were kids, in tribute to one of their favorite movies. The position players in the BBL were not required to report to their teams' spring training sites until the next day, but Ryan was like most in that he couldn't wait to get things started. He threw on his uniform, and although it was just a batting practice jersey, he couldn't help but run his hand across the B-O-S-T-O-N lettering stitched across the front. This was his sixth season in the BBL, but putting on his uniform, especially for the first time in a season, put him right back into his childhood. Grabbing a couple of bats from his equipment bag, he headed for the cages.

If a ballplayer could only do one facet of the game, it's a safe bet it would be hitting. Taking some hacks was the way to go, even more so at this time of the year. As long as a player could find someone to throw, or someone to feed the pitching machine, he could stand in that cage and swing away forever. Walking up to the nearest batting area, Hannegan got his first chance of the season to see the Boston manager, Dudley Perryton.

"Hey, D.P., I guess those rumors of you being lynched by the fans weren't true. Your neck looks like it's stretched a bit though."

"I wouldn't have any trouble with the damn fans if Simonton wouldn't saddle me with horseshit talent like you."

The Colonials' skipper grabbed Hannegan in a big bear hug. Perryton was a players' manager, a former player who had ridden the physical and emotional roller coaster that is a baseball season and appreciated its difficulty. Simonton was Paul Simonton III, a stuffed-shirt bean counter who also happened to be the general manager for the Colonials. Downhome Dudley Perryton was one of the throwbacks. He may have spent the better part of the last thirty-five summers in the major metropolitan cities of the BBL, but every winter it was back to little Hargrove out in the Texas panhandle. He was forward-thinking enough to have a laptop with him in the dugout, but Perryton knew from experience that the essence encompassing the psyche of a ballplayer isn't always found on some computer printout.

"D.P., is it true when they talk about the bright lights of Hargrove, they have to close the door on the phone booth?" Ryan kept a straight face with difficulty.

"My mama told me someday God would punish me for all the aggravation I caused her as a child. Lord, she was right because it started the moment I got stuck with you."

"Somebody told me the Number One pickup line in Hargrove is 'Hey, I think we're related!'"

Perryton gave Hannegan the middle finger salute, but he did it with a smile.

"It wouldn't be so bad if I could find a spot for you in the lineup, Ryan, but there's nothing here for a no-bat, no-glove, no-speed talent like you. Get your ass in there and hit."

Actually the Boston field boss was thrilled to have a veteran player like Hannegan on the club. Ryan was someone who could do a variety of things without bitching about playing time or publicity. Longtime Boston center fielder, Terry Howe, had retired at the end of last season, and many thought Hannegan would get the first chance to replace him.

Perryton and Hannegan had crossed paths fourteen years earlier when D.P. was a first year manager after his long playing career in the BBL, and Hannegan was just beginning his time in professional baseball after being drafted out of Loyola Marymount by the St. Louis Rivermen.

"Excuse me, Skip — do you have a moment?"

"Sure, Hannegan, what can I do for you?"

"It's been more of an adjustment than I thought going from the aluminum bat, and I was wondering if I could get in some extra hitting with you."

Hannegan led the NCAA in hitting in his final collegiate season, batting .477. With his nice, compact swing and his good speed, Ryan was getting some extra base hits at his first level of pro baseball, but driving the ball wasn't happening as often as he wanted, or felt he needed.

"Sure, Ryan, that's what I'm here for. Tell you what, stop by Sarah's and pick me up some cheeseburgers tomorrow and I'll meet you for some extra hitting at lunch time."

Dudley Perryton loved his young player's dogged determination to succeed; Hannegan reminded D.P. of himself in his early days as a pro player. In the searing heat and oppressive humidity of Carolina summer afternoons, or amidst the late night swarms of mosquitoes and black flies, the pair spent hours working on skills or just talking about the game. The relationship lasted just one year because Hannegan was part of a giant multi-player trade by Saint Louis in the ensuing off season. Nevertheless, a bond was formed and it had reconnected when Ryan joined Perryton's Colonials the previous year.

Ryan settled in at the batting cage, pawing the dirt with his left foot to get a good toehold while smoothing out the landing area for his right. A quick tug on the right sleeve of his batting practice jersey, a tap to the top of his batting helmet and Hannegan was ready to go.

"Let 'em fly, Tommy."

Tommy Gladstone, the team's third base coach, was manning the pitching machine. The ball made a swooshing sound as it passed through the spinning tires that propel the ball toward the batter, followed an instant later by a loud crack as polished ash met horsehide.

"That's the way to sting it, Ryno!"

For about ten minutes, the rhythmic cadence of swoosh and thwack was all that was heard, except for a positive comment here and there from the Boston manager. With a good sweat starting to develop, along with just a slight tingling sensation in his hands, Hannegan took his first break to allow fellow outfielder, Gary Gorski, to get in some work, too.

"Not bad, Ryan. Even for cage work, you had good tempo, like you were seeing the ball real well."

"I did a lot of work this off season, D. P. Not too many shots left for me, so I want to make the most of this one."

The Boston skipper nodded in agreement; he knew the pressure would be immense this season. There's always the pressure to win, and that was particularly true with the Boston fans and their beloved C's. Some said following the Colonials was like a religion in Boston and throughout New England. D. P. Perryton knew it was much more serious than that. The Colonials always seemed to be competitive, but not enough in comparison to their hated rivals: the New York Horsemen. Their failures had become known as the Jinx.

Whatever plans Hannegan or Perryton might have had for Ryan to be an everyday player changed in early November when Paul Simonton announced the signing of Junichi Nakata. Junichi was the latest Asian star ready to make an impact in the BBL. Junichi powered the Yokohama Yellow Tails in the Japanese Oceanic League to several titles. With solid talent in the field, speed on the bases and great results with the bat, the Japanese star was the complete package. The Los Angeles Stars had been the odds-on favorite to land the outfielder, but Simonton was able to convince Junichi to make his American debut in a Colonials' uniform.

"Have you met Junichi yet, Skipper?"

"I talked with him on the phone. Simonton told me I didn't need to be there for the official signing."

"Figures ... I guess he wanted the focus to be only on him, D.P. You know how it is when you're a baseball genius."

Perryton shrugged his shoulders.

"He didn't have any problem putting the load on me when he said Junichi was going to be the final piece to the puzzle. How the hell does he know? We haven't even played a game yet."

The Colonials had been one of the founding franchises of the Baseball Big Leagues and despite numerous appearances in the playoffs, they had not won The Showdown for several generations. Some fans believed it was payback time for the role Colonials players had in a gambling scandal in the 1920s. Through the years, it was a critical injury late in the season or some weird misfortune in the playoffs that always seemed to deny the C's victory. The cruelest of all came when Mother Nature conspired against the Colonials with a sudden gust of wind that blew Max Gharrity's lazy fly ball over the Blue Pier in the ninth inning of Game 7 of The Showdown to give the Denver Mountaineers a come-from-behind win four seasons ago. The Jinx was real in New England, and Perryton's burden was to somehow find a way to overcome it.

"No doubt about it, son. That damn jinx plagues me worse than the indigestion I get from those Cheese Big Beefys I eat at my brother-in-law's drive-in back in Hargrove."

Hannegan reached over and rubbed his manager's midsection.

"D.P., the indigestion couldn't be that bad. It sure looks like you had a bunch of Big Beefys this winter."

"Blow it out your ass, Hannegan. Even at my age, I could still outrun you."

The Boston skipper was close to being right. He was one of the fastest players in his era in the BBL. His nickname came not just from his initials, but because Perryton led the BBL for several seasons for grounding into the fewest double plays. Teammates dubbed him with the abbreviation for the twin kill as a tribute to his ability to avoid them. One season, D. P. Perryton grounded into just one double play in almost six hundred plate appearances.

Hannegan stepped back into the batting cage for another session, leaving his manager to contemplate the season ahead. Back in the clubhouse following the workout, Ryan renewed his acquaintance with some of his teammates. One player dominated the clubhouse, literally and figuratively: veteran pitcher Ellis Nance. The right-hander cast a large shadow at six feet nine inches and two hundred seventy-five pounds.

"Y'all ready for this?"

Nance had a voice that pealed like thunder.

"This old man is always ready, and I expect y'all to be ready 'cuz this is the year we end this goddamn jinx!"

Ellis Nance was thirty-nine, but he could still bring a ninety-plus miles per hour fastball to the plate and his breaking ball had a knee-buckling trajectory that had humbled many a hitter during his seventeen years in the BBL. Nance, however, was more than just a pitcher; he was an athlete of the highest caliber.

The Big E was as feared in the fall as he was in the spring during his college days at Ohio State. He played a defensive end/outside linebacker spot for the Buckeyes, and was named a first team All-American as a senior when he led the nation with an incredible twenty-six sacks in eleven games. In the spring of that year, while he was helping the Ohio State baseball team reach the college playoffs, the Indianapolis Racers selected Nance in the PFA draft. The Colonials had drafted him the previous June, and most sports fans expected Ellis to head that way when he graduated. The Racers still felt, however, it was a worthwhile gamble.

"I am pleased the Racers have chosen me. It's a great organization and I will be proud to wear their uniform."

Twenty-two year old Ellis Nance was addressing the media in a conference room at the Ohio State football complex.

"I have also been honored to be chosen to be a part of the Boston Colonials baseball team. I love baseball, but I also love to play football and it would be hard to choose between them."

The media had gathered on this late spring afternoon to learn what Nance's ultimate choice would be.

"I am informing both organizations of my decision. I will play both sports, or I will not play for either team."

Momentarily stunned, the reporters questioned if this was just a contractual ploy to boost the offers from the Racers and the Colonials. Holding up a piece of paper, Nance continued.

"I have also been humbled by acceptance into the School of Law here at Ohio State University. Should both teams not agree to my wishes, I will return here to Columbus this fall to begin my training to become an attorney."

The Colonials and the Racers, in time, acceded to his demand because each could not afford the risk of giving up such a talented player. For several seasons Ellis Nance mowed them down from the mound and from his outside linebacker position. Eventually however, the year-round process took its toll. To the delight of the Colonials and their followers he chose baseball, and though he was now nearing the end of a glorious career, Nance remained one of the game's best.

The rangy right-hander was still holding court when Ryan entered the shower area.

"None of you could be as strong as me — or as pretty — so y'all had to shoot the juice to try and catch up. Now the General's going to nail you when y'all have to piss in the cup tomorrow at the physicals. That includes you, Doc, and your buddy, too."

"Come on, Big E, look at me. I worked hard to get a body this bad. Do you think I would mess it up with something that might get me into shape?"

Soos came out from under the spray of his shower and walked over to where Ryan was standing.

"Now Hannegan here I'm not so sure of. You know they say the juice makes your package shrink and look at Ryno here. Hung like a mule. Oh, I'm sorry, I forgot. He's Irish; that explains everything."

Ryan laughed while shoving his friend back toward his shower.

"Don't drop your soap, Ellis. There's gotta be a reason Doc is such an expert on a guy's package. We're lucky they won't be taking stool samples tomorrow because he's so full of it we'd be stuck in line for hours."

Soos sailed a bottle of shampoo playfully in Hannegan's direction, along with a few F-bombs, as the rest of the players in the shower room hooted. Ryan Hannegan was back in his element. If it could just last at least one more season . . . if it only could last.

· THREE ·

AMONG THE CHANGES in the BBL initiated by the new commissioner was a shortened spring training period. There were now only four weeks of prep time before the season got underway in mid-April. Previously, spring training lasted six to seven weeks, more than enough time for the regulars to get ready and for the wannabes to discover their limitations. The margin for error in this spring training had disappeared for Ryan Hannegan.

The new timeline also meant many players did not bring their families as in previous springs, and most were staying at the same hotel near their training facility. The Gulfport Royale, the best resort hotel in the Fort Myers area, was the team headquarters for the Colonials. Ryan Hannegan checked into a huge suite with a host of amenities. Being a baseball nomad, especially since his divorce, he felt at home in a hotel as much as any other place. The television in the bedroom was tuned to DBC as Hannegan was changing to go out to dinner with Doc Soos.

"Here in Scottsdale, the Gold Rush front office is hopeful veteran third baseman . . ." The female announcer's voice filled the room.

Jayvee DellVecchio was giving the first of her spring training reports on that night's early edition of *Sports Roundup*. Hannegan glanced over several times as DellVecchio described activities from her day at the training camp of the San Francisco Gold Rush. Ryan mused to himself as she spoke authoritatively. She does know her stuff, I'll give her that. And, damn, she is a keeper. Anytime you want to do a little one-on-one,

Miss DellVecchio! Right, like she would be looking for an exclusive from the great Ryan Hannegan. He felt sheepish as he tucked in his shirt and grinned wryly at his reflection.

As pleasant as it was to contemplate a little one-on-one with Jayvee DellVecchio, Ryan's attention drifted to the portable freezer he had brought with him, and the picture of his eleven-year-old daughter, Michaela, sitting on the dresser.

Michaela was the best thing that had ever happened to Ryan. Ryan had met his ex-wife, Deirdre, during his journey through the minor leagues. He had dated in high school and college, but he had never really been in a serious relationship. On a rare off-night in Tampa when he was playing for one of the Minneapolis Lumberjacks' minor league teams, Ryan and some of his friends had decided to build a little team unity at a local tavern. Hannegan, turning away from the bar, had nearly run over a woman, resulting in both their drinks slipping out of their hands and spilling everywhere. Ryan was totally discomfited for a brief minute. He grabbed some paper napkins from the bar and began to pat the sleeve of the woman's blue chiffon dress. He noticed a delicate tennis bracelet twinkling on her narrow wrist. He could also smell the aroma of the fragrance she wore. It was the same as a gardenia in bloom, like his mother had grown when he was a child.

"Oh, I'm sorry. I got you, didn't I?" He got another napkin and kept blotting her sleeve.

"I'm fine . . . I guess I wasn't watching where I was going." She smiled up at him gratefully, not at all provoked.

"No, I was the one going like crazy without looking. Well, anyway, hi, my name's Ryan. Let me buy you another drink."

"Hi. I'm Deirdre. You don't have to, but that's very nice."

"I don't think I've seen you here in the Swinging Door before? Do you come here very often, uh, . . . Deirdre, is it?"

"First time. See those girls over there giggling at us? We were at a bridal shower and decided to stop in for a drink. Are you from around here?" She shook her head, declining more napkin repair.

"Kinda." Ryan lowered his voice almost to a whisper. "I play baseball for the Tampa Tarpons."

"Baseball? I'm not much of a fan, but I'll bet that's interesting." She had noticed his shyness and felt more at ease, as a result.

Hannegan invited Deirdre to sit with him at a nearby table and she agreed, evoking more giggles from her girlfriends and hoots from his teammates. The pair became engrossed in a conversation that lasted for the rest of the evening. That chance meeting turned into a whirlwind romance, and they were married a few months later, in the offseason.

Deirdre admired Ryan's drive to succeed, but she wasn't prepared for the arduous trek many players must endure to make it to the BBL and the resulting impact on a family life. Mrs. Ryan Hannegan struggled with the frustrating disappointments that can be the life of a minor league baseball couple, and Michaela's birth only made it more difficult.

"This can't keep going on, Ryan. You're never home, and when you are, you spend more time playing with Michaela than you do taking any interest in me."

Ryan had moved into the Detroit T-Birds' organization, after three and a half years with the Minneapolis Lumberjacks minor league teams. His progress was consistently slow.

"That's not fair, Deirdre. I love being with you, but I never seem to get enough time with Michaela. I told you when we got married a baseball life has some tough times to live through before you hit the jackpot."

"So where's the jackpot? All I've seen is one bad apartment after another with nothing to do." Her scowl and her whine had become permanent features, or so it seemed to Ryan.

"Maybe if you tried to learn the game a little better, you would enjoy going to the ballpark and being with the other guys' families." He spoke softly but he knew she could hear every word.

"Don't start with me about that. Baseball didn't mean much to me before we met, and there has been little to change my mind since. It's bad enough you've got our daughter brainwashed so she thinks there is nothing but baseball! Sometimes it's like I'm not even in the room when the two of you start talking about it." Deirdre's tone of voice was close to shrill.

"I have to talk with someone in this family because it's obvious you don't care what is happening with me or, apparently, what's happening with us." He folded his hands together and looked unblinkingly into her face, his expression grave and somber. He knew he was out of their comfort zone but he had grown impatient, waiting for something to change.

"I do care, Ryan, and that's why you have to give up this silly dream. I know you think you can be a big leaguer, but maybe it's not going to happen. Look at Diane and Dave Borkowski. He got out of the game and they're doing just fine. I'm sure you could find something else that would make you happy."

"This is what makes me happy, Deirdre. It's going to happen. I just have to stay with it until it does."

That argument repeated itself throughout the summer in Riverside, California, where Ryan was playing for the T-Birds AAA team. In truth, the games and the road trips became a blessing because the forced separations kept the peace. Ryan and Deirdre had come to the realization they may have rushed into their marriage, and other than their mutual love for their daughter, they had little else in common. With the season winding down, Deirdre demanded Ryan give up his baseball career or she and Michaela were leaving.

"How can you even think about making me do that? I'm so close!"

"But we're not, Ryan. I can't live like this anymore."

"This is what I do! This is who I am! I have to keep going."

"Then do it without Michaela and me."

Deirdre Hannegan filed for divorce that October, and Ryan did not contest any part of it, except to make certain he got to see Michaela as much as possible during baseball's offseason. He had been faithful with his child support, and to her credit, Deirdre did not ask for a big jump in his alimony payments when Ryan made the BBL for good with the T-Birds the spring after the divorce. Deirdre got remarried the following year; Owen was a good guy who treated Michaela well. They even allowed Ryan to have Michaela with him when the New York Gothams, Ryan's team at the start of last season, made their annual family trip. That was the only time players were allowed to have family members accompany them on the team charter. Father and daughter had a blast, thoroughly enjoying each other's company.

Michaela was a baseball nut; she loved everything about the game. She learned to read and do math as much by checking out box scores as she did with any of her lessons in school. Father and daughter were always hanging out at the batting cages or just playing catch whenever Michaela spent time with Ryan. Michaela not only could tell you the lineup of almost every team in the big leagues, but she also had opinions on whether or not a manager really knew what he was doing.

"Daddy, you have to let me talk with Mr. Perryton. If he wants to beat New York or Baltimore, he's got to make some changes." She did not lack for confidence, even at her young age.

"We'll see, Michaela. I'm sure Mr. Perryton would appreciate your input, but he's probably busy right now."

She had her favorites, of course. Her comment recently that Kevin Tompkins of the Dallas Wranglers was "s-o-o-o-o hot" told Ryan his little girl wasn't just thinking about a player's batting average anymore. Best of all, Michaela believed her dad was the best player in the game.

"You just haven't caught a break. If a manager would put you in the lineup and leave you there, they'd see what I see. I know it!"

Unfortunately for Ryan, he had yet to find the manager who would put him in the lineup and just "leave him there." Nevertheless, this baseball duo of father and daughter remained true to the game they loved.

My Number One fan. That's my Michaela! Hannegan grinned as he gazed at her smiling face beaming from the picture. *Is this my last chance, Kiddo?* So often he talked to her picture when she wasn't around. He missed the feeling of having a "family."

At age thirty-five, Ryan had admitted to himself he might not be the best roster option for a ball club like the Colonials unless he were very productive over the next four weeks. His eyes drifted over to the portable freezer a few feet away on the floor in the bedroom and he grimaced, shaking his head. After a long pause, he shifted his gaze away, grabbed the remote to flick off the television, and headed out the door to find a restaurant.

Terry Howe's retirement last October seemed to have provided Ryan Hannegan with his best chance yet to be an everyday player. The addition of Junichi Nakata had changed all that. Ryan had a career batting average of .285, but he had hit just 55 homers. That wasn't enough power to make most teams comfortable with him as a corner outfielder where he would be expected to provide much of a team's run production. He had the speed and the defensive ability to be a solid center fielder, but Junichi had been a center fielder in Japan, and it was a safe bet Paul Simonton had directed D.P. Perryton to play him there. Showing a growing strength for four weeks would be crucial for Ryan if he was to stick with the Colonials.

A fountain of youth is what I need, he thought to himself.

Ryan had returned to the bedroom in his hotel suite, contemplating what lay hidden in the locked freezer several feet away. His dinner with Dennis Soos and some of the other guys had been a good distraction, but back alone in his suite, the doubts and fears had re-materialized. He went over to the freezer, fiddled with the combination, flipping the latch that popped open with a hiss. He reached into the refrigerated container and pulled out one of three thick, plastic bags filled with a dark crimson substance. Rolling the bag between his hands, Hannegan sat down on the edge of the bed. In the back of his mind he could sense the sound his spikes make whenever he stepped from the outfield grass onto the warning track.

"What am I doing? Is making it worth all this? Did that poor kid, Sandoval, think about that before he hit the wall?" Ryan flopped back on the bed and let his memory take him back through earlier days. He rubbed his eyes with one hand, breathing deeply.

It began innocently enough in early December when Hannegan got a call from Dale Flandera, an old teammate from the T-Birds, who now worked with the Players' Association.

"Hey, Flando, what's happening? Long time, no hear from . . ."

"Listen, Ryan, I was just on the phone with your buddy, Doc, and he said I should give you a call. I had somebody cancel on me for our fantasy camp in Florida next week, and I need someone to fill in. Doc says you would be great."

"I don't know about that. Isn't that camp just for all-star guys?"

"Not necessarily . . . and besides, Doc says you've got lots of great stories, and the people who come to these things love the bull sessions at night. We'll pay you ten grand and all of your expenses."

"The money sounds great. If you think I would be okay, sure, why not."

Fantasy camps had become a popular vehicle for BBL teams and the Players' Association to raise money for their designated charities. Men, and some women, usually in their forties and fifties, paid big bucks to relive their youth by playing baseball for a week at the spring training sites of various teams. The baseball played wasn't very good, but the campers were re-living their childhoods, and they loved the experience. One camper put it best:

"It's like being twelve again, with one huge difference: you're allowed to drink beer!"

A big part of the week was sitting around with the baseball people at the hotel in the evenings, hoisting a few, and listening to the stories. A Kangaroo Kourt where the campers get fined for some miscue during that day's games only added to the fun. Ryan's team was filled with the usual crowd that attended these camps, with one notable exception. His name was Vladimir Titov, an expatriate from what used to be the Soviet Union. 'Mad Vlad', as Ryan dubbed him early in camp for his maniacal way of chasing after fly balls, was built like a Siberian grizzly at almost six feet five inches tall and nearly three hundred pounds. He couldn't play defense, but, oh my, could the big man hit.

"Mad Vlad, what are you doing trying to play baseball? I didn't know anyone from Russia knew this game?" Ryan said, as they walked off one of the fields following that morning's action.

"Glasnost, my friend," responded Titov in excellent English tinged with a Russian accent.

"When they had all that talk of détente between our two countries, America sent some coaches over to help us prepare a team for the Olympics. I had been a wrestler in our sports federation, and they picked people like me and other athletes to see if we could play this game."

The Russian flipped his glove into the air and began making swings with the big-barreled bat he was also carrying.

"I never could get a good feel for the catching of the ball, but I loved to — how do you say it — take some hacks!"

Ryan laughed. Vladimir Titov had plenty of defensive shortcomings, but he could sting the baseball.

"I must say that I am impressed, Vlad. You're easily the best hitter here. How did you learn to do it so well?"

"Soviet science, Ryanovich! Someday I will let you in on my little secret."

Hannegan was an active participant in the evening bull sessions with the campers. He loved telling baseball stories, and with his long run through the minor leagues before finally reaching the BBL, he had plenty of them to tell. Titov was there every night, soaking up the tales of hi-jinks on and off the field as told by Ryan and the other baseball people. Hannegan, meanwhile, was captivated by the Russian's accounts of some of his athletic experiences and life overall in the Soviet Union. Ryan also discovered Titov shared his passion for playing cards.

"Ryanovich, my friend, would you be interested in a friendly game of gin?"

Hannegan and Titov were leaving the pool area where that night's gabfest had just finished.

"And what do you mean by *friendly*, Vlad?"

"Something small. Say five dollars a point."

"Small? Sounds like you're trying to set me up."

"But, of course, Ryanovich. Is there any other way?"

The pair headed to a corner booth in the hotel's lobby bar. Ryan drank bottled beer as they played, while Titov consumed vodka in prodigious portions and seemed none the worse for it. The Russian's ability to play cards soon convinced Ryan he'd better be on top of his game or it would be a costly evening. The play was spirited, the drinks endless, and as the night wore on, Hannegan reveled in the company of Mad Vlad.

"Vlad, what was it really like to be an athlete in Russia? Didn't you guys get treated like kings?"

"It was nothing like the American professional athlete, but we did have things better than the rest of our comrades. Many of us had cars. We had nice flats and money to do things most others could not afford. Best of all, we had plenty of good food, and we did not have to spend hours waiting in long lines to get it."

Titov flipped a card onto the discard pile, then continued.

"I did well in our national competitions in wrestling, but I never got the Olympic recognition because of the boycott by your country in 1980 and then when we did not come to the Olympic Games in Los Angeles in 1984. No matter how we did against the rest of the world, we always measured ourselves against the Americans. That was why I was happy to be selected to be a part of the baseball program. We wanted desperately to beat the Americans at their own game." He narrowed his pale green eyes angrily for a moment, then suddenly grinned, his mood changing as quickly as a cloud's shadow passing over the land.

"I remember trying out for the U.S. team for the L.A. games. I was just a freshman in college then, but I didn't make the squad. By the time the Seoul Olympics rolled around in eighty-eight, I was already into my minor league career. Some of the guys who have played in the Games have told me it was a real thrill."

Titov hammered back what remained of a tumbler full of vodka and waved to the waitress to bring another round of drinks for both.

"What made you leave, Vlad? I know things are different politically, but it seems like athletes still get better treatment than others."

"Without question, Ryanovich, but that changes dramatically when your competitive days are over. Unless you become a part of your sport's governing body, or the head coach for one of the teams, the — how do you say it — "fringe bennies" drop off. I wasn't cut out to be a coach, and besides, I saw enough of the outside world when I did compete to know I wanted to be a part of that instead, if you know what I mean?"

"I hear you. The extras are nice. I'm going to miss that when my playing days are done. I just hope that doesn't happen too soon for me."

"Gin!" exclaimed the Russian as he laid down his cards, took a big gulp of the vodka the waitress had just brought, and then laughed heartily.

Hannegan grimaced as he counted the points in his hand. He realized this could get very expensive. But, he decided, you have to like the guy. And he added to himself, it's only money.

"Ryanovich, why all the talk about your baseball days being over? Are you not one of the top players? Isn't that why you are here teaching all of us?"

"Thanks for the vote of confidence. Maybe I should make you my agent. Actually, I was a last-minute replacement for Nick Hamilton from Baltimore. Right now I'm just trying not to be permanently replaced in this crazy game."

After a long, finishing hit on his longneck bottle of beer, Ryan continued.

"I am probably close to the same situation you were in when you left home, except I don't want to give up yet on playing. I don't think I'm the coaching type, so I keep chasing the dream."

"You keep chasing that dream, Ryan Hannegan! I want to die an old, happy man with LOTS of money, so I too am still chasing my dream!"

"At least you're going to be happier and a little richer before the night is over if I don't start getting better cards," Ryan replied to another call of 'Gin' by Titov. "If this wasn't a friendly game, I might wonder if you're doing something with these cards."

"I am," laughed the Russian. "I am beating you at one of your own games. Once again the power of Mother Russia shows its domination to the world!"

"Right — that's why your old country is broke and you're over here living in the American lap of luxury. By the way, I know this camp is not cheap; did you have any trouble coming up with the cash for it, if you don't mind my asking?"

"Not at all, my friend. It was a gift from my Uncle Yegor, for doing some services for him. He knows how I love to hit the ball, so this is my reward. Uncle Yegor was the man who brought me over to America."

"And what does Uncle Yegor do that allows him to send his nephew to a baseball camp that costs more than ten grand?"

The Russian raised his right index finger as a sign for Hannegan to wait a moment. With that, he reached into a bowl of peanuts sitting on the table and proceeded to fill his cheeks with them, like a giant-sized squirrel.

"He's just an honest businessman," proclaimed Titov in an awful Marlon Brando-as-the-Godfather impression, tinged with his Russian accent, and with bits of peanuts spraying across the table. "He makes offers you can't refuse," he added before nearly choking on the peanuts during the laughter that followed. Fortunately, Titov caught his breath, and after spitting out the remainder of the peanuts, resumed his hearty laughter.

"Your Uncle Yegor is Russian mob?"

"That is just what your news people say when they talk about any Russian who is financially successful when he comes to this country. In Russia, Uncle Yegor was a fixer. If you needed something — like an extra meat ration for a holiday dinner — then Uncle Yegor was able to fix it for you. Everyone loved Uncle Yegor there, and he takes care of those of us who have joined him since he came to this country."

Ryan perceived his new Russian friend did not want to go into any further details about his uncle's background, so he diplomatically steered the conversation in a different direction. The evening continued with more drinks and more good card playing from Titov. When Hannegan decided it was time to call it a night, he was down several hundred dollars. The Russian waved him away from paying off — or from picking up the rather substantial bar tab — with the offer to do it again later in the week. They hooked up several more times before the fantasy camp concluded, but Ryan's luck at cards didn't get any better against the skill of his counterpart.

The day before Hannegan was to leave for spring training in Florida, an overnight delivery service truck pulled into the driveway of his home in southern California. Ryan signed for the parcel and brought the large box back into the house. When he opened the container, he found a slightly smaller package inside, packed with dry ice, and with a small note attached to it:

Chase your dream!
Uncle Yegor

Suddenly, the phone rang.
"Ryanovich, did you receive your package?"
"Mad Vlad, what the hell is this?"
"Soviet science, my friend, so you can hit the ball like a Russian!"
Soviet science? Ryan rolled one of the plastic bags in his hands as he sat up on his bed in the hotel in Fort Myers. Do I have the American guts to use it?

In the latter half of the twentieth century — when sport and science began to merge — the Eastern Bloc countries were at the forefront in research. The propaganda value was immense any time they could beat the West in competitions on the world stage. The use of steroids, human growth hormones and other drugs became a part of the development process for the Eastern athletes. In an effort to keep pace, other countries began to cross the line into similar questionable practices, forcing the worldwide athletic federations to initiate drug-testing programs in an attempt to clean up their sports.

Research then turned to performance boosters that might not be as easily detected in the testing programs. Blood doping, a method of increasing the oxygen-carrying capacity in the blood of an athlete, became one of the newest tools. It was difficult to say with certainty that an athlete with a high blood count was blood doping since some athletes who train at high altitude, or others genetically predisposed, could also have a higher red blood cell count. Synthetically produced erythropoetin, or EPO, which produced similar results without some of the potential risks in the blood doping process, became another popular method. It was a continuing challenge for sports officials to police such activities.

"Ryan Hannegan, my good friend, I have sent you my secret to help you in your chase to be the big baseball star," Vladimir Titov had said in their phone conversation when the mysterious package had arrived. He added, "Do you remember when you asked how I could be such a good hitter of the baseball? I told you then it was a secret, one I am now sharing with you."

A baseball season is often described as a marathon because of the large number of games played, but ballplayers don't usually go through the same body-taxing experiences as high endurance athletes, even if the schedule is considered grueling. For that reason, the benefits of practices such as blood doping or EPO would not seem as appropriate for the sport since it relies more on reaction, explosive bursts of power, and hand-to-eye coordination rather than endurance. What if, however, there was a way to fortify the fast-twitch muscles needed in a hand-to-eye coordination sport like baseball with the endurance properties of slow-twitch muscles? What if a treatment could be created that would enable the body's to change muscle fiber type? It might allow a world-class athlete to augment the appropriate muscle type needed for his sport with characteristics of another muscle type.

Yegor Karpin was a fixer, Vladimir Titov had said so. When something was needed, he was able to provide it. The package that had arrived at his home earlier in the week, some of its contents which Ryan now held in his hands, was the gift from his new Russian friend and his uncle.

Ryan was appreciative but very fearful of the restrictions against doping. "They are cracking down big time this year, Mad Vlad. If I get caught doing anything illegal, I'm busted, and that would mean my career!"

"You hurt me, Ryanovich. Do you honestly believe that I would put you in any jeopardy? There is nothing in that package that is against the rules, or unsafe. Let's just say it is a special Russian cocktail, courtesy of Uncle Yegor. It will help you as it has helped others in your situation."

The Russian explained to the still skeptical Hannegan what was in the package. Titov assured him it was a natural process that could not be detected by baseball's testing program, no matter how sophisticated the system might be.

Ryan held the packet and let his thoughts come to the surface of his conscious mind. "Why didn't I just throw this stuff away when I first got it? Why are Titov and his uncle so interested in helping me? These people always have a reason for what they do." Now as Ryan contemplated making, perhaps, the most difficult decision of his professional life, the last words of the phone conversation with Vladimir Titov rang in his head.

"Just think of it this way, Ryanovich ... I am making you an offer you cannot refuse."

What did Brando say about the Don someday needing a favor in return? Why does Mad Vlad want to do this for me, and what am I supposed to deliver for him? He had seen the Russian smash the ball throughout the fantasy camp — almost like a pro — and Hannegan knew Titov did not have the same baseball skills as he did. Could Mad Vlad's Soviet science really make a difference? The season was less than four weeks away.

Ryan glanced over at the picture of his daughter sitting on the dresser. *Well, Kiddo, what do you think I should do? You always tell me it will happen if I get the chance, but time is running out for getting my chance!*

Ryan looked down at the plastic bag and again rolled it slowly in his hands, watching the thick, crimson fluid swish from side to side. Then he looked up again at the photograph.

"Michaela, you're all I've really got. I want you to be proud of your old man! I guess I have to do what I have to do."

Official reporting day for the players meant physical examinations. These exams, however, are not like the ones given by a family doctor. The players undergo a battery of tests checking every aspect of a player's physical condition. Orthopedic surgeons test the flexibility and range of body joints and x-ray areas if previous surgeries had been performed before cross-referencing that information with the medical history of the player. Some teams have players perform a series of exercises to compare their condition and strength with that of seasons past. Vision and hearing are checked, and with the new policies in baseball, blood and urine samples are taken for toxicology analysis. At the end of the lengthy process, each Boston player has a one-on-one session with Dr. Loren Myers, the head of medical services for the Colonials.

Dr. Myers had examined Ryan perfunctorily when he was acquired by Boston late last season, but this was the first time Hannegan had gone through the full work-up with the medical personnel of the Colonials.

"Good to see you again, Ryan. The numbers here on your chart indicate you had a most productive off-season."

"Thanks, Dr. Myers, good to see you, too. Yeah, I really got after it over the winter. Not many pages left on the calendar, you know."

"Quite impressive, I must say. Your flexibility and strength numbers have jumped compared to what you registered with the Gothams last spring. The blood test and the urinalysis won't be back for a couple of days. We aren't going to find any problems there are we, Ryan?"

"Not a chance, Doc! Baseball means everything to me, and I want to keep on playing. Do you think I would risk getting caught trying something that would have the General punching my ticket for an early release?"

"I am not making any accusations, Ryan. I just don't know you very well, so when I see significant changes in a player's physical profile from one season to the next, it does raise a red flag. The commissioner's office is quite specific about coming down hard on any chemical violations this season, and we want all of our players to be clean."

"Hey, Dr. Myers, I understand your concerns. This team has got enough going on with the Jinx and all. I'm sure they don't need Hoppy going after 'em for somebody juicing. You're looking at a guy who is as clean as they come."

The physician nodded and then went back to studying Hannegan's chart.

"I am glad to hear that, Ryan. Let's hope the blood and urine samples back up your claim. I must say, however, these numbers are impressive. Tell me how, at your age, were you able to improve your eyesight? Did you have laser surgery done?"

"No, Doc, I got turned on to a new vision training program that's really made a difference. I've got Dennis Soos and some of the other guys trying it now, but I think they feel it's a bunch of mumbo-jumbo."

Many professional athletes have undergone LASIK surgery in recent years. Done properly, an athlete, or any qualified candidate for that matter, can improve his vision in a quick procedure, with little or no pain, and a fast recovery period. Not every one is a good candidate for this procedure, however, and Ryan Hannegan was in that category. When his ophthalmologist told him his corneal tissue was too thin for the laser procedure, Hannegan began searching for other answers. One evening surfing the Internet, Ryan came across the Bates Method.

Dr. William Bates, a New York ophthalmologist in the early 1900s, believed he could improve a person's vision through a series of eye exercises. Most eye practitioners do not subscribe to such theories, but some followers have adopted his program. Ryan found a Bates Method doctor and underwent the training. Like his teammates, he found some of the exercises pretty goofy, but he stayed with them since he had nothing to lose. In his workouts before he came to Florida, and in the hitting session that had taken place yesterday, Ryan had begun to notice a significant improvement in that area.

"I guess my eyesight means you CAN teach an old ballplayer some new tricks. Anything else you need to know, Dr. Myers?"

"No, that takes care of things for now, Ryan. Good to see you again and best of luck this season."

"You got it, Doc! See ya' around the ballpark."

With a big smile, Ryan left the Colonials' team doctor in the meeting room and headed toward his locker in the clubhouse. As soon as he closed the door, the color drained from his face. Ryan wasn't the best at deception — his ex-wife could always catch him in some flimsy cover-up. Hannegan was moving into uncharted territory now, and at moments like this, he didn't know if he was going to be able to pull it off. Thank goodness the team had a workout scheduled. Just focus on baseball, he told himself; that's all Ryan wanted to do right now.

The official opening of practice also meant the first day for Junichi in a Colonials' uniform. The star from Japan had arrived in Florida the previous evening, along with more reporters and camera people than Ryan had ever seen crowding around one player. When stars from Asia had begun to play in the BBL in recent years, a large number of media came as well to follow their every move for their fans back home. It would be no different with Junichi and the Colonials.

"Can you believe that entourage?" Ryan yelled over to Mark Allen, Boston's starting catcher, as the team was going through its stretching exercises in the outfield grass. "It looks like there are at least fifty paparazzi! Do you think they'll be with us all year?"

"You better get used to it. I was playing with the Stars back when Takayuki Inamoto came over from the Tokyo Tigers. I felt sorry for the guy. I don't think he could take a crap without cameras clicking and a dozen reporters ready to write about the whole thing."

The Colonials already had a large contingent of reporters. The Colonials were a regional team, with reporters from all over New England keeping track of their ups and downs. The group covering the Colonials was passionate about baseball. Just like the fans, they seemed to rise and fall emotionally with whatever was happening with the team. It was their passion that had taken Boston's history of playoff failures and lifted it to the cult status of a jinx.

"We might as well wear our uniforms home after the games. If these guys are added to the home gang in Boston, there's no way we're even going to be able to move in the clubhouse."

Kevin Kyle, the Colonials' second baseman, who was working through his stretches on the other side of Hannegan, joined in.

"It'll give Terry Tate material for a column or two. Not that he needs a reason to comment about something."

Kyle was a native, a Southie from South Boston, and he was a crowd favorite at Patriots' Harbor. Terry Tate had been the lead columnist for many years with the *Boston Journal*, and Kyle had grown up reading Tate's viewpoints on all that was good and bad about sports in Boston. Tate could get grouchy in his columns, but no one could doubt his passion for the hometown teams.

"I like the guy," Ryan answered. "At least it seems like he knows what he is talking about — more than some of the guys who follow us around these days."

"No disagreement there, but just remember not to get on his bad side or he can crucify you. If you're up front with him, he'll give you a fair shake. But if he ever finds out you crossed him, well, I just wouldn't do that if I were you."

Ryan filed the information away for future reference. In truth, he had had little contact with Terry Tate up to this point. His relatively undistinguished career left Tate no reason to get to know Hannegan, and other than a brief introduction to him by Dennis Soos after the trade last August, Ryan hadn't done much more than nod in the sportswriter's direction whenever their paths had crossed. Nothing was going to change that today since all of the media's focus was on Junichi.

"Welcome to America, Junichi. Are you ready to go?"

The Japanese star bowed to the reporter that had asked the question and then surprised the crowd around him by responding in perfect English.

"It is a great honor to be in the Baseball Big Leagues and to be wearing the uniform of the Boston Colonials."

Junichi then turned to the Japanese media on hand and repeated his answer in his native tongue. This was a change in the usual ritual where Asian imports to the BBL would usually speak to the U.S. media through an interpreter.

"To be a teammate of great players like Ellis Nance and Ramòn Morientes is a humbling experience. I hope I can measure up to them and the other great players who have been Colonials."

He had a quick smile that made him quite photogenic, and a flair for knowing when to be coy and when to be forthcoming. It was obvious Junichi would be the next sensation if he were able to do anything out on the field. The Japanese media claimed he was the greatest baseball player ever in their country, and at first glance, Junichi looked ready to fulfill the potential expected of him.

He's bigger than I thought, Ryan realized as he walked up to him behind the cage during batting practice. Ryan glanced at him out of the corner of his eye. He was at least six-two and about two hundred pounds, and he looked like his body was poured out. *But what kind of guy is he? It's one thing to dazzle the media, but we're the ones who have to live with him all season.* Ryan hoped to himself the Japanese player would be compatible.

"Hello, I am Junichi Nakata," said the outfielder in perfect, if slightly accented, English as he extended his hand to Hannegan. "It is a privilege to meet you. I look forward to being your teammate."

Ryan shook hands firmly with Junichi, taken aback somewhat by the Japanese player's introduction. His previous experiences with the Asian players in baseball usually had them keeping to themselves, not mingling with the other players too much until they had been around for awhile.

"Good to have you with us, Junichi. I don't know how much of a privilege it is for you to meet me. You're the big star; I'm just trying to hang on in this game."

"I know all about you, Ryan Hannegan. The LMU Lions, right? Led the universities in hits, I think?"

"We say colleges around here, but how would you know anything about that? Nobody knows about that stuff, except maybe my daughter. What's your hobby? Reading old BBL media guides?"

Junichi smiled.

"As a boy in Nikko back home, I would watch the American university, I mean college, games on DBC-Asia. You were quite good."

Hannegan turned to Marty Fergus, another of the Colonials' players standing around the batting cage, and said, "You gotta love a guy like this. He's the first one to recognize the true talent I bring to this ball club."

"And when they allow us to swing aluminum bats, Ryan, you'll be the king of them all."

"Kiss my ass, Fergus! You'll find out this year."

Putting his arm around the Japanese star, Hannegan continued.

"With my boy, Junichi, here, we're going to be like Batman and Robin. Just grab hold of our capes, men, and we're going to take the C's where they've never been, to a Showdown championship."

"Who gets to be Batman? I think you would look so sweet in Robin's tights, Ryan."

Everyone around the batting cage roared with laughter. Junichi was going to fit in nicely. *How can I not like this guy, even if he's taking my job?* As the teasing and horseplay continued around the cage, Ryan's mind wandered back to his hotel room where a freezer full of opportunity and maybe calamity waited.

"That was quite a show you put on this afternoon," offered Dennis Soos as he dug into his steak that night at dinner. "It seemed like the old days back at LMU when you had everything going. Sometimes I wondered how you ever managed to stay eligible."

"You know me, Doc. I'm just a poor, little country boy trying to fit in with all you fancy people."

"Horse shit, Ryno. Country boy by way of Manhattan Beach. I swear, if you didn't like baseball so much, you would have ended up doing those infomercials on TV, convincing people to send you money to learn how they could make a fortune by selling the lint out of their navels. Or worse, you might have ended up being a politician, and then we all would have been screwed."

Hannegan smiled back at his friend as he sipped on his beer and reached for another buffalo wing.

"What can I say, Doc? I just love to get everybody's juices flowing."

Baseball players, like most athletes, are competitive, and Ryan Hannegan was no exception. For many players, nothing seemed to fire their interest away from the field more than card games and betting pools. The down time in baseball can be lengthy and card games made the time pass more enjoyably, whether it was hanging around the clubhouse in the afternoon before a night game or getting through the charter flight from one city to the next. It was a tradition as old as chewing tobacco in baseball, and was a great way for a player to get to know his teammates better, and if a guy was sharp with the cards he was dealt, it was a nice way to pick up a little extra cash.

The other popular BBL clubhouse pastime was the betting pool.

Basketball and hockey playoffs, auto racing, the Triple Crown horse races, golf tournaments — you name it — and the players probably had a pool going over its outcome. Ryan loved the clubhouse pools, and over the years, he usually wound up as the director of the action. He was reluctant to jump into that position with the Colonials because he was one of the new guys, but he grabbed the lead here in Florida at the urging of Dennis Soos.

"It's time to see if you girls have any *cajones*," Ryan shouted above the post-workout din in the Colonials' clubhouse. "The college basketball tournament starts tomorrow as you know, and I am here to see who has the INTESTINAL FORTITUDE — and more importantly — the CASH to be a PLAYER!"

Ellis Nance took the leap.

"Count me in, Bro'. Me and my Buckeyes are going to take it all!"

"What's the game?" countered Kevin Kyle. "And what's the tariff?"

"I'm glad you asked that, my friend. I'll tell you what I'm going to do. We are going to have the best game going since the last one I ran in the southeast part of northwest South Dakota."

By this time Hannegan had climbed up on a stool by the food table, and with broad gestures and wild-eyed wonder, he captured the attention of everyone in the clubhouse.

"We are not going to have just one pool. That's chump change, my friends. We are going to have two pools. And we're not going to have just two winners, no sir! We are going to have three cash-outs in each pool. But this isn't for the faint of heart, my dear flingers and mashers of the old horsehide. You have to be daring, and that probably leaves you out, Doc. You have to be smart and not just bet with your heart — sorry about that, Big E. And you have to be willing to fork over a little cash, so that means open up that wallet, Junichi. I know you've get some yen to throw around."

"What's in it for you, Hannegan?" yelled Nick Ertle, one of Boston's starting pitchers.

"Just the simple satisfaction of seeing my teammates have a good time — and ten percent off the top."

That comment brought an avalanche of towels, jock straps and other laundry airborne in Hannegan's direction.

"Seriously, all the money goes to the winners. The first pool is a random drawing for teams with an entry fee of two hundred dollars per draw. The winner gets fifty percent of the money, second gets thirty, and third takes home twenty. You can buy an additional team after everybody gets the chance to pick one, and you can sell your pick if someone wants to pay your price. The second pool is out of respect for the large gentleman over there," Ryan said as he pointed in the direction of Ellis Nance. "Five hundred big ones gets you the team of your choice. No more than two bets per team, so it's first-come, first-served and we'll have the same payouts as the other pool."

Raising his right hand solemnly, Hannegan headed for his big finish.

"As your humble servant, I conclude my presentation with one small request: SHOW ME THE MONEY!"

A cheer went up in the clubhouse, and everyone began to gather around Ryan, money in hand, ready to make a play. Ryan had struck a positive chord, and as it had happened with every team on which he played, the action and excitement generated helped give him a feeling of belonging.

"I don't get it, Ryno," mumbled Dennis Soos as he gobbled down a steak so rare it wasn't even warm. "In the clubhouse today, you were the king. You had everybody eating out of your hand. Tell me why I don't see that same guy when we're out on the field."

Soos ripped off another chunk of steak and crammed it into his mouth.

"In college you practically sprinted to the plate; you couldn't wait to hit. There wasn't a pitcher in the leagues you were afraid of. There wasn't a pitch you couldn't read and blast. What happened to that guy?"

"I wish I knew, Doc. That has been the story of my career. D.P. was great trying to straighten me out back in rookie ball, but then I got dealt to the Lumberjacks' organization, and they were clueless. It was hard getting comfortable there, and I guess I started tinkering with things. Whatever it was, I lost my confidence."

"No kidding. I couldn't believe it was you the first time I saw you playing for Murfreesboro. You looked so mechanical; no more of that 'see the ball, hit the ball.' You sure weren't having much fun."

"I know. I mean even in college I knew I wasn't going to be a guy who was going to hit a bunch of homers each year, but I always felt I could drive the ball as well as anybody. It got so the pop in my bat was gone. Yeah, yeah, I know. Warning track power. There's not much of a market for a slap hitter unless he runs like a cheetah with his ass on fire."

Soos picked up a French fry and bounced it off Hannegan's forehead.

"Your problem is right there, that lump that sits on top your shoulders. There's nothing wrong with your swing, at least from what I've been seeing. Man, you've been stroking it ever since we got down here."

"It has felt good. I did a bunch of different things over the winter to try to get better. Do you really think it shows?"

"Ryan, do you remember that Tom Cruise movie when we were in high school, *Risky Business*?"

"Are you kidding? That babe — I can't think of her name — was so hot. When they got it on during the train ride — man, that was the best!"

"All right, tiger, take a cold shower. I'm talking about when Cruise's character was talking with his friend about what Cruise was going to do while his parents were away."

"You lost me, Doc."

"The friend was ripping Cruise because he was too uptight, saying he wasn't willing to take any risks, you know, 'Risky Business.' Anyway, the guy tells Cruise sometimes in your life you just need to say 'What the Fuck!' Just let it go and do what feels right."

"That's what you need to do, Ryno. Just say 'What the Fuck' and let it go. I think if you get back to putting the W-T-F, the what the fuck, into your game, you're going to feel a whole lot better . . . and it's going to show in your play."

"W-T-F, huh? Might as well give it a shot. I've got Mr. Japan on one side and a calendar that won't slow down on the other. It wouldn't hurt, I guess, if I give it a little W-T-F."

"There's another problem though, Doc. My stomach."

"Something wrong with your belly, Ryan?"

"Yeah, I get sick every time I have to look at that ugly face of yours," Ryan snickered as he fired an answering shot with a chicken bone at his friend's head.

· FOUR ·

THE SHORTENED SPRING training schedule allowed the Baseball Big Leagues only about a week of team drills before the exhibition games got underway. The players didn't mind limiting their time in Florida or Arizona. Guys come to camp in shape, and they were usually antsy about getting started with a couple of weeks left anyway. Now they could jump right into playing games and be ready for the official schedule by April fifteenth.

Ryan Hannegan wouldn't have minded an extra week or two to impress management. He had performed well in the drills the first week. He hit the ball with authority in batting practice, and that continued against live pitching in the two intra-squad games played over the weekend. Now it was finally time to face a different uniform as the Colonials traveled north to Clearwater for an exhibition contest with the Philadelphia Quakers.

"Man, talk about getting it together, Ryno," Dennis Soos said as they rode together on the bus up Interstate 75 from Fort Myers toward Clearwater. "I haven't seen you hit like this, not since back at LMU. I guess my pep talk is paying off!"

"You keep thinking that, Doc," Hannegan replied, thankful his friend believed his advice over dinner last week was the reason for Ryan's early success. "I'm seeing the ball real well, better than I have in a couple of years. I guess all those vision exercises were worth it."

"I don't know anything about your seeing things better. What I see is you're quick to the ball. Shit, you're hitting inside the ball and with some sting, too! I'm not the only one noticing it, either. I even overheard that prick, Simonton, talking about you with D.P. the other day."

Hannegan leaned back and stared up at the ceiling of the bus before answering.

"Prick or not, Simonton is the guy I have to show something to. I know D.P.'s on my side, but I don't think our general manager thinks of me as much more than a bag of extra baseballs."

Paul Simonton III was part of a new wave of baseball executives. An accounting major in college, Paul Simonton was a fantasy baseball freak, reveling in the numbers side of the game. Using his family's financial and social connections, he made his entry into the baseball industry straight out of college in a low-level marketing position with the New York Gothams. A relentless work rate got him noticed, and soon he received the chance to move into the personnel side of the business.

Simonton was a statistics maniac. He knew the offensive output of even the most obscure players in the team's organization and he loved to make projections based strictly on those facts and figures. Simonton ended up with a pretty good batting average when it came to those predictions, enhancing his reputation. He was hired as the director of minor league operations for the Philadelphia Quakers and continued success there culminated in his rise to the top when the Colonials named him their general manager, the youngest in the Baseball Big Leagues. The media dubbed him the Baseball Boy Wizard. Simonton wore the title like a crown.

"Hell, he feels that way about everybody, Ryan. I think he would move anybody on this team — except maybe his boy, Junichi — if their numbers didn't add up on his Boy Wizard charts. I hate that son of a bitch!"

"Gee, Doc, tell us how you really feel."

It was no secret Soos had little regard for the team's general manager. He grudgingly gave credit to Paul Simonton for making some smart transactions the past several seasons, and for starting to rebuild what had been a thin farm system for the Colonials. Soos was like D.P. Perryton, however, a baseball lifer who saw the game as more than just statistics. Soos had won defensive honors at third base the last four seasons running, and he was the hitter in the Colonials lineup that always seemed to make the opposition pay when a pitcher let his guard down. Just as D.P. always said, it's the little things that win ball games. Doc did that as well as anyone on the club.

"Doesn't it bother you, Dennis, that you don't take better care of yourself?" Paul Simonton once asked him.

"You mean you aren't impressed with this body?"

Simonton ignored Doc's attempt at humor.

"There is an image that should go with this game. Great players should look the part, not be like some schmuck off the street. I believe appearance plays an important role in success or failure."

"Well, excuse me if I don't fit your profile, Mr. Simonton. I always thought the only thing that mattered at the end of the game was whether or not the result ended up under the W or the L column."

The Boston general manager showed no reaction to the response from Doc Soos. *These players,* thought Simonton, *what do they know anyway? They're just looking for their next freebie, or an undeserved raise in their next contract. If I had had the chance, I would have shown them how a player is supposed to look and is supposed to act.*

Statistics drive the game of baseball for many fans — including some front office executives — but numbers never give the complete picture. Success at one level of the minors doesn't always guarantee big numbers at the next, and that pattern only grows stronger as a player climbs the game's ladder. The same is true when it comes to scouting prospects where a player's physical dimensions and speed readouts take on as much importance as game skills. Longtime baseball people shake their heads when new wave talent evaluators limit themselves to the numbers. A veteran scout, Pops Hillier, once made the following observation:

"The guy looks like a Greek god and he could probably win the decathlon at the Olympics. But nobody stops to find out anymore if he can play the goddamn game!"

The bottom line was all that mattered to Paul Simonton. The stats told the story. Simonton had loved playing baseball as a child; he just wasn't very good at it. At six foot three and two hundred pounds, Simonton had an athletic build, but it had not translated into success. No matter how much effort he made in team sports as a youth, the results never came. To compensate, he threw himself into running, pounding the pavement as diligently as he poured over the latest statistical printouts. The miles piled up, but the sting of failing at the sport he truly loved didn't go away. If he couldn't play the game on the field, he would devise a way to win on his terms.

"The guy has no heart. All he cares about are his damn numbers," Doc continued. "I'm not saying stats don't count, but there's a feel to this game, and that comes from being around the game, from being out on the field."

Paul Simonton downplayed the value of playing experience in the decision-making process, saying the proper analysis of the numbers could often achieve, or surpass, the results of having a feel for the game.

"I'd like to take his numbers and shove them where the sun don't shine. D.P. has forgotten more baseball than that suit will ever know, no matter what his computer printout tells him. But his highness, the Wizard, takes all the credit when we win. If Simonton doesn't like how I feel, then he can kiss my ass and trade me someplace else!" Doc could afford to complain about his general manager because he had the respect of his teammates in the clubhouse, and just as importantly, the love of the die-hard Colonial fans. To trade off one of the team's most popular players would be difficult, even for a bottom-line guy like Paul Simonton. Besides, at least for now, Soos' numbers showed up very well in the Simonton baseball ledger, even if he didn't fit the general manager's profile of what a player should look like.

Ryan had been listening attentively to his friend's convictions. "I'm just going to give it my best shot, Doc, starting today with the Quakers and whenever D.P. gets me some at-bats. What was your advice, a little WTF? That's my plan, and we'll just see what happens."

"That's what I'm talking about, Ryno! We'll show Simonton and the rest of them what the boys from LMU can do now that we're finally back together." Dennis Soos settled back into his seat on the bus, closed his eyes and smiled contentedly.

Those pleasant thoughts about good times with his college teammate certainly looked right in the early stages of exhibition play. Replacing Junichi in the fifth inning of that first spring game against Philadelphia, Hannegan collected a pair of hits and made a nice running catch of a drive to right center. The trend continued throughout the first week of spring games with Hannegan stroking the ball with authority and flashing the leather in the field. Junichi was drawing the bulk of the attention because he too was starting off well, but Ryan's efforts weren't flying under the radar of the media completely.

"Paul, can you comment on the good play here in Florida by Ryan Hannegan?"

Paul Simonton relished the chance to show off his take on the game. He felt superior to most of the people assigned to the coverage of the Colonials, and he enjoyed his daily sessions with the media.

"It certainly has been a pleasant surprise. As you may recall, I worked hard to acquire him from the Gothams last summer to help us in our playoff chase. My choice looks even better now in view of the numbers here this spring. And he gives Dudley veteran help off the bench because of his versatility."

Terry Tate didn't bother to question the young general manager's version of Hannegan's acquisition. That was last season.

"It seems you may have an overload of talent out there in the outfield, Paul. Besides Junichi, you've got Gorski and Cook, and now Hannegan plus your kid prospects, Ian Cahill and Drew Gannon. You can't keep them all on your major roster. What are your plans?" The reporter licked the tip of his pencil and prepared to write.

"A team can never have enough depth. There are still two weeks of spring training to sort things out. Cahill and Gannon have options remaining, and you never know what surprises turn up that can force a move."

Simonton paused for effect and then continued.

"I'll crunch the numbers at the appropriate time and make the right decision."

Tate and some of the other listeners rolled their eyes at the Boston G-M's arrogance, but said nothing. Simonton then excused himself to head to an interview with Jayvee DellVecchio. The DBC's *Totally Baseball* crew was on hand that day in Fort Myers to do its preseason preview of the Colonials. Paul Simonton was looking forward to embellishing his Boy Wizard reputation on the national platform that DBC Television would provide.

The presence of the DBC crew raised the level of interest for the Colonials players as well. Ballplayers get used to their daily interaction with the media during the course of a season, but the national network people are a different element. The increased exposure is obvious, but it is also important to the players because of the reaction from their peers. Catching the day's highlights on the DBC's late show of *Sports Roundup* was part of the daily regimen for almost everyone involved with baseball, and the special emphasis the *Totally Baseball* show provided the sport was the bonus exposure that everyone sought. Jayvee DellVecchio's appearance that day added another element, too.

"She is a FOX!" exclaimed Eric Polick, one of the utility infielders for the Colonials, as the players sat in the dugout before that day's exhibition game with the New York Horsemen.

Dennis Soos dug an elbow into his teammate.

"Roll your tongue back up into your mouth, Polick! She's way out of your league."

Ellis Nance, sitting alongside Doc Soos, echoed the general feeling in the dugout.

"My kids would say she's hip, which I guess is a good thing. I must admit it's pretty damned rare to find someone who looks that good and knows that much about the game."

"I'd be happy to give her some game."

"She'd chew you up, Eric, that is if she even acknowledged your presence," Ryan Hannegan added to the conversation. "Believe me, that lady knows what she's doing and God help anything or anybody keeping her from taking care of business."

"Right, like she would give *you* the time of day, Hannegan. You're just a bench jockey like I am. Anyway, if she's ever actually met you, I doubt she'd remember it."

Ryan simply smiled and made no response as the players watched DellVecchio wrap up her interview with Paul Simonton. Shaking hands with the Boston general manager, Jayvee left the area behind home plate where she had been taping and made her way past the Boston dugout. Recognizing Ellis Nance among the Boston players sitting there, she smiled and called out to him.

"Big E! It's nice to see you again. How's the family?"

"They're just great. But Kaayla's almost fifteen now, and the way the boys hover around her is gonna give me gray hair."

"I don't think you have anything to worry about, Ellis. Somehow, I think those potential suitors are well aware of who Kaayla's dad is."

"And, I guess, when I'm not around, her not-so-little brother can keep an eye on things for me. Jamir is already over six-two and he's only twelve."

"Is he going to play football or baseball? Or is he going to be like Dad and play both?" Jayvee had her hands on her hips, smiling at Ellis.

"Not a chance. He got all of my wife's brains, and he wants to be a computer engineer, that is if he doesn't decide to become the next great African-American golfer."

Jayvee chuckled and then reminded Nance and Dennis Soos she needed to do interviews with them following the day's game. With a wave, she left the dugout area to head to the ramp leading up through the stands to the press box area in Fort Myers. Every pair of eyes in the Boston dugout followed her departure until they lost sight of her. Her youthful backside and her almost-strutting walk was enough to draw stares until she was out of sight. Her navy blue form-fitting Chanel pantsuit with the snow-white jabot was stunning. As was she.

"Yumpin' Yimenny — vhat a vhoman!" exclaimed Ryan in a mock Scandinavian accent, making everyone laugh.

The game against New York was the first meeting of the spring between the two longtime rivals. If the Colonials represented the frustrations of always being close, then the Horsemen symbolized success. The New

York franchise, after a slow beginning, had become the flagship of the BBL. Their string of achievements began when Randolph Irving Noyes, the great-great nephew of the author Washington Irving, bought the team in the early days of the Depression. He changed their nickname from the Flying Dutchmen to the Horsemen in tribute to the main character in one of his ancestor's famous novels. As the Horsemen slowly dominated the American Conference — and all of the big leagues for that matter — their logo of the Headless Horseman became the most respected or most reviled symbol in baseball. If you were a fan of the Colonials, nothing was more irritating than the sight of that Headless Horseman.

Players throughout baseball were aware of the emotional aspects of this Boston-New York rivalry, but it was brought home full-force to those who become members of either team. The Horsemen carried themselves with a certain swagger that comes with the accumulation of so many championships. Contrast that with the pressure to win when a player wore B-O-S-T-O-N across his jersey chest. Boston fans let a Colonial player know, most assuredly, that his sole duty in baseball was to beat those damned Horsemen! Exhibition game or not, the full house on hand to watch in Fort Myers was testament to the depth of the rivalry.

In the dugout, Boston second baseman, Kevin Kyle, fiddled with the laces of his glove, but his mind wasn't on defense. The fiery little infielder turned to Ryan with a questioning look.

"Man, I don't know what it is with Pickens, but he's always got my number. Skipper says you've got the right approach for him. What the hell is it that you do?"

"Close my eyes and hope," Ryan responded with a shrug.

Buddy Pickens was a four-time winner of the American Conference's Most Valuable Pitcher award. Pickens and Ellis Nance were considered the top two pitchers in the A-C, and the New York ace always seemed to dominate the Colonials. Ironically, Hannegan had been successful in his battles with Buddy Pickens through the years with other teams, hitting well over three hundred and with a couple of homers. D.P. Perryton had Ryan in the lineup in an attempt to take advantage of that success and because of the fine spring he had been having thus far.

"Honestly Kev, I try not to do too much, maybe choke up just a tad and take the pitch wherever he puts it. The man throws the ball so damn hard so he supplies all the power. All you need to do is make decent contact."

"Works for me, then. The way you're whacking the ball this spring I'll believe anything you tell me. Come on, let's take it to them. I don't care if this counts or not. I hate these sons of bitches."

Kyle bounded off the bench to take his place in the field for the game's start. Angel Correa, a twenty-two year old flamethrower from the Dominican Republic, was getting the call from D.P. Perryton in this matchup. Correa had been inserted into the Colonials' starting rotation in late June last season when injuries forced the team to give the relatively untested rookie a shot. Paul Simonton had fast-tracked the young man through the Boston minor leagues system, and Correa did not disappoint, winning nine games against just two losses in his rookie campaign. Perryton had Correa penciled in as his number two starter behind Ellis Nance.

There were concerns about the readiness of the pitchers due to the contracted spring schedule, but both Correa and Pickens looked in mid-season form. Neither side mustered any serious scoring threats until the Colonials began to get something cooking in the fourth. Kevin Kyle led off the inning with a bunt single and Junichi followed with a ringing double to right center, moving Kyle to third. With first base open, the Horsemen elected to intentionally walk the Boston cleanup hitter, Ramon Morientes, to create a force situation at any base. That brought Ryan Hannegan to the plate.

Hannegan had grounded out weakly his first at-bat when Pickens had busted him inside with a good cut fastball. A similar approach seemed likely here in the hopes of getting Ryan to hit a double play grounder. Pickens missed inside with his first pitch however, and then Hannegan fouled off the next offering that was up and in. Conventional pitching wisdom could have seen Pickens work away with his next pitch to get Hannegan set up for another pitch inside, but Buddy Pickens didn't get to be one of the most feared pitchers in the BBL by always following convention. Instead he tried to triple-up with another cut fastball in on the hands of Hannegan. Using a compact inside-out stroke like he usually did against hard-throwing right-handers, Hannegan served the ball over the left side of the New York infield for a single, scoring Kyle from third and the flying Junichi from second. Two to nothing Colonials and the Fort Myers crowd went wild.

Ryan tipped his batting helmet to the cheers of the fans and then noticed Pickens glaring over at him while the Horsemen' ace was hammering the rosin bag into the ground at the back of the mound.

"C'mon, Pickens, it's spring training for chrissakes. Lighten up. We're just having some fun." Ryan smiled cordially.

Pickens responded with a middle finger salute for Hannegan. Pickens had the reputation of making retribution for every redress he felt he suffered at the hands of a hitter. That usually meant the guilty party would be hitting the deck from a pitch buzzed inside, no matter how long it might be until they next met.

"I guess that's the way it's going to be, then. That'll make it interesting when we see these assholes the next time." Hannegan muttered to himself, shrugged his shoulders and walked out to his lead.

Angel Correa was still on the hill for Boston as the game moved into the fifth inning. Dudley Perryton felt Correa needed the work to keep his conditioning at the max for the start of the season in two weeks. Unfortunately for the Colonials, it was one inning too many. With two outs, Horsemen center fielder, Nelson Cuevas, chopped a ball off the hard dirt in front of home plate. Correa leaped high to grab the bounder, but when he returned to earth, his right leg crumpled with a nasty-sounding crack. Pete Hudec, the Boston trainer, raced onto the field before the umpires had even called for time. It was obvious Correa had done something serious from the way the young Dominican was howling in pain and by the fact that his leg was definitely misaligned. Correa's day was done and his future prospects looked grim.

Even with the injury to one of their top pitchers, the day was a good one for the Colonials. Boston knocked off New York four to one, and with the lone off-day of spring training set for tomorrow, the Colonials were in a celebrating mood when they hit the clubhouse following the game.

"Ryan, what's the game plan for tonight?" bellowed Ellis Nance across the room as he chomped on a soft taco from the postgame spread.

Ellis was referring to the college basketball championship game being contested that evening, and the Big E's beloved Ohio State Buckeyes were in the game. Nance had a piece of the action in both of Ryan's betting pools. He was big-time into his alma mater, and his school had the chance to win him some serious cash and major bragging rights if they could triumph over their opponents.

"I've got it all worked out."

Hannegan jumped up on a stool near the food table to get the attention of everyone in the room.

"Tonight's the payoff for our college hoops pool. And since tomorrow is an off-day, it will be party time for everybody, even if your team is out of it."

"It'll be crying time for the Big E when my BC boys take it all," shouted out Kevin Kyle in his nasally South Boston accent.

"In your dreams, little man, in your dreams! I doubt if they even know how to play basketball in Boston!"

The heckling had the potential to increase and go on for a long time. Ellis was ready to respond when Hannegan cut him off.

"Cool it, guys. Listen. Here's the deal. I worked it out with the hotel and they're giving us one of their big conference rooms on the second floor. We'll have a big-screen TV, a full bar and plenty of food. It's our party, so let's not invite half the Gulf Coast, okay? You can bring some people if you want, but let's keep it small if we can. That means make sure anyone you invite is of legal age and no pros, Hwang, if you know what I'm saying."

Hannegan made his last comment toward the Colonials' bullpen ace, Hwang Sang Hwan, who was from South Korea. Wang blushed and smiled at Ryan. He was one of the few players who had his family with him in Florida, and he would have been the last player on the team to be involved with someone. Everyone respected the Korean, but he was often the target for teasing that he was a real ladies' man, when the complete opposite was the case.

"Tip-off is around nine o'clock tonight, so the action will get started around eight thirty. It's the Tarpon Room on the second floor. Jumping off the stool, Ryan concluded, "I expect everyone to be there . . . team photo at half time!"

· FIVE ·

The catering and decorating for the party that evening was over the top. The Gulfport Royale personnel outdid themselves. It wasn't a big screen TV; it was more like half a wall. The television was situated at one end of the Tarpon Room, with a large bar at the opposite end, manned by three bartenders. In between the two action spots, the hotel had arranged tables and seating for about one hundred and fifty people. They were prepared for the team inviting more than their share of friends. The food spread, with beef, shrimp, chicken and every kind of finger food imaginable, would have satisfied several teams, not just the Colonials. The several chefs had earned their enviable reputations with this one display of culinary splendor. It was a good thing the ballclub had the day off the following day because it was a certainty they would be slow-moving after this feast.

"Hello, boys, c'mon in..."

Hannegan was at the door before the game began, greeting teammates and making certain there were no party crashers.

"Everybody has a chance to win tonight, even if the Eagles and the Buckeyes aren't your teams. Pick a square; they're twenty bucks a pop with at least two winners, and we've got some side bets going, too."

Hannegan escorted the partygoers over to a large dry-erase board near the door displaying all the possible betting choices available.

"I'm telling you it's the luck of the Irish," Kevin Kyle said. "I get BC in the pool and now they're in the title game. It's going to be our night."

Kyle had actually drawn the team he wanted, Boston College, in the blind-draw pool, and he convinced Hector Santana, the team's bullpen coach, and Pete Hudec to join him in the five-hundred dollar pool.

"Junichi, my friend. So glad you decided to make it."

The newest Colonial had with him several friends from among the Japanese media covering his every move, including an attractive young lady. This night was going to be a new experience for them, but they were eager to participate.

"Ryan Hannegan, master ballplayer and now gracious host!" Junichi beamed at his new American friend and mentor.

"I don't know about any of that master ballplayer crap, Ju, but here's the skinny. It's very simple. You give me as much money as I think you should, and then you eat and drink enough so you don't ever remember giving it to me. Then I'll be sure I can afford my daughter's college tuition someday."

Junichi smiled, bowed with a flourish that seemed more European than Japanese, and then peeled off several fifty-dollar bills from a money clip and tossed them in Hannegan's direction.

"Ryan, I almost believe you are serious."

"Oh, but I am, Junichi. As anyone can plainly see, you never, ever gave me any money tonight."

Hannegan deftly took the fifties and made them disappear with some sleight-of-hand he had learned as a youngster. Junichi Nakata gasped and then laughed along with his teammate. It was going to be that kind of evening. The routine continued with the other players and guests as they arrived, and soon the room was humming with activity.

"Let's get with it, chumps."

Ellis Nance had a CD player on a table blaring the Ohio State fight song. He was cajoling several teammates into trying to learn the words.

"I don't care if it's a football song; we're going to do this. *'Our honor defend, so we'll fight to the end for O-HI-O!'*"

Kevin Kyle was attempting the same with his Boston College boosters, but without success. Maybe it was because he was a foot shorter and a hundred pounds lighter than Ellis Nance, or maybe because Kyle wasn't sure he knew the Boston College fight song, but whatever the reason, the struggle to perform the BC theme song collapsed in laughter.

More than one hundred people were in the Tarpon Room, enjoying themselves thoroughly, ready for the opening tip-off. Just then Dennis Soos arrived with a surprise.

"Ryno, you know Jayvee DellVecchio from DBC Television..." Dennis half-turned, holding one of his hands palm up to usher the lovely young lady at his side toward Ryan.

"Who doesn't, Doc, but I am sure she wouldn't know much about me. Nice to see you again, Jayvee."

"I am familiar with you, Mr. Hannegan. I see you're making some noise this spring, trying to make D.P. find a place for you to play. Nice job today, although you must know that Buddy Pickens never forgets. He's a bull elephant."

Ryan smiled. "Yeah, I know. I'm just trying to win a job. I wasn't trying to show him up. I know better than that."

"You'd better be ready the next time you see him. It's good for me, though. It will give us something extra to talk about when you face them during the season."

"I hope I get the chance to be dusted off. That'll mean D.P. is giving me some playing time. Anyway, what brings you here with this bum?"

"Kiss my ass, Ryno," Soos chuckled.

"Whistle so I'll know which end it is," Ryan muttered, grinning.

Jayvee scowled at their toilet humor and decided to ignore it. "When I finished my interview with Doc, he asked if I was going to watch the game tonight. I had planned on doing some work and order room service when Doc persuaded me to come here. He said you knew how to throw a party. I'm reserving judgment on that." She looked from Soos to Hannegan and back again, smiling, expectant, but totally self-possessed.

"It's great to have you join us; we're going to have some fun!" Hannegan offered his arm to Jayvee to escort her into the room while his teammates hooted good-naturedly. Ryan smiled broadly, knowing just about any guy in the room would gladly change places with him if they could.

With Dennis Soos trailing behind, he led Jayvee to a table in the back near the bar where they joined Ellis Nance, Kevin Kyle, and Pete Hudec.

"Another Buckeye fan joins us," exclaimed Ellis Nance. "Your Cleveland roots are going to come through here, aren't they, Jayvee?"

"She can't root for your hayseeds, Big E," countered Kevin Kyle. "She lives on the East Coast now and she went to an Ivy League school, so she has to be for BC."

"Sorry, Kevin, but the Big E's right. I'll always be an Ohio girl down deep, so I have to root for the Buckeyes. It was sweet of you to want me on your team, though."

DellVecchio leaned over and planted a kiss on Kyle's cheek causing his face to turn nearly as red as the shock of hair on top of his head. The banter continued between Kyle and Nance as Hannegan brought some plates of food to the table and then went off to take care of the drink orders for the group. The game got underway, and the electricity in the room picked up immediately. Ohio State had been the top-ranked team for most of the season, while Boston College barely made the post-season competition. BC got hot in the tournament however, and now they were one win away from an improbable title. It was expected to be just the kind of David versus Goliath battle fans loved.

When Hannegan returned with the drinks, everyone was concentrating on the game. He grabbed the lone empty seat alongside Jayvee and sat down. During an early time out in the first half, Jayvee struck up a conversation.

"So, are you really the mastermind behind tonight's extravaganza? It's very impressive!"

"Thanks. Doc and I have been doing things like this ever since we were kids back in college. You should see Doc's Super Bowl bash. He fancies himself as quite the cook, and I have to admit he puts on quite a show."

"That's right! I had forgotten! You two played together on those good Loyola Marymount teams back in the eighties. It must be nice to get the chance to be teammates again, here with the Colonials."

"We give each other grief all the time," Ryan said with a grin as he delivered a playful elbow to Dennis Soos who was sitting on Hannegan's other side. Ducking a friendly jab at his jaw in return, he continued.

"But it is special to be together again. I've watched Doc play great for a long time; he's earned all the attention he gets. He deserves a Showdown championship ring before he hangs it up. Big E too. They got real close a couple of years ago, and I know they want to get back and win it."

Hannegan ate a forkful of pasta from his plate. "Me, I just want to contribute to that. I've never really played for a contender, and I don't know how many chances I have left. It would be the best if we could achieve that here."

"Just keep delivering for D.P. like you did today, and I am sure he'll find a place for you."

Jayvee smiled and then motioned to Hannegan indicating he had a spot of sauce on his face. Red-faced, Ryan wiped it away.

"Is it that important, to make a name for yourself in this game?"

"It's important to any player who puts on a uniform. I think the pressure really goes up a notch when you can see your career heading toward the stretch." He paused and stared deep into Jayvee's unblinking hazel eyes. "But I have to tell you, Jayvee, as great as it would be to win a championship and to be a factor in winning it, it would be even better to see what it would mean to my daughter, Michaela. She thinks her old man is the best. It shows you what kids know."

Jayvee was intrigued as she listened to Hannegan talk about his daughter and their relationship. It was amazing, she thought to herself. *It's been more than twenty years, but it sounds like he's talking about Dad and me. That was always so much fun: Dad and me and baseball. I do miss that.*

The talk between the two deepened, interrupted only when the action of the basketball game drew their attention, or when Ryan did an update on whatever betting pool was being resolved by the score of the game at that time. It was obvious they were enjoying each other's company. The game had everyone's attention as it reached its closing moments. The underdog Boston College Eagles had led through most of the contest by controlling the tempo of the game and with incredible shooting success from three-point range. However, Ohio State's superior size inside — their big man, Curtis Swain, was having a monster game — was wearing down BC as the game moved toward the finish.

"Four seconds left ... Matt Miller again trying to extend BC's two point advantage. Here's his second attempt ... no good ... Swain with the rebound and he gets if off to Becker ..."

The crowd was on its feet in the Tarpon Room, and the noise was almost as loud as in the arena down in Atlanta where the game was being played.

"Kirby Becker is dashing up the far sidelines; two seconds, one second... he lets if fly..."

The Buckeyes' point guard launched a forty-five footer just before the buzzer sounded. The shot crashed off the backboard, spun around the rim several times, and then, unbelievably, dropped through the net.

"Buckeyes win! The Buckeyes win!!"

Ellis Nance, all six foot nine of him, stood atop his chair screaming loudly. Kris Fucci, a Boston pitcher who had teamed up with Nance in one of the betting pools, was spraying him with beer. Meanwhile, Kevin Kyle slumped in his seat in disbelief.

"I don't freakin' believe it. We stick it to those guys for the entire game, and then some little shit that's no bigger than me kills us!"

"Oh, I don't know. I think he is a little bigger than you, Kev."

"Screw you, Doc; we can have a go anytime you want."

"Easy, Kevin, I was just giving you some crap."

"I know man, sorry about that. It's just that I can't believe we lost."

Ellis Nance walked over to Kyle and picked him up in a giant bear hug that had the diminutive second baseman half-laughing and half-groaning from the embrace. His squirming to get away from his large teammate only made the scene funnier and everyone laughed uproariously. Eventually, Kyle settled down and he was returned to his feet. He slapped Nance with a strong handshake and congratulated Big E on his alma mater's triumph. Euphoric in victory, Nance was ready to party.

"Shots all around... to celebrate my Buckeyes doing it!"

Those at the table, especially Jayvee, tried to protest, but Ellis Nance would have none of that. He waved to one of the bartenders who came to the table with a tray of shot glasses filled with a purple concoction: Raspberry Kamikazes. The disadvantage of celebrating with a man the size of Ellis Nance was that his ability to handle alcohol would probably be better than everyone else. Whenever another group of people came over to congratulate him, Big E would order another round. For Hannegan, Jayvee, Doc, and several others, this pattern happened five times before they could finally convince Nance it was time to slow down.

Ryan went to the front of the room by the big screen to get everyone's attention. He slipped momentarily as he climbed a chair.

"What's a matter, Ryan? Having trouble staying up with the Big E?" Nance turned to the crowd and spread his rather large wingspan. "Y'all had trouble staying with me and my Buckeyes, and that's just the way it should be. We're number one. No, I'm number one."

Doc Soos ripped off a large belch in response and everyone roared.

"You're absolutely right, Big E," Ryan said as he tried to regain control of himself and the party. "As tonight's big winner, it is my privilege to show you the money."

Hannegan handed Nance an envelope with a large wad of cash that represented the winnings for the Big E and his partner in the pools, Kris Fucci. Ryan passed out envelopes to the other winners from the scores pool as well as taking care of the runner-up and third place finishers.

"We're not done yet, my friends. The Palladium next door has invited us to continue our party and the drinks are on them."

Hannegan threw a bunch of free drink tickets into the air, setting off a mad scramble for the cards.

"Whaddya say, Jayvee? Should we join everybody next door?" He was daring her to accept.

"I'd love to, but I have an early flight tomorrow back to New York so we can edit the preview package on you Colonials. Besides, after those rounds of shots, I am not sure how long I would last, anyway. Things are starting to move a little fast in here as it is."

"Then let me take you back to your hotel. That's the least I can do."

"That won't be difficult; I am staying right here up on the eleventh floor."

"No kidding! I'm up on eleven too. Even I can't get lost taking you there."

Ryan and Jayvee walked a little unsteadily to the elevator, talking and laughing all the way. As they rode up to their floor, Jayvee thanked him for a great time. Ryan smiled down at her, noticing the golden flecks in her eyes, loving the whiffs of her cologne that made his head reel more than the drinks did.

"I didn't know what to expect out of all of this myself, but it was certainly a lot more fun than watching the game by myself in my room."

"You're not a bad guy, Ryan Hannegan . . . after talking to you for just a little while, I felt like I knew you already."

"You never know what surprises life can bring. I have to tell you I had a great time too. You're even better than I imagined you would be. You know how we ballplayers do like to fantasize . . ."

"I'll take that as a wonderful compliment, Mr. Hannegan."

The two walked down the eleventh floor hallway not speaking, but Jayvee did hold Ryan's arm. Upon reaching her door, she turned to him.

"I look forward to the next time our paths cross. You guys have to admit I hung with the big boys pretty well tonight, even with all those shots."

She leaned over and kissed Hannegan on the cheek. Turning away, she inserted the magnetic card into her door lock.

"You were great. Normally we just hang with the best, you know, the Varsity. But tonight we didn't mind settling for the JV's."

Jayvee DellVecchio froze, then spun around and slapped a startled Ryan Hannegan across the face. But her next move was even more astonishing; she kissed him hard on the mouth and dragged Ryan by his shirt into her room.

Jayvee DellVecchio woke with a start, the way someone does when their bearings are anything but centered. She sat up on one elbow and looked around, feeling like she was still dreaming. She tugged the sheet up around her neck, bemused she was nude but still suffused in a warm afterglow. The slight buzz of a developing headache was going off, and her clothes were strewn about her hotel suite. On one side of the bed the glaring light of the clock radio told her it was time to start getting her things together, and in a hurry, too, if she was to make her sunrise flight back to the City. On the other side lay a softly snoring Ryan Hannegan.

What in God's name are you doing, girl? You can't be crazy enough to get yourself involved with a ballplayer? She began to lecture herself in her mind, like her own corrective parent.

Of course there had been men in Jayvee's life. She was a healthy woman and she enjoyed dating as much as anyone, but baseball players had never been on the agenda. Not because of any potential conflicts for Jayvee; it was more that the players were too intimidated to consider the prospect. After all, she was Mike DellVecchio's daughter as well as the host for *Totally Baseball*.

Jayvee stared at Ryan's tousled hair and longed to run her fingers through it. She studied the darkness of his eyelashes curled against his cheeks and she longed to kiss his eyelids awake. She mused to herself as she watched him sleeping and decided he was kind of cute. And he didn't try to make a big deal about who he was, or who I was. They had talked about a number of different things during the course of the game, and it was very comfortable, she had to admit. *I wish I could remember all that we talked about. Damn that Big E and those shots.*

She glanced over at the clock and knew she needed to get going, but she let her head sink back down into the pillow instead. Her thoughts raced back to the moment at the door when Ryan made the comment about being with the JV's. She hadn't heard that since Little League days back in Cleveland a lifetime ago. How could he know about that? Was he there? He couldn't have been because he talked last night about high school and college ball out in California. But he knew it too well, as if he had been waiting all these years to use it again. Could he really have been there?

Jayvee did know that his remark hit her like a bucket of cold water, and the whack across his face was an instinctive reaction. Less clear was why she kissed him, kissed him hard. *Damn you, Big E.* Then what followed the moment at her door began to come back through the hangover fog and a small smile creased Jayvee's face.

After the initial shock, Ryan was eager to respond to Jayvee's advance. They stumbled into her suite still locked at the lips. Her mouth opened slightly and his tongue slipped forward in exploration. Their hands searched each other's bodies eagerly, caressing each angle and curve. Ryan wanted desperately to tear away her clothing, but he had enough sense to know he would not gain any points by destroying some designer clothing, no matter how passionate things were. Instead he slowly undid the buttons on her silk blouse, lingering as each movement revealed more of her. This only increased their passion, except her response was faster and more furious as she fumbled with his belt buckle.

With their clothes scattered about the room, Jayvee and Ryan had fallen onto the bed in a steamy embrace. Her body was even more beautiful than he had fantasized. It was the perfect combination of athleticism and femininity. Ryan leaned down to kiss her breasts and she arched her back to welcome his exploring lips. Moaning slightly, Jayvee continued to explore his body, discovering quickly, he was fully aroused. As they came together, both gasped loudly and then found the rhythm that only lovers know. With building intensity they traded the control of their actions back and forth until they could contain their passion no longer. One final burst of intensity and then they collapsed, fully spent, into each other's arms.

The beauty of their lovemaking was enhanced by their physical fitness, and in almost no time, they resumed with even greater and deeper waves of desire. Touch and smell and taste and sight, the senses were all alive as they explored every inch of each other. When the climax arrived the second time, Jayvee and Ryan could only hope the walls of the Gulfport Royale had sufficient soundproofing. Totally exhausted, the pair fell into a blissful sleep.

The ardor of their unexpected dalliance however, had now been replaced by the reality of the upcoming day for Jayvee as she rose again from the pillow to contemplate her situation. Her thoughts began to sound like a reprimand. This is just a one-time thing. It's no big deal — just two people doing something that felt right at the time. But a simple brush-off of the night's activities didn't sit right for her. Alcohol or not, it wasn't like her to do something spontaneous when it came to sex, no matter how enjoyable it might be. *Had it really been that long and have I been missing something?*

Jayvee got up from the bed and began to collect her clothes. Her head was whirling with thoughts even through the dull ache from all that alcohol just a few hours before. Her father, the man who set the tempo for so much of her life, had passed away three years earlier from cancer. She had yet to get over it; perhaps she never would. In response, Jayvee had thrown herself into her work with even more dedication, cementing her reputation as one of baseball's best commentators. Was that effort also some defensive wall building? Was she pouring all of her emotions and energy into a job, into a sport, rather than into another person?

Jayvee grabbed her travel bag and stuffed the discarded clothes into the bottom. She liked to dress casually for her frequent plane trips, so a Cornell t-shirt and some warm-ups would do the trick for this morning's flight. The remaining clothes from the closet and dresser followed the others into the bag. Jayvee sat in a chair and bent down to tie her sneakers, which increased the buzz in her head a few decibels. She went into the bathroom to collect her makeup and toiletries and brush the tangles out of her long dark hair. A splash of water in the face to clear away the cobwebs was followed by a quick brush of the teeth to kill the stale taste she had in her mouth.

"Is this all about missing Dad?" she whispered to her reflection in the mirror. "I've never been with a ballplayer like this; could there be something more to it?"

Jayvee threw some more water on her face and shook her head. Now she was sounding like a shrink, and that was a little too weird to contemplate at this time of the morning. Nevertheless, the baseball connection kept going through her head as she finished packing her things. Her father had been such an important part of her life. She had to admit the void he left had never come close to being filled. She sat down at the desk and wrote a note to Ryan that she then placed gently on the pillow next to his.

The alarm clock alongside told her time was running out to make her flight. Still, she lingered. *He is cute and last night was spectacular. What am I doing? Get your butt in gear, Jayvee.* Quietly, Jayvee headed out the door for the elevator and a taxi downstairs. It was going to be close.

Several hours later, Ryan slowly opened his eyes. He had that awful cottonmouth taste from too much alcohol and sleeping with his mouth open. It took him a moment to realize he wasn't in his own room, and another to realize Jayvee was not in bed with him. In fact, it appeared she wasn't in the room at all, since the bathroom door was open and the light was off. Rising up to sit on the edge of the bed, he found the note she had left.

Ryan,

Sorry for the quick departure, but if I didn't make my flight there was going to be hell to pay. Just close the door after you leave. I have already checked out. Don't worry, I put the Do Not Disturb sign on the door.

I had a very nice, albeit, surprising time with you last night. You are a sweet guy — much nicer, apparently, than that brat from years ago in Little League.

Good luck with the season . . . I hope it turns out to be as good as you want it to be. Maybe we will get a chance to get together again someplace down the road.

All the Best,
Jayvee

P.S. Take care of Michaela. I have a soft spot for the daughters of ballplayers.

Ryan, easing back down onto his pillow, let the note drop to his chest. He closed his eyes, but broke into a broad smile. Things certainly seemed different than just twenty-four hours earlier. His love life had not been great since his divorce, and he had reached the stage in his baseball career where the groupies were not that interested in him, and vice-versa. Lately, all his emotions had been tied up with Michaela, Mad Vlad, and his final chance at the big-time in the BBL. Last night's connection with Jayvee DellVecchio came out of nowhere, for both of them apparently.

Then he rolled over onto the pillow that had been Jayvee's and inhaled deeply the fragrance she had left behind. Roses and musk.

"Ain't nothing like that smell, baby!" Ryan said aloud, feeling like he hadn't felt in years.

· SIX ·

THE FINAL TEN days of spring training in Florida and Arizona were pretty much a whirlwind. The shortened spring schedule did not seem like it would be a problem when the BBL made its changes in the off-season. Reality can be a sobering thing however, when a team feels it is not as prepared as it would like to be. Such was the situation facing D.P. Perryton, Paul Simonton, and the Colonials.

The news was bad. Angel Correa had torn both his anterior cruciate ligament and medial collateral ligaments. It would be several weeks before the swelling could subside, postponing any immediate surgical fix. The preliminary indications were that Cuevas likely would require a full reconstruction of his damaged knee. That meant he was done for at least this season — if not longer — and it left the Colonials with a big hole in their starting rotation.

"I don't think we need to overreact, Dudley. My research indicates we can find a replacement for Correa from within the organization."

The young boss walked with his veteran baseball manager along the warning track of the main field at the Fort Myers complex. The Colonials had won their exhibition game earlier that afternoon against the New York Gothams, but it meant little to the leaders of the team.

"Fucci's numbers look good and maybe Freddie Antonelli can be this year's Angel."

Kris Fucci, the young left-hander who had been working out of the bullpen as the long man and a spot starter, could be moved up into the rotation. Antonelli had been Boston's top draft choice out of Holy Cross two years earlier, and he was rapidly moving up in the organization.

"My problem with any of the kids, Paul, is that we're messing with the whole rotation if we move them up."

"You don't think Fucci or Antonelli can handle it?"

"Kris is fine in the spot we have him in right now, and we got lucky when we rushed Angel last year. I don't think we can count on that again with the Antonelli kid."

Shadows from the scoreboard and the palm trees behind it had crossed the track and were lengthening across the field. The season was one day closer and Boston needed to do something.

"My calculations tell me you might be right about rushing Antonelli, but the numbers say Fucci could handle it."

D.P. Perryton had learned not to overreact to Simonton's claims about the accuracy of his statistical projections. He had to work with the guy, and like it or not, he had to make certain he wasn't the fall guy if a decision based strictly on the numbers didn't work. Perryton put his arm around the shoulders of his general manager and felt Simonton stiffen. D.P. knew the fatherly approach didn't always work with his hard-edged boss, but he was going to try every angle.

"Your numbers, Paul, usually show up well, and I think Kris Fucci is going to become a good starter someday, but he's not my only concern. With Angel out, we'd have to move up Gomez, Haddad, and Ertle. I don't think Raul and Darren are mentally tough enough yet to handle being second and third in our rotation."

Fans frequently debate how a manager makes out his lineup, yet they don't seem to put the same analysis into how a manager sets up his starting rotation. The road map to success for a baseball club is usually found through pitching, and the right alignment of the starting rotation is crucial to making that happen.

"Crunch the numbers for me, Paul. There's got to be somebody out there who needs something we have. Find me a number two."

Rumors spread quickly in baseball, especially at spring training where the teams are close together and scouts are everywhere. Potential trade partners with the Colonials added even more eyes and ears to their entourages at the remaining spring games for Boston, searching for talent they could grab from the C's if a swap was made. The same was true for Paul Simonton and his staff as they fanned out in Florida and Arizona to look at the pitching talent available... and at what price. The activity didn't stop when the games ended; cell phones were working long into the night, checking out possible trades and buys.

Now on the Colonials' last day in Florida before heading to Dallas for the regular season's opener, the trade rumors intensified. The best spring of his career made Ryan the Boston media's best guess to be part of a deal to acquire more pitching. Hannegan had moved around quite a bit in his baseball career, so a trade would not be something new. For Ryan's part, however, he wanted to remain with the Colonials. There was a good mesh of personalities with this team, and the promise of a good season had him eager to be a part of it.

Walking off the field toward the clubhouse down the right field line after the final spring game against Kansas City, Dennis Soos jogged up alongside Hannegan.

"Boy, am I glad that's over... though I must admit it's been fun with the way we've been playing. Now we've got to carry it over to the games that matter."

"This is a good ball club, Doc. I haven't played on too many contenders in my career, but there sure is a good feel about this one. I hope I'm around for it."

"Me, too, you worthless excuse for a ballplayer," Soos teased as he knocked off Hannegan's cap. "Who am I going to give shit to if they ship you out of here? Seriously, man, you've done everything you possibly could. It's too bad about Angel; you would have been a sure shot to stick around here if he hadn't gotten hurt."

"Dennis, I have learned, painfully at times, that nothing has been a sure thing in my career. Whatever happens is whatever happens."

The pair walked into the clubhouse where the scene was organized chaos. The Colonials were flying out on a charter in several hours, and the team's director of travel, Billy Seghi, was trying to keep the process of moving the team from spring training to the regular season at least somewhat together. The players had all checked out of the Gulfport Royale that morning, and their personal belongings were already loaded onto a large rental truck. Equipment manager Jimmy Walsh and a small army of clubhouse attendants, bat boys, and others were standing by to load up the players' baseball gear and the other equipment needed for the opening road trip to Dallas and Kansas City.

Ryan Hannegan sat at his locker, slowly stuffing shoes, bats, gloves and other gear into his equipment bag. All of Ryan's off-season preparations — the Bates Method, the special workouts, the promise of Mad Vlad's gift of Soviet science — had culminated in the best spring training results of his career. Still, he couldn't help wondering if his Boston equipment bag would soon be joining the others in the closet back home, replaced by a new bag with a new team logo on the side. It had always been about just getting the chance to show what he could really do in the BBL. It didn't matter what team before. But now it did matter; this clubhouse was the right fit, and this was the place where he wanted to play.

"Hey, Ryan. D.P. wants to see you in his office."

Hannegan looked up to see Tommy Gladstone. He shot a glance at Dennis Soos. Doc quickly turned away, not wanting to see his friend's face as he got up to learn his fate.

Walking into Perryton's office, Ryan found Paul Simonton also was there. Perfect! If Simonton is here, then for sure I am heading out of here.

"Sit down, Ryno," D. P. Perryton instructed, pointing to a chair on one side of his desk in the cramped quarters that served as his office during spring training. "We wanted to talk with you before you heard it from anybody else."

Hannegan's heart sank as he dropped into the chair. He avoided eye contact with the general manager of the Colonials because he was certain Simonton had been the one to pull the plug. D.P. looked pretty serious, so it had to be bad news.

"The name of the game in this business is productivity," Paul Simonton began. "The numbers tell the story."

Ryan listened to the haughty baseball executive's words, and he remembered Dennis Soos' comment about where he would like to put Simonton's numbers. He stifled a smile. Good old Doc, he always gets right to the heart of things.

"We feel we are in a position to be serious contenders this year, not only for the post season, but to get back to The Showdown. The facts are clear that we have a quality lineup, and until two weeks ago, a pitching staff to go along with our offense. Mr. Correa's injury upset the formula I had put together with Dudley, and it has forced us to make a big move. Within the last hour, we have concluded a deal with the Los Angeles Stars to acquire pitcher Keith Lash."

Los Angeles; at least I could live at home during the season. Ryan was steeling himself to deal with whatever came down.

Keith Lash was a veteran pitcher, and if Ellis Nance was the symbol of an experienced pitcher who could still bring the heat, then Keith Lash was the poster boy for the junk ballers. Players said that a Lash fastball couldn't break a pane of glass, but the way he changed speeds and arm angles made his pitches just as tough to hit as the Big E's. The Stars needed offense, and they were willing to trade the left hander if the deal was right. Keith Lash . . . well, he was a nice pickup for the club.

"To gain a player of Keith Lash's caliber, we had to pay a significant price because teams knew what our situation was. To that end, we have sent Gary Gorski and two of our top prospects to the Stars."

Ryan's head jerked up when he heard those words. What did he say? Gorski? Gary Gorski had been Boston's starting left fielder for the past three years. He was not a spectacular player, but he had done a solid job during that time. Only when Hannegan looked over at D.P. Perryton and saw the big grin on his manager's face did Ryan truly believe he was sticking with the Colonials.

"We have been impressed with how things have gone with you this spring, Ryan," D.P. Perryton said. "Your veteran experience can be a big help to this ballclub, and if you can hit like you have so far, then that's even better for us."

Perryton got up from behind his desk and came over to where Hannegan was sitting.

"Paul and I talked things over this morning with Junichi before we made the deal, and Junichi suggested he move to left field to allow you to take over in center. He believes we will be better defensively with that kind of alignment, and I agree with him."

"Here's your chance, Ryan . . . make the most of it."

Hannegan jumped up from the chair and slapped Perryton on the back. He vigorously shook Paul Simonton's hand, surprising the general manager.

"Thanks, D.P. And you, too, Mr. Simonton. I promise I'm going to make this deal work for the Colonials."

Rushing out of the office, Ryan nearly ran over Dennis Soos, who was waiting just beyond the hallway in the clubhouse.

"Your worst nightmare has come true, Doc; you're stuck with me!"

Hannegan grabbed Soos in a bear hug, practically shouting into his friend's face.

"They sent Gorski to the Stars for Keith Lash!"

"Lash? That's great! He is a bitch to hit. I faced him in the All-Star game a couple of seasons ago, and I wanted nothing to do with all that junk he throws. It's embarrassing not to be able to hit that stuff. I don't know if he even throws it eighty."

The news spread like a grass fire in August around the clubhouse. Players get conditioned to teammates coming and going, and although they would miss having Gary Gorski on their team, just like Dennis Soos, they knew the addition of Keith Lash would be significant for the Colonials. Ryan went over to Junichi to thank him for his comments to D.P., and he promised to buy him a dinner at the next opportunity. Hannegan then returned to his locker to finish packing up his gear, but now in a much different frame of mind.

Later in the evening at the hotel in Dallas, he watched the coverage of the trade on that night's edition of *Totally Baseball*.

"Terry Tate, your take on this deal, please?" The commentator was smiling.

"There was little doubt, Jayvee, that the Colonials needed pitching help, and Lash fills a need."

"Did they give up too much?"

"Gorski is solid while the kids Gannon and Miller have a chance to be good players. But really, Boston didn't have any other choice."

"Thanks, Terry."

Turning to another camera for a close-up, Jayvee wrapped up her show.

"The Colonials have shored up the weakness in their rotation, but we will have to see what happens to their offensive production with Junichi and Ryan Hannegan replacing Gary Gorski and the retired Terry Howe. We know all about Junichi's status in Japan, and spring training seemed to show it will translate well here in America. Ryan Hannegan has been a journeyman for most of his BBL career, but Boston will need him to produce if they are to win the fight in the Northeast Division with New York and Baltimore. The question in New England tonight, and for all of the BBL for that matter, is can Ryan Hannegan keep up with the big boys?"

Jayvee then wrapped up that night's show with the usual closing material and a knockout smile. Her comment about playing with the big boys was a message meant only for one person.

Ryan fell back on his hotel bed and laughed.

"Yumpin' Yimeney, vhat a vhoman!"

Opening Day is that special time when fans renew their love affair with The Game. Baseball is a race of marathon length perversely played out at a maddening pace. On Opening Day, however, that relentless march slows to allow all who love the game to savor each element of its annual re-birth.

Ryan Hannegan could only wish for a leisurely appreciation of this Opening Day in New England. The Colonials had spent the first week of the season on the road, playing in Dallas and Kansas City. The team's charter had not landed at Logan Airport in Boston until the early hours of Friday morning. A limousine took him to the condo he had leased from last season, and he crashed for a few hours' sleep. When the alarm clock rang all too soon, a quick dash around the condo was spent trying to find things in the boxes that had arrived there from home and from spring training.

Frustrated in his search for his favorite jacket, Ryan grabbed another coat and pushed some of the boxes out of the way to make a larger path through the room. The doorbell rang.

Hannegan headed out the front door, following the driver he had hired into a waiting limo. If his Michaela's flight landed on time, he could probably hurry back through the Sumner Tunnel and be at the ballpark by the one p.m. reporting time for the home opener.

"Crown Air Flight Six-Four-Seven-Nine from Tampa, Florida has landed at Gate Forty-Five. Passengers deplaning can be met outside the security checkpoint at Concourse C. Baggage may be claimed downstairs at Carousel Nine." The impersonal voice boomed from the loudspeaker.

Ryan hadn't seen his daughter, since the Christmas holidays. When his ex-wife, Deirdre, remarried, she had moved back to the Tampa area to be near her family. Ryan missed seeing Michaela more frequently, but a professional baseball player's lifestyle was not particularly beneficial for a young girl, especially during the school year. Besides, Deirdre had always done a good job with their daughter.

Ryan was wired as he scanned the crowd of arriving passengers, periodically glancing at his watch. *We've got to get moving if I'm going to make the ballpark on time.* Finally, he spotted her walking with a representative from the airline. *That can't be my little girl*, he thought to himself. She couldn't have changed that much in four months. Michaela's squeal of delight when she passed the security checkpoint and leapt into his arms told him that she certainly was his daughter, but she had a new look.

"Who is this strange, young lady accosting me in the Boston airport? I came to meet a Michaela Hannegan, but WHO IS THIS?"

"Stop it, Daddy!" Michaela giggled as she kissed her father. "You know it's me; it's just that I am starting to mature."

"Can you see my bra?" she asked, stepping away from Ryan. "Isn't it cool? Mom helped me pick it out. I wanted to go to Victoria's Secret, but she said not yet."

"Michaela, please! Let's not talk about that in public, not with your father anyway. And what is that on your face?"

She groaned but batted her eyes to show off her makeup.

"You know very well what this is. Mom said I could. All the other girls in my class are starting to . . ."

"That may be true, Kiddo, but in some things your old man can be pretty conservative. This is something I will have to discuss with your mother."

Michaela made a face and started to complain again, but her father's expression told her this was neither the time nor the place to continue the argument. Jumping up to wrap her arms around Ryan's neck again, she changed the subject to something they were both excited about.

"I can't believe I'm here for the home opener. They have the coolest ballpark here. How do we get there? When do we leave? Where am I sitting?"

Ryan had all he could do to answer the rat-a-tat stream of questions from his daughter as they scurried down the escalator to baggage claim. Once they collected her bags, it was into the limo for the trip to the ballpark. Michaela was more than excited. She was with her dad in Boston, for Opening Day! Wait until she told the girls back home about this!

The late morning traffic from Logan through the Sumner Tunnel wasn't out of the ordinary, although Ryan fretted at each pause in the flow. He was anxious to get Michaela situated once they arrived at the ballpark. Michaela didn't mind the occasional traffic snarls.

"Sarah . . . you're never going to believe where I am! In the back of a limo!" Michaela was enjoying the opportunity to use the phone in the passenger section of the luxury car.

"Yes, 'dahling'," she continued, pretending to be sophisticated as she sipped a soft drink. "My driver is taking me into town."

Hannegan groaned but he was happy to see how much she was enjoying herself. They finally cleared the tunnel and headed toward Patriots' Harbor Park. The car pulled up in front of the players' entrance, and a crowd of Colonials' fans had already gathered at the fence to greet the players as they arrived.

"Yo, Hannegan! Ya' really pahked that one in KC last night!"

Ryan smiled in acknowledgment of a fan's reaction to his first home run of the season in the win over the Blues, and he reached to sign the Boston hat that was extended to him. He continued moving along the line of fans, signing autographs on all kinds of things, while Michaela smiled proudly at her father, hanging onto the tail of his sport coat with her right hand. Moving inside after signing a dozen or so autographs, Hannegan led his daughter toward the room set aside for the players' families.

"Look, Daddy, there's Mrs. Soos and Mary Ann."

Michaela ran ahead of Hannegan to hug the wife of Doc Soos and her daughter, who was the same age as Michaela. Satisfied she was all set for the day's activities, he kissed his daughter on the cheek and headed for the Colonials clubhouse.

Though the ball club did not get much sleep overnight, thanks to the late return from Kansas City, the atmosphere in the clubhouse was palpable with excitement. Players may appear blasé at times about special events, but few can ignore the extra boost the home opener gives, especially in a baseball hotbed like Boston. Opening Day might as well be declared a holiday because just about everyone treats it that way. Most of his teammates were already dressed, ready to head out the tunnel to the field for batting practice when Ryan arrived. The crush of media and front office personnel made the scene even more crowded than usual, and it had taken Hannegan a moment to locate his locker. His nameplate was wrapped in a wreath that had been made by knotting his uniform pants and batting practice jersey together.

"Welcome home, Ryno . . ."

He could hear Doc's comment and accompanying cackle drifting up from the nearby tunnel that led out to the field.

Patriots' Harbor Park, or just The Harbor to the fans, was one of the great baseball facilities in the country. Built during the 1920s, The Harbor held about forty thousand people, and it seemed like every fan was sitting right on top of the field. Some luxury suites had been added in recent years, but overall, the ballpark had not changed much over time. Patriots' Harbor was situated on Boston Harbor between the Long Wharf and the Christopher Columbus Waterfront Park, just a short walk off the famous Freedom Trail. The nearby Faneuil Hall/Quincy Market area was a popular pre-game stop for many fans.

Don Cunningham was the owner of the Colonials when Patriots' Harbor Park was constructed. Cunningham was in the shipping business, and he thought building the new ballpark in a place where he could also promote his other enterprises made perfect sense. With downtown Boston on one side and its harbor on the other, Cunningham had the ballpark laid out so a working pier could be incorporated right into the design. The pier had several levels and it was painted the corporate color for Cunningham Shipping: a deep, royal blue. Cunningham Shipping was one of the larger merchant marine fleets in this country, but the company also was heavily involved in ferry services around Boston. One of its ferry lines worked the pier at the ballpark. His family had long since given up its ownership of the Colonials, but Don Cunningham's Blue Pier would always be the signature architectural statement of Patriots' Harbor Park.

Boston and Cleveland concluded their pre-game drills in rapid order. The Ironmen had also arrived in the early morning hours, so both teams used the batting and fielding drills to work the kinks out as much as anything else. Finally, it was time for the introductions of each team member. Some of the Boston players razzed the Ironmen as they watched from the third base dugout during the presentation of the Cleveland team.

"Hey, Jimmy, haven't you ever heard of a low-carb diet?"

"Up yours, Keith," responded Cleveland first baseman Jimmy Craddock with a grin to his former Los Angeles teammate, Keith Lash. "Now that you're in a real league, be prepared to have your lunch handed to you."

"Bring it on, big boy, bring it on."

Now it was the Colonials' turn. The introductions began with the coaches and training staff, followed by the reserve players and pitchers. The manager and the starting lineup were saved for the finish to allow the crowd's intensity to build. Hannegan had been in a starting lineup several times for home openers during his BBL career, but today felt different. Here he was in Boston, one of baseball's best places, and Michaela was on hand to see him get recognized. Following the introduction of the Boston skipper, D.P. Perryton, the public address announcer unveiled the C's starting lineup like he was at a heavyweight title bout.

"Leading off, the Haitian Hurricane, #13, shortstop, Fernando Horrado..."

"Batting second, the pride of South Boston and Boston College, #4... second baseman... Kevin Kyle!"

"He's made an impact already... one of the greatest hitters ever produced in the Far East... in left field... #99... JOOOOO-NEEEE-CHEEE!"

The crowd exploded as Junichi ran out of the dugout toward his teammates standing along the third base line. After exchanging some bumped fists with several of them, Junichi turned to face the crowd, bowed deeply, and then broke into a big grin as he waved his hat to the fans. They only screamed all the louder. At last the ovation died down and the stadium announcer resumed.

"The cleanup hitter . . . he has more home runs over the last three years than any other Boston hitter . . . #24, first baseman . . . Ramòn Morientes!" The announcer rolled his R's effectively, and the crowd loved it.

"The captain of the Colonials . . . the best fielding third baseman in the game today . . . batting fifth . . . #14 . . . Dennis Soos!"

Ryan slapped his friend on the back as Soos clambered up the steps of the dugout accompanied by the roar from a thousand throats. There was no doubt Doc was a crowd favorite in Boston. Now it was his turn. Oh God, whatever you do, Hannegan, don't trip over your own feet.

"Hitting in the sixth position . . . playing center field . . . #47 . . . Ryan Hannegan."

Nothing fancy, but what else could be expected. After the obligatory run down the line, slapping hands, Ryan turned to face the crowd when he reached his spot. *Where's Michaela? There she is. Great smile, Kiddo. I guess the old man is okay in your book.*

The introductions continued with right fielder, J.R. Cook, and Mark Allen, the catcher. The Colonials' starting pitcher that day, Ellis Nance, was the last to be recognized, and he received a thunderous salute from the crowd as he continued his warm-ups out in the bullpen. Boston was ready and so were the Colonials. It was going to be a great year . . . it just had to be.

This season was the one hundredth for the Baseball Big Leagues, and each player on the Opening Day rosters received a small gold medallion to commemorate the event. Here in Boston, the new commissioner was on hand to present the medals. As General Hopkins made his way along the line of Boston players, Ryan was surprised to realize the General was not quite as big as he appeared to be on television. Yet when Hopkins reached Hannegan's spot to present the medallion, an aura of power emanated from the man.

"Congratulations, Mr. Hannegan," the General said as he handed Ryan the medallion with his left hand while firmly shaking hands with his right.

"Nice job last night . . . it looked like Martinez hung you a slider."

Before Ryan could respond, the general moved on to J.R. Cook, the next Boston player. *Well, I'll be damned,* thought Ryan in amazement. *I guess Hoppy really does follow the game. The man does his homework; put that in the old memory bank, Ryan.*

The pre-game activities concluded with a wonderful rendition of the national anthem by a well-known opera singer from the Boston area and with the ceremonial first pitch. This year it was handled by about a dozen children whose fathers had lost their lives in a catastrophic fire that had occurred in the Boston area the previous winter. There were more than a few misty eyes watching that, including those of a number of the players.

Ellis Nance had won the season's opener in Dallas with a strong performance, and he began his first home start in similar fashion. Cleveland mustered just a weak flare single to left in their first turn through the lineup, and Nance had registered three strikeouts. Players loved to play behind the big pitcher, not just because he was talented, but also because he was a fast worker.

Conor O'Toole, the ace of the Ironmen staff, was similarly effective in the early going. Ramòn Morientes had driven a ball to the base of the Blue Pier to end the first inning, but, except for a walk to Kevin Kyle, O'Toole had not allowed another base runner. In Hannegan's first at-bat, O'Toole got him out in front on an off-speed pitch, and Ryan had tapped an easy come-backer to the Cleveland starter.

With one out in the bottom of the fourth, Junichi timed an off-speed offering from O'Toole and laced it into left-center for Boston's first hit. The Japanese star promptly stole second base on the next pitch. The huge crowd, waiting for a reason to yell, screamed themselves silly for their newest hero.

"... That's ball four. Morientes draws the walk to put two on with one out ..."

Tom Kingery, the radio broadcaster for the Colonials, had been the voice of baseball for more than a generation in Boston and his play-by-play was resonating around The Harbor.

"... Tough spot for O'Toole now; Dennis Soos has been one of the best clutch hitters in the game for a number of years ... O'Toole comes set ... checks the runners ... and the pitch ... POPPED HIM UP ... O'Toole jammed the Doctor ... Fernandez has it ... that's a big out number two ..."

As Ryan advanced to the plate, Soos yelled some encouragement. "Let 'er rip, Ryno. No time like now for a little W-T-F!"

Hannegan grinned and then proceeded to dig in at home plate. *Be patient, Ryan. He's going to try and get you again with something off-speed. Look for your pitch.* Hannegan grabbed a good toehold at the back of the left-hand batter's box, made the familiar tug on his right sleeve and tap to the top of his helmet, and he was ready to go. The first pitch was a fastball up and in that moved him off the plate. O'Toole followed by changing speeds, working a backdoor slider that found the outside corner to even the count. Another off-speed pitch, but Ryan's rip sliced just a few feet foul in the left field corner.

"Time, please."

Hannegan stepped out of the batter's box, and took a glance down to Tommy Gladstone for a sign from the third base coach. Digging back in with another tug and a tap, he awaited O'Toole's next delivery. It was a fastball, but it didn't get in or get up enough for the Cleveland pitcher's purposes.

". . . a swing and a smash . . . FAIR as it screams down the right field line . . ."

The ball took off on a line over the head of Jimmy Craddock before Craddock had the chance to react to it. The Cleveland outfield defense was bunched up the middle, but Ryan's hit drove into the right field corner at the base of the Blue Pier and then got hung up there. By the time the Ironmen defense recovered and got the ball back into the infield, Junichi and Ramòn Morientes had scored, and Hannegan had gone headfirst into the bag at third with a triple.

"Atta boy, Ryno. That's the old W-T-F."

Ryan got up on one knee to dust himself off while Dennis Soos was on the top step of the dugout, motioning with his hands like he was firing a pair of six-shooters just like they had done for each other when they were college teammates. The capacity crowd screamed with joy. Three pitches later, J.R. Cook blooped a single to center, and Hannegan jogged home with the Colonials third run of the inning. Ryan had the chance to give a quick wink to Michaela as he moved back toward the dugout where he received congratulations from his teammates.

Ellis Nance, meanwhile, continued his domination of the Cleveland offense. Spotting his fastball on both sides of the plate — and mixing in his still-devastating curve ball — Nance had limited the Ironmen to just three hits through the first seven innings, and he had fanned nine. If Nance was heading toward the twilight of his career, it was not evident on this sun-drenched afternoon in Boston.

The Boston advantage grew to four to nothing when Junichi led off the bottom of the sixth inning with his first BBL home run, a no-doubter carrying well over the Blue Pier and into the harbor. When the ball soared out of sight, it touched off another celebration for the Colonials' fans. *Make A Splash* flashed on the scoreboard located above the center field bleachers while Junichi circled the bases. A Beach Boys' tune blared through the sound system, and the fans clapped along rhythmically. Animation of a colonial figure riding a surfboard came next on the big message screen, and Ryan shook his head at the sight.

"Like people surf in Boston Harbor," he said to Dennis Soos as they applauded Junichi on the top step of the Colonials' dugout.

"It's all about the marketing, my friend."

If marketing was going to be the way in baseball, then it sure looked like Junichi was the hot, new product to sell. In less than a week of baseball, he had already become a chart-topper for the baseball-mad fans of New England. Junichi reached home plate and stopped to make a grand bow to the crowd that only heightened their frenzy. Junichi Nakata might be new to the BBL, but he knew all about how to market himself.

Boston maintained its four to nothing advantage over Cleveland through eight innings. D.P. Perryton turned to the bullpen to finish up in the ninth; it was the break Cleveland was looking for, and the Ironmen struck quickly for a pair of runs against reliever Jeff Hennessey. Perryton was hoping to rest his closer, Hwang Sang Hwan, since he had used the little Korean fireballer three times already in this first week. A walk and another hit brought in a third run, however, and by the time Perryton could bring his bullpen ace into the game, the Ironmen had the bases loaded with only one out.

Wang completed his warm-up tosses, and then stepped off the pitching rubber. He looked over to Dennis Soos, who was relaying signs to the infield to set the defense for the various possibilities.

"It's easy, Wang. Just get us a ground ball to turn two and we'll get out of here."

The Colonials' closer nodded to the encouragement.

"Okay, boys," Soos said to the rest of his teammates aligned around the diamond, "we've got a force anywhere; play it smart."

The options were a little different in the outfield. There a fielder must play deep enough to cut off the alleys and keep a ball from sailing over his head. The Colonials in this situation wanted to keep the go-ahead run at second base from scoring, or if possible, advancing to third. At the same time, an outfielder wants to be in position to make a throw to the plate on a fly ball that is not hit quite as far.

Hwang Sang Hwan climbed back up atop the mound and toed the rubber as he looked in for the sign from his catcher. Jimmy Craddock, the left-handed-hitting first baseman for Cleveland, was at the plate. The Colonials' outfield was positioned medium deep and swung around a little toward left since they didn't feel Craddock could pull Wang's fastball. Players and fans have seen this situation thousands of times through the years, but its frequency doesn't take away from the drama, from the anticipation.

Wang delivered a fastball in the ninety-five miles per hour range, about knee high on the outer half of the plate. Craddock sliced a hard liner to left that had trouble written all over it.

"In! In!"

Hannegan screamed at Junichi in left field, but it was unlikely his teammate could hear him above the noise of the crowd. Joe Otto, the Cleveland base runner at third broke momentarily for the plate before heading back to the bag to tag up if the ball was caught. Junichi came racing in and speared the ball at about knee level. His momentum was not going to be slowed, however, so he flipped the ball to his bare hand as he was falling forward. Placing his glove on the ground as his momentum continued, Junichi performed a one-hand forward flip, and when his feet hit the ground, he fired a seed towards the plate. The ball arrived in Mark Allen's glove just an instant before Otto came crashing into him. When the Cleveland runner wasn't able to dislodge the ball with the impact, the Colonials had their victory.

"Are you shittin' me?" Ryan didn't even know he had spoken aloud.

He stood motionless in the outfield. *People can't do that, but that sunnavabitch did it!*

A volcano of volume spewed forth in an ovation that might not ever be duplicated at The Harbor. The Boston players gathered around Junichi in short left field, slapping his back, pounding his head, and pumping his hand in congratulations while the noise from the crowd cascaded over them in waves. On this Opening Day in Boston fan and player alike had seen something that would live for ages in the annals of the game.

The hubbub did not really subside even after the players retreated to the clubhouse. Reporters and news crews clamored around Junichi's locker, each one trying to get his own slant on the play capping off this glorious debut in Boston. The startling defensive play overshadowed Junichi's own offensive contributions and the fine efforts turned in by Ellis Nance and Ryan Hannegan. In fact, Ryan's two for three day with a pair of runs batted in went all but unnoticed by the assembled media.

"Nice job, Hannegan."

Terry Tate tapped Hannegan on the knee with his notepad and nodded congratulations as Tate made his way toward Junichi's locker. Ryan didn't care. His number one fan had been there, and she was waiting for him just outside.

"Daddy, did you see that? How did he do that? That's the most unbelievable thing I've ever seen"

"Yes, Michaela, I was right there. It was pretty special."

Before his daughter could resume her questioning, Ryan used one of his sleight-of-hand tricks to make the centennial anniversary medallion he had received from General Hopkins magically appear around his daughter's neck.

"This is so cool, Daddy!" she said as she held the medallion in her hands, running a finger over the design etched into it. "What are you going to do with it? Where are you going to put it?"

"I think it looks great right where it is, Kiddo. It's yours if you promise to take care of it and not lose it . . . or give it to some boy."

"DADDY! This is great . . . What a game! You were terrific . . . and now this medal. What could top this?"

"How about a big lobster at Mateskon's down the street? Of course, I don't have any money, so you'll have to buy. I'm sure your mother won't mind."

"Don't start," Michaela scolded as she gave her father a big hug.

Ryan helped her collect the rest of her things, grabbed her by the hand, and turned to head toward the exit. As they began their walk down the hallway, a familiar voice called out from behind.

"So, this is the famous Michaela Hannegan?"

Father and daughter whirled in surprise to find Jayvee DellVecchio smiling back at them. Ryan was pleased to see Jayvee; it was the first time he had seen her since their evening in Fort Myers.

"You're Jayvee DellVecchio! I watch you every night when my mom lets me stay up late. Sometimes I sneak downstairs to watch when she's already asleep. I can't believe I am really talking to you! Wait a minute; how do you know my name?"

"I told you she goes a mile-a-minute once she gets started. I didn't know you were coming today?"

"One at a time . . . I'm getting the Hannegan double-team!"

Jayvee reached out and shook Michaela's hand.

"It is very nice to meet you. I am a friend of your father's, and he's told me all about you. I thought he was talking about me the way he described your love for baseball. When I was your age, all I could think about was either playing baseball or watching my dad play for the Ironmen."

"Your dad was Mike DellVecchio . . . I've read all about him. He was a great player."

Michaela looked like she would burst with pride over Jayvee's comparison of their childhoods. She wasn't just getting to meet somebody famous from TV; this person was saying that she was like her. *Wait until I tell the girls back home*, she thought to herself.

"And as for you, Mr. Hannegan . . . first of all, thanks for all the flowers, although you have the gossip mill running overtime at DBC. My desk looks like a florist shop, and everyone is talking about my secret admirer. I tell them it's probably some wacko stalker!"

Ryan had sent flowers to Jayvee's office that first morning after, and had continued to do so every couple of days since. The pair had exchanged some e-mails and played phone tag, but this was the first time they had talked since the night in Fort Myers.

"Thank you very much for the wacko label. It's nice to know you think so much of me."

"Daddy, I didn't know you were sending flowers to Jayvee! What else do you want to tell me?"

"I want to tell you to mind your own business," he said playfully. Turning back towards Jayvee, Ryan added: "It is great to see you . . . I didn't know you were coming to the game today?"

"Well, you were playing Dad's old team, and I still root for the Ironmen. I thought it would be interesting to see Junichi's debut here in Boston, and he sure didn't disappoint."

"No kidding . . . I have never seen someone make a play like he did in the ninth. People aren't supposed to be able to do that"

"Excuse me. I'm hungry, so if you want to talk baseball, let's do it in a restaurant. You are going to ask Jayvee to join us, aren't you, Daddy? Or do I have to do everything around here?"

She turned to Jayvee, whose cheeks were rosier than usual.

"You'll have to excuse my father; he's a little slow at these kinds of things."

With that, Ryan picked up his daughter and flipped her upside down, shaking her mischievously. Michaela howled with laughter. Hannegan knew his daughter must be impressed with Jayvee because she usually didn't give up her private time with him so readily. Smiling over at Jayvee, while still playing around with his daughter, Ryan asked Jayvee a question.

"We're headed to one of the seafood places nearby. This is last minute and you probably have things to do, but would you like to join us?"

"I'd love to. We're doing the show here in Boston tonight, and as long as I can get back here by nine o'clock to start the run-throughs, it shouldn't be a problem."

With that settled, Ryan returned his daughter upright, and the three of them headed for the exit and dinner nearby. Michaela, to no one's surprise, dominated the dinner conversation.

"It must be so cool to be on TV. Do you ever get nervous? Did you go to all the games with your dad when you were my age? Who's your favorite player now?"

Ryan enjoyed watching the give-and-take between the two baseball daughters. It was remarkable how quickly they developed a rapport with each other. He did manage some conversation with Jayvee when his daughter directed her concentration toward trying to remove the meat from her lobster. Just as they did at the party in Fort Myers, Ryan and Jayvee found it easy to be together.

"Shoot, look at the time. I wish I could stay longer, but duty calls."

Ryan was pleased by Jayvee's disappointment at having to cut the evening short. She kissed Ryan on the cheek as she got up to leave, drawing a long "o-o-o-o-h" from Michaela and a resulting napkin thrown in his daughter's face by Hannegan.

"Call me at the office when you can, but please no more flowers."

"Okay, I'll slow down. I'll give you a call next week."

That response drew another reaction from his daughter, and their conversation in the car on the ride back home was dominated by Michaela's opinion of Jayvee.

"Isn't she just the greatest, Daddy? She's the best baseball announcer I know."

"And how many announcers do you know, Miss Hannegan?"

"You know what I mean. And how about when she said I reminded her of herself when she was a young girl? Wait 'til I tell everyone back home. And I think she likes you, too."

"That's enough, young lady. We have become friends through our jobs. Let's not make too much of this."

Ryan shook his head in wonder. *What makes a woman — even at age eleven — look for a romantic angle? Still I must admit that I am interested; I probably haven't felt like this since I started going out with Deirdre.*

Arriving at the condo, Michaela raced ahead with Ryan's key to open the door while he carried in her things. Since it was her first time at his place in Boston, Michaela ran from room to room, checking things out, making observations all the while.

"This is Michaela Hannegan reporting; welcome to tonight's edition of Cribs. Tonight we are in the home of Boston Colonials star, Ryan Hannegan."

Ryan groaned at his daughter's comments, but after a whirlwind eighteen hours he was too tired to do anything but collapse on the nearby couch. The condo was still in a state of semi-chaos with boxes everywhere as Michaela continued her running commentary. Ryan sank into the couch with a grunt. *Where does she get all that energy?* All he wanted to do was close his eyes and recharge his batteries. But that was not to be.

"What's this, Daddy? It looks really weird."

Ryan's stomach filled with dread. His daughter had dragged into the living area the refrigerated case that contained the Soviet science. Mad Vlad had told him it would be a dream fulfiller. At this moment, it seemed more like a nightmare.

· SEVEN ·

HANNEGAN SOMEHOW came up with an explanation for the freezer box that satisfied his daughter's curiosity. He took the case from her, promising himself it would stay out of sight for the rest of Michaela's visit. The weekend went well for the Colonials. Keith Lash won his first game as a Boston player in a 6-1 complete game nine-hitter on Saturday. On Sunday, the Cs flexed their muscles, blowing Cleveland out of the water with seventeen hits, including five homers, in a 14-5 rout in game one of a doubleheader. Ryan Hannegan was right in the middle of things, going four for five in the game, including his second homer of the season. His opposite field shot into the seats in left was the finishing blow of a back-to-back-to-back sequence of long balls from Ramon Morientes, Dennis Soos, and Hannegan. In the nightcap, Cleveland finally won a game, but Ryan extended his hitting streak to six games with a base hit in the fifth inning of the loss. He had gone eight for sixteen in the first four games of the series.

"Daddy, why were those Cleveland players so mad?"

Ryan and Michaela were sitting at the dining table in his condo, happily munching on a giant pizza following the Saturday game.

"Kiddo, when a guy like Keith Lash is pitching well, you get very frustrated."

"Why?"

Hannegan grinned before answering. *Just like when you were small, Michaela . . . always with the questions.*

"Well, Mr. Lash doesn't throw quite as fast as some of the other pitchers, so as a hitter you figure he would be easy. Instead, he makes you look silly because of the way his ball moves. You see the ball coming, but you just don't get a good piece of it."

"I bet you'd get a good piece of it."

"You keep thinking that, Michaela. I'm just glad that Keith Lash is on our side."

That's the way it went on Saturday and Sunday: father and daughter talking about the game they loved. Most of the time anyway.

"Did you call Jayvee yet?"

"Michaela . . ."

"Well, you did say you were going to call here, and I bet she is expecting you to."

"When I need advice on romance from my daughter I will ask for it."

"But, Daddy . . ."

"Michaela, that's enough."

The Jayvee issue put to the side, the pair spent the weekend nights watching videos. Hannegan had rented two comedies that had both of them laughing until their sides hurt. Monday morning he was back at Logan Airport putting his daughter on a plane home to Florida. Hannegan always hated to see Michaela leave, but this was the most difficult yet. It had been their best weekend together since . . . well, Ryan couldn't remember a better time with his daughter.

"What am I going to do now that my good luck charm is leaving town? I may never get another hit without you, Kiddo."

"I don't want to go, Daddy," Michaela said while playing with the centennial medallion that hung around her neck. "Maybe you can get Mom to let me miss school for the rest of the year so I can stay here with you. We do make a great team!"

"School's too important . . . you know that. Besides you would miss your friends, and I wouldn't have anyone to watch you when I went on road trips. Summer vacation will come soon enough, and we'll get back together. Now give me a kiss so that this nice lady can take you to the plane."

"I love you, Daddy. Remember to call me whenever you can, and don't forget about IM'ing me on my computer."

"I love you too. I will call you tonight after the game if it's not too late. Say hello to your mother and Owen for me."

Michaela started down the jetway with the Crown Air flight attendant and then turned back to Hannegan.

"And don't forget Jayvee! She's expecting you to call."

An exasperated Ryan Hannegan waved to his daughter to keep going. There was no doubt that Michaela was going to do everything in her power to foster a relationship between her father and the host of *Totally Baseball*. His daughter's matchmaking notwithstanding, Ryan had a call to Jayvee DellVecchio on his list of things to do that day. With a final look back, Michaela waved to her father and turned the corner of the jetway to enter the airplane.

The rest of the month of April went well for Ryan and the Colonials. If a quick start was needed to be successful, then Boston's 11-6 record fit the game plan. Only the 12-5 mark of the St. Louis Rivermen was a better beginning than the Colonials. Here's how the two divisions of the A-C shaped up following the opening month of the season:

AMERICAN CONFERENCE

Northeast Division			Midwest Division		
	W-L	GB		W-L	GB
Boston	11-6	—	St. Louis	12-5	—
New York	10-7	1	Chicago	10-7	2
Baltimore	9-8	2	Dallas	8-9	4
Cleveland	8-9	3	Minneapolis	8-9	4
Detroit	7-10	4	Kansas City	8-9	4

The initial weeks had been great for Hannegan. He had been in the starting lineup for all but two of Boston's games, and it had been the best fourteen days offensively of his career. Hannegan had a batting average of .317, collecting twenty hits in those early games. Even more impressive was that eight of those hits had been for extra bases including three home runs. Ryan's personal high in homers was eleven, so his power numbers were definitely ahead of his usual pace. He was not the story in baseball, however.

"The top selling dish on baseball's menu this month definitely has an Asian flavor to it."

Terry Tate, the *Boston Journal* columnist, was a regular contributor to the *Totally Baseball* show.

"If Junichi Nakata keeps up this kind of performance, we might have our first Triple Crown winner in decades."

"Do you really think that's possible, Terry?" Jayvee DellVecchio asked.

"He leads the American Conference in batting, he's second in homers, and he's also on top in RBI's. With the protection he's got in that Boston lineup, people will have to pitch to him."

If that wasn't enough, Junichi was handling the media circus that had grown larger by the day with quiet calm. Likewise, the baseball import had fit in easily with the rest of his Boston teammates. In short, he had been a lightning rod for all the good things happening to the Colonials.

The month of May presented a difficult challenge for the C's: an eleven-game road trip from Baltimore to New York, and ultimately St. Louis. The brief two-game set at The Hollow with the Horsemen would be its usual wild affair, and St. Louis had gotten off to the best start in the conference. The schedule makers had done Boston no favors with sixteen of their first twenty-three games away from home. The players were grateful for the off-day to catch their breath after the games in Baltimore, especially in New York with all of its diversions.

The trip to New York was a welcome one for Ryan because it would allow him to see Jayvee DellVecchio again, this time without Michaela as a chaperone. Ryan and Jayvee had talked several times since their dinner together in Boston, and they had made plans for a quick meal between Jayvee's shows at DBC that Tuesday. No one outside of his daughter knew something might be developing with them, and both wanted to keep it that way.

"Let's go to McArdle's on 58th. It's not far from the studios so I won't have to rush off right away."

"Sounds great. I will see you there about seven-thirty."

Hannegan grabbed a table near the back, beyond a bar with its clientele of regulars. The room had a typical New York bistro feel to it: well-appointed and with lighting tastefully allowing for discretion for those diners who sought such an atmosphere. This will be perfect, he decided. No one will know we're here.

Jayvee DellVecchio came through the front door shortly after Ryan's vodka and cranberry had arrived. The hostess directed her to the table where Ryan was sitting, and she gave him her wonderful smile in recognition. She looks even better than the last time I saw her. Rising to greet her, Hannegan leaned forward to kiss her on the cheek, only to be surprised when Jayvee planted a full one on his lips. She laughed at his startled expression.

"I wasn't going to do that when your daughter was with us. But I did want you to know I have appreciated your thoughtfulness, Mr. Hannegan."

"You look great. I have been looking forward to this since we set the date last week. I couldn't wait to see you again."

"I've enjoyed every time we've been together . . . except maybe that FIRST time we met. I've been dying to put this whole thing together, since we apparently did meet when we were kids."

Ryan seated Jayvee and signaled for the waiter to get her drink order. Jayvee asked for a glass of white wine since she still had a show to do that evening. When the waiter departed, she resumed her friendly interrogation of Hannegan.

"I couldn't figure it out that night in Fort Myers how you knew about the whole JV thing from Little League. They did a piece on me in *People* once about my nickname, but I never went into any real details. I looked up your bio in the Colonials' media guide and there was nothing in there about your being from Cleveland. But you knew exactly what went on at home plate."

The waiter had returned with Jayvee's wine, momentarily halting the conversation.

"When I got the flowers that first time at work, and it was signed from the Lakewood Eagles of the Four Corners League, I knew I had to get the whole story. So what gives, Hannegan?"

"We moved around a lot when I was small. My dad worked for an engineering firm that was connected to the automotive and aeronautical industries. The family moved several times before we came to Cleveland, and at the end of that summer when we played in that same Little League, we moved again to southern California. We finally stayed in one place there, and that's what I really considered home. My family all lives out there . . . except for Michaela who lives with her mother in Florida."

"You would have had no reason to remember me from that summer; what were we, ten? Anyway . . . I knew all about you, from that Little League World Series right on through your job now with DBC. Hell, you were Mike DellVecchio's kid; who wouldn't remember you?"

"So why didn't you say anything to me sooner?"

"Right, like I'm going to run right up to the host of *Totally Baseball* and say remember me? I kicked around in the minors for eight years, and my numbers here haven't exactly been all-star. You had no reason to have any interest in me, and I wasn't going to challenge that."

Again, the pair paused in their conversation for the waiter's return to take their dinner orders. Jayvee ordered the sole stuffed with scallops and crabmeat while Ryan selected veal parmesan. Doc Soos always teased Hannegan saying he couldn't really be Irish since he ordered Italian food almost every time he had dinner in a restaurant. The waiter brought a fresh vodka and cranberry for Ryan, and then the pair resumed their conversation.

"Okay, I'll buy the argument that you weren't really in a situation to connect with me beforehand, so what made you decide to hit me with that line when you took me back to my hotel room that night?"

Ryan blushed, surprising himself a little, and paused a moment before answering.

"I don't know, really. Maybe it was some deep psychological thing that was dying to get out . . . or maybe it was all those purple lightning shots from the Big E."

"Don't remind me about those shots. I think I cursed Ellis for two days because of the hangover!"

Hannegan dug into his veal when their dinners came. "This is a good place, Jayvee." He spun a forkful of spaghetti and popped it into his mouth with a slurp that had a final strand of pasta leave a spot of sauce on his nose. Jayvee giggled and then reached over to wipe it away with her napkin. Being together felt right, for both of them.

"Now it's my turn. I understand the slap — hell, I probably deserved it — but what happened next came out of nowhere, not that I'm complaining, mind you."

"I'm still trying to figure that out myself. Believe it or not, I've never been involved with a ballplayer before, so this is new territory for me, from what happened that night, right up to us being here now."

"So we're involved?"

Jayvee blushed without answering, but her body language told Hannegan what he wanted to hear. As they continued to eat, the conversation flowed in the way it does when things are starting to develop between two people. It was a delightful time that might have found them together by evening's end, if not for her work obligations. Before the bill came, another surprise hit.

"Ryanovich!"

Advancing to their table was Hannegan's Russian friend from the fantasy camp, Vladimir Titov. He was accompanied by an older gentleman.

"My good friend, I knew you were in town, but what good fortune to run across you here. I had planned on reaching you at your hotel to congratulate you for your fine play, but now I can do it in person."

He eyed Jayvee appreciatively. "But first you must introduce me to your friend here. Someone this beautiful has to be Russian."

"Vladimir Titov, may I introduce to you Ms. Jessica DellVecchio. Jayvee, this is my friend, and I use the term loosely, Vladimir Titov."

Titov took Jayvee's hand in the European fashion and kissed it.

"Of course, the lovely woman from the baseball show. What are you doing with a dog like Ryanovich when you could fulfill your every fantasy with me?"

Jayvee laughed and told the Russian that it was a pleasure to meet him. The flamboyant Titov turned to introduce his companion. Dressed more conservatively, the older gentleman looked like a slightly smaller version of the Russian.

"My friends, I would like you to meet my Uncle Yegor."

Yegor Karpin kissed Jayvee's hand in the same manner as his nephew then followed with a firm handshake for Hannegan.

"It is a wonderful pleasure to meet such fine young people. Mr. Hannegan, you are to be congratulated for your performance in this season. I hope that our small gift to you has been a help. We have been keeping a close eye on you."

Hannegan blanched at the remark by the older gentleman, but then forced a smile and mumbled thanks in reply. The group exchanged some small talk for a few more moments before the Russian pair moved toward a table on the other side of the restaurant.

"Chase that dream, Ryanovich . . . I am counting on you!"

Vladimir Titov's departing comment whacked Ryan right between the eyes.

A reporter's instincts alerted Jayvee immediately.

"Do you know who that older man is? That's Yegor Karpin . . . they say he's Russian mob. What was he talking about? His small gift?"

Hannegan quickly began to build a defense.

"I worked the Players' Association's fantasy camp last winter, and Vladimir was one of the players I coached. We had a lot of laughs together during the week, and he was always bragging about Soviet superiority. I guess the Cold War hasn't really ended for some people."

"So what was the gift?"

"I called him Mad Vlad because he was a maniac chasing fly balls in the outfield. But the man could hit! He blasted a bomb off Mac Davis in the game between the campers and the coaches."

"The gift, Hannegan?"

"Oh yeah, right. One day during the camp, I asked him how he was such a good hitter, and he told me it was a Soviet secret. Then, just before I left home for spring training, Vlad sends me this package with the secret in it."

"What was it . . . some kind of special equipment, some training program?"

"I wish. It was a concoction that smelled just awful. Probably a bunch of herbs mixed in something that smelled like beets. It must be the Russian's version of Popeye's spinach."

"What are you supposed to do with it? Is it safe?"

Hannegan pushed up his left sleeve at the wrist.

"Wow, look at the time. You better get going or you'll be late for your show!"

It was obvious Jayvee wanted to know more about Ryan's relationship with the Russians, but she was running late. She gave Ryan a long kiss and warm embrace, and then dashed out of the restaurant. Ryan settled the tab with the waiter and headed back to his hotel. He decided that a walk back would be preferable to a cab ride.

His inner voice was a condemnation. *You're into it now, Hannegan. She's not going to forget about this. What are you going to do about it?*

The pedestrian and street traffic was still active in the city that never sleeps, but Hannegan was oblivious to it all. For Ryan, there was only a smell of foreboding and a noise similar to baseball spikes crunching on a warning track echoing in the back of his head.

· EIGHT ·

THE RIVALRY BETWEEN the New York Horsemen and the Boston Colonials was the most competitive in the Baseball Big Leagues, if not in all professional sports. The intensity was felt on the field, in the stands, where the spectators were sometimes known to take their enthusiasm a little too far, and even in the press box, that supposed bastion of impartiality.

Terry Tate was a native of Boston, and his reporting for the *Boston Journal* was colored by his great affection for his hometown and its team. He was not afraid to be critical, but it was evident there was an emotional pull the Colonials had on him. His column in the *Journal* that early May morning spoke of the enthusiasm generated by the Colonials' good start, and the underlying fear of the Jinx rising up to extinguish the dream again.

Woodrow Wilson Watson of the *New York Tribune-World*, on the other hand, mirrored the self-confidence that seemed to be almost God-given to the Horsemen. He often expressed his conviction that he was among the rare few who had the insight to truly understand a situation. As the Internet became popular, Watson adopted a secondary byline to play upon the connection between his initials and the cyberspace mother lode of information. For those who knew him, the affectation was appropriate to his personality.

Watson was not averse to sticking his needle into the Horsemen when he deemed it necessary, and his column in that day's *Tribune-World* all but demanded the Horsemen begin their return to the top of the Northeast Division in earnest.

ENOUGH ALREADY

Woodrow Wilson Watson, *New York Tribune-World*
www.TheTruth.com

NEW YORK (AP) I cannot remember exactly if it was Copernicus or Galileo because it has been some time since I studied those learned gentlemen in school. If my memory is still functioning properly, however, I believe this pair of mathematicians developed ideas about order in the universe. Both men described the role the sun plays at the center of what we now call the solar system. The same principles can be applied to the world we know as the Baseball Big Leagues.

Certainly there are those strange phenomena such as last season when the Horsemen were not at the heart of the baseball universe, but many of us believe that is an aberration to what should be the natural order of the sport. Let's be frank. Baseball makes more sense when a New York team, especially the Horsemen, is the focus of our attention. This philosophy might be objectionable in certain circles, but Galileo and Copernicus had their enemies, too.

With that in mind, it is incumbent upon the Horsemen to return to their rightful place and this series with the Colonials that begins tonight needs to be the starting point. Speaking of setting things right, I look forward to tonight's meeting between Buddy Pickens and Ryan Hannegan of Boston. Hannegan is one of the surprises in this early season, a meteoric beginning that does not fit the profile of his BBL career. To compound his disruption of the natural order of the sport, this never-was had the audacity to insult one of the greatest pitchers ever with a display of unfounded showmanship during a spring training matchup in this rivalry. Let's hope that Mr. Pickens takes the proper step to set things right, if you know what I mean. It all begins tonight. Anything less than success will be unacceptable.

The stadium for the Horsemen is called The Hollow in tribute to the team's nickname, and it is located right along the Hudson River, although considerably farther downstream than the original Sleepy Hollow. The ballpark's atmosphere was already charged for batting practice although the game wouldn't start for several hours. This was the first of twenty meetings between the Horsemen and the Colonials.

"Here we go, Horsemen, here we go!"

"Boston Sucks, Boston Sucks!"

"Fuhgettaboutit, Colonials. You ain't got nuthin'."

The fans were as hot as fresh popcorn and their tongues flapped with venom. The game was a sellout, and many of the New York faithful had turned out early, clad in their Horsemen regalia of black and orange with the logo of the Headless Horseman riding a flame-breathing steed. Frankly, it was the most impressive in the BBL. A few Boston supporters bravely wore the royal blue and ruby red colors of the Colonials. Most of the interaction between the fans was good-natured, but at least a few Boston caps with the logo of the interlocking letters B and C and a tri-corner hat cocked on top of the B would be snatched off the heads of poor Colonial fans and stomped upon by New York supporters.

Ryan Hannegan had gotten a taste of a pennant chase for the first time in his career when he joined the Colonials the previous August, but there had been only two games left on the schedule with New York, and both of those were in Boston. This would be his first experience with the rivalry in New York City, and the first time he would be a central figure in the drama.

Ryan had heard more than a few "You're going down!" calls from New York hecklers as he went through his pre-game warm-ups, and Junichi was another target of the wrath of the Horsemen's followers. After Pickens disposed of Fernando Horrado and Kevin Kyle easily at the beginning of the game, the action was momentarily halted when a literal storm of sushi hit the field from the upper deck. Those Horsemen fans might be vulgar and politically incorrect, but they deserved some credit for imagination. This was a new experience for Junichi, but he handled it with the same calm and grace he had shown with everything he had encountered so far in the BBL. Unfortunately, he couldn't handle Buddy Pickens in his first at-bat that evening as the big right hander struck him out with a nasty split finger fastball to end the top of the first inning.

"Let's go get-em, Big E. This is our time."

Boston manager, D.P. Perryton, had adjusted his rotation to get Ellis Nance and Keith Lash as his starters for the two games in New York, but he was apprehensive about having Nance change to seven days between starts when he had been pitching every fifth day. The concern seemed warranted in the bottom of the first when the Big E walked a pair of New Yorkers and pitched consistently from behind in the count.

"...Casey Hegan laces a ball to left-center...It's going to split Hannegan and Junichi... Cuevas comes around to score and here comes Kesicki headed to the plate... that'll make it 2-0 New York."

It might have been more if Dennis Soos hadn't speared a line dive with a diving grab at third to end the inning. Ramòn Morientes grounded out to begin the second frame, and the noise in the stadium grew to a deafening level when Ryan Hannegan was announced as the next hitter. If the Horsemen's fans had forgotten about Ryan's encounter with Buddy Pickens in spring training, Woody Watson's column in the *Tribune-World* refreshed their memories like a sharp stick in an ant bed.

Ryan approached the batter's box and began his ritual. It was always the same: dig a good toehold with his left foot to settle into the box, then a tug on the right sleeve, a tap to the top of his batting helmet, a few practice swings and he was ready to go. Hannegan asked for time from the home plate umpire, however, just before Pickens started into his windup.

"Excuse me, Mr. Pickens." Ryan said with a small grin on his face. "How about we settle this whole respect thing?"

Hannegan surprised everyone by hitting the deck as if Pickens had just buzzed him with an inside fastball. Ryan got back up, dusted himself off, and then looked out at Pickens.

"What do you think? Will that work?"

The New York fireballer answered the question by plunking Hannegan squarely between the four and the seven on the back of his Boston jersey with his first pitch, clocked at ninety-five miles an hour.

"Now things are square, asshole!" The pitcher was furious.

Both benches came to the top steps of their dugouts, but not out onto the field. Ryan slowly made his way down the first baseline, never reacting to the stinging pain he felt in the middle of his back. Instead, he smiled at the New York pitcher, tipped his cap, and then blew him a kiss. This infuriated Buddy Pickens who reacted by extending the middle finger of his right hand at the Boston outfielder.

Ryan just grinned. "Yeah, that's the first time you've hit me, Buddy. I'm kinda looking forward to the next time you do it. They tell me you count like this when the numbers get higher..."

Hannegan started pawing the ground with his right foot like counting show horses do. Pickens went crazy, threw down his glove and began to come at Hannegan. Casey Hegan, the Horsemen's first baseman, jumped between the two to keep a fight from breaking out as now both benches, as well as the bullpens, emptied out onto the field. After a little milling around by the two teams, order was restored and the game was resumed without any ejection being made, although both benches were officially warned against any more deliberate throwing at hitters.

The incident with Hannegan must have cost Pickens some of his concentration, even with all of his BBL experience, and he made a mistake with the next hitter, Dennis Soos.

"There's a swing and drive... WAY BACK AND GONE TO THE BLEACHERS IN THE LEFT... Pickens hung Soos a curve ball and the good Doctor was all over it..."

D.P. Perryton had flip-flopped Hannegan and Soos in the batting order because of Ryan's hot start, and Soos' game-tying two-run homer was an early payoff. The game remained a two-all standoff heading into the fifth inning when Ryan Hannegan was due to lead off. Buddy Pickens had regained his composure and rhythm, setting down seven in a row since the Soos homer, but he fell behind in the count, two balls and no strikes to Ryan. With Hegan playing back and guarding the line at first, Hannegan surprised the New York defense with a beautiful drag bunt just past the reach of Pickens who had lumbered off the mound trying to grab it.

"Damn you, Hannegan... you're a chicken-shit!" yelled a frustrated Pickens as Ryan pounded through the bag at first for a leadoff hit.

Knowing it was probably going to be a low-scoring game, D.P. Perryton had Dennis Soos sacrifice Hannegan to second. J.R. Cook couldn't bring the runner home, however, and flied out to left field. Peter Beckwith, the New York skipper, then elected to walk Mark Allen, the number eight hitter for Boston, to bring Ellis Nance to the plate.

"Beckwith is going with the safe strategy. Let Pickens take care of his opposite number and choke off the rally."

It was only the beginning of May, but Tom Kingery's description already had an edge to it that usually came out only as the playoffs drew closer.

"... Here's his first pitch to Nance ... Swing and a shot towards left-center ... that's going to drop in for a hit. Hannegan is heading home and the Big E helps himself with an RBI hit to make it 3-2, Boston."

Pickens was hotter than a sidewalk in August in his hometown of Jasper, Texas, but the problems this inning had all been his. He got a small sip of revenge when he struck out Hannegan in the sixth inning with a couple of men on base, but he was still on the short end of the scoreboard when he departed for a pinch hitter in the bottom of the eighth. Ellis Nance had been brilliant since his shaky first inning, retiring fourteen New Yorkers in a row at one point. More impressively, the radar gun was still clocking his fastball around ninety-four in the eighth inning.

"Two outs here in the ninth with Junichi still out there at second. Hannegan comes to the plate, a left handed hitter facing the right hander, Chris Jewett. First base is open, but it looks like the Horsemen are going to pitch to him. Jewett fires — and there's a drive to deep right ... oh, man, he really crushed that one — it's gone to the upper deck. Up above the ozone, folks! Touch 'em all time for Ryan Hannegan — what a game for the Boston center fielder ..."

Following the five to two Boston victory, Terry Tate and Woody Watson appeared on Jayvee DellVecchio's DBC show later in the evening.

"Terry, winning tonight's game seemed to be more important to the Colonials than the Horsemen."

"I wouldn't go so far as to say that, Jayvee, but there is no question there is a new atmosphere in the Boston clubhouse."

"Is that the result of this strong start?"

Tate leaned forward, putting his elbows on the studio desk as if he wanted Jayvee to be the only one to hear his answer.

"A good beginning is always important, but I think it's more about what's happening inside that clubhouse. Junichi has brought a strong presence and his obvious talent, but I also believe Ryan Hannegan has made a difference."

Jayvee made no visible reaction, but she was pleased Terry Tate was recognizing what Ryan has done so far.

"In what way has Hannegan impacted Boston?"

"He's the first Colonials player in recent years, in my opinion, to have an answer for the bullying tactics of Buddy Pickens."

"You're out of line, Tate," Woody Watson interjected.

"Hang on, Woodrow, you'll get your chance. What I mean is Buddy Pickens, to his credit throughout his career, has controlled the atmosphere of a game with his talent and with his dominant personality. I think the Colonials are now saying what the hell to Pickens for the first time in a long time . . . and I attribute that to Ryan Hannegan standing up to him in Florida and again tonight."

The color had risen in Woody Watson's face; he was chomping at the bit to respond.

"May I remind my esteemed colleague from Boston that there have been fewer than twenty games played thus far. In addition, the Horsemen have nineteen games remaining in this rivalry, a rivalry thoroughly dominated by the Horsemen over time."

The director for *Totally Baseball* cut to a shot of Jayvee so she could ask a question, but Woody Watson was not about to relinquish the spotlight.

"Of greater importance here, as I wrote about in my column this morning, is the current atmosphere in the New York clubhouse."

Watson, a frequent contributor to a number of panel discussion shows on television, waited for the director to return to a close-up of him. Once he saw his face on the monitor next to one of the cameras, the New York columnist continued.

"The Horsemen have a built-in advantage over most BBL teams, one that is the result of winning more championships than any other organization. But when they do not use the power of that tradition to intimidate other teams, they are just another ball club."

The color in his face was now in full bloom, creating an interesting contrast to the wavy white hair on his head. With a flourish, Woodrow Wilson Watson delivered his parting salvo.

"This is fair warning for the Horsemen and their fans. Remember who you are and what you represent. Anything less than a full effort is unacceptable. Watch out! If this keeps up, you'll end up like that witch in *The Wizard of Oz* and have the sky fall on you."

"Woody, that was Henny Penny worrying about the sky falling. It was a house that fell on the Wicked Witch."

Watson waved off Jayvee's correction with a dismissive look, but Terry Tate chuckled at her effort. Without question, there was a Boston-New York rivalry in the press box as well.

Whether it was the Wizard of Oz or Henny Penny, trouble fell out of the sky for the Horsemen Thursday afternoon. At a hastily called media conference at BBL headquarters, General Hopkins had some disturbing news.

"I regretfully report the drug testing program we have initiated this season in the Baseball Big Leagues has come up with a positive test result. In a cooperative arrangement between BBL management and the Players Association, we have been administering drug testing on a regular schedule as well as randomly. We were gratified the scheduled testing conducted at the beginning of spring training resulted in negative readings across the board. Unfortunately, in the first series of random tests, which took place over this past weekend, a positive reading occurred. David Bock of the New York Horsemen was found to have one of the BBL's banned substances in his bloodstream. As part of the agreement with the Players Association, a testing facility independent of the BBL also analyzed the sample and concurred with the results our labs found."

General Hopkins paused. Several reporters raised their hands to ask questions, but quickly lowered them when the commissioner's expression told them he wasn't finished with his message.

"When I accepted the leadership of this great game, I promised the

American public we would do all that was necessary to restore the integrity of the BBL. I intend to fulfill that pledge. As a result, Mr. Bock has been suspended for the next sixty days without pay, effective immediately. During that time he will not be allowed to work out with his team, and he will be subject to a series of additional drug tests. Since this is his first offense, he will be reinstated to the Horsemen upon the completion of the sixty days, provided there are no additional infractions. Should Mr. Bock test positive at any time during his suspension period, he will be ineligible to play for the remainder of the season, with the possibility of permanent suspension."

A suspension of this length was new to baseball for such an offense. There was, however, much more to the new drug policy for the Baseball Big Leagues.

"In addition, I have decided the Horsemen will not be able to replace Mr. Bock on their active roster during the length of his suspension. It is the responsibility of each team to educate their players on the dangers of supplement use and to monitor these athletes to ensure they play clean. It is the only way, in my opinion, we can get the cooperation necessary from all sides to clear up this problem in our sport."

The penalty of making the Horsemen play one player short for next two months astonished the reporters. In the question-and-answer period that followed, General Hopkins emphasized the power he had been given to make these kinds of decisions.

"What was the reaction from the Horsemen?"

"Certainly they were not happy to have one of their players not abide by the supplement policy that has been put into place. All the owners know we cannot make exceptions if this program is going to work."

"And they agreed to the roster loss of a player for sixty days?"

"The Horsemen did ask if a substantial financial penalty could be issued instead, but ultimately they agreed to my mandate. I am hoping the severity of the penalty creates an understanding with each team where EVERYONE has a stake in removing improper supplement use from the clubhouse. If not, they will pay the price."

Some of the Colonials watched the news conference from the visitors' clubhouse at The Hollow. Talk had been going on around batting cages and in clubhouses throughout the spring as players wondered who would make the first false step. New York, of course, was the archrival for the Colonials, so they weren't unhappy that the decision handed down by the new commissioner would certainly impact the Horsemen.

"I'm glad Hoppy stuck it to 'em," Dennis Soos said to the group of players standing around the television watching General Hopkins make his statement. "There have been too many goddamn cheaters in this game, and it's about time we did something about it!"

Ellis Nance echoed the sentiments of the Boston team captain.

"The General was talking a big game when he got the job, and I guess he was serious when he said he was going to clean things up."

"Can you imagine what's going on over in the other clubhouse right now?" added Kevin Kyle. "I bet there are some pretty pissed off people; imagine playing one guy short for two months! That is going to be a bitch."

"Screw 'em," snapped Dennis Soos. "They wouldn't have any sympathy for us if one of our guys tested positive."

Ryan Hannegan stared silently at the television while his teammates discussed the situation. They all knew there was a chance some guys might get caught trying to beat the new system, but Hannegan never thought General Hopkins would penalize a whole team for an infraction. The implications were immense.

"Hey, you all right, Ryno? You look like you've just seen a ghost."

"Sure, I'm okay, Doc. I was just thinking about Dave Bock. Losing two months pay is really going to hurt his family. I wonder if he thought about that when he started taking the stuff."

"Well, I wonder if he thought about his teammates when he decided to cheat. They're going to spend the next two months paying for his stupidity."

Hannegan managed a wan smile for his friend, and then walked away from the television area back to his locker. His inner voice was back again, replete with guilt and paranoia. *And when Dave Bock comes back, I wonder how he's going to be treated. I'll bet he's gonna have some guys in his face when he returns.*

Hannegan didn't even want to consider that happening to him. He finished putting on his batting practice gear and grabbed a bat for an early session in the batting cages below the grandstands at The Hollow.

The game that evening in New York was almost surreal. The Horsemen and their fans acted like zombies, dazed by what had occurred earlier. The fans not stunned by the blow to their beloved Horsemen hurled invectives at the Boston players, accusing the Colonials of somehow conspiring with the commissioner against the Horsemen. It didn't make any difference to Keith Lash as he completely befuddled the sleepwalking New Yorkers. The veteran soft-tosser pitched a six-hit shutout, and needed only eighty-three pitches to accomplish the task. The game would not have lasted even two hours except the Colonials pounded Rick Shoemaker, the New York starter, and four other pitchers for a season high twenty-six hits. Every Colonial player that saw action collected a hit, including Lash. Horrado, Junichi and Hannegan all had four hits apiece in a 19-0 rout that could have been worse.

The worst shellacking ever administered to the Horsemen pushed Boston's lead to three games over their rivals, and the media gave wide coverage to the potential connection between the suspension of Dave Bock and the margin of victory.

"Gentlemen, how long do you think it will take for New York to recover from all of this?" Jayvee was very much in control in front of the camera. She was impeccably dressed, as usual, with not one hair out of place. She was the ultimate professional.

Woody Watson and Terry Tate were again the featured guests on *Totally Baseball*.

"It's a two-fold problem," Terry Tate jumped in before Watson could respond. "They may recover from the emotional blow, but the big question is how will they fill the void in their lineup without Bock's powerful bat?"

"Young lady," Woody Watson responded, "we must look at the big picture here. I am curious that the Horsemen would be the first team singled out for General Hopkins' wrath."

Terry Tate leaned back in his chair and shook his head at his colleague's stance.

"I hope this new commissioner is not using the flagship of this sport just to verify his authority. He'd better be as vigilant with the other teams or this reporter will be suspicious of his efforts."

"If that's the way you're going to be, Woody," answered Terry Tate, "then what happened today couldn't have happened to a better team."

The Colonials couldn't maintain their momentum after New York, however, and they dropped three of four games in St. Louis to the Midwest Division-leading Rivermen. Returning to Boston, a nine-game homestand began with another loss, this time to the Chicago Blaze. They were able to gain a split the following evening behind solid pitching from Darren Haddad. The Horsemen in the meantime, had regained some of their resolve and won four of six on their eleven-game trip. The Horsemen arrived for a rematch series with the Colonials — this time a five-game affair at Patriots' Harbor — again trailing Boston by just one game in the Northeast Division.

If the Colonials were going through their first down cycle of the season, it had not affected Ryan Hannegan. He had posted a .344 batting average through the team's first twenty-five games which put him among the elite in the American Conference. His twenty-four runs batted in also had him among the leaders. For the first time since his college days, Ryan's baseball exploits were drawing attention, publicity that carried mixed blessings, along with an undercurrent of dread.

"Down goes, Hannegan..."

Tom Kingery sounded like he was describing a boxing match.

"Boy, that's about the fourth or fifth time this week someone has tried to intimidate the C's hottest hitter. Welcome to the spotlight, Ryan."

Such notoriety also carried weight with members of the press as Hannegan observed at the Friday night opener with New York. Emerging out of the tunnel from the Colonials clubhouse for batting practice, he found a cadre of writers and radio-TV types in the dugout awaiting his appearance. Ryan smiled and nodded in acknowledgment to some of the people he knew. Grabbing his bat out of the bat rack, he began to work his way toward the batting cage while the interrogation began.

"Hey, Ryan, you got a minute for a couple of questions?"

"Hannegan! You ready for Pickens again this weekend?"

"What happened in St. Louis? Can you guys take it to the Horsemen like you did last week?"

Fortunately, Bobby Greene, the Colonials media relations man, stepped in to temporarily halt the inquiries.

"No interviews without advance notice, boys, until Ryan finishes his workout on the field. Ryan, you okay to talk after BP?"

Hannegan shrugged his shoulders and nodded affirmatively and then ran onto the field for the pre-game work. He got in his hitting in the cage, and then spent most of the remaining batting practice time shagging flies in the outfield. When it was New York's turn for pre-game, Ryan returned to the dugout area and found his waiting audience had shrunk. Ryan smiled as he recognized Terry Tate among the group that remained, but his smile froze as he realized Woody Watson was also there.

"Fire away, guys," Hannegan said, attempting to put on a pleasant front, "... what is it they say? Any publicity is good publicity?"

"Ryan, this is your best start ever in the BBL. What's made the difference?"

"Terry, I think it has been several things. I got a chance here because the injury to Angel forced a trade, and D.P. showed he had the confidence in me to be able to contribute. I also spent more time working on things in the off-season to get ready than I ever have before, and so far, it is paying off."

"What are you doing differently than in seasons past?" another reporter asked.

"Nothing in particular, really, except I am seeing the ball better thanks to these eye exercises I've been doing the past six months. And, obviously, my confidence is up. It's a lot easier to play this game when you know you're going to be in the lineup almost every day. Then if things go badly a few games, you don't worry about whether you're going to be yanked out of the lineup. That makes a big difference."

Woody Watson interrupted.

"Would you care to comment about Dave Bock's suspension last week?"

"I feel sorry for his family because of the financial loss and the negative publicity, but General Hopkins said he was going to crack down and apparently he means it."

"Do you think there is any connection between what Bock was allegedly doing and the success you are having for the first time in your career?"

What an asshole! Ryan took a deep breath and quietly responded. "I won't even dignify that with an answer."

"But you're not denying anything either?"

Ryan glared at the veteran newspaperman for a long time without speaking.

Finally, he turned to the rest of the people gathered there.

"Thanks for your interest. I need to head back inside now."

Raul Gomez was getting the start in the opener, squaring off against New York's little left hander, Rock Hunter. Gomez had begun the season well, winning three of his first four opportunities, equaling Nance and Lash for the team lead in victories. The night against the Horsemen, however, didn't go the way of his previous outings, and New York was up six to nothing when D.P. Perryton lifted him midway through the fifth inning. Hunter, meanwhile, was especially sharp early.

"... Horrado on third, Morientes on first — two outs and a two-two count on Hannegan. Here's the little lefty's pitch ... SWING AND A MISS ... Hunter strikes out Hannegan on a beautiful changeup to retire the side. It's one to nothing New York after one ..."

The fans at Patriots Harbor were becoming increasingly nervous until the C's finally started clicking in the bottom of the sixth. Kevin Kyle led off the frame with a single, and Junichi followed with a two-run homer off the foul pole in left. Hannegan walked with one out, and Doc Soos followed with a single, but with the big Boston crowd screaming for more, Hunter recovered and got Cook and Allen out to kill the rally.

Hank Cummings had come out of the bullpen in relief of Gomez in the fifth, and he held New York scoreless through the seventh. In the bottom of the inning, Junichi hit Hunter's first pitch over the Blue Pier in right. Before the strains of Beach Boys music and the yells of "Make

A Splash" had faded, Ramòn Morientes followed with a double to right-center, and Hannegan brought the big first baseman home with a ringing single to right. Hunter was able to choke off the continuing Colonials' comeback, but with the score now six to four, the full house at The Harbor had reason to believe this one was not over.

"What a finish we've got brewing here at the Harbor..."

Tom Kingery, the Boston broadcaster, was as revved up as the capacity crowd. The Colonials were mounting another rally in the bottom of the ninth.

"Kris Fucci did a great game keeping New York off the board, and now the C's have the great Matt Lerner on the ropes."

Kris Fucci followed Cummings out of the bullpen, and he pitched scoreless eighth and ninth innings for Boston. The Horsemen' Matt Lerner was considered the best stopper in the American Conference.

"Bobby Applebee, the pinch hitter who got it started is at third — Horrado is at second, representing the tying run; ... no balls and two strikes the count on Ramòn Morientes... Lerner comes set... here's the pitch. Up and in and the ball gets away... wait a minute, home plate umpire Bill Wazevich says the ball hit Morientes' helmet... that'll load the bases! How about that!"

Hannegan was the next hitter and he took a deep breath as he walked towards the plate. His mind tried to calm him down. Stay relaxed now, Ryan. It's not like you've been in something like this before.

Lerner was a fastball pitcher, but his easy delivery and the late movement of his pitches made him especially difficult to hit. Lerner had a strong, sinking fastball, which a pitcher gets by gripping the ball parallel with the seams of the baseball. When it comes spinning to the plate, just two seams cut through the air which gives the ball its sinking action and its name: the two-seam fastball. When the grip is across the ball's seams, four seams work the spinning, and the ball appears to rise as it comes to the plate. In the vernacular of the players, Lerner's two-seamer was filthy, while his four-seamer just exploded.

Hannegan settled into the left-hand batter's box as Patriots Harbor reverberated like a den of din.

"... Lerner comes set ... the pitch ... fastball, outside corner at the knees ... a called strike one."

"Bases full of C's...two outs...Horsemen up 6-4. Lerner has his sign and he's ready again. He fires. SWING AND A MISS...98 miles per hour upstairs and Hannegan wasn't even close."

The Boston outfielder stepped out of the batter's box to collect his thoughts. *Come on, Ryan, relax.* He stared at the bat between his large fists. He mentally strained to make the crowd noise vanish. *This guy is tough enough; don't make it any easier for him. Concentrate on what you have to do.* He glanced over to the on-deck circle where Dennis Soos was giving him their six-gun salute and mouthing his W-T-F mantra. Ryan smiled.

Climbing back in, he took the 0-2 pitch as Lerner wasted one, an off-speed pitch away. The New Yorker then followed with a two-seamer, a borderline pitch Hannegan was just able to chop foul down the third base side. Another four-seam fastball pushed Hannegan back from the plate, evening the count at two balls and two strikes. Once more, Ryan asked for time to step out of the batter's box. Slowly he settled back into his position...got a good toehold with the back foot...a tug on the right sleeve of the jersey...a tap on the top of the helmet...a few practice swings, come on...bring it.

"Hannegan's hanging in there...Applebee and The Hurricane can run, so a base hit can tie it up...Lerner's ready again..."

Lerner elected to go with another four-seam fastball up and in at Hannegan, but as the ball hurtled to the plate, Ryan swore later it was spinning so slowly he could almost read Hoppy Hopkins's signature on the baseball. When hardwood meets horsehide in perfect synchronicity, the action seems almost effortless.

"...Oh, he crushed that one...deep to right...that ball's GOIN' AND IT AIN'T COMING BACK...over the Pier...the Colonials win on Ryan Hannegan's grand slam!"

He had done it to the hated Horsemen. The Beach Boys' "Fun, Fun, Fun" blasted from The Harbor's sound system, and Hannegan practically danced along with the music as he circled the bases. His teammates poured out of the dugout to gather at home plate and as he stepped on the dish, they proceeded to pummel him playfully. When the celebration finally subsided, Ryan looked up to the press box and spotted Woody Watson. He gave the New York writer a derisive salute. That's probably a mistake, he thought, but the hell with it. He had cleared the Blue Pier for the first time when it mattered . . . he had made a splash . . . this was the best moment of his Baseball Big Leagues career.

The jubilation of the Boston players continued in their clubhouse, calming down only when the media horde entered to get their post-game comments from the players and D. P. Perryton. The focus was on Ryan Hannegan to no one's surprise, and Ryan enjoyed the attention, although he was disappointed Woody Watson had not come down from the press box for another potential confrontation. No matter, nothing could take away from the high he was riding on at the moment.

With deadlines approaching, the media eventually headed back to their laptops and remote trucks, allowing Hannegan time, finally, to pull off his uniform. His teammates had either departed already, or were in the process of doing so, since tomorrow was going to be an afternoon game. Pete Hudec, the C's trainer, was still there — he was usually the last to leave — and called out to Ryan.

"Hey, Ryno. I need to see you before you get outta here."

"No problem, Blade. I'm heading to the showers now."

After a steaming soak for about ten minutes, Ryan checked in at the training room where he found Hudec in conference with the team's doctor, Loren Myers, and someone Ryan did not recognize.

"Ryan," Pete Hudec began, " . . you know Doctor Myers." Gesturing to the other gentleman standing there, he added: ". . . and this is Jack McDermott."

Hannegan shook hands with Dr. Myers and McDermott who introduced himself to the Boston outfielder.

"Mr. Hannegan, I represent the commissioner's office as part of its security team. I am a retired agent of the Federal Bureau of Investigation . . . "

Ryan nodded to the representative for General Hopkins, but he made no other response as the former lawman continued.

"As part of the agreement between the Baseball Big Leagues and your Players Association, I am here to supervise a drug screening. We expect your complete cooperation."

Again, Hannegan nodded in response as whatever remaining color he had under his skin slowly drained from his face. Doctor Loren Myers explained to him he would need to take a small blood sample. Completing that, the Colonials' team physician handed Ryan a plastic sample bottle.

"I realize this might be a little awkward for you, Ryan, but Mr. McDermott and I must accompany you when you give us your urine sample in order to ensure it is a valid one. I represent the best interests of the Boston Colonials, and of course, Mr. McDermott does so for the commissioner's office. We both must be present to verify its authenticity."

"No sweat," Ryan responded, forcing himself to give his audience a big grin. "The only problem I see is that you and our good buddy here might feel a little inadequate when you observe my magnificent equipment."

Neither man reacted to his lame attempt at some humor, not that Ryan really expected they would anyway. As the trio stood impassively, waiting for Hannegan to head to the bathroom, Ryan's mood changed.

"You know, it's very interesting that you're here to give me one of these tests now. If I weren't having this kind of season, you wouldn't give a damn about me. Have some success, and suddenly everyone believes you must be cheating. You people really PISS ME OFF!"

Again, Dr. Myers, Pete Hudec, and Jack McDermott made no response to Hannegan, so he headed to the bathroom area, with the doctor and the lawman right behind him. So this is the way it's going to be ... everything I do is going to be scrutinized now. He didn't know if he should be angry or afraid.

It was a subdued Ryan Hannegan ready for the games on Saturday and Sunday. D.P. Perryton sat him down for the nightcap of the doubleheader on Sunday after he had collected just two hits in eight at-bats in the previous two games. New York won on Saturday, and the two teams split in the doubleheader with their aces, Ellis Nance and Buddy Pickens, getting the wins for their respective teams. The media reports played up the dramatic win on Friday night, but thankfully for Hannegan, there was no mention of his drug screening, not even in the big Sunday notes columns, a regular feature of the major newspapers around the country. The Baseball Big Leagues had promised the Players Association confidentiality for the random drug tests and they had made good on that promise, at least in Ryan's case anyway.

"Blade, have you heard anything yet?" Hannegan popped his head into the trainer's room when he came to the ballpark early Monday afternoon.

"Not a word, Ryan. I figure no news is good news."

Feeling better about his situation, Hannegan finished up the series with New York by driving in a pair of runs with two doubles on a three for five night at the plate. The Colonials won the Monday finale, eight to four, to open up a two-game lead over their chief rivals in the Northeast Division. Boston followed that with a sweep of their two-game set with last year's division winners, the Baltimore Crabbers, despite Nick Hamilton hitting for the cycle in one of the games for Baltimore. The two victories meant the C's went six and three on the homestand, and, coupled with New York's loss on Wednesday, Boston's lead over the Horsemen had grown to three games. Momentum was on the side of the Colonials as they prepped for their toughest trip of the season: a twelve-game journey through Cleveland, Detroit, and Chicago.

"Everything okay, Ryno?" Dennis Soos asked his friend as they packed their bags in the Boston clubhouse for the upcoming trip. "You seemed a little out of it over the weekend. Anything wrong?"

"I guess I celebrated a little too much after Friday night. I don't seem to recover as quickly as I used to . . ."

"You are an old fart, that's for sure, but I didn't think that was the reason. Man, you were lost in space on Saturday."

"I don't know . . . sometimes I keep thinking about when this bubble is going to burst. This is new territory for me."

"Don't give me that crap about bubbles bursting. You're hitting .351 . . . leading the conference in batting. All you have to do is keep believing in yourself. You've got all the tools . . . just let it go."

Ryan smiled at his friend without answering, but Soos had hit the right nerve.

"C'mon, Ryno...W-T-F...just remember the good doctor's philosophy and everything will be just fine. Speaking of W-T-F . . . I think I deserve a fee or something for how well you're playing. None of this would be happening if it wasn't for me."

"Yes, Doc . . . it's all because of you. And next you're going to tell me you invented the Internet . . . and that you're going to save the environment, too."

"Kiss my ass, Ryno. So what do you say — buy me dinner on Saturday night and we'll call it even."

"It will have to be in Chicago. I've got something else I've got to do, Saturday night in Cleveland."

Soos rose from the stool in front of his locker, put on the sports coat that was hanging there, and started toward the clubhouse door. Turning back to Hannegan, Soos broke into a large smile.

"That's right! I forgot . . . you have a rendezvous with a certain member of the media that has to take priority over anything you might want to do with your best friend."

Hannegan was flabbergasted. It was true that he had made plans to go out with Jayvee that night because she was going to be in Cleveland to help celebrate her mother's birthday. But he hadn't told anyone about his plans.

"How in the hell did you know about that?"

"Who knows what lusty thoughts lurk in the minds of dirty old men — or in this case — never-were outfielders? Only the Doctor knows, only the Doctor knows."

Soos let loose a hearty cackle and walked out the door of the clubhouse.

· NINE ·

THE ROAD TRIP got off to a fine start in Cleveland on a Friday night as the Colonials won their fourth straight game, defeating the Ironmen six to one behind the solid pitching of veteran righthander, Nick Ertle. Ryan Hannegan had two more hits and another run batted in to stay atop the A-C in hitting at .359, and his RBI total of thirty-two had him in the top five in that category as well. Despite the continued success, that wasn't what had Ryan feeling good as Boston took batting practice before the Saturday afternoon game.

"Look at that shit-eating grin," Doc Soos teased as they stood alongside the cage waiting for their next turn to hit. "I used to look like that, in junior high, waiting to get a little action in somebody's basement."

"Doc, the way I feel right now, nothing you could say can bother me. Even your ugly mug looks good!"

With that, Hannegan leaned over towards Soos, grabbed his teammate's face with both hands and looked like he was about to plant a big wet one flush on Doc's lips.

Soos playfully pushed Ryan away.

"Get away from me, you asshole."

"Everything all right, gentlemen?" Boston manager D.P. Perryton asked from the other side of the batting cage.

"No problem, Skipper. It's just our lover boy here who is all hopped up because he thinks he's going to get some tonight."

"How about we concentrate on getting something this afternoon off O'Toole?"

"You got it, D.P."

Hannegan returned a push at Doc.

"You heard the man, Doc. Let's keep our focus on the game, shall we?"

Soos returned a middle finger salute at his friend, but with a large smile on his face.

It was remarkable the relationship between Ryan and Jayvee had developed at all, considering how difficult their demanding schedules were. They had been with each other just a few times, but Ryan felt like he had known Jayvee all of his life. They constantly shared e-mails, and he was grateful he had one of those unlimited calling plans for his cell phone.

If he was distracted, Hannegan didn't show it during the game, banging a two-out single to score Fernando Horrado with the game's first run and later adding his second triple of the season to drive home another run. He was now averaging a run batted in for each Boston game played, production he had not shown at any other time in his career. On this beautiful mid-May afternoon in Cleveland, Hannegan, Junichi, and Ramòn Morientes combined for eight hits, including a pair of homers by Morientes, in a 12-2 romp over the Ironmen. Ellis Nance cruised through eight innings to win his fifth decision of the campaign.

"Ryan-san," Junichi called to Hannegan adding the Japanese term that denotes respect and friendship. "What are you doing?"

Hannegan was in one of the meeting rooms in the visitors' clubhouse doing the Bates Method eye exercises following the game.

"Just a little trick I learned last winter. I don't know if it makes any difference, but things are going well, so I'm not going to change my routine. Around here we like to say if it ain't broke, don't fix it."

"Back home, I would think you would be in deep prayer to the gods."

"Not me. I'm not really the religious type."

"In Japan, our beliefs tell us all people are basically good, and if we follow the gods' ways and avoid the evil spirits, things will turn out right. You have *makoto*, Ryan-san. That means you have a true heart which comes from following the gods' ways . . . even if you don't realize you are doing it. I think that makes you religious."

"I appreciate the thought, but I don't know that I deserve it. If anybody has a true heart, it's you, Junichi. It's been unbelievable how you have handled all the pressure . . . and how well you have fit in here."

Junichi bowed slightly to Hannegan.

"I have never been bothered by the media. They have their job and I have mine. If you have *musuhi*, my uncle always told me, everything will be just fine."

"Your uncle . . . moo-shoe?"

Junichi laughed.

"Musuhi — it means to have the powers of harmony. My uncle is a Shinto priest, and he always taught our family there is a way for all things and all people to work together. I have tried to carry that philosophy with me throughout my life."

"Well, it sure works. You were the biggest thing in baseball in your country, and it looks like you're going to do the same thing over here!"

Again, Junichi bowed slightly to his teammate.

"You would be surprised, Ryan-san, but you are the talk of Japan. All the stories are about this player who is outdoing the great Junichi."

"Hey, it's the other way around, my Japanese friend."

Hannegan got up from the chair, put his arm around Junichi, and began to walk back toward the main clubhouse area.

"By the time pitchers get done with you and Ramòn, they're too distracted to worry about a nobody like me."

"This is the Ryan Hannegan, the hitter from American college baseball I remember watching. Yet, you are always the one to minimize your accomplishments. Ryan-san, if I didn't know any better, I would think you have some Japanese in you."

"The only Japanese in me is some good sushi. But from you I take that as a great compliment."

For added emphasis, Hannegan bowed to his teammate as best as he could in the Japanese tradition. Junichi smiled, and returned a bow in Ryan's direction.

"Just keep the magic going, Ryan-san. Perhaps this will help?" He handed Hannegan a small medallion.

"What is it?"

"It is called a *Mamori*. I received it from my uncle before I left Japan. It is supposed to help heal and protect anyone who possesses it."

Ryan was deeply touched by Junichi's gift, and he gave his teammate a hug catching the Japanese star by surprise. Slightly embarrassed, Junichi stepped back, bowed slightly one more time, and headed back to his own locker. Ryan was humbled by the expression of friendship. His Japanese teammate was a great ballplayer and an even better man. *Hannegan, it doesn't get any better than this! First place, the best you've ever played, and now you're going to spend the evening with one terrific lady.* Feeling like a giddy teenager before a date, Hannegan spent a little extra time primping in front of the mirror before heading out of the ballpark for the short walk back to the team hotel.

The blue Taurus pulled up to the front of the hotel right on time, with Jayvee at the wheel. As he crossed the lobby, Ryan Hannegan had seen only Dennis Soos, who gave him an exaggerated wink. The unpretentious car would draw no attention from any of his teammates, should they be outside the hotel, and that was just the way Ryan liked it. He and Jayvee were both content to keep their growing relationship under wraps for as long as possible.

"Wow, quite a ride," Ryan said, climbing into the car and placing a light kiss on Jayvee's lips.

"Don't give me any grief, Hannegan. Dad did Ford commercials here in town forever. I can't help it if my mother stays loyal to them."

"You know I'm just teasing — it's probably better this way — less obvious. So where are we going?"

"There's a nice little Italian place on the west side that I've always loved. I thought we could go there."

"Sounds great," said Hannegan as he settled into his seat for the ride. "You know how I feel about Italian food."

Jayvee tooled the car through the downtown area and out onto the freeway for the drive to the west side of her hometown. Ryan remarked that he didn't remember this highway from the time he lived in Cleveland as a youth, and she pointed out it had been put in when she was in high school. After about ten minutes on the freeway, Jayvee exited in what appeared to be a largely residential area.

"Hey, this looks like the old neighborhood."

Jayvee just smiled in response as she kept driving along a road undergoing construction, forcing the traffic to be only one lane.

"And that's where we played army and went sled-riding as kids," Hannegan continued, pointing to a wooded area that dropped down below the far side of the construction area. "What did we use to call it — the Valley wasn't it?"

"They call it the Metroparks now," she answered as she turned the car down a side street that ran alongside a school. At one of the last driveways on the cul-de-sac, Jayvee pulled in the car and parked.

"Here we are: Chez DellVecchio!"

"You're kidding! We're at your mother's house?"

Before Hannegan could say anything else, the front door opened and out came Jayvee's mother. Clare DellVecchio was in her sixties, but she looked much younger. Jayvee had been telling Ryan how active her mother was with golf, tennis, and a number of other things, and as Clare hugged her daughter, Ryan could plainly see that all that activity made a difference: she still looked great. And Ryan knew where Jayvee's beauty genes had come from.

"So let me see this young man who has my daughter talking so crazy." Ignoring her daughter's protest, Clare greeted Ryan as he exited the car. "Nice to meet you, Mr. Hannegan. I must say, Jessica, he looks even better in person than he does on TV. It's about time you dated an Irishman."

Red-faced, Ryan moved to shake the hand of Jayvee's mom, only to be further surprised when she politely kissed him on the cheek instead.

"Nice to meet you, Mrs. DellVecchio. Jayvee . . . I mean, Jessica, has told me a lot about you."

"You can call her Jayvee, Ryan, everyone else does. With her father gone, I believe I'm the only one who still calls her Jessica — except maybe for the nuns next door," she added, gesturing towards the school that abutted the DellVecchio's property.

Hannegan smiled in reply as Jayvee walked where the two were standing.

"Now that you have thoroughly embarrassed me, Mother, maybe I should take Ryan someplace else."

"Don't be silly. I've got enough food in there to feed the whole ball team. What would I do with it?"

"You are hungry I hope, Ryan. My maiden name is Gibbons, but Jessica's father made me an Italian a long time ago."

Clare DellVecchio slipped her arms around the waists of her two guests and escorted them into the house. She wasn't exaggerating about the food; she had laid out a feast that looked like it could serve thirty. There were appetizer dishes of fried calamari and bruschetta, but that was just the beginning. The main course was stuffed manicotti, filled with cheeses, spinach and spices, and covered with a wonderful tomato sauce. A plate of Italian sausage and meatballs as well as a salad of mixed greens accompanied the main dish. It was nirvana for an Italian food aficionado like Hannegan.

"So, out with it, Mrs. DellVecchio. What kind of baby was Jayvee?"

Like a dutiful mother, Clare reached over and dabbed some sauce from Hannegan's face with her napkin. "She was the most beautiful baby in the world . . . unfortunately, she grew up."

Jayvee groaned at her mother, but made no other reply.

"Actually, Ryan, Jessica was a joy throughout her childhood. We had this wonderful neighborhood for her to grow up in. I wouldn't have traded it for anything."

Clare DellVecchio placed her right hand on Jayvee's arm and rubbed it tenderly. Her daughter returned the gesture with equal affection.

"Mother, tell Ryan how you found this place."

Herb Chandler was Mike DellVecchio's teammate with the Cleveland Ironmen and his best friend. Herb's wife, Nancy, was in the real estate business, and she helped find the house for the DellVecchios when Clare was pregnant with Jayvee. They loved the house and the neighborhood, a cul-de-sac filled with families, made the choice even better. Even with a winter home in Florida, Clare DellVecchio had no intention of moving to a smaller place despite her daughter's encouragement to do so.

"It was the perfect place for a family and it still is. We never had to worry about Jessica. There were always children around; she never needed to go far to find something to do. And when she got older, she baby-sat for the next group of little ones." Clare pointed out the window. "Jessica went to high school right there. In fact, she was always hopping the fence to avoid being late for school and she would do it even though she was wearing a skirt as part of her uniform. I don't know who was more shocked — the nuns or her father!"

Jayvee laughed and then began her own story, recollecting an incident from her past. Ryan watched the interaction between mother and daughter. Jayvee may have inherited her athletic prowess and her love for baseball from her father, but she was much more like her mother than she realized.

"Now, Mr. Hannegan," Mrs. DellVecchio said as she rose from the table, "it's time for the real reason why my daughter suggested I make dinner tonight."

"Did you really do it, Mom? Come on, Ryan, help me with these dishes. You're going to love this."

Hannegan and Jayvee cleared the table and loaded the dishwasher. Meanwhile, Mrs. DellVecchio busied herself with the preparations for dessert. She took out cups and saucers for coffee and aperitif glasses for the bottle of anisette that she had removed from a cupboard. As Jayvee and Ryan carried them back out to the dining room, Clare removed a bowl filled with a creamy concoction from the refrigerator and grabbed a covered plate that had been sitting on the counter. With everything arranged at the table, the trio sat back down for the big unveiling.

"Mother, I can't believe you took the time to do this."

"You are always asking me to make some when you come home, Jessica, and I thought Ryan here was worth the trouble. You seem to think he is anyway."

Blushing slightly but ignoring her mother's comment, Jayvee turned to Ryan.

"You are about to have one of the best eating experiences of your life. I don't know why I didn't weigh five hundred pounds when I was a kid. These are the most incredible . . ."

"Because I wouldn't let you," Clare interrupted, removing the plate's cover to reveal a small pile of homemade pastry shells.

"These are Mom's canolis. Ryan, you have never tasted anything like them!"

Ryan thought what he had eaten already was pretty special as he watched Jayvee take the pastry shells and stuff them with the contents of the bowl. She handed him one of the cannolis, and the first bite sent off an explosion of delighted taste buds in his mouth. The pastry shell was so delicate it dissolved in an instant, while the filling was sinfully rich, with the added surprise of chocolate chips inside.

"Aren't they the best? I love it when Mom adds the chocolate chips."

Hannegan was in such bliss that his only response was to take another one from the plate, bringing a smile of satisfaction to Clare DellVecchio's face.

"I don't know about my daughter, but someone who enjoys my cooking as much as you do, Ryan, is welcome at my table anytime."

Trying vainly to look somewhat polite as he used his hand to wipe off excess filling from his face, then lick it off his fingers, Ryan finally managed to speak.

"Mrs. DellVecchio, I have been to a lot of great restaurants in my life, but I know I haven't eaten any better than I have tonight. Jayvee's right. How did all of you keep from weighing five hundred pounds apiece?"

"We didn't eat like this every night, Ryan, but that's nice of you to say."

The conversation went on about the good food while they ate the remaining canolis. Hannegan had never been much for after-dinner drinks, but the anisette was the perfect complement to the canolis and the coffee. When they had eaten the final crumb, Ryan guessed he must have had at least four of Mrs. DellVecchio's masterpieces. The remaining dishes were cleared away, and the three of them moved into the DellVecchio's cozy family room.

"So, Mrs. DellVecchio. Give me the real low-down on Jayvee."

"Would you like to see the picture albums and the scrapbooks?"

"Mother!"

Nothing was going to stop Clare DellVecchio from pulling out the details of her daughter's childhood, and Hannegan loved it. He had read about some of Jayvee's exploits, but he hadn't fully appreciated before what a gifted athlete she had been. It was another element to add to Ryan's growing fascination for her. He was also hoping to see some of the scrapbooks Clare DellVecchio had made of her husband's career, but with the night getting late, they decided to save that for another visit.

"Thanks for everything, Mrs. DellVecchio. The food was spectacular, and with those grade school pictures with the braces and the pigtails, I've got plenty of ammunition to keep your daughter in line."

Jayvee punched Ryan in the shoulder as he leaned forward to give Clare a warm hug.

"Come see me anytime you're in town, Ryan, with or without Jessica."

"And I love you too, Mother," Jayvee said with a sigh although she followed Ryan's hug with an even larger one of her own, followed by a big kiss for her mother.

The car was quiet as they began the drive back to the freeway, although Jayvee had taken one hand off the wheel and placed it on top of Ryan's. They had to take a detour because of the road construction on the way back to the freeway. Driving slowly, Ryan noticed another landmark from the past.

"Jayvee! Stop the car! Isn't that the park?"

It was the city playground and park where they had played Little League nearly twenty-five years ago. At his urging, Jayvee turned the car into a parking lot that ran alongside the edge of the playground. It had been a warm spring, and the weather was still nice as the pair, hand in hand, took a stroll down a path filled with distant memories. Before long, their walk through the deserted park reached the sandlot area of their youth.

"Here's where it started. With all the eligible men in the world, how in the hell did I end up with a snot-nosed brat from my childhood?"

"And you love it," Ryan replied, pulling Jayvee to him and kissing her tenderly. Her response told him that she did. When the kiss finally ended with the two of them still embracing, Ryan looked into Jayvee's eyes and began to hum a tune that she couldn't quite place.

"What are you doing, Hannegan?"

"Do you remember when . . . ," Ryan softly crooned. "You know, Van Morrison."

"You, my brown-eyed girl . . . ," he sang while reaching up under her top to undo her bra.

"Are you crazy, Ryan? What if someone sees us? You don't think my mother won't know what we've been doing if I go home with grass stains on my clothes?"

"Making love in the green grass behind the stadium with you . . . ," he sang as he gently lowered her to the ground.

· TEN ·

THE COLONIALS HAD forged much of their lead in the American Conference's Northeast Division by dominating the Cleveland Ironmen in six of their first seven matchups, and in game one of the doubleheader on this Sunday, Hannegan made sure the trend continued. An RBI single in the first was followed by a double that drove in another run in the third. Another double and two more singles finished off the game, including another run batted in, the first time in his pro career Hannegan had gone five for five. The back end of the doubleheader and the series finale Monday evening did not go as well for Boston, but overall it was outstanding for Ryan. He went twelve for twenty-one with a home run and seven runs batted in. His .394 average was the best in baseball, and he was second in the American Conference with his 38 RBI.

The short charter flight from Cleveland to Detroit, the team's next stop, was a lively one, even with the two straight losses. A baseball player has to have a little different psyche than his other professional sports brothers. The grind of so many games during a season, with so many individual situations within each one of those games, demands a ballplayer has to have a little bit of amnesia. With three-quarters of the season yet to go, and seven games remaining on this road swing alone, the Colonials had already put the two losses in Cleveland behind them.

"Hey, Bro, whassup for tomorrow?"

"I've got some serious plans with the casinos. My meal money is just itching for those blackjack tables."

An off-day in Detroit would be a welcome break for the team, especially with the casinos in operation right by the hotel district in downtown Detroit. In the BBL, each player receives seventy-five dollars per day in meal money for the games away from home. The money is to be used for incidental expenses such as tips, cab fares or meals not provided by the teams at the ballparks. That money, in cash, is delivered to each player by the team's director of travel at the start of the trip. This was the Colonials' longest of the season — eleven days — meaning Billy Seghi handed each Cs player $825 when they boarded the plane in Boston last Thursday.

The flight from Cleveland took less than a half hour and the bus ride to the hotel was equally brief on the post-midnight deserted Detroit freeways. When a baseball team travels, it's different than for most on the road. There is no waiting in line to check in at the front desk. Usually a table is arranged with all the room keys for the members of the traveling party. A player, coach or even a member of the media if he is traveling with the team, just grabbed his room key and that was it. Often, the hotel may set out water, soft drinks, fruit and other snacks for the group. Hannegan had picked up his room key, along with some pretzels and a Dr. Pepper, and was headed for the elevators when D.P. Perryton grabbed him.

"Ryno . . . you got a minute?"

"Sure, what's up, Skip?"

"Are you headed to the casinos tonight?"

"Nah. Big E finagled a tee time for us at the TPC up in Dearborn tomorrow. I'm shutting it down to be ready for that. I can't wait to play it . . . I hear it's a great track!"

"What time?"

"Not until after one . . . it's ladies' day until then."

"Can you meet me for breakfast tomorrow? Not too early though. Tommy and I are going over to play some blackjack for a bit. How's ten-thirty sound?"

"No problem, D.P. Anything wrong?"

"No. No big deal. I just haven't really caught up with you on a few things since the season got underway. You know how things start to steam roll once we get started."

"Ten-thirty will be fine, Skip. See you in the morning."

Hannegan slapped his manager on the back and walked to the elevators for the ride up to his room on the ninth floor. The players' personal luggage, along with all the baseball gear, was loaded from the plane onto a truck to be brought to the hotel or the ballpark. Since the luggage truck had not yet arrived, Ryan flipped open his laptop to check his e-mail when he reached his room. Both Jayvee and Michaela had left messages for him. Jayvee's e-mail was a follow-up to their Sunday night conversation when she had returned to New York.

"Ryan Hannegan, you are the craziest man I have ever known. I can't believe at my age, you had me rolling around in the grass."

"And you put up such a fight. As I recall, you sure sounded like you were enjoying yourself."

"That's not the point. What if someone saw us? And what if I went home and my mother wanted to know why I've got grass stains on my clothes?"

"Don't let Mom know her little girl was doing something naughty."

"Hannegan!"

"Take it easy . . . I'm just teasing. I can't help it, Miss DellVecchio, but I find you irresistible."

"Well, you are pretty cute yourself . . . I must admit that, among other things!"

The banter between the two continued until Jayvee told him she was tired and going to bed.

"Oh, one more thing. While I was waiting for my luggage at the airport, I bumped into your friend, Woody Watson."

"He's not my friend, that asshole."

"He doesn't do much for me, either. Anyway he was boasting about some big exclusive he has. I wonder what it could be?"

"I don't have a clue and if it concerns that prick, I'm not interested anyway."

The subsequent e-mail was more of the same exchange:

I forgot to tell you on the phone last night about all the questions my mother had about you. She must be slipping because, somehow you left a good impression on her. When she told me I'd better hang on to you, I thought I was going to be sick! (Just kidding!) Anyway, back to business. What happened tonight? You guys have owned Dad's old team. At least you got a hit, so that's good. Good luck in Detroit. Call me when you get a chance, and remember, let's make some plans for later, when I get back from my trip.

Ryan began his Internet response on a light note, complaining about a bruise in his lower back from a rock in the grass during their lovemaking. He credited Park Sun Hong with mixing speeds well in shutting down their offense that night. Most of his message was spent telling Jayvee again how much he enjoyed the time they had had together on Saturday. He had been with Jayvee just forty-eight hours ago, but he was already missing her terribly.

His daughter's e-mail was typical Michaela:

Daddy . . . what was D.P. thinking? He had to sacrifice in the 6th. Where did he learn to manage?

Hannegan chuckled. Does she ever give it a rest? I'll be sure to ask D.P. tomorrow morning, Kiddo.

But you were good again tonight. I bet you're going to make the All-Star team. Just like I always knew you would. Did you know, Daddy, that no one in the BBL has hit .400 since Mike DellVecchio did it in 1971? I know you can do it, and then it will make me just like Jayvee.

Cool your jets, Michaela, Hannegan typed out on his laptop. Yes, I am happy with how things had gone so far in the season, but it was too early to be thinking about the All-Star Game or hitting .400. All-Star voting? I've never had any reason before to even consider it. As for hitting .400, it's crazy to even think along those lines.

He finished his response with some questions about what was going on in Michaela's life, with a gentle reminder to keep at the books since school still had several weeks yet to go. Just as he clicked on the send button, there was a knock on his door. That had to be a bellman with his luggage. One fifteen already. Time to hit the rack; tomorrow was going to be a great day.

Ryan was startled the next morning when he looked at the alarm clock on the bedside table and the numbers blinked ten twenty-five. He had not set it when he went to bed because he always got up early. Damn these thick hotel curtains; you can never tell what time it is, not by the amount of light outside, anyway. Hannegan was supposed to meet Dudley Perryton in five minutes. I must have been more tired than I thought. He grabbed a warm-up suit out of his suitcase, tossed on the clothes, slipped into a pair of running shoes, and bolted for the elevator. It wouldn't be a big deal for D.P., but still Ryan didn't like being late.

The hotel coffee shop was deserted for the most part since it was that slow time between the breakfast rush and the lunchtime crowd. Dudley Perryton spotted Ryan as he came into the dining area and waved to him from a table on the far side of the dining area. Ryan smiled in recognition and crossed the room to join his manager.

"Sorry I'm late, D.P. I can't believe I overslept. I never do that anymore."

"You're not late. I was just having some coffee and reading the papers."

"How did it go last night? Did you and Tommy clean up?"

"Are you kidding? I would have been better off just giving them my money as I walked in the door. It would have taken less time."

A waitress came over with some coffee and the pair busied themselves with the menu. Ryan had his back to the rest of the dining room, so he didn't see the approach of someone who was going to join their breakfast conversation.

"You were several minutes late, Mr. Hannegan. I hope this is not an indication you are losing your edge."

The voice belonged to Paul Simonton, the Colonials' general manager, and Ryan was more than surprised to see him. Where the hell did he come from? He wasn't on the charter. Our baseball boy genius is not one to take a low profile, so why was he here?

"Wouldn't you know, Mr. Simonton, I shut it down last night to catch up on my sleep, and I ended up grabbing more Z's than I expected. I guess when things are going good you sleep like a baby. I hope I sleep like this all season." Ryan kept his tone of voice friendly and respectful.

"We'll see; that's why we are meeting here this morning."

The undercurrent of a threat was surprising, even for Simonton's usual manner, and Hannegan didn't like the sound of it.

"Let's not make things so melodramatic, Paul."

D.P. Perryton turned back toward Ryan to detail the reasons for the meeting.

"Ryno, I thought it would be best if you and I got together informally to discuss a situation that has come up. Paul wanted to be a part of this however, so we decided it would be best to do this on an off-day. I didn't want your teammates or the media to get the wrong idea."

"What the hell are you talking about, D.P? Last night you said it was no big deal, and now it sounds like we're trading nuclear secrets."

Simonton slammed his fist down on the table hard enough to catch the attention of the hostess at the front of the coffee shop. "It is a serious matter, Hannegan. I hope you haven't done something that will impact all of us."

"Please, Paul, let me lay this out for Ryan without things getting heated up."

Simonton leaned back in his chair, not happy to be pushed out of the lead, but acquiescing to his manager's wishes . . . for the moment anyway.

"Ryan, do you remember the drug test you took recently?"

Hannegan could feel his body tensing as he heard the question about the drug test, but he did his best to remain calm.

"Sure Skip, but when I didn't hear anything back after a couple days, I figured there was nothing to worry about. Why? Should there be?"

"There were some irregularities that are hard to explain. Apparently your red blood cell count was higher than normal and that set off some warning bells for the testing lab."

"Are they trying to say I am juicing or something just because my blood numbers don't add up?" The color rose in Hannegan's face. If they were going to go after him, he was not going to let it happen without a fight.

"Those aren't the only numbers that don't add up," Simonton interrupted again. "I have calculated the results in your career, and your numbers this year don't fit your profile. While I am happy with what it has meant for the Colonials, I am concerned that there must be another hidden element involved here for you to have this kind of success."

"THAT'S BULLSHIT! A guy finally puts together the kind of season he has worked for his whole career, and once it happens everyone thinks you're cheating. I CAN'T FREAKIN' BELIEVE IT."

D.P. tried to calm his upset player.

"No one is accusing you of cheating, Ryan. In fact, the Commissioner's Office is taking no official action on the matter. The ball club just wants to be clear with you on all of this because of the implications for the team if there is anything wrong. You know what's happened with the Horsemen."

After an initial burst of success, Boston's rival had struggled to score since Dave Bock's sixty-day suspension for the positive test for steroids. Bock's absence from the Horsemen's lineup, as well as the inability to replace him on the roster, created a power shortage that might not be overcome until his return in August. What was happening in New York was making every team more vigilant about supervising their players — just as Hoppy Hopkins had envisioned.

"I know all about Bock and what's happening with the Horsemen. Do you think I would want to screw up the best chance I've ever had in my career to be a part of a pennant winner?"

"We go way back, Ryno, and I want to give you the benefit of a doubt. That's why I suggested to Paul here that we try to keep this whole matter between us. We just wanted to let you know the league has some concerns about your test, but nothing for which they are going to take any action."

"I have some concerns too," Paul Simonton cut in again. "I have staked my professional reputation on putting together a pennant winner the right way, and I am not going to have that damaged by some run-of-the-mill player who thinks he can have his moment of glory by cutting some corners."

It was bad enough for the Boston G.M. that he had to deal with old school fools like his manager, but to him this Hannegan was just like so many players he had met through the years. The guy had never lived up to the numbers he projected out of college and now because he's off to a good start, he thinks he's everything. Simonton was convinced things would have been different if he had been on the team.

His jealousy and conceit were not lost on Ryan.

"Heaven forbid this run-of-the-mill player damages your reputation. Excuse my bluntness, Mr. Simonton, but you can KISS MY ASS!"

With that, Hannegan pushed away from the table, slammed down his napkin, and stormed out of the coffee shop. It wasn't the brightest thing he had ever done in his life, but he knew Paul Simonton was too much of a baseball pragmatist to take some action against him, not while he was leading the conference in hitting.

Ryan's thoughts were racing through his head. Damn, I thought nothing would happen when nobody said anything to me about the test. If it comes out that something's up with my blood, everyone is going to question what I've done so far. I knew something like this could happen when Mad Vlad sent me that stuff.

Hannegan was distracted when he played golf with his teammates that afternoon, but they didn't seem to notice. He had to give Doc Soos a couple of strokes per side, based on their handicaps, and Ryan's lack of focus led to a long day on the links.

The voice in Ryan's head kept shouting alternatives. "I wish I could tell Doc what happened — he would have enjoyed the part where I told Simonton to kiss my ass — but it's not something I can talk about right now. Doc is going to love bragging about beating me on the course, though. I'll never hear the end of this."

Ryan's difficulties continued on the field. He took an 0-fer in the first game of the twi-nighter with the T-Birds and committed his first error of the season. He didn't play in the second game, but it got no better on Thursday or in the first two contests in Chicago. The Colonials won two of the three tilts, but Hannegan had now gone without a hit since he got a single in his first at-bat on Monday in Cleveland: a string of nineteen straight without reaching safety. Forty-five points had been knocked off his batting average, and Ryan was pressing at the plate for the first time.

"You could use some help here, Hannegan. But who do I turn to? Sure, Doc would be on my side, but what about the rest of them? They saw what happened to New York because of Dave Bock. If this stuff comes out about my blood count, they're gonna be thinking the same thing is going to happen to them. And I'll be dead meat."

Ryan had gone through tough stretches during his professional career — most players do. The first six months after the divorce from Deirdre and the separation from Michaela had been a painful experience. But over the past few months, the strengthening bond with his daughter and his developments with Jayvee had put Ryan in a wonderful place, reflected in his success on the field. Now, with the possible questions about his drug test, he was in a tailspin. Worst of all, there was no immediate source of comfort. Dennis Soos had a sister living in the Chicago area, so he was busy with family matters when they were away from the ballpark. Michaela was on a weekend camping trip with her Girl Scout troop, and DBC had sent Jayvee to the Caribbean to do a profile on some of the top Hispanic prospects for the upcoming amateur draft. She did not expect to get back to New York before the end of next week.

Hannegan sat alone in his room in one of Chicago's high-rise luxury hotels, feeling miserable. The television was on — a hockey playoff game that had gone into double overtime — but he hardly noticed it as he toyed with his plate of food. Doubt had found a toehold in Ryan Hannegan's psyche, and for the moment, he had no one to help drive it away. Once again, the crunching sound of baseball spikes on the cinders of a warning track echoed softly in the back of his head.

· ELEVEN ·

AN EXTRA BOOST?

Woody Watson, *New York Tribune-World*
www.TheTruth.com

NEW YORK (AP) Car owners and their drivers on the racing circuits are always looking for some special additive that will provide that additional burst to carry them to a checkered flag. The question in the Baseball Big Leagues these days is whether one of this season's early surprises has chosen a similar path?

According to informed sources, concerns have been raised over the results of a drug test administered to Ryan Hannegan of the Boston Colonials. The BBL and its Players Association had reached an agreement last fall stipulating several mandatory drug tests for all employees, as well as allowing for random testing during the course of the season. One such random test detected traces of a steroid in Dave Bock of the New York Horsemen, resulting in a sixty-day suspension for the outfielder and the loss of one player from the active roster of his team during his suspension.

The Baseball Big Leagues has refused comment regarding the results of these random tests, nor will they officially comment on the names of players who might be involved in the random testing due to the confidentiality issues that were part of their agreement with the Players Association. Nevertheless, people, who have asked not to be identified, have advised us Hannegan is the player whose test has come under scrutiny.

The random test administered to Hannegan did not detect any banned or questionable substances according to our insiders, but there were some surprises. The information obtained reveals the Boston player had an elevated red blood cell count: a level surprising the testing labs employed by the BBL. The samples and the preliminary results were then sent to labs in Lausanne, Switzerland where they do much of the drug testing for the International Olympic Committee. Those findings were in agreement with the preliminary report and they are consistent with those that might be found in an athlete that was engaged in the practice of blood doping. Blood doping, the practice of storing blood and then reinserting it into an athlete shortly before major events, has been a problem in recent Olympic competitions.

The inside information which we have obtained did not make any conclusions about the possible benefits of a higher red blood count for a professional baseball player. The questions raised however, by the test's results demand answers, especially in light of Commissioner Hopkins's intent to clean up the sport and the penalties already exacted against Dave Bock and the New York Horsemen.

Ryan Hannegan walked into the visitors' clubhouse in Chicago, his brain bubbling with worry. *Man, it's cold as a witch's tit in here. I guess they've seen the papers, too.* He had read Watson's story that morning and it ruined the good Spanish omelet he was eating in the hotel's coffee shop. *I can just imagine that S-O-B enjoying every minute of writing that column.* If the players hadn't seen Woody Watson's syndicated column reprinted in the Chicago newspapers, they certainly had watched as the story was being thoroughly dissected on the various DBC programs coming from the giant television in the corner of the clubhouse.

Dennis Soos had not yet arrived, so Hannegan allies were scarce as he walked to his locker on the far side of the clubhouse.

Tossing his bag into the bottom of his locker, Hannegan slumped into his chair. So much for the tests being privileged information. The television reports were featuring reactions from Paul Simonton and Henry Lamirand, the executive director of the players' group.

"I am outraged at the release of these confidential test results," Lamirand told reporters. "Ownership assured us safeguards would be in place to prevent such an occurrence as this, otherwise we would have never agreed to the testing program in the first place. I would hope General Hopkins launches an investigation to determine who is responsible for giving out such information."

Ryan sat in front of his locker, pulling off his shoes and socks. Glancing over at the big screen, he saw Paul Simonton giving his statement from his home in the suburbs of Boston.

"I am shocked a story like this would appear. It is an affront to all the Colonials stand for. I plan on filing a formal protest with the Commissioner's Office."

Ryan's head began to pound as his mind screamed words he couldn't say aloud. *Look at that sunnavabitch. He's all upset that there was a leak, but he's not saying anything about me. Telling everyone what he would do to prevent leaks, but not a goddamn word supporting or defending me. If I didn't know better, I'd bet that asshole was the one who gave the information to Watson.*

It had been a distancing week for Hannegan with some of his teammates as they steered away from him while he struggled to pull out of his batting slump. With this morning's revelations, things had gotten downright frosty, until Dennis Soos walked into the room.

"Feels like a morgue in here. We're in first place for chrissakes, and you guys act like the world is coming to an end."

Soos walked over to Hannegan's locker and yanked him up off his stool. "Do you guys really think this dumb Irishman could actually figure out a way to cheat? You know that prick Watson is just trying to stick it to us to help his damn Horsemen. C'mon . . . look at him. Ryno is so bad he has to take a Viagra just to get enough of a leaner so he doesn't piss on himself when he takes a leak!" He shoved Hannegan back down on his stool and wiped his hands together briskly.

The Colonials players laughed and the atmosphere lightened throughout the clubhouse. Marty Fergus went over and switched stations on the giant TV, and the move met with nods of approval from several Boston players. The crisis was momentarily over and it was an issue forgotten because there was a game to play.

"Thanks, Doc... I felt like I was the invited guest to an ambush."

"Just tell me, Ryno, there is nothing to all of this."

"You know me, Doc. Do you think I would be stupid enough to get caught doing something like that? I've got no idea why my blood count was screwed up."

Both players had gotten out of their street clothes and were in the process of putting on their batting practice gear.

"Like I told D.P. and Simonton in Detroit on Tuesday, why do they suddenly decide I am doing something against the rules? Just because I'm finally having a good year? This is all bullshit."

"D.P. knows about it?"

"Yeah... he and Simonton were the ones who told me I had some kind of inconsistency with my red blood cells when they gave me one of those tests. But D.P. told me the commissioner wasn't going to do anything about it since, technically, there is nothing in the rules against having more red blood cells than normal."

Dennis Soos paused in the middle of looping his belt into his uniform pants.

"Yet Watson still tries to make a big deal out of it. I know the guy is good at what he does, but I wonder where he is able to get this kind of information... especially with someone like the General in charge?"

"I've got a pretty good idea." Ryan went on to tell his teammate about his confrontation with the team's general manager at the Tuesday breakfast, including his big blowup at the end.

"And the way he talked this morning, Doc, it wouldn't surprise me at all if he were the one who gave the info to Woody Watson."

"The bastard is devious enough to do something like that. He doesn't like to be shown up. I know he would love to get rid of me if he could, so you're probably on his hit list just because we're friends. He wants to win, but he wants it so the spotlight is on him more than anybody else."

"I guess I just have to keep playing well. That way he won't be able to get rid of me. That'll make his life miserable."

"Well, then let's get it going, Mr. 0-for-the-Week," Soos said as he prodded Hannegan's chest with the barrel end of one of his bats. "We need your sweet swing again, Ryno, and no funny business off the field."

Soos headed off to the trainer's room with his departing warning hitting home to Hannegan. Even Doc was concerned; he was saying, "the spotlight is definitely on you now, Hannegan." I've got to get the magic again, but what are they going to think if I do? The thought sent a shiver down his spine.

In the game that afternoon, Hannegan's hitless string came to an end at twenty-two when he doubled home Junichi in the eighth inning. The RBI proved to be the game winner in a three to two win over the Blaze. He was able to collect his third triple of the season in the Monday night holiday game, a five to one triumph that featured another strong pitching performance from Raul Gomez. More importantly, the Colonials went eight and four on the longest trip of their season to maintain their advantage over their closest pursuers, New York and Baltimore. Back home, Boston swept three games from the Minneapolis Lumberjacks. Hannegan had things going in the set, and now he was back to second in the batting race at .349, and his homer total was just two shy of his career best with more than ninety games left to play.

One of baseball's oldest axioms is that a team doesn't get a real feel for its chances until it has played forty to fifty games. With nearly seven weeks of the season complete, the Colonials were playing better than .600 baseball and leading the Northeast Division of the American Conference.

AMERICAN CONFERENCE

Northeast Division			Midwest Division		
	W-L	GB		W-L	GB
Boston	30-19	—	Saint Louis	29-20	—
Baltimore	28-21	2	Dallas	28-21	1
New York	26-23	4	Chicago	25-24	4
Cleveland	24-25	6	Minneapolis	23-26	6
Detroit	21-28	9	Kansas City	21-28	8

If things had improved again on the field for Ryan Hannegan, the same could not be said for the reception he was receiving from a few of his teammates and from some of the fans. The little speech in Chicago by Dennis Soos had helped, but there were still several players who were wondering about Ryan's new-found success this season.

"I guess it's 'guilty until proven innocent', Doc."

Hannegan's entrance into the home clubhouse had gotten a frozen reception from some of the other players.

"Don't let those assholes get to you, Ryno. They're just worried something like what happened in New York is going to happen to us. They'll get over it."

"You really think so? I don't know a lot of these guys like you do."

"Listen. If you keep hitting and we keep winning, they won't care if you're Hannibal Lecter."

Woody Watson had continued to apply the pressure on Hannegan with a series of articles in the *Tribune-World*. From detailed outlines of blood doping incidents in international competitions through the years to the potential benefits from the practice, the New York newspaperman had not backed off on his attack. He demanded the BBL take some action since this appeared to be a violation in spirit, if not in deed, with the sport's drug policies.

On Friday, General Hopkins held a news conference in New York. A full contingent of the media was on hand and DBC television was carrying the news conference live. Promptly at four o'clock, a stern-faced Michael Hopkins strode to a phalanx of microphones as camera motors whirred and strobes flashed. Henry Lamirand, the executive director of the Players' Association was flanked to the General's left, while a rather sullen Paul Simonton was on his right.

"Ladies and gentlemen, I thank you for coming on such short notice. I have a statement to make and then I will be available for a brief period of time to answer your questions. When I was asked to take on the position as baseball's chief executive, I did it with the understanding I would have the control to implement changes we all felt would be beneficial to the sport. When problems arise, my modus operandi has been to deal with them swiftly and decisively. This wonderful game was in danger of being sullied by the unchecked use of supplements and other elements that could diminish the integrity of baseball and, just as importantly, threaten the health of our players. Unfortunately, we saw that happen with Omar Sandoval last season."

Gesturing toward Henry Lamirand, Hoppy Hopkins continued.

"Thanks to the cooperation of the Players' Association, we were able to institute a drug testing program we believed would stem the tide of illegal and unethical practices in regards to supplement use and, in time, remove it from our game altogether. Such a program, however, can not be implemented unless the privacy of such testing is preserved."

The General paused for a moment before leaning forward on the podium, extending his right hand and pointing his index finger toward the assembled media.

"I was involved in conflicts in my career during which I had to send young men into harm's way in order to preserve the American ideals we so cherish. Among those ideals is the right to privacy and the freedom from prosecution in the press without just cause."

Hopkins' eyes were ablaze, his face flushed; many in the room flinched involuntarily.

"A breach of security costs lives in the military and lapses in judgment allowing the public dissemination of information can ruin careers."

Bits of spittle formed at the edges of Michael Hopkins's mouth, and some spewed out as he spoke. He glanced at Paul Simonton who ducked his head like a reprimanded child.

"I will not allow someone's sanctimonious agenda impact what we are trying to accomplish. If someone in this great game takes a misstep, we will deal with it in the proper manner. But I will not tolerate someone trying to dictate policy to me."

General Hopkins slammed his hand down on the podium.

"It is the command I have been given, and it is one I will execute WITHOUT EQUIVOCATION!"

With that, the game's most powerful figure turned and walked away from the podium even though he had said he would remain to answer questions. The shell-shocked media in the room didn't even notice.

Woody Watson was seated at the front of the assembly, and tried to maintain a strong front. He hadn't experienced anything like this since he was a young man being reprimanded by his father. "That's fine, General Hopkins," he muttered to himself. "I will back off . . . for now. But I know that no-name player is guilty and I'm going to nail him."

Ryan had watched the general's speech with a number of his teammates in the home clubhouse at Patriots' Harbor. Several glanced in his direction, while others commented on the fiery nature of the commissioner's comments. Hannegan said nothing as he dressed slowly for batting practice for that night's game with Dallas. Glancing up, he saw Terry Tate of the *Journal* advancing toward him from across the room. A feeling of dread washed over him.

"Hey, Ryan . . . do you have a minute?"

"I guess so, Terry, but I have no comment about Watson's columns this week or the General's speech, if that's what you're looking for."

"Forget about that pompous jerk Watson. He's mad his always-sperfect Horsemen have come up dirty, and now he wants to drag the Colonials down with them."

"Okay, go ahead."

"Any idea as to why you came up with that kind of blood count?"

"Jesus Christ, Terry . . ."

Hannegan started to turn away from the Boston reporter.

"Take it easy, Ryan. What I mean is, sometimes it can be genetics."

"I don't follow."

Having stopped Hannegan's departure, Tate sat down on the stool next to Ryan's locker, hoping, successfully it turned out, the player would sit back down and listen to his theory.

"There are many cases where ethnic groups have a different blood make-up than what is considered normal. You know, like the African distance runners in the Olympics. All those Kenyans and Ethiopians had higher-than-average red blood counts; maybe that's the case with you?"

"Are you kidding? In case you haven't looked closely, I don't exactly fit that profile. Besides, I hate running distances. First to home is about as far as I ever want to go."

Tate was momentarily frustrated, but he pressed on.

"Perhaps there is some genetic reason in your family's background? I was wondering if you would mind if I talked with your parents."

Hannegan dropped his head momentarily and then looked back up in Tate's direction.

"Mom died when I was finishing high school. But my dad is living out in California. I don't know if he would be of any value, but go ahead and try."

Terry Tate got the phone number of Ryan's father, thanked him for the go-ahead, and then headed for the clubhouse exit. Ryan wondered how his dad would react when Tate called him? He decided to give him a call himself. Ryan was not particularly close with his father; Patrick Hannegan had been consumed by his job and left much of the parenting to his wife.

Erika Hannegan had been a good athlete as a youngster, so she loved taking her children to all their practices and games wherever the family was living at the time. She figured being a part of the teams in the neighborhood was the best way for her children to make new friends in each new city on their cross-country odyssey. Her sudden death from a cerebral aneurysm when Hannegan was a senior in high school had devastated him.

Ryan decided he'd better call his father and give him a heads up. He knew if his mother was still around, she'd be calling every day to tell him what he was doing right or wrong.

The series with the Wranglers on the weekend was the first time Boston had seen Dallas since the opening of the season and the Wranglers were the hottest team at the moment. Kevin Tompkins, their all-star shortstop, had taken over the lead in the batting race, and Dallas had gone 20-12 in May to pull to within one game of St. Louis in the Midwest Division. Friday night the Wranglers knocked Raul Gomez out of the game before many of the fans had settled into their seats at Patriots' Harbor. Kevin Tompkins' first inning grand slam set Dallas off and running. Four other Boston pitchers fared no better in a sixteen to three trouncing that was easily the worst in a number of seasons for the Cs, and even their most die-hard fans were heading for the exits long before the final out.

The two teams were back at it the following afternoon, and the same results unfolded. The seven to one loss made it three of the last five in the dumper at home, and a few of the Boston faithful expressed their displeasure at their heroes.

"Come on, you bums; don't start fading on us already!"

"What's the story, Soos? Are you the grinch who lost the pennant?"

"Ertle, if you're going to retire, do it before you pitch, not while you're out on the mound."

"Hey, Hannegan, what's the matter? Did your shipment get sent to the wrong dugout?"

Ryan winced at the fan's crack. He had gotten a hit in each of the two losses, but he stranded base runners in his three other at-bats in the Saturday game, including a strikeout with the bases loaded when the game was still up for grabs. He was as disappointed as the fans over the team's lack of production, but he had hoped — foolishly perhaps — the blood issue wouldn't be used against him.

The home clubhouse was unusually subdued after the second loss to the Wranglers. The few players who even bothered with the food picked at the post-game buffet aimlessly. Whether it was just a tough stretch for the Colonials' offense, running into a hot team, or the uncertainty raised by the Watson articles regarding Hannegan, that fragile element called confidence appeared to be draining from the club. Tomorrow they would face Rory Clark, the Wranglers' number one pitcher who had yet to lose a game in the season, while Boston had to juggle its rotation and use Hank Cummings as a starter for the first time in more than a month. Things did not look promising for the hometown nine.

Hannegan didn't waste much time getting dressed following the game, although he still had no real place to go. Jayvee was finally getting back from the Caribbean — but not until late that night in New York — so it would be another quiet, introspective evening. Heading for the clubhouse exit, he spied Junichi in a meditative pose on the stool in front of his locker. The Japanese star opened his eyes to see Hannegan looking his way and a small smile creased his face.

"Ju, I would give anything to have the calm you've got going right now."

"But you can have it, too, Ryan-san . . ."

"Not me, Ju. I'm the duck on the pond that looks like everything is great on the surface, but underwater his legs are paddling like crazy. I'm working to find your peace, but I'm not sure I'm going anywhere."

"What about your new philosophy? What does Doc call it . . . WTF?"

Hannegan chuckled in response.

"Doc's ideas are okay, but sometimes you need SOMETHING to get you going again, and right now I not sure where to look."

"Look in your pocket . . ."

Instinctively Hannegan reached into the right pocket of his slacks, and among the change there he felt something: the small charm Junichi had given him in Cleveland two weeks earlier. What had Junichi called it? In an instant, he remembered. It was a "mamori."

"Your uncle's mamori . . . it's supposed to help isn't it?"

Ryan extended his hand towards Junichi.

Junichi rose from his stool, closed Hannegan's hand around the small charm, and then grabbed him by the shoulders.

"Ryan-san, a small piece of metal will not protect a man . . . only when the man knows what it means can the mamori offer protection to its owner."

"I don't understand?"

Junichi removed his hands from Hannegan's shoulders and placed one over the hand that held the charm. With the other, he pointed to Ryan's heart.

"Doc is not so far off. True peace comes when a man lets go, confident he is doing right and doing the best he can. When you let go, Ryan-san, you are capable of doing the best you can . . . without fear . . . without regret. That is when a man is truly protected because he is who he is, right here."

Tapping with his right index finger at Hannegan's heart while he made that last comment, Junichi unfolded the hand that held the mamori. Holding it on edge between his fingers, he raised the charm to eye level.

"I believe the mamori protects because it reminds me of who I am. It is the spark that kindles the fire of my being. It is the symbol telling me to let go and do the very best I can. And when I do, there is no failure regardless of the result. I am at peace."

He then placed the medallion back into Ryan's hand, bowed slightly, and turned back to his locker. Ryan watched his teammate for a moment then looked down at the small piece of metal in his hand. He squeezed his hand into a tight fist until the edges of the mamori made an indentation in his palm, almost as if he was trying to will some magic from the charm into his own psyche. He decided tomorrow would be another day, another opportunity to be the player he wanted to be.

The evening was quiet for Ryan. He grabbed some Chinese take-out on the way home because he didn't feel like cooking and he picked at the food while he sat at the table in the dining area of his condo and tried to balance his checkbook. The long trip on the road put him out of sync as far as paying bills went, and now it was already the second of June with some obligations from May still left unpaid. Ryan was glad for the distraction as it made the time pass by more rapidly. Around nine o'clock, his phone rang.

"Hi, Daddy!"

"Hey, Kiddo. So what are we doing wrong now?"

"Forget about that, Daddy, I know you are going to turn it around any day now, I can feel it."

"Now you're giving ME a pep talk. I thought I was the parent here?"

"You know what I mean. You're too good of a player not to snap out of it . . . and the Colonials, too."

Without realizing it at first, Hannegan was playing with the Japanese medallion in his pocket while Michaela attempted to boost his spirits.

"Whatever you say, Michaela. As long as I've got you, I'm going to be just fine."

"Always and forever, Daddy. I can't wait to see you."

"Me too, Kiddo. Less than two weeks left and it'll fly by. School okay?"

"Almost done. Gawd, I can't wait until it's over."

Hannegan laughed.

"It's not that bad. Finish up strong and we'll talk later this week. I love you, baby."

"Me too, Daddy. Don't forget to IM me."

Hanging up the phone, he pulled the mamori out of his pocket. Maybe you're right, Ju. *The protection comes by knowing how to let go and just let the true you take over.* Michaela had made him feel better, and some of the tension that had built up since his confrontation in Detroit with Paul Simonton began to fade away. He tossed the medallion into the air and caught it. With an ironic smile, he put the mamori back in his pocket and returned to his bill-paying chores.

Hannegan finally completed his paperwork around eleven o'clock, and he clicked off his CD player that had been providing some background music and turned on the television to watch the late edition of *Sports Roundup*. He had just settled on his couch when the phone rang.

"I leave you alone for a little while and you let all hell break loose. What's going on, Hannegan?"

"Hello, Jayvee, what a lovely way to tell me you're back."

"Sorry, it's just that I'm a little fried right now. It's bad enough they sent me to places in the Dominican where indoor plumbing is only a rumor, but I come back to find Woody Watson has painted his bull's-eye squarely on your chest. I guess you were the big exclusive he was bragging about that night at LaGuardia."

Ryan detailed his meeting in Detroit with Perryton and Simonton, the articles by Woody Watson, and the reaction it created from fans and a few of his teammates. He finished with a recap of General Hopkins' tirade at his news conference on Friday.

"You let it get to you, didn't you? I know baseball always has a way of keeping you humble, but you can't tell me your little batting skid was just a swing flaw or facing some good pitching..."

"You're right. I did let it get to me and I started pressing."

"Well, stop feeling sorry for yourself... you're too good a player for that. Dad always used to tell me you've got to pull the real you out from underneath when troubles start to pile up and just let it go."

"Michaela and Junichi told me pretty much the same thing."

"Well, they're right..."

Ryan reached into his pocket and again felt the mamori. Junichi said it would create a spark, and as he listened to Jayvee's words of encouragement, Hannegan could swear he could feel heat flowing from the medallion.

"I wish I was there tonight so I could slap some sense into you, Hannegan."

"I wish you were here too, but I can think of something else you could do for me."

"Relax, dear. There will be plenty of time for that when we get together."

"And when will that be?"

"Not until we get all these reports from the Caribbean done, and then you're going back out on the road again, aren't you?"

"It's nice to see that you're keeping tabs on me, Miss DellVecchio. I hate our schedules."

"I feel the same way. Hopefully I can get up to Boston the next weekend you guys are home, or when you come to New York at the end of the month."

"It can't be soon enough. I hope you know how I feel about you."

"Listen, you dumb Irishman, do you think I would let you have your way with me on some sandlot if I didn't feel that way, too? Heaven help me now that I have fallen for a ballplayer."

They both laughed and the conversation went on as Jayvee told him about her experiences during the assignment in the Caribbean. The playful digs flew back and forth as the pair settled into a familiar and comfortable rhythm of trusting friendship. It was nearly midnight when Jayvee finally begged off because her energy was all but gone after a hectic return home. She had one request as they finished.

"Ryan, promise me that you will always be honest with me. I don't think we can last if I don't have trust in you, and you in me."

"I will never do anything to hurt you, Jayvee. I made mistakes my first time around, and I don't want to repeat them. You're the best thing that has happened to me in a long time, and I am not going to screw this up."

"Just be the person you are and things will be just fine. Knock 'em dead tomorrow and call me tomorrow night."

Hannegan promised to do just that and hung up the phone. The spark was now a glow, and as he went to bed, Ryan was convinced tomorrow would be a great day. It turned out he didn't even have to wait until he got to Patriots' Harbor on Sunday morning; Terry Tate's column on page one of the sports section in the *Boston Journal* took care of that.

FAMILY TIES

Terry Tate, *Boston Journal*

Boston (AP) If you are a regular reader of this newspaper, you have seen my mug affixed to the top of this column more times than you might need to see. My wife may still appreciate that middle-aged, slightly overweight, balding visage, but for the rest of you it's not likely to be memorable. Now my Aunt Cathy will tell you how much I look like my Uncle Joe, or my mother will remark how, on occasion, my mannerisms echo those of my late father. And heaven forbid my two lovely daughters follow their father's physical path to mid-life rather than their mother's.

My point is obvious: none of us comes from a singular mold; we are all products of the family members who have come before us. That's why the name Günter Karlsen is an important one for the fans of the Colonials.

Who is Günter Karlsen? He was a dairy farmer from Nordseter, Norway, who immigrated to this country shortly after World War I. He settled in Brattleboro, Vermont, to raise his family of three sons and two daughters. In 1924, at the age of thirty-nine, Günter Karlsen became a U.S. citizen, and he went on to represent this country in the first Winter Olympics, held that year in Chamonix, France. A cross-country skier since he was able to walk, Karlsen competed in the 50k race, finishing a respectable twenty-fifth in a field of much younger competitors.

Boy, that's great, Terry, but what does that have to do with the Colonials? Günter Karlsen's oldest son, Erik, had one child, a daughter, Erika, her father's namesake, and she was a fine athlete like her grandfather. In 1962 she married a budding young engineer, and four years later her middle child was born: Ryan Hannegan.

There has been much media speculation in the last week regarding allegations that the Boston center fielder had an abnormal red blood count when he underwent a random drug test recently, as mandated by the Baseball Big Leagues. One of my esteemed colleagues has taken it upon himself to paint our local boy as someone who has skirted the new regulations in baseball... if not broken them altogether. It might have served him well to consider genetic possibilities as an explanation, but perhaps, the strong Irish flavor to Ryan Hannegan caused him to seek only answers that would benefit his cause.

I am not saying here that Ryan Hannegan is ready for the next Winter Games, but there is scientific evidence available showing competitors from the Scandinavian countries, as well as the African runners in the Summer Games, have a red blood count elevated above what is considered a normal level. Unfortunately, Ryan's mother passed away suddenly at the age of forty-two, and neither she nor Hannegan's great-grandfather is around to possibly confirm a genetic connection to the blood count in the Colonials' player's test that is causing so much speculation.

Baseball has decided to take no action against Ryan Hannegan because there is no reason to do so. It's time for others who are trying to make a case here to back off as well, although I don't see that happening. Rather all of us should give this young man the benefit of the doubt, and let him carry on with the best season yet in his pro career. And the next time Ryan Hannegan seems to run forever to chase down a long fly — or continues his phenomenal success at the plate — all those who love the Colonials should look up to the sky and say: Thank you, Great-Grandpa Günter!

Well, I'll be damned. Dad always said that the athleticism in the family came from Mom, but I never thought much about it. How cool is that? Great-grandpa in the Olympics. Hannegan finished off his coffee and got ready to head to the ballpark. There was a little more spring in his step as he came into the clubhouse that Sunday morning, and he laughed when Eric Polick yelled "Yumpin' Yimeney" to him. It was time for a little W-T-F and Junichi's eastern peace and tranquillity.

That afternoon Dallas was going with its ace, flame-throwing Rory Clark. Clark had emerged as a top candidate for Pitcher of the Year honors by running off eight straight wins to begin the year. One of those victories came against Boston in the second game of the season when he fanned a dozen Colonials. Clark dominated in the first inning, fanning the top of the Boston order — Horrado, Kyle, and Junichi — on just twelve pitches. Hank Cummings had shown his rust as a starter in the top of the frame, walking one Wrangler, hitting another, and giving up a pair of runs before retiring the side. It went better in the second with a 1-2-3 inning.

After Ramòn Morientes grounded out to begin the Colonials' half of the second, it was Ryan's turn.

"... Hannegan now the batter for the Cs. Ryan went one for four when he faced Clark back in April..."

Tom Kingery, was settling in just like the rest of the full house in The Harbor, waiting to see how their best hitter on the season would fare against the conference's hottest pitcher.

"... Clark misses with a changeup away — one ball and one strike — a cutter inside to run the count to two and one..."

Hannegan paused to adjust his batting gloves. Well, that's different. Four pitches and he hasn't thrown me the gas yet. But it's coming... oh man, I know it's coming.

"... Rory Clark has his sign and goes into his windup. Here's the pitch. This ball is drilled, no, hammered to deep right — 'way out of here and gone into the water. Oh my! That's as long a ball as I've seen hit this year."

The wags in the press box estimated the distance at almost five hundred feet. All Ryan knew was he had never hit a ball that far before in his life. The score remained two to one Dallas through the middle innings. Rory Clark had allowed only one other hit through the first six innings: a bunt single by Junichi in the fourth, but he was stranded at second when Clark fanned Hannegan to end the inning. Hank Cummings, meanwhile, staggered his way through six innings, allowing base runners in every frame except the second, but somehow managing to keep Dallas from adding to its lead.

Jeff Hennessey came on to work the seventh and got himself into trouble. He retired the first two Wranglers, but a walk and a pair of hits loaded the bases for Kevin Tompkins, the current batting leader in the conference. Tompkins was one of the poster boys of baseball. At age twenty-six, he had been in the big leagues for five seasons already, and he was the complete package. Tompkins had contributed to Hank Cummings' problems in the first inning, and he could put a major hurt on the Colonials with a big hit here.

Hannegan, like the other outfielders was taking his defensive position for Tompkins' at-bat. *Let's see where they want me to play this guy? Tommy's waving me to play him straight up — okay, I guess so.* As Hannegan moved into place in center field he couldn't help but take a glance to his right. Patriots' Harbor had some quirky dimensions because of the Blue Pier, and one of them was a vast expanse in left-center. It was about four hundred feet to straightaway center field, but it went back to almost 430 feet for a large section of left center before jutting back in to more normal distances in left. Tompkins certainly had the ability to drive a ball there and the Boston defensive alignment in the outfield would make it hard to catch a ball hit in that direction.

Jeff Hennessey's command of his pitches was not sharp, leaving the C's with little choice but to play Tompkins straight away and hope Hennessey could hit his spots. With the count two balls and two strikes, Boston catcher, Mark Allen, called for a slider away, hoping to get Tompkins to hit a ground ball if he tried to pull the pitch. Hennessey missed badly on the plate, however, a hanging slider, and Tompkins jumped on it. If he didn't get all of it, he got plenty and the drive was heading toward that great triangle of green space in left-center.

Oh, shit. Here we go. Hannegan got a good jump on the ball, but he could run a long time into that gap and still not catch up to it. Stay up ball, give me a chance. The crunch of his spikes on the track warned him the wall was coming up fast. With a final grunt, Ryan left his feet and reached for the ball as he crashed into the wall.

The recoil off the padding — thicker now in every BBL ballpark since the death of Omar Sandoval — sent him tumbling over backward. Climbing to his feet, Hannegan raised his glove, with the ball still safely inside. As the umpires signaled the final out of the inning, the full house of Boston faithful let out a giant roar. Running off the field with a supporting arm around his shoulders from Junichi and several bumped fists from other teammates, Ryan also got a unique ovation from the fans.

"Günter, Günter!"

That had to be a first at Patriots' Harbor: nearly forty thousand people yelling the name of his long-dead ancestor. Ryan tipped his cap to the cheering fans and then pointed in acknowledgement to Terry Tate up in the press box. The cheering had hardly died down when Junichi brought the crowd back up on its feet with a double, his second hit of the day and only the third allowed by Rory Clark. Junichi remained at second as Clark fanned Ramòn Morientes for his ninth punch-out. Now it was Hannegan's turn.

The Dallas flamethrower decided not to mess around this time, going to his gas right from the start. The adrenaline was flowing for Ryan however, and he got enough on the fastball to lift it into the air in left where it floated down in the third row of the bleachers just beyond the reach of the Wranglers' leftfielder. It was Hannegan's second home run of the day which gave him eleven on the season, equaling his career high. The crowd took up the Günter chants again as he circled the bases and demanded a curtain call after he had descended into the dugout.

The two-run round-tripper would turn out to be the game-winning blow as Dallas went down in order in the final two innings. It had been a crazy couple of weeks for Ryan, but that was something to worry about at a later time. For the moment, he was back in baseball heaven.

· TWELVE ·

THE SUNDAY THRILL was not long lasting for the Colonials. For the first two weeks of June, the Colonials went seven up and seven down, allowing the Baltimore Crabbers to pass them in the Northeast Division standings. The Crabbers were coming to Boston for a four-game weekend series at The Harbor, and there was a buzz in town about the set, although not up to the level achieved whenever the Horsemen paid a visit.

Like the Dallas Wranglers with Kevin Tompkins, Baltimore was led by one of the game's role models, Nick Hamilton. It has been well documented how Hamilton overcame some childhood physical obstacles to become one of baseball's most feared sluggers. A perennial top vote getter in the fans' balloting for the All-Star Game, Hamilton would be a lock for the midsummer classic the following month in Los Angeles.

Regardless of the importance of the Baltimore series, it was going to be a big weekend for Ryan Hannegan because his Michaela was coming for a visit. School was done for the summer, and she couldn't wait to make another trip to Boston. Father and daughter had not seen each other since Michaela's visit in April, but they had been in constant contact by phone or email. His self-proclaimed baseball expert of a daughter was coming to help push the Colonials back on the winning track. Ryan smiled to himself thinking he'd better keep her away from D.P., the manager. He wouldn't stand a chance.

Ryan had always regretted their time apart, even before his divorce, and those feelings had grown now that Michaela was getting older. He had missed her birthday again — and couldn't believe she was twelve already. And she was really getting to be fun to be with. This was a painful reality for a baseball-playing father, especially a divorced one. One of Hannegan's friends, who was also divorced, had worked a trade to Philadelphia so he could be closer to his children.

Michaela exited through the security area in the company of a representative for Crown Air. He was shocked when he recognized her. She seemed even more grownup than when he had seen her a couple of months earlier.

"Hey, Kiddo, you look great... and look at that tan," Ryan said as he gave her a huge hug.

Michaela planted a big kiss on Hannegan's cheek with a squeal of "Daddy" before regaining her newfound maturity to say, "I mean Dad."

"What's this? I'm no longer Daddy?"

"All the other girls never say Daddy anymore. I'm growing up, you know; you shouldn't treat me like a child."

Hannegan picked up her backpack and they began their walk to the baggage claim area to retrieve her suitcase. He couldn't help but notice the teen magazine tucked among the various sports periodicals in the outside pocket of the pack. The hormones had begun to rage for his daughter, and Ryan knew he was just going to have to get used to it.

"I'm sorry, Kiddo, I didn't realize I was treating you like a child."

"Like just now; you called me 'Kiddo', so you must think I'm a kid. I'll be an official teenager in less than a year."

"Don't remind me, Michaela. Look, I've been calling you 'Kiddo' since you were old enough to respond to it. I thought it was better than 'Honey' or 'Sweetie'; it was my nickname for you. I love calling you 'Kiddo'. But if you want me to stop, I'll work at it."

Michaela looked up at him and he saw there was still a lot of little girl left in that face. She dropped her head for a moment before returning his gaze.

"I didn't know it meant that much to you. It's okay... you can still call me Kiddo." She paused for a moment and then added: "I love you, Daddy!"

"And I love you too, Kiddo. Dad is okay — I'll get used to it — but I draw the line at 'Father'."

Ryan tried to look serious, but Michaela easily saw through it, and with a giggle, she put her arm around her father's waist and they headed toward the parking garage. It was going to be a great visit; both of them knew it.

The evening was ideal at Patriots' Harbor: temperatures were in the low seventies and a small breeze slipped in off the water to make things even more pleasant. The place was packed with fans ready to do battle with Baltimore, especially with Keith Lash on the mound. The veteran junkballer was having one of his best seasons with eight wins against only three losses. This would be the first time Baltimore had ever faced Lash, and it was not easy visualizing his "slow-slower-slowest" style until it had been seen in person.

Lash took care of the Crabbers early in the game with complete ease, needing just forty-five pitches in the first four innings. Glenn Hoffmann, the Baltimore starter, was equally strong, keeping the Colonials off the board through the same span, allowing only hits to Junichi and Hannegan while striking out five. The first challenge to the dominance of Keith Lash came in the fifth when Baltimore's cleanup hitter, Nick Hamilton, led off the inning. Lash notched a called strike to begin the sequence, but then Hamilton began to foul off every pitch that was even close to the strike zone. Souvenir baseball after souvenir baseball found its way into the grandstands in a remarkable display of bat control by one of the American Conference's most feared hitters.

"What a battle we've got going here... Keith Lash used just forty-five pitches get his first twelve outs and already here in the fifth with Nick Hamilton he's thrown ten..."

Tom Kingery's voice resonated from the loudspeakers on the main concourse of Patriots' Harbor and from small radios being used by Colonials' fans throughout the ballpark.

"Lash ready again... here's the windup and the pitch — just a little outside. Boy, how could Hamilton lay off that one? That runs the count full... three balls and two strikes — nobody on, nobody out... top of the fifth... folks, this is reminiscent of a day in baseball history when Manager Connie Mack of the Philadelphia Athletics named Howard Ehmke as his starting pitcher... Ehmke was a novice but Mack finally put him in against the Cubs... using his curves and change-ups, he won 3-1, fanning out 13 Cubs and in the ninth, runners on first and third, two out, the count three and two against the pinch hitter ... Ehmke took a big breath and let it fly, a fastball. The hitter swung and missed. It was Ehmke's greatest moment in baseball ... and his last."

The modern sports fan is supposed to wants lots of action in a game, but you wouldn't know it from the atmosphere in Boston. A scoreless battle at its midpoint, yet most of the crowd was leaning forward in its seats, awaiting the next pitch.

"Keith Lash takes a long look in to catcher Mark Allen ... this will make a dirty dozen he has flung plateward at Hamilton. He's got the sign he wants ... takes a deep breath ... and here's the pitch. Hot smash, back up the middle ... it's headed for centerfield — wait a minute, Kyle's got it on the backhand — he leaps — his throw to first ... IN TIME! WHAT A PLAY!"

The crowd roared in appreciation, and the superstitious among the fans breathed a sigh of relief: the thirteenth Baltimore hitter had been retired. Keith Lash went behind the mound to wipe the perspiration off his brow and to give a thankful nod to his second baseman for the fine play. Climbing back up the hill, Lash set down the next two hitters with ease, needing only four more pitches to end the inning.

Hoffmann was as sharp as his Boston counterpart, blowing away Soos, Cook, and Allen in the fifth. Lash had another 1-2-3 in the top of the sixth; now things were getting interesting: eighteen Crabbers in a row set down. A murmur was building in The Harbor.

The nuances in the game of baseball are a significant part of its beauty. The ballet around the bag at second when an infield is turning a double play, the awesome display of strength when a slugger belts a monstrous home run, and the bemusement of a pitcher when he badly fools a hitter are just a few of those elements. So too are the game's superstitions. Many a player has been known to keep wearing the same article of clothing during a streak until his luck runs out or the smell drives his teammates crazy. Some clubs have taken to wearing the pants legs of the uniforms up like the players of old because it coincided with a run of success. How many times does a player go out of his way to avoid stepping on the first or third base lines as he runs on and off the field in order to avoid the curse supposed to come with contact on those chalk stripes in that situation?

Perhaps the biggest superstition is how a team treats its pitcher in the midst of a potential no-hitter. A pitcher sits with the rest of his teammates in the dugout when his team is batting, but he usually keeps to himself. This allows him to rest and re-focus on his pitching plans for the following inning. When a no-hitter is in progress, baseball superstition demands no mention be made of it in the dugout and more importantly, that the rest of the team stay away from the pitcher, lest they jinx him.

Keith Lash was not a conventional pitcher, what with his off-speed deliveries and quirky motions, and he wasn't following standards in this situation either. He struck out on three pitches when he led off the bottom of the sixth inning and then took his spot in the dugout. Getting up from the bench after a moment, he sauntered down the dugout where Doc Soos sat with his head down, working on the lacing of his glove.

"Hey, Doc . . . how's it going?"

Dennis Soos looked up from his tinkering, shocked that Keith was talking to him, or to anybody for that matter. Doc stared at him, his mouth agape, astonished the guy didn't seem to know he wasn't supposed to talk when he was pitching a no-hitter.

"Can you believe I haven't allowed a base runner yet? I can't remember the last time I've gone this far in a game without giving up a hit."

Lash had an *aw-shucks* look like he was playing in a Sunday beer league. The color was totally gone from Doc's face, however, and his mouth was open so wide he probably could have swallowed a baseball without any difficulty. All activity in the dugout ceased like a freeze frame in a movie. Even Junichi who was heading out to the on deck circle stopped in the middle of putting on his batting helmet. Baseball superstitions were a part of the game in Japan as well.

"Lighten up, guys, it's not like I'm pitching a perfect game or anything . . . oh, wait a minute, I guess I am. Isn't that a gas?"

Now his teammates were convinced Lash had totally lost his mind, and if they could, they would have taken seats in the stands rather than sit in the dugout with him. He can talk about it all he wants, but they weren't going to be the ones to ruin things by testing the superstition. When the bottom of the sixth came to an end, the Boston players rushed out to their positions, fearful they would be hit by lightning had they stayed in the dugout a moment longer.

It did not affect Keith Lash. The seventh inning was just like the previous six: three up and three down, and none of the outs registered with any great difficulty. Knowing they were potentially witnessing history, the Boston fans chanted "Let's go C's" rather than singing *Take Me Out to the Ballgame* during the seventh inning stretch. Tension and anticipation filled the ballpark.

Baltimore's Hoffmann had been matching Lash pitch for pitch, but he walked Ramòn Morientes to begin the inning. He induced Hannegan to hit into a fielder's choice that just missed being a double play, and then did the same in the at-bat by Doc Soos. On Hoffmann's next pitch, however, J.R. Cook belted it into the crowd standing atop the Blue Pier in right. Patriots' Harbor exploded: the C's now had their runs.

The crowd was into every Keith Lash pitch in the top of the eighth, screaming with joy at each strike, booing loudly when the home plate umpire had the audacity to call a ball.

"Here we go again, Keith Lash and Nick Hamilton . . . it was a twelve-pitch at-bat back in the fifth when Kevin Kyle made the defensive play of the game to retire the Baltimore slugger . . ."

Press box observers noted after the game that Tom Kingery uncharacteristically stood up in his radio booth to call the final outs of the game.

". . . two and two on Hamilton . . . here's the pitch from Lash . . . on the ground toward third . . . backhanded by the Doctor . . . his throw to Morientes in plenty of time, Hamilton is out number one. That's twenty-two in a row set down by Keith Lash."

Twenty-three and twenty-four followed in quick order on a soft fly to Junichi in left and a three pitch strikeout, the called third strike a floater that dropped over the plate at no more than sixty miles per hour.

Lash led off the last of the eighth to a thunderous ovation from the full house, and he was quickly out on a comebacker to his counterpart. When he returned to the dugout, his teammates jammed into a corner away from their superstition-defying pitcher, and if he moved toward any of them, they scattered in the opposite direction. Kevin Kyle singled with two outs, but the side was retired when Junichi flied out to deep center. Glenn Hoffmann got a nice round of applause as he headed to the dugout. A four-hitter deserves notice, but the Baltimore pitcher was only a supporting character on this night.

Everyone was standing for the ninth inning . . . except those who sat with their heads down, too nervous to watch. Each Boston player in the field behind Lash fought contradictory thoughts: ready to make a play to keep the string going, and yet hoping the ball gets hit to somebody else. The nonchalant Lash, meanwhile, smiled at his nervous teammates, and then set down the first two hitters on a grounder to short and a fly ball to right. One out to go.

"Marty Schreiber is going to pinch hit for Hoffmann; Schreiber's a good fastball hitter, but I don't think he's going to see any heat here. Lash is ready . . . here's the pitch . . . strike called. Oh, what a curve ball that was . . . the lefty looked like he dropped that one on the plate from out of the sky . . ."

The closest thing that Schreiber would see to a fastball — a little cutter — came next, but it was in at his feet and not a ball he could swing at even if he wanted to. The count was one and one. The Baltimore hitter got crossed up again on Lash's next offering, anticipating something away and instead finding himself handcuffed by a slider he barely managed to foul away. One ball and two strikes. Everyone was on their toes, from the players in the field to the peanut vendor in the last row of the upper deck, straining forward in anticipation of this next pitch.

"I can't hear myself think! This place is going crazy!"

Tom Kingery had his hands on the ledge of his radio booth, leaning his head out the window like he wanted to jump out on the field and join in on the action.

". . . one ball, two strikes, two outs, nobody on, top of the ninth . . . two nothing Boston as Keith Lash is perhaps one pitch away from baseball immortality . . . he nods to the sign from Mark Allen . . . here's the windup . . . here's the pitch . . . POPPED HIM UP! He threw him a changeup . . . J.R. Cook settles under it in short right . . . he's got it. A PERFECT GAME! KEITH LASH HAS JUST THROWN A PERFECT GAME!"

Pandemonium broke loose at Patriots' Harbor. Lash was mobbed by his Boston teammates on the mound as they poured out from the dugout and in from the bullpen, while the crowd clapped, hollered, stamped their feet, and did whatever else they could think of to salute the man who had enabled them to witness history. Twenty-seven up and twenty-seven down: a perfect game. The team's celebration moved into the clubhouse, but the fans would not leave without several curtain calls from Keith Lash. Even the normally laid-back Lash was overwhelmed by the tremendous display of support from the fans. That rarest of baseball rarities pulled the Colonials back into a first place tie in the division with the Crabbers.

"Daddy, that was unbelievable. I've never, ever seen a no-hitter, not even on TV — and now I've seen a perfect game!"

Michaela Hannegan couldn't stop talking on the drive home.

"I know what you mean, Kiddo. That's only the second no-no I've been a part of, and that was my first perfect game, too."

"Did you know that it was just the seventeenth perfect game in the history of the Baseball Big Leagues?"

"I would have no idea about that, Michaela, but if you say so, I believe it."

The perfect game remained the principal topic of conversation the next day when Michaela and her father went to see some of the sights of Boston.

"... and how 'bout that curve ball he threw to Schreiber in the ninth?"

"Michaela Hannegan! That is enough. We are going to do some sightseeing ..."

"But, Daddy, this is like school stuff. I'm on my vacation."

Hannegan glared at his daughter and the protests ceased. Ryan had been a history major in school, so he wanted his daughter to appreciate and learn about some of the places around Boston significant in the early historical development of this country. In time, Michaela got into it and the pair had a great day together. Ryan was actually disappointed when he had to cut things short in order to get to the ballpark for that evening's game.

The second game with Baltimore did not go as well as the previous Friday night. Nick Ertle struggled with his control, and the Crabbers hammered him. Led by Nick Hamilton's three hits, including a long-distance homer well over the Blue Pier into Boston Harbor, Baltimore evened the series with a nine to four victory. Even in the loss, Ryan Hannegan played well, collecting two more hits and driving in his fifty-fourth run of the season.

"Nick just didn't have it tonight," Michaela said to her father as they walked to his car in the players' lot following the contest.

Hannegan was always amused at how comfortable children feel using the first name of an adult of some public renown. They would never dare call a teacher or some other adult in authority by their first name, but it was no big deal when it came to athletes, movie stars, singers and the like. Michaela had been calling Jayvee by her first name almost from the moment they met on Opening Day because she had gotten to know Jayvee through her work on television. Now here, she was treating Nick Ertle like she was one of his contemporaries, even though all of Ertle's children were older than Michaela.

"Yes, Michaela, MISTER Ertle had a tough game this evening, but that's a pretty good team he was facing."

"You're telling me, Dad, the Crabbers can really mash the ball. But we'll get 'em tomorrow . . . you just watch."

"'Mash the ball'? 'We'? Whatever you say, Michaela."

The day spent sightseeing and a long night at the ballpark took its toll on his daughter — no matter how many times she told Hannegan she should be treated like a teenager — and she fell asleep in the car during the short drive back to his condominium. She was still in bed on Sunday morning when he got ready to head back to Patriots' Harbor for game three of the series.

"Michaela, I'm going now. I called Mrs. Soos and she'll come by a little later to pick you up for the game."

She mumbled "good luck" and almost immediately fell back to sleep.

Ryan realized she must be very tired, since it was not like her to miss going to the ballpark early. Before the game was about to start, Hannegan noticed Michaela was not in the seats with Lisa Soos. He quickly headed to the edge of the grandstands, where Lisa was sitting.

"Where's Michaela? Is she all right? She's not sick is she?"

"Relax, Ryan, she's fine. Michaela said she was a little tired from yesterday." Lisa put her hand on Hannegan's arm in a soothing gesture. You must have run that poor girl ragged, what with the sightseeing and everything else. I told her to keep the door locked and just watch the game on television. Everything will be fine, Ryan."

"I don't know ... I've never left her alone before ... Maybe I should ask D.P. to pull me out of the lineup so I can go check on her."

"She's twelve now! A few hours by herself won't be a big deal. Don't turn into a helicopter daddy, for Pete's sake! Don't hover and smother. Big mistake."

"Are you sure?"

"Believe me, Ryan ... just concentrate on the game. Michaela will surprise you. You'll see."

Lisa added a wink to her last comment, but with his concerns, Hannegan didn't even notice. His concentration wavered throughout the game as he took the collar — a baseball euphemism for a batter going hitless for a game. Fortunately, Kris Fucci was in focus and he shut down the Crabbers. The southpaw wasn't perfect like Keith Lash on Friday, but he blanked Baltimore in the seven innings he worked. Hwang Sang Hwan got the final six outs in a 3-0 beauty. The Korean flamethrower might not talk too much, but his fastball could more than carry a conversation. Hwan was leading the American Conference in saves.

Hannegan dressed quickly following the game, anxious to get home to check on his daughter. He had talked to Michaela briefly after his conversation with Lisa Soos, and he had even gone back into the clubhouse in the fifth inning to make another call home. Michaela sounded fine, and in fact, the stereo was blasting in the background. I guess everything's okay. Nevertheless, he was hurrying to get home, and although traffic never really eases up in Boston, it wasn't a bad trip. Reaching to put the key in the lock on the front door of his condo, Ryan could hear the stereo belting out the latest song by one of those boy groups that had suddenly drawn the attention of his twelve year old. He hoped the neighbors didn't mind. It wasn't exactly the music of choice for the people who lived in his development.

Inside, the music from the stereo was being challenged by the noise of pots rattling and a general hubbub coming from his kitchen.

"Michaela Hannegan! What is going . . ."

Hannegan stopped in mid-sentence as he made his way around the corner into the kitchen. There in the midst of the biggest mess he had ever seen in his kitchen stood his daughter . . . and Jayvee! The two were splotched with flour and several other ingredients he couldn't identify. The shocked expression on his face drew giggles from both of them.

"Hi, Daddy. Sorry I didn't come to the game, but me and Jayvee thought we would surprise you."

"Jayvee and I. Yes, this is certainly a surprise. And as for you, Miss DellVecchio . . . I know you have many talents, but judging from this flour blizzard, I don't think working in a kitchen is one of them."

"Back off, Irishman," Jayvee answered with that wonderful lilting laugh of hers while trying to look threatening with the wooden spoon she brandished. "I may have spent more time with my dad and baseball, but I did learn a few things from my mother. Michaela and I have everything under control . . . You'll see."

With that, Hannegan's two women shooed him out of the kitchen with the ultimatum not to return until they had finished their preparations. Finally, after more noise, giggles, and one serious-sounding crash, dinner was finally ready. The wait was worth it: a casserole of chicken and noodles with mushrooms and cheese that had Hannegan clamoring for seconds almost immediately. Jayvee and Ryan had a nice Chardonnay to go with the meal that also included a Caesar salad, while Michaela tried to show she was growing in sophistication by insisting she have a wine glass for her soft drink.

"Nice job today, Hannegan. Tom Kingery said you looked lost at the plate."

"Thank you for that, Jayvee," he responded, trying to take a serious tone. "I was worried about a certain someone who was SUPPOSED to be alone."

"Don't blame me, Daddy. It was Jayvee's idea."

"Traitor," Jayvee answered as she reached over and tickled Michaela. The two of them both laughed and Ryan had to smile as well. Ryan's relationship with Jayvee was growing with each passing day, and he couldn't help but see the development between his daughter and Jayvee, too.

Despite their gap in age, the pair were becoming like sisters, sharing experiences, and at least toward Ryan anyway, plotting conspiracies amid giggles and whispers.

"That was great, ladies, actually delicious! Is there any dessert? I'm a growing boy, you know."

More giggles and whispers.

"Okay, what's going on?"

Jayvee and Michaela looked at each other, trying to decide who was going to tell. Finally, Jayvee decided to do it.

"I was going to make you a cake, but Michaela said you liked ice cream and pie more."

Hannegan's daughter nodded in affirmation to what Jayvee was saying.

"She also told me that red raspberry was your favorite, so that's what we decided to make. We got everything together and I put Michaela in charge of rolling out the dough. She really had to work at it, but we finally got it together and put it in the pie tin. I must admit that it looked great when it came out of the oven."

The pair looked at each other and began again to giggle. Before Hannegan could find out what was so funny, Jayvee and Michaela retreated to the kitchen, only to return quickly with a homemade raspberry pie.

"Hey, that looks great. Slice me up a big piece, please."

More giggles.

"Come on, stop the inside jokes. What do the two of you find so funny?"

The giggling finally stopped and Jayvee continued.

"Here's the knife. You do the honors."

Hannegan took the utensil from Jayvee and plunged it into the crust ... or at least he tried to.

"What the hell happened? It's like a rock."

Jayvee nodded to Michaela who ran off to the kitchen and then returned moments later with another pie.

"This is round two."

"What happened?"

"After Michaela and I let the pie cool, we decided to have a little taste ... and that's when the fun began."

"The fun?"

"I couldn't cut the pie, just like you couldn't. Michaela was telling me I must have lost all my muscle. Then she tried and the same thing happened."

More giggling.

"I still don't understand?"

"We forgot to put in shortening when we made the dough. No wonder, Michaela had such a hard time rolling it out. When you bake just salt and water and flour you get ..."

"Paste, Daddy. That's why we couldn't cut it. We ended up with cement."

"You'd have trouble cutting it with a chainsaw."

Now Hannegan joined in on the laughter. The second pie turned out to be delicious, especially warmed in the microwave and then topped with a generous helping of vanilla ice cream. Hannegan had two pieces. They all helped do the dishes complete with flying suds, dish rags, and a water fight. It was going to be one of those evenings.

With the kitchen work finally completed, the trio moved back to the dining table for a game of Monopoly. Michaela always enjoyed playing it with Ryan, and Jayvee was happy to join in the competition. Competitive it was, particularly when the girls decided to become partners and drive Hannegan into bankruptcy. When he was eliminated, they turned on each other until Michaela eventually prevailed.

"You didn't have to let her win, you know," Hannegan said as an aside to Jayvee when they collected the cards and pieces at game's end.

"I didn't! She won fair and square. I think you have a budding tycoon on your hands. She is quite the cutthroat."

When the game was put away, the ladies announced Jayvee was going to stay for the night and take the train back to New York in the morning.

"Mom always lets me have sleepovers at home. I hope you don't mind?"

Hannegan was thrilled Jayvee was staying over, but he knew it would have to be the girls in one bedroom and himself in the other.

"Go make some popcorn, Dad, and pick out a video. Jayvee and me are going to put our PJ's on."

"Jayvee and I, Michaela Hannegan. I don't care if it IS summer vacation, you're still going to use good grammar."

The pair looked at each other and giggled again as they headed off to the bedroom to change. What are they laughing about now? He went to the kitchen to make the popcorn, returning with a big bowl that he set on the coffee table in front of the couch. A quick search through his collection of videos produced a movie that would be appropriate.

"Dad, are you ready?"

"Ready for what?"

"Hang on, Hannegan," said Jayvee. "Close your eyes until we come out and tell you to open them."

With still more giggles, Jayvee and Michaela returned to the living room area where Ryan waited with his eyes closed.

"Okay... on the count of three you can open your eyes. One... two... three!"

Hannegan opened his eyes to see his daughter and the love of his life wearing identical nightshirts with the Colonials' logo on the front of the royal blue tops. They turned like fashion models to reveal the backs of the nightwear and Ryan saw his name and number on them, just like on his uniform.

"Wow! You guys look great."

Michaela and Jayvee came over to Hannegan for a three-way hug. Settling on the couch — with Jayvee on one side of Ryan and Michaela on the other — they watched the video and munched on the popcorn. They howled at the movie, even though it was one they all had seen before. Hannegan held the bowl in his lap, and his favorite females snuggled up to him on either side. It was the perfect way to end the evening. Despite her best efforts, Michaela eventually began to doze off before the movie was done.

"Time for bed, Kiddo..."

"But I'm not tired. I want to see the end."

"Michaela, you've been asleep for the last ten minutes. We can watch the rest another time."

"Okay. Jayvee, can you help me get ready?"

"Sure, partner. Let's go."

They kissed Ryan, almost simultaneously on each cheek, and then scampered off to the bathroom to make final preparations for bed. Faces washed and teeth brushed, the pair returned to say good night.

"I'm sorry I missed the game today, Dad, but it was okay to do this surprise, wasn't it?"

"It was a wonderful surprise, Michaela. You were a terrific hostess." Hugging her father tightly, Michaela continued: "I love you, Daddy!"

"Oh, so it's alright to be 'Daddy' again?"

Michaela stuck out her tongue at her father, and then hugged him again. Jayvee came over and kissed Hannegan lightly on the lips, drawing a reaction from his daughter. Now it was Hannegan's turn to stick out his tongue at Michaela, and she giggled loudly. With that, Jayvee and Michaela grabbed each other's hand and went off to the bedroom. Ryan turned off the television, did some last minute straightening of the living room, turned on his security system, and called it an evening himself.

Sometime during the night, Hannegan stirred; convinced that he could still smell the sweet fragrance of Jayvee, the same aroma he first noticed that night in Fort Myers. He realized he wasn't alone in his bed.

"We have to be quiet, Ryan. I don't think we want to wake up Michaela." Jayvee leaned over and kissed Hannegan on the mouth.

"Don't worry. When Michaela falls asleep, it's impossible to get her up."

"As opposed to her father," Jayvee said with a laugh as she reached down to caress an already aroused Hannegan. They made love more gently than they had at any time previously, and then after a conversation in whispers, they did it again until they both fell asleep in each other's arms.

Hannegan awoke with a start. What time was it? He heard the television from the living room. Jayvee must have gone back to the other bedroom. *I hope Michaela was asleep. I'm not ready to explain that yet.* Throwing on a t-shirt and a pair of athletic shorts, Ryan exited the bedroom.

"Good morning, Dad. Did I wake you ... I'm sorry."

Michaela was on the couch watching, what else, *Sports Roundup* on DBC.

"It's fine, Michaela. Where's Jayvee?"

"She must have been really tired, Daddy, because she was still asleep when I got up a little while ago. Jayvee showed me how to work the coffee maker ... can I make some?"

Hannegan told her that would be great, and Michaela ran off into the kitchen. Ryan turned back to his daughter's bedroom as he heard the door open. Jayvee came out, still sleepy and with a disheveled appearance that made Ryan laugh.

"Don't laugh at me, Hannegan . . . I'm not a morning person. Get some coffee in me, and I'll be fine."

"Michaela is taking care of that right now. But you might want to check out how you look before she returns."

"Why? Do you think she suspects something? She looked sound asleep when I got back to the bedroom."

"I'm sure she was, but I still think she is going to have some questions when she sees how you're dressed."

Jayvee looked down to her nightshirt and realized she had it on inside out. That would be tough to explain. She bolted for the bathroom and closed the door just before Michaela returned from the kitchen. The trio enjoyed breakfast together, and then Jayvee went off to get her things packed for the trip back to the city. The ride from Hannegan's condo to the train station passed quickly, and the girls sang along with the music from one of Michaela's CD's that was playing. When it was time for Jayvee's departure, Michaela had tears in her eyes, surprising but delighting Hannegan.

"I don't want you to go, Jayvee. Can't you stay a little longer?"

"I wish I could, sweetheart, but I have to get back to work.

Jayvee brushed away the tears from Michaela's cheeks and gave her a big hug.

"You have my e-mail address now, so we can stay in touch, and here's my cell phone number if you need some girl advice your Mom or Dad can't give you."

Michaela's eyes brightened as she took the piece of paper from Jayvee and put it in her pocket.

"I'll e-mail you every day, Jayvee."

"Easy there, Kiddo. Jayvee's a busy woman. Once in a while will be fine."

"Don't worry, Ryan, I don't mind. You've got quite a young lady here. I wish I could say the same for her old man."

Before Hannegan could protest the dig, Jayvee kissed him lightly but thoroughly on the lips, drawing another reaction from Michaela, and then ran off to catch her train. Father and daughter missed her the minute she was out of sight.

· THIRTEEN ·

THE FINISH TO the Baltimore series went well as Darren Haddad won for the first time in the month of June. Hannegan tallied just one hit, but he did score on a double by Bobby Applebee in a 9-3 stroll allowing Boston to regain a game advantage on Baltimore in the division and a three-game edge on third place New York. The Northeast Division historically had the best title chases, and it appeared this season would produce more of the same. The Colonials still had thirteen games on the schedule with the Horsemen, and there were nine left with the Crabbers. It was going to be interesting.

Tuesdays are the designated off-days for the American Conference, and on the Hannegans decided to explore Cape Cod.

"What are we going to do first, Daddy?"

"To the beach, of course. You'll find it's a little different than down home in Florida or when you come to visit me in L.A."

"Just as long as we don't have to do any more school stuff."

"Relax, Michaela. It's going to be fun."

The pair got out of Boston right after the morning rush of traffic, and it was a smooth ride to the Cape. The conversation was steady between the two, but like a typical twelve-year-old, Michaela bounced from one subject to another. She had talked about boys since her arrival, which Ryan had noticed was now competing with baseball as the principal focus in her life. They fought playfully for control of the car's music system, alternating between Hannegan's oldies' station and the latest pop and hip-hop favorites of his daughter's. Before they realized it, they had reached their destination.

They had a great time on the beach. Michaela discovered the waters of Nantucket Sound were much colder than what she was accustomed to back home, but she adjusted quickly.

"Michaela, what are you doing?"

"Nothing, Daddy..."

They were stretched out side by side, lounging on beach towels, people-watching other beach visitors.

"It looks like you're checking out those boys over there."

"P-uh-leese, Dad. I am not."

Michaela rolled away from her father, but in the direction of the boys.

Ryan smiled ruefully, detecting the obvious interest of his daughter for the young males. He decided her teenage years were probably going to kill him. Hannegan let out a wistful sigh. It seemed like only yesterday that he and Deirdre had brought Michaela home from the hospital, and in a blink of an eye she was growing up.

Two of the boys walked over to the Hannegans' spot and began talking with Michaela. One of the boys was wearing a Colonials cap.

"Hey, I know you. You're Ryan Hannegan. Petey, this is Ryan Hannegan, the C's centerfielder!"

Petey and his friend asked for autographs and had all kinds of baseball questions for Ryan. Michaela beamed as her father smiled and answered the boys' questions as if he had all the time in the world, just for them. They finally went on their way, waving good-bye to Michaela and Ryan as they jogged off down the beach.

After another hour of relaxing and listening to the waves, the pair visited the John F. Kennedy Museum in Hyannis. Kennedy had been assassinated just a few years before Hannegan was born, and he always remembered his mother talking about those tragic days.

"President Kennedy was your grandmother's favorite, Kiddo. She really loved how he was so involved in sports."

"We read about President Kennedy in social studies last year. This is so cool to see all these pictures."

The Kennedy family spent much of their free time on the Cape, and the museum had an ample collection of photographs of the family at play. Hannegan put his arm around his daughter as they walked along the gallery.

"In college, Kiddo, I majored in history. I remember in one class where we talked a lot about what might have happened if President Kennedy hadn't been assassinated."

"Why was he killed, Daddy?"

"That's a tough question to answer, Michaela. I don't know if they will ever know for sure. The man who they say shot President Kennedy was killed two days later before saying anything about it."

"I know; we studied that, too. It's all so sad."

"You're right. Let's hope we all learn something from it and it never happens again."

It was gratifying for Hannegan to be able to take some of the country's history out of the schoolbooks and make it come alive for his daughter. The day on the Cape concluded with a stop at one of the many seafood restaurants in the area.

"We're on Cape Cod, Daddy. We have to have lobsters."

"You women are always so expensive, picking the priciest thing on the menu."

Michaela stuck her tongue out.

"That's because we deserve it. We're going to have lobsters."

"Okay ... but I'm not wearing one of those bibs."

"Daddy!"

Hannegan knew his daughter wouldn't back off, so he acquiesced and let the waiter tie a bib around his neck when the meals arrived. They made a mess, but they had a blast. Michaela fell asleep on the drive back into Boston wearing a very contented smile on her face.

Cleveland was next for the Colonials, the final two games of this homestand before a four-game weekend in New York. Hannegan was eager to face the Ironmen: he was having unbelievable success against them with a .488 batting average, a pair of homers, and twelve RBI in the first nine games. The hot streak continued as he went three for five with another homer and two more runs driven home. That didn't give Ryan much comfort, however, because Cleveland came back to beat them for the third straight time, eight to six. And that wasn't even the bad news.

"...top of the sixth, five to three, Cleveland. Ellis Nance has not been sharp tonight, but the C's are still in this one..."

The Big E had walked four men and allowed a pair of homers, but he managed to work out of three separate jams to keep the game close.

"Joe Otto to lead it off for the Ironmen. He's got a double and a single already off Nance, and he's been on every pitch..."

Otto rocketed the Big E's first offering of the inning toward the hole on the right side of the infield. Ramòn Morientes was not a great defensive player at first base, but he sprawled to his right to knock down the hot smash.

"What a stop by Morientes! The ball rolls away, but now he's got it — and from down on his knees he flips to Nance covering at the bag..."

Morientes's throw was slightly off-line, and it drew his Boston teammate into the path of Otto where the two big men had a violent collision. Otto went flying into foul territory, while Nance crumpled in the infield dirt just beyond first base.

"Wow! What a train wreck that was! The Big E has rolled onto his back in the dirt by the bag and he's holding his right leg. Otto looks like he's out cold as the Cleveland trainer works on him. The Colonials got the out, but let's hope it doesn't cost them."

Joe Otto got the worst of his run-in with Ellis Nance, the former football All-American. The Cleveland outfielder was taken off the field on a stretcher with a concussion, from catching Nance's shoulder on his chin. There was some rib damage as well. It was not much better for Ellis Nance. He had been able to snare the throw from Ramòn Morientes to register the out, but he landed awkwardly with his right foot on first base when he had to extend for the ball. In the ensuing collision with Joe Otto, the Big E rolled his right ankle badly. The veteran pitcher was helped off the field, in a great deal of pain.

"The news is not great, but I guess it could be worse."

D.P. Perryton was holding his postgame gathering with the media and everyone wanted to know the status of Boston's ace pitcher.

"The X-rays were negative, but Ellis has a substantial amount of swelling. Blade calls it a *high ankle sprain,* whatever that means exactly. He told me he can't really do much except pack it in lots of ice until the swelling goes down."

"How long do you think he will be out?"

"Blade didn't want to make a guess, but he told me these things sometimes can drag out for four to six weeks."

"What's this going to do to the team?" Michaela asked as she walked with Hannegan from the clubhouse following the game. "The Big E is the best pitcher in baseball. What are we going to do without him?"

"We will do the best we can until he gets back. Injuries are a part of the game, and the good teams make the adjustments."

Adjustments can be made in terms of filling a roster spot and having someone else move into Nance's place in the starting rotation, but how would the Colonials react to being without one of their team leaders? Although he would still be with the ballclub during his rehabilitation, his absence on the field would be painfully noticeable. The Big E brought a presence with him every time he pitched, an aura that raised the morale level of his teammates and brought more than a touch of intimidation to the opposition.

Thursday brought the end of the homestand and Michaela's visit to Boston. Things were a little more complicated this time since Hannegan also had to get his own travel gear ready before taking his daughter to the airport. Michaela seemed to bring more stuff each visit, and she would be departing with even more. Finally squaring away his daughter's things, Ryan began to throw his own clothes and shaving kit into a suitcase. He knew it was going to be a race to get to the airport in time and he hoped the traffic wouldn't be as heavy as usual. Just as he locked his carry-on, the doorbell rang.

"Michaela, see who's at the front door."

"Dad, it's a delivery man with a package."

"Just sign for it, Kiddo, and I will take care of it in a minute."

His packing complete, Hannegan ducked into the second bedroom to make sure Michaela hadn't forgotten anything. Grabbing her suitcase along with his, he headed for the front door where she stood waiting for him, inspecting the package that had been delivered.

"Daddy, there's this really weird name on this package. It says it was sent to you by someone called Vee-lad-eye-meer. It's kinda heavy, and I couldn't move it, so I left it here where the delivery man set it down. Are you going to see what it is?"

"Don't worry about it, Kiddo ... we don't have time if we're going to get you to the airport. Here, take your suitcase and backpack to the car. I'll put this away, and then I'll meet you outside."

Michaela did as she was told while Hannegan carried the box into the kitchen. He knew what was inside the package, and he wasn't certain if the refrigerated container would keep the contents safe until his return from New York late Monday night. Cutting open the cardboard box, he removed the container and set in on the floor in front of the refrigerator. The top came open with a hiss when he unlocked the latches. Just like the first delivery back in the spring, there were three sealed clear bags made out of heavy duty plastic inside the case. Each bag was filled with a scarlet red substance, at least a pint of the thick liquid. Hannegan hesitated before reaching into the container to remove its contents. He placed each bag on the lower shelf of the refrigerator and had just closed the door when Michaela burst back inside.

"Let's go, Dad! I don't want to miss my plane," she called from the front foyer.

"On my way."

Ryan hurriedly exited the kitchen, his thoughts racing. *Michaela does not need to see that stuff. She asked too many questions when she found the other container back in April. I've got to talk with Mad Vlad, but how the hell do I do that? I don't even have his number.*

With his insides churning, Hannegan raced down the hallway and out the door toward his car. His Johnston & Murphy loafers made a rat-a-tat sound across the ceramic tile and then on the concrete pathway outside. All Ryan could hear, however, was a crunching sound. And with each step, impending trouble seemed that much closer.

Hannegan made the airport in time for his daughter's flight and then it was straight to the ballpark for the finale with the Ironmen. Keith Lash was gone before the fourth inning — his shortest outing since coming to the Colonials — and the Boston offense didn't have much either. The seven-two loss to the Ironmen dropped the Colonials back into second place as Baltimore swept their two games with the Kansas City Blues.

The trip to New York was a short one, but it was still almost one o'clock by the time the team arrived at their hotel in mid-town Manhattan. Ryan checked into his room, but didn't even bother to unpack his suitcase when a bellman brought it up from downstairs. He flipped open his laptop and found messages from Michaela and Jayvee when he logged on the Internet. He spent some time sending messages back to both of them and then clicked off his computer.

Hannegan threw back the spread and lay down on the bed. Except for his shoes that he had taken off as soon as he had entered the room, he was fully clothed. He clicked on the television. The programming at this late hour wasn't very stimulating, and Ryan's thoughts kept drifting to the Soviet science that was sitting in his refrigerator back in Boston. Some infomercial about the latest product that slices and dices finally enabled him to drift off to sleep in the early morning hours.

The sound of the telephone ringing jarred him awake. Nine-thirty! He was shocked at the time and couldn't remember the last time he had slept in his clothes, cold sober anyway.

"Hello . . ." His voice was froggy with sleep when he spoke into the receiver.

"Ryanovich, my good friend. Are you okay?"

Mad Vlad. The call was not unexpected.

"No, I'm fine, Vlad. It just took me too long to fall asleep last night, so I'm a little slow this morning."

"I know my shipment arrived. Just checking in to protect my investment!"

Hannegan shivered at the Russian's response.

"Protecting your investment? Haven't you been following this whole thing about my blood count? The league is watching my every step, and this Watson guy here in New York would like nothing better than to catch me doing something wrong. Now you send me more stuff. Are you CRAZY?"

"Ryanovich! Relax my good friend. They didn't find anything against the rules the first time, and they won't if they test again. Another triumph for the ingenuity of Mother Russia!"

"Things are going great for me, Mad Vlad. I don't think I need the stuff. Why did you send me more?"

"Like I said, I am protecting my investment."

The Russian's lighthearted mood turned serious.

"Right now, there is more than one hundred thousand dollars that says the Boston Colonials will win The Showdown and Ryan Hannegan will win the American Conference batting championship."

Hannegan was floored. Baseball was as concerned about gambling as they were about the supplement abuse.

"Vlad, we get a lecture from the league every spring about gambling and associating with gamblers. You're trying to kill me, aren't you?"

"You wound me, Ryanovich. Do you think I am not smart enough to know that? I took care of all my transactions with ... how do politicians say it ... oh, yes, through intermediaries."

Oddsmakers had the Colonials at ten to one odds to win The Showdown before the season began. Should Boston win it all, Titov could collect more than a million dollars. Hannegan had no idea what the odds would be for his winning a batting title.

"No offense to you, or your Uncle Yegor, but you guys DO have a reputation. If you make a bet on me, that's going to raise some eyebrows."

"You have no concerns in that regard, my friend. I can guarantee no one will make the connection. I am quite excited about my prospects. I even got the Criterion in Vegas to take a special wager."

The Criterion Resort and Casino in Las Vegas was reputed to be the top sports book in the world, handling millions of dollars in wagers on a daily basis. The casino was spectacular, its golf course was championship caliber, and the treatment their guests received couldn't be topped.

"The Criterion? R.C.O'Dwyer's place? That guy hogs the limelight more than anybody I've ever seen. Not exactly the place for staying under the radar, Vlad."

"But, Ryanovich, I knew he would take my bet. It was too delicious for him to pass up."

R.C.O'Dwyer was as well known as any of the celebrities that frequented his establishment. O'Dwyer had the reputation of never turning down a bet on anything, no matter the stakes, as long as he felt the wager was on the up-and-up.

"I told them I wanted to make a wager that Ryan Hannegan would hit .400. They were hesitant, but when I reminded them of their reputation for taking any bet, they agreed."

"Are you nuts, you crazy Russian? I could get suspended by baseball if they believed I had a connection with gambling and gamblers."

"I have no intention of making public our connection to each other and these wagers. But I hope you realize I must protect my investment by having the ability to reveal our situation if you do not give your best efforts in this regard."

"My best efforts?"

"That means using the additional help I have provided you with to continue the success you have achieved already this season. After all, I am sure you would not want that beautiful woman who works on the television to know her hero is not perfect."

Jayvee? There's no way Ryan would want her to know anything more about Mad Vlad. And Michaela? Would she understand? There wasn't much of a choice as far as Ryan was concerned.

"Don't push me, Vlad. I will do my part. Make sure you do yours."

"You can count on my discretion, my friend. I too have a reputation to maintain."

"But Vlad, why would you make a bet that I would hit .400? That hasn't been done in over thirty years."

"I have faith in you, Ryanovich . . . and in my Soviet science. You will make history."

"How much was the bet?"

"The most they would let me. Ten thousand dollars at a hundred to one odds."

Hannegan gasped.

"Chase your dream, Ryanovich, and you will help provide for mine!"

With that, the Russian hung up the phone. Hannegan rolled onto his back and stared up at the ceiling in the room still darkened by the drawn curtains. His mind was filled with thoughts of the deceptions, complications and pressures that lay ahead.

"Ain't nothing like that smell," he said to no one in the deserted room. "The smell of fear!"

Hannegan arrived early at the visitors' clubhouse in The Hollow that afternoon.

"Hey, Ryan, come here for a minute."

Pete Hudec was yelling from the training room.

"What's up, Blade?"

Hannegan stopped in mid-sentence when he found Dr. Loren Myers and Jack McDermott, the security chief from the Commissioner's Office with Pete Hudec. They told him he had been singled out for another random drug test. Ryan half-expected this to happen again sometime, so he didn't make a fuss over the blood and urine samples as he had done earlier in the season. When the tests were complete, Hannegan moved toward his locker only to be headed off by his manager.

"Ryno, just wanted to let you know I'm giving you the night off."

"I'm feeling okay, D.P. You don't have to do that."

"I know that, but I need to give Cahill some ABs. This will help you stay fresh."

"You're the manager — whatever you want."

Dudley Perryton motioned for Hannegan to come into his office, close the door and sit down.

"Ryan, I know you had to take the test again today. I saw Dr. Myers and the commissioner's man with The Blade. Let's hope things stay confidential this time."

"I was hoping all the stuff Terry Tate wrote might cool things off, but I didn't really expect they'd give me a free pass the rest of the season."

"You can't let it affect you, son. Keep your focus on the field and just let all of this play itself out."

Hannegan let out a long sigh and then smiled at his boss.

"Like I said, you're the skipper. You're probably right . . . I could use a night off to recharge the batteries. Thanks, D.P."

The losses to Cleveland had dropped Boston behind Baltimore in the division race, and New York now trailed the Colonials by just two games. Raul Gomez drew the starting assignment for game one, trying to turn around a tough month. Gomez was tentative, however, allowing the Horsemen's Casey Hegan to whack a two-run homer in the first inning, and he let Nelson Cuevas jump-start another New York rally. The Horsemen led four to nothing after three innings and cruised to a six to two win.

Boston's offense remained listless Saturday afternoon. Darren Haddad pitched well, but the righthander got little support in a three to one loss. The injury to Ellis Nance appeared to have taken the spirit out of the ballclub. With the loss, Boston was now tied with the Horsemen for second place, and when Baltimore won later in the evening, the steps up to first place grew to four games.

The message light on the phone was lit when Hannegan returned to his hotel room; it was from Jayvee. Hannegan punched in the buttons of her phone number.

"Hi, Jayvee. I got your message. I'm heading down in a minute to grab a cab. What do you want to do about dinner?"

"Would you mind terribly if we just crashed here? I'm whipped from work and I would love to just veg."

"Sure, that's fine. Do you want me to pick up something?"

"That's okay. There's a nice Chinese place right around the corner. I can order some takeout. Do you like Chinese?"

"Sounds good. Order Kung Pao chicken and some Won Ton."

"This will be fun. We can relax here and keep a low profile."

"I know . . . heaven forbid the star of DBC be seen hanging out with some lowlife ball player."

"Just get your ass over here, Hannegan, before I find someone better."

Hannegan caught a cab in front of the team's hotel in mid-town Manhattan. Saturday night traffic was typical New York, but eventually the cabbie got to Jayvee's place on East Seventy-seventh, along the river. She buzzed him in through the security gate and was waiting in her doorway when he got off the elevator on the third floor. She was barefoot, wearing jeans and a Cornell Softball t-shirt, and Hannegan couldn't remember seeing anyone more beautiful. They embraced as they kissed when they got inside, and perhaps Ryan hugged a little longer and a little tighter than Jayvee expected.

"You okay? I know you guys have been losing lately, but . . . are you all right?"

Hannegan nudged Jayvee's chin with a gentle fist and gave her a *don't worry about it* look. He knew he couldn't tell her about getting another package from Vlad. He didn't want her to know anything about Vlad, period.

"It's no big deal; we're just scuffling right now, what with the Big E going down and the Crabbers so hot. I'll be fine, especially now that I'm with you."

He broke out a smile and then reached out to caress Jayvee's breasts and got a laugh and a tender slap across the hands for his effort. Another kiss — a quick one this time — and the somber atmosphere was broken. It was Hannegan's first time at Jayvee's apartment, and she gave him a quick tour.

"It's not the biggest place in the world," she said as they ended up in the kitchen, "but it's more than enough for me since I'm gone most of the time anyway."

"And judging by your efforts with Michaela last weekend, you don't use THIS room very much."

"Watch it. From the looks of those pots and pans at your place, you're not exactly a gourmet chef yourself."

"I'll give you that one; but whoever is in charge of the food here, let's get going. I'm hungry."

As if on cue, the doorbell rang with the delivery of the Chinese food. It wasn't fancy, but there was plenty of it, and they sat at the table eating right out of the cartons.

"This stuff is pretty good," Ryan said as he slurped a noodle from his soup."

"You're such a slob, Ryan. Am I going spend all my time cleaning up after you?"

"You should be so lucky."

Jayvee stuck out her tongue, but then smiled. The pair had settled into a comfortable routine with each other. After eating, they moved into Jayvee's living room.

"What's next on the agenda, Julie?"

"Julie?"

"You know — the cruise director on the Love Boat."

Jayvee grabbed one of the pillows from her couch and threw it at Ryan.

"Something is seriously wrong with you, Hannegan. Do you let anybody else live in that world of yours?" she added with a laugh. "I picked up that DVD you talked about wanting to see, but now I don't know if I'm safe with you."

Hannegan rushed over and tackled Jayvee onto the couch, tickling her until she begged for mercy. Releasing her, Ryan picked up the DVD and put it into the player.

"I'm going to get you for that," Jayvee said to him as he returned to the couch.

"I can only hope."

Ryan put his feet up on the coffee table in front of the sofa.

"Make yourself at home," Jayvee scolded, although she nestled under his arm with her head on his chest. Before the movie had ended, she had fallen asleep, gently snoring, which made him smile.

He wondered why it couldn't just stay like this? No press, no pressure . . . just the two of them.

"Jayvee, wake up. The movie's over; it's time for me to go."

"You don't have to . . ."

"You know there is nothing I would enjoy more than staying here, Ms. DellVecchio, but this is for the best."

"You must be getting old, Hannegan, if you're willing to pass up a night of passion."

"Are you kidding? You've been asleep half the night already. I'd have better luck with one of the streetwalkers in front of the hotel."

Jayvee again stuck her tongue out at Ryan, but put her arm around his waist as she walked him to the door. He held her closely as they stood in the doorway, neither wanting him to leave, but knowing that he should. He had arrived earlier that evening with his world in turmoil, but in the past few hours, she had taken the tension away. He couldn't imagine life without her.

"I'll be at the game tomorrow," Jayvee said in between some warm kisses. "Let me know what the plans are for after the game. Do you think we can go someplace without attracting any attention?"

"Hey, Lady, this is your town. Find us some little Italian spot, and you'll have me forever."

"Forever . . . maybe I'd better think about this," she answered while squeezing him more tightly with her arms wrapped around his waist.

With that, they kissed once more before Ryan reluctantly departed.

In the game at The Hollow on Sunday afternoon, Rock Hunter befuddled Hannegan, putting the collar on Hannegan in an 0 for four that included two strikeouts. It went better for the rest of the Colonials, however, as Junichi and Mark Allen each hit a two-run homer off the little lefty. Nick Ertle, Old Reliable, as D.P. Perryton liked to call the veteran, won for the first time in two weeks, handcuffing the Horsemen for seven innings in the four to one Boston win. It enabled the C's to reclaim their advantage on New York, and they gained a game on the Crabbers who lost to Minneapolis. Needless to say, the post-game atmosphere was much lighter in the visitors' clubhouse.

"Ryno, big day out there. You were really stinging the ball!"

"I believe the box score will also reveal a certain third baseman who can't run fast enough to get out of his own way hit into a couple of double plays."

"You got me there, asshole. You know, when you win, it really doesn't matter as much does it?"

"And that's why, Doc, we've got to keep grabbing W's, especially from these guys."

The conversation continued for the two long-time friends through a quick stop in the trainer's room and then their postgame showers. Toweling off back in front of their lockers, Soos extended an invitation to Hannegan.

"What are you doing tonight? Do you want to join Lisa and me for some Italian, maybe grab a pizza someplace?"

Hannegan hesitated before answering, and his friend knew why. Leaning over to Ryan in order to whisper, Doc continued.

"Hey, I know you might have plans with Jayvee, but Lisa would like to meet her. Besides it's not much of a secret in our house. Your daughter has been talking about her to my Mary Ann for awhile now."

"That Michaela! I knew I couldn't count on her to keep a secret; she likes Jayvee too much to keep quiet to her friends."

"C'mon, Ryno. I bet she wouldn't mind if you asked her. I'm sure Jayvee might find someplace where no one will know us anyway."

"I doubt anyone would recognize an old has-been like you, but, hey, the top hitter in the American Conference always attracts a crowd."

"Bite me, you S-O-B. I don't know how you're doing it; you must be cheating or something."

Hannegan grimaced momentarily at Doc's last comment, but then quickly smiled to show him the friendly shot was a good one.

"Let me call Jayvee and see what she thinks."

Jayvee had been down on the field before the game, but she and Hannegan went out of their way to avoid each other except on one occasion when Jayvee was talking with a group of Boston players that included Ryan.

"Sounds great. I would love to go out with Doc and his wife. I know a little place where we can just blend in with the crowd."

Jayvee gave him directions to a restaurant on the Upper East Side of Manhattan, and they agreed to meet there around six-thirty.

Bastulli's was even better than Jayvee described it. The place was not that small, and most interestingly, it had an authentic bocce court behind the restaurant.

"I can understand why you've wanted to keep a low profile with Ryan," Doc said to Jayvee. "People have been locked up for associating with lowlife like him."

"That would make sense," Jayvee shot back, "since you're always bragging you've taught Ryan everything he knows."

The banter among the foursome continued through a dinner of salad, a giant pizza loaded with all the fixings, and two bottles of Chianti. Lisa and Jayvee hit it off — Hannegan knew they would — and the conversation was filled with stories and lots of laughs. Following dinner, they headed out back to watch the bocce players. The four of them had more wine, and it wasn't long before the competitive spirits started flowing, too.

"C'mon, Ryno, this looks like fun. We can take them."

"Have you ever played this game before?"

"No sweat, bro, we can do it. Let's go, ladies . . . the pros from Dover are taking over."

Lisa wasn't overly competitive, but the other three certainly were, filling the backyard area with groans or cries of delight whenever a play was made.

"DellVecchio! You're half-Italian . . . you've got to be able to play this game better."

"Don't give me shit, Hannegan. I'm carrying your ass here."

One time, Ryan grabbed Jayvee from behind just as she was about to make one of her tosses, and she reacted by threatening to bean him with one of the large wooden balls. They had a great time. Finally giving up the court, the four of them went back inside for a nightcap.

"Here's my number," Lisa Soos said to Jayvee later as they hugged outside the restaurant. "Heaven knows, you're going to need a friendly ear if you're going to hang around these two knuckleheads," she added, pointing to her husband and Ryan.

"C'mon, Lisa, I thought we were friends," Ryan groaned.

"Ignore her, Ryan, I always do," Doc put in, drawing a momentary glare from his wife. "Here's a cab. We've got room, Jayvee, we'll ride you back to your place."

"Thanks, Doc, but my apartment is just a short walk from here. Besides, your friend there might get the crazy idea that he would be welcome to stay."

Now it was Ryan's turn to be exasperated, although that quickly disappeared when Jayvee gave him a soft, but meaningful kiss that drew a response from Dennis Soos and the ensuing elbow into her husband's ribs from Lisa. With a wave, Jayvee turned and headed up the block to return home.

The following morning, Hannegan was awakened by another phone call.

"Get out of bed, old man."

"Good morning to you, too, Jayvee. What's up?"

"I'm running to work, but be sure to pick up a copy of the *Tribune-World*. There's something interesting on page seven."

"Hang on a sec; there's one outside my door."

Hannegan retrieved the paper and then returned to the bed, found the right page and began to read.

What attractive sports anchor was seen last night kissing what baseball hero on the streets of our fair city? Both seemed quite comfortable in each other's company. An interesting double play combination, don't you think?

Accompanying the gossip note was a picture of Jayvee and Ryan together on the sidewalk in front of Bastulli's.

"So much for our low profile," Ryan said. "I didn't even see a photographer?"

"Are you kidding? Think what this will do to my reputation."

"Is this going be a problem?"

"Relax. I'm actually glad it's out in the open."

"What about work? Maybe some people will think you'll be compromised by us being together."

"If you slip up, Irishman, they don't have to worry . . . I'll be all over your ass!"

"You're always after my ass anyway."

"Well, it is one of your best features."

The ribbing from his teammates when Hannegan arrived at the ballpark that afternoon was expected, and the hecklers among the New York faithful also tried to ride the Boston center fielder, but it seemed as if Ryan was energized by their catcalls. He knocked out three hits in the series finale, driving home two runs in a seven to five Colonials' win. His American Conference-leading batting average was now at .361, and his homers and RBI totals were already career highs with twelve and sixty . . . and they had just passed the halfway point in the 140-game schedule. The short flight back to Boston was spirited. The split with the Horsemen kept them two up on New York and still more than within striking distance of division-leading Baltimore. Tomorrow was an off-day, followed by a quick three-gamer with the struggling Detroit T-Birds. There was good news for Hannegan when he arrived at the ballpark on Tuesday.

"Ryan, I think you're in."

It was the Colonials' assistant PR man, Bart Danburg, holding up a computer printout.

"These are the latest updates on the All-Star voting, and it looks like you've got a great chance to be in the starting lineup. Junichi, too."

Danburg showed Hannegan the figures, which had the two Boston outfielders far in front of the other vote-getters at their positions in the American Conference.

The All-Star game! It was hard for Ryan to believe it. That was about the last thing he thought would happen before this season started. And it was going to be in L.A, so his family could come. He couldn't remember the last time his father saw him play in person.

The divisions of the BBL are geographically based, and the American Conference teams don't go any farther west than Dallas. Outside of one series last year when he was with the New York Gothams, Ryan had never played a professional game in Los Angeles. Since his father had developed a fear of flying, the only way Ryan's games were seen by Patrick Hannegan was through the satellite system his son had purchased for him several years earlier.

"Hey, Ju," Ryan called across the room to his teammate. "This thing really does work."

Hannegan was holding the mamori, the religious medallion that Junichi Nakata had given him earlier in the season. He then respectfully bowed in as good an interpretation as he could of the Japanese honorific tradition. Ju returned the bow and then gave Ryan the double six-gun salute that Ryan often shared with Dennis Soos. Both players smiled, thrilled they would almost certainly be going to the All-Star Game together.

Sitting in front of his locker, Dennis Soos added his congratulations, but with the usual edge for his best friend.

"The All-Star game? As a starter? Now I'm positive the world is coming to an end."

Hannegan good-naturedly flipped the bird at Doc, accompanied by a huge smile.

"I should at least get a commission for this. If it wasn't for my pep talks in spring training, you would have gone nowhere this season. By the way, did you get an All-Star Game bonus written into your contract?"

"Hey, Doc, I was just happy to get a contract over the winter. I wasn't going to worry about all-star bonuses."

"Too bad, Ryno . . . I guess now I'll have to start negotiating your contracts, too. It seems like I've got to do all the thinking for both of us."

"You just keep doing the thinking, Butch; that's what you're good at."

Hannegan and Soos both loved the movie *Butch Cassidy and the*

Sundance Kid, and they had even taken to calling themselves Butch and Sundance back in college.

As for the games on the homestand, the Colonials continued their sing-song pattern of play, losing two of three to the lowly T-Birds and then splitting a four game series with St. Louis. Saturday's game marked the end of June for Boston, a truly forgettable month. The team had a mark of 14-15 over the past thirty days, and in the process, had allowed Baltimore to take a firm grip on first place in the Northeast Division and New York to once again pull into a tie for second.

The following Tuesday, official notice came that Hannegan and teammates Junichi and Keith Lash had been selected to the American Conference team for the All-Star Game. There wasn't time for celebrating since the club was on a plane for the final road trip before the All-Star hiatus. It would be a difficult stretch of seven games in five days at Kansas City and Dallas. The Colonials won all three contests in Kansas City, but that was negated in Dallas when the Wranglers won on Friday and Saturday nights.

Kevin Kyle was not happy as he sat in the visitors' dugout before the Sunday doubleheader.

"This is BULLSHIT."

Playing two games in the daytime in Dallas in the middle of the summer was a scheduling fluke. In order to make certain every All-Star made it to Los Angeles on that evening, all the Sunday games were afternoon affairs. Junichi, Keith Lash and Ryan Hannegan would have preferred flying out early Monday morning, but those were the ground rules. It meant the Wranglers and the Colonials would spend a sweltering afternoon in the Texas heat. It was not the quirk in the schedule however, that had Kevin Kyle as hot as the conditions in Dallas.

"We better start sucking it up. We've been playing like crap for more than a month now. We need to make someone pay, and this is as good of a place as any to start."

Spurred by their bantam infielder, Boston grabbed the first game with the Wranglers. Jeff Hennessey made an emergency start, and he benefited from a four-run first inning on the way to a seven to four win. The game featured some rising tensions between the two clubs. Perhaps it was because of the torrid temperatures; maybe it was the result of the long grind of a baseball season, but things began to get chippy.

"Ground ball, slowly hit towards second... Kyle flips to Horrado for one... on to Morientes, that's two for the price of one..."

"Wait a minute, we've got Conway and Horrado chest to chest out at second. Conway came into the bag with a little extra action, and The Hurricane is letting him know he didn't appreciate it..."

When J.R. Cook returned the favor to the Wranglers' star, Kevin Tompkins, in the top of the next inning, both benches emptied. Order was restored quickly, but the tone had been set for the rest of the day.

The temperature on the field for the second game was well over one hundred degrees. There was a steady wind blowing, but it was more like a shot from a blast furnace than a cooling breeze. The fans were baking in the stands, and there wasn't much in the way of relief for the players in the dugouts. Everyone was uncomfortable.

Dudley Perryton had to use Hank Cummings, another spot starter, for the nightcap. Most descriptions of Hank usually included the adjective crusty. Cummings was the type of player who didn't talk much, even to teammates, and he had the reputation for not taking crap from anybody.

Right from the first Dallas hitter, Cummings had batters jumping away from fastballs up and in, or going jelly-kneed from breaking balls that appeared headed for their noggins before dipping down into the strike zone. The edginess from game one was still there, and both sides increased their barking at each other whenever a batter had to hit the dirt. The tension escalated in the third inning when Fernando Horrado got tangled up with Jeff Sibel on a bunt up the first baseline. Horrado bounced up screaming at the Dallas pitcher who just shoved Boston's leadoff hitter away. That action emptied the dugouts and bullpens again, but order was restored without any ejections.

The sacred code in baseball is that you protect your teammates, and even if he wasn't very friendly with the members of his own team, Hank Cummings knew he was supposed to do his part. Cummings plunked Fred Jansen, the first batter he saw when he went back out to the mound. Jansen was immediately restrained by Boston's backup catcher, Robbie Rigo, to prevent a fight, and home plate umpire Bill Wazevich issued a warning to both benches. Regardless of the warning, the barking continued.

"You're a chicken shit, Cummings," Jansen yelled from first as he took his lead.

"Any time, Fred, anytime."

Cummings let fly a stream of tobacco juice in Jansen's direction and then proceeded to aggravate the Wranglers' player by continually making throws over to first base. Fred Jansen kept diving into the Dallas dust to get back to the bag, and mixed in with all the perspiration from the intense heat, his uniform was quickly becoming mud-caked.

"Throw a goddamn pitch will you? It's so damned hot out here, asshole, my fillings are melting."

Hank Cummings response was to throw over to first base five more times. This further soured Jansen's disposition as well as the Dallas fans growing impatient at the lack of action while they cooked in their seats.

"... Cummings comes set again, finally he delivers to the plate. Swing and a ground ball to short; Horrado to second for one, on to first, it's a double play."

Kevin Kyle's relay throw to first low-bridged Fred Jansen to make certain the Wrangler didn't try to wipe him out as the second baseman made his pivot.

"What the fuck do you think you're doing, Kyle?"

"Kiss my ass, Jansen. Quit your bitchin' and get off the field."

"Up yours, little man, up yours."

Hank Cummings disposed of the next hitter to end the inning, but it was obvious the fireworks weren't over.

"... Junichi leads it off for the C's. I don't know how they play this over in Japan, but I hope he doesn't get too comfortable at the plate!"

Tom Kingery's commentary had a foreboding ring to it. After getting a called strike one with a pitch at the knees on the outside corner, Sibel was going to push the Boston switch-hitter off the plate with a little chin music. Perhaps the Wranglers' righthander held onto the ball just a little too long, or Junichi didn't think he would get a pitch up and in following Bill Wazevich's ejection threat, but big trouble was at hand.

"... Sibel fires a fastball up and in, and it hit him. Junichi goes down. Boy, I hope that got him on the helmet because you could hear the contact all the way up here in the pressbox..."

The ball did not catch the helmet; it hit the Japanese star squarely on the cheekbone just below his right eye. Junichi dropped at the plate like a tree felled by a lumberjack. The blood flow was immediate, making the B-O-S-T-O-N lettering on the front of his uniform almost undistinguishable. Several Dallas players quickly ran to the mound to form a protective circle around Jeff Sibel in anticipation of a fight, but the Boston players raced to home plate instead, hoping to help their injured teammate.

Amazingly, Junichi never lost consciousness, but the swelling was immediate, all but closing his right eye. In addition, his nose was turning an ugly purple from the impact of the ball; it was possibly broken as well. Peter Hudec was finally able to stanch the bleeding, turning several towels red in the process, and he and several Boston players assisted Junichi to the clubhouse where an ambulance waited outside to take him to a nearby hospital.

Jeff Sibel and his manager, Charlie Lydon, were ejected, and it seemed whatever energy was left in this game departed along with them. The Wranglers gained a split in the doubleheader, with a four to two win. For Boston, they had lost more than just a game. Coupled with the earlier injury to Ellis Nance, the Colonials now found themselves missing two important cogs in their machine.

Hannegan numbly sat in his first class seat as his plane climbed from the Dallas airport toward its Los Angeles destination. He couldn't stop thinking about poor Ju. He wondered how long he was going to be out? Would he would be gone for the rest of the season? A second half without Junichi was a situation the C's did not want to consider, and for Hannegan, no Ju would mean even more of the focus would be on him.

As he sat on the plane, that second dose of Soviet science that lay in his refrigerator back in Boston dominated his thoughts. The complications were more than he needed, so with a final hit on his beer, Ryan tried to get some sleep for the rest of the flight. Sleep was hard to come by however, even at thirty-five thousand feet. The maddening crunch was growing louder in his head.

· FOURTEEN ·

Of all the professional sports, baseball's annual All-Star game seems to have the most to offer. Professional football's game is played at the completion of the season, either with players who haven't played for weeks since the regular campaign was finished, or with those whose energy levels are all but gone from the pressure and physical toll of the playoffs. In pro basketball, the matchup of the best players takes place at midseason, just like in baseball, but defense is only talked about, making the game an exhibition of offensive theatrics. Baseball's All-Star Game, however, usually produces most of the elements of good baseball.

Ryan Hannegan might have reason to be distracted by all the events of recent weeks, but he got caught up in the All-Star festivities once he arrived in Los Angeles that Sunday evening. Michaela wasn't going to miss being there in person for her father's first All-Star appearance, so when it became official he was playing, Ryan flew her out early so she could stay with his sister, Eileen. Eileen had two daughters, Colleen and Cecilia, who were around the same age as Michaela. The whole family was waiting for him at the airport: his father, Michaela, Eileen and her family, as well as his big brother, Dan, his wife, Tina, and their three boys, including the baby, Jimmy, asleep on his father's shoulder, when Ryan passed through security.

"There he is, my All-Star Dad!"

Michaela ran up to hug her father, followed by her cousins who gathered around them.

"Dad, we went to Magic Mountain, the beach, Pancho's, Warner Brothers..."

"Slow down, Michaela, you can tell me all about it, but let me say hi to everyone first."

Hannegan turned to his sister and gave her a kiss.

"I apologize, Eileen, you must be going crazy with the three girls. My head hurts and I just got here."

"It's been great, Ryan, really it has. The girls don't get together as much as they should, so they've had fun since the first moment Michaela arrived."

"Colleen introduced me to some boys, Daddy, and they were really cute."

"Don't tell me that. And as for you, Miss Colleen... what are you doing to your uncle? Giving him gray hair before his time?"

Colleen blushed, but then gave her uncle a hug as did her younger sister. Hannegan next moved on to greet his brother's family, decked out in Boston T-shirts with his name and number on the backs. Ryan had sent some autographed baseballs and bats to his nephews earlier in the season, so he was as good as Santa Claus as far as they were concerned. Meanwhile, the Hannegan patriarch stood off to the side, impassively watching the various greetings. At last, Ryan walked over to his father where he was met with the usual gesture of affection from Patrick Hannegan: a firm handshake.

"Hey, Dad. You didn't have to come to the airport. I could have seen you back at Eileen's house."

Patrick Hannegan was an engineer, and his life reflected that with an orderly, reserved approach to things. He loved his children and his grandchildren; he was just a person who didn't let his guard down very often.

"Did you think I'd miss anything to do with my son being an All-Star? Your mother would have been so proud," Patrick Hannegan said softly with the hint of a tear in his eye.

Ryan startled his father by impulsively hugging him, but the elder Hannegan, after some momentary stiffness, relaxed and returned the gesture.

"Wow! Get your camera, Eileen," Dan Hannegan let out. "We may never get a shot of the old man like this again."

The elder Hannegan pulled away from his middle child, red with embarrassment but also with a stern look at his oldest son. It only lasted for a moment, however, and soon he joined in laughter with the rest of the family over Dan's joke. Making sure that everyone was there — Dan's boys were notorious for running all over the place — the family moved toward the baggage area to collect the rest of Ryan's things.

"Are you sure it won't be too much of a problem to stay with you, Eileen? Michaela and I can stay at my place."

"That's silly. You've got it closed up for the season, and you're only going to be here for a couple of days anyway. If they're not making you stay at the hotel, we're not going to miss the chance to spend extra time with you. Besides, the girls love having Michaela here, and the logistics will be easier."

All-Star Monday was a great day for everyone. Hannegan was able to bring his nieces and nephews into the clubhouse along with Michaela, leaving the girls momentarily speechless for the only time during his stay in Los Angeles.

"Ohmigod, it's Becka. I've got all her records."

"Look Colleen, there's Jason, he's so hot."

Several movie and television celebrities were awaiting the charity softball game that was part of the activities and the kids were thrilled to get autographs.

"Uncle Ryan, come here. Look I'm Dante Russo."

One of Hannegan's nephews had found the locker of the St. Louis slugger and he was gamely trying to swing one of Russo's bats.

"Daddy... here's your locker. Check out your jersey. This is so cool."

Michaela and his nieces and nephews enjoyed walking around the room, reading the nameplates of the various players atop the lockers, and occasionally, reaching up to touch one of the jerseys that hung there.

Of course, Jayvee was there to cover the events for *Totally Baseball*. She spotted Michaela in the crowd where the Hannegan family was seated for the celebrity softball game, and she walked over during a break after the game.

"Jayvee... Jayvee, over here. See, I told you I know her."

Michaela was bursting with pride while she introduced Jayvee to her cousins.

"Everybody, this is Jayvee DellVecchio. She's the lady on TV and she knows everything there is to know about baseball. Isn't that right, Jayvee?"

"If you say so, Michaela. And who are all these people?"

"This is my cousin, Colleen and this is her sister, Cecilia . . . and those are my cousins, Ian and Kevin."

Jayvee talked with the children and then introduced herself to the rest of the family.

"If my brother is as crazy about you as Michaela is, then there's hope for him yet."

"Thank you, Eileen. Michaela is a wonderful young lady. I was an only child, so it's been fun being her big sister, so to speak. Now, as for your brother . . ."

Jayvee made a face like she had just tasted something sour. Ryan's family was defensive until they caught on to her joke.

"Tell me about it," Dan Hannegan laughed. "He was a pain in the butt growing up. You'd better steer clear of that guy."

Ryan walked over in the midst of the bantering between Jayvee and his family, not realizing, initially, that he was the butt of their laughter. Jayvee was getting along fine, just as he hoped. Her responsibilities meant Jayvee wouldn't have much time with Ryan, but that was just as well since she thought it was important he share this experience with his family. It also meant the pair could avoid adding to the gossip about their relationship.

The children of the all-stars were allowed to be with their fathers on the field during the home-run hitting contest. Hannegan had taken Michaela on the field a number of times at various ballparks, but always when they were deserted. Now she was getting the chance here at Hollywood Haven to be there with the greatest names in the game today.

"Hey, Kev. Come here a minute will you."

"Don't, Daddy . . . don't bring him over."

"Kevin, I want you to meet your biggest fan. You'd think it would be her old man, but I guess I'm not cute enough."

"DADDY!"

Both Kevin Tompkins and Michaela blushed at Hannegan's comment. The Dallas Wranglers' star was very gracious to Michaela, even posing for a picture certain to find a prominent place on her dresser back home.

His daughter punched him in the arm after Tompkins left, but Ryan knew she was thrilled to have met one of her favorite players.

All the extra events passed rapidly, and before Hannegan could believe it, it was game time on Tuesday evening. Each All-Star wore the cap of his particular team, with a commemorative All-Star insignia on the side. Standing in the visitors' dugout with the rest of his teammates for the game, Hannegan rubbed his fingers across the American Conference logo on his jersey. Thank goodness, Eileen is here. Katie Kodak was the family's nickname for her and it was her job to fill up the family album. Ryan wasn't one for taking pictures, but tonight was certainly an exception.

The trainers and various coaches for the A-C squad were introduced to the sellout throng, followed by the extra players. Keith Lash got a big round of applause from the fans in tribute to his work with the Stars in years past. Following the introduction of the Crabbers' skipper, Tom Kiczek, the Stars' public address announcer was ready to rev up the crowd.

"Leading off for the American Conference ... from the Baltimore Crabbers ... speedy second baseman, Carlos Valeron!"

"Batting second and currently the second highest batting average in the A-C, ... a four-time All-Star already, ... from the Dallas Wranglers, ... shortstop, Kevin Tompkins!"

The crowd reacted strongly to Tompkins, not only because he was the MVP in the conference the past season, but because he had also grown up in Los Angeles, playing ball out in the Valley.

"The number three hitter is one of the great ambassadors of the game ... and an outstanding player as well ... this is the tenth straight season that he has been voted a starter by you, the fans — also from the Crabbers — right fielder, Nick Hamilton!"

Like the other players, Nick Hamilton ran out of the third base dugout to join his teammates along the baseline, facing the grandstands. While he slapped hands up and down the line, the Los Angeles faithful responded with a loud ovation.

"Hitting cleanup for the American Conference, he has led all of baseball in home runs the past five seasons ... — and he is doing it again this year — from the St. Louis Rivermen, let's hear it for first baseman, Dante Russo!"

As Dante Russo came out onto the field to the cheers of the crowd, Ryan Hannegan stepped up to the second step of the dugout — he was next. He thought, *What a long, strange trip this has been. No way was this ever going to happen.* A representative from the DBC had his hand on Ryan's right arm, ready to give him the signal to take his place with his All-Star teammates ... as if Hannegan didn't know his cue.

"In the five hole for the American Conference — he has already posted career numbers in homers and runs batted in, and his .355 batting average is the best in all of baseball — from Loyola Marymount right here in L.A. and from the Boston Colonials — centerfielder, Ryan Hannegan!"

While not with the same level of applause as some of the other players, Ryan was greeted warmly. He imagined some of his friends from high school and college were sprinkled among the capacity crowd. After the run along the assembled American Conference personnel, Hannegan took his place on the third base line and waved to the crowd. He was able to see his family cheering wildly, his daughter with her hand over her mouth, almost in disbelief, and his father beaming more proudly than at any time Ryan could remember in his life. Looking skyward momentarily, Hannegan remembered his father's words from Sunday night and smiled. *You're right, Dad. If only Mom could have been here. That would have been perfect.*

The announcements continued with the remainder of the American Conference starters, and then the same process was repeated for the National Conference stars. The current rage in pop music sang The Star Spangled Banner. The roar of the crowd at the song's end was momentarily overwhelmed by the noise of a squadron of fighter jets that did a fly-by over the stadium. It was time to play ball.

The game itself was a blur for Hannegan. He popped out to second in his first at-bat, but he belted a double up the alley in right-center in the fourth to plate a run. Tom Kiczek replaced him with Joe Otto of the Ironmen in the fifth, and Ryan spent the rest of the night soaking up as much of the evening as he could. There was a post-game party for the baseball families, and Ryan was happy to have his gang with him for the celebration. They didn't stay long because the children were getting tired, and that was just as well since he had an early flight for the cross-country trip back to Boston tomorrow morning. Fortunately his sister's house was in Manhattan Beach, close to the Los Angeles airport. Ryan said his good-byes to the family before they went to bed so they wouldn't have to get up when he left the house around 5:30 a.m. That included his daughter, Michaela, who was going to stay with her cousins for a few more days.

As he usually did when he was on the road, Hannegan packed most of his things before going to bed in order to sleep almost until just before it was time to leave. The alarm went off shortly after five. Damn, I think I rolled over once. Ryan could hear his brother-in-law rummaging in the kitchen as he headed to the bathroom for a quick shave and a run through with the toothbrush to get rid of his morning breath. He slipped on some sweats, tossed his shaving kit into his bag with the rest of his things, and made his way downstairs. He could smell the welcome aroma of just-brewed coffee, but Ryan was surprised it wasn't Tom in the kitchen.

"Dad, what are you doing here? I thought Tom was going to take me to the airport?"

Patrick Hannegan smiled as he handed his son a travel mug of steaming java.

"When you get to be my age, Ryan, you will understand sleep is a sometimes thing, what with going to the bathroom too often and other things. I am usually up by this time of the morning anyway, so I told Tom he could sleep in and that I would run you over to the airport. C'mon, we better get going."

The ride to the airport was without conversation for the most part, something to which Ryan was well accustomed. Patrick Hannegan, a D-Day participant when he was just eighteen, took a stoic approach to life like so many of his generation. He married late and was well into his thirties by the time he and Erika had children. Ryan and his brother and sister knew their father loved them; he just had a more difficult time expressing it. The car pulled up to the curb at the departure area, and there was a bustle of activity even at this early hour. Hannegan was ready to hop out when his father reached out to put his hand on his son's arm.

"I hope you know how proud I am of you, Ryan?"

"Yeah, I know, Dad. It was really special that you and Danny and Eileen could be here for all of this. I didn't think I'd ever get to play in one of these things."

"It was wonderful. With you being back east, I don't get to see you play much . . . except on the dish."

Patrick Hannegan paused for a moment before continuing.

"But you should be used to that. I don't think I saw many of your games growing up either . . . there was always something going on. Thank God for your mother."

"Dad, we understood, we all did. You were trying to take care of us, so we knew you couldn't be around all the time. When you were there — just like these past couple days — it was great. Besides, we always had Mom, and I think she was tougher on us than any coach could have been."

"Your mother was quite an athlete, and I don't think I have ever known a woman who cared as much about sports as she did."

Ryan smiled softly as he watched his father's gaze drift off to memories of earlier days. A child naturally assumes his parents love each other, but sometimes it's not always outwardly expressed. *Look at him. It's been nearly twenty years since she died, and he still loves her. I don't think I ever noticed that before.* It was a side to his father Ryan had rarely seen. Coming back from his reverie, Patrick Hannegan looked closely into his son's eyes.

"This may sound maudlin, Son, but your mother made everything right for me. I miss her more with each passing day. I know it didn't work out for you with Deirdre, but I see what a wonderful dad you are to my granddaughter, and I am very proud."

"I don't know much about the young lady I met this week, but maybe she's the one for you like your mother was for me."

"Jayvee is special, Dad, and I am going to do my best to see that she keeps me around. She would have given Mom a run for her money when it comes to loving sports."

The elder Hannegan smiled at his son's comments. The conversation was then interrupted by a knock on the window. Airports do not like parked cars remaining at the curb too long these days, and a police officer was telling the Hannegans it was time to move along. Ryan was reaching into the back seat to grab a small travel bag when his father surprised him with a hug. It was the second time in the past several days that these men had embraced, but this time it was Ryan who was caught off guard. *The old man is still full of surprises . . . but it feels good.* After retrieving his suitcase from the trunk, Hannegan leaned back into the car through the passenger side window.

"By the way, Dad, thanks for the information you gave Terry Tate for that article he wrote about Mom's grandfather. It really took the heat off me."

"I don't pretend to understand what that blood stuff is all about, but if it helped, then I'm glad."

Hannegan smiled and then grasped his father's right hand firmly. As he began to pull away from the handshake, Patrick Hannegan held onto it for a moment longer.

"Ryan . . . just remember, do the right thing."

Hannegan nodded to his father and then unhooked from Patrick Hannegan's grip. As the car pulled away, he remained standing at the curb. *He hasn't said something like that since he dropped me at the college dorm freshman year. Do the right thing.* He wanted to cry out to his father, "What is the right thing, Dad . . . for me?"

The flight back to Boston was supposed to be nearly full, but the first class area was empty when Ryan climbed aboard. Settling in, Hannegan fell asleep almost immediately — he didn't even remember the takeoff when he awoke several hours later. *That coffee's kicked in.* He needed to find the bathroom.

There were only three other people in a first class section that could hold about twenty, and one of them was D.P. Perryton. Tapping his manager on the shoulder as he passed by him in the aisle, Hannegan gestured indicating he would be right back. Returning a short time later, Ryan found D.P. engrossed in reading the latest edition of *USA Today*. Seeing Hannegan, the skipper of the Colonials tossed the newspaper onto a pile of other papers and magazines on the seat next to him.

"Excuse me," the flight attendant interrupted. "Would you like your breakfast now?"

She had let Hannegan sleep through the meal service, and he was grateful he could still get something to eat. Perryton only wanted a fresh cup of coffee. As she departed, D.P. gestured for Ryan to sit down, but Hannegan chose to remain standing in order to stretch out the kinks from his earlier snooze.

"I was very proud of you last night, Ryno. It has been a long time for both of us from those days in the Carolina League, but you've stuck with it."

"I tell you, Skip, that was something last night, wasn't it? I know guys talk about it — and I have seen plenty of the games on television — but nothing really prepares you for that experience."

"If you think that was something . . . just wait until you experience the playoffs, if we can get there."

Perryton's comments meant a lot to Hannegan. Even with the separation of years between the two times D.P. was his manager, Ryan felt Perryton was his baseball father.

"It's not going to be easy without Ju and the Big E. Any news?"

"Good and bad. Pete Hudec told me on the phone yesterday he thinks Ellis will be back in about three weeks. The ankle is progressing, but Big E is going to need some time to get his arm back in shape since he hasn't been able to do much throwing."

"And Ju?"

"Not so good. He broke the orbital bone around his right eye, and there are concerns about some damage to his sinus passages and his nose. He was fortunate there was no damage to the eye itself . . . as far as they can tell because he's still pretty swollen there."

Hannegan grimaced. *No way would I want to take one in the face.*

"They're going to keep him in the hospital for at least several more days. They've got some specialist to do the surgery when the time is right, and Simonton told me they might bring in a doctor from Japan, too."

"Specialists? That sounds serious."

"It is, Ryan. I'm not sure we can count on Junichi coming back before the season's over."

"Then what's the game plan, D.P., if I can ask?"

"My plan is to put a no-bat, no-glove, no-speed talent like you in the three hole."

Perryton made his comment with a slight chuckle, but his intent was clear: he was counting on Ryan to pick up the slack. The number three position in a team's batting order is usually reserved for its best all-around hitter. Out of the three hole, that batter gives a team the chance to create a big rally behind the table-setters at the top of the lineup, and he causes pitching matchup problems when paired with a team's cleanup hitter.

"If I hit you third, it gives me protection for Ramon on both sides because I can move Doc up into the five spot. He's hit there before, so it won't be a big deal for him. You can do it, Ryno. I know you can."

"Thanks, Skip. I hope you feel that way a couple weeks from now."

"If we can just keep our heads above water through the rest of the month, we'll get Ellis back and then we can make a run down the stretch."

The flight attendant had Hannegan's breakfast ready, so he headed back to his seat, leaving his manager to contemplate whatever lay ahead. Ryan wolfed down the breakfast — he was hungry enough to even enjoy airplane food — and he passed the remainder of the flight reading a paperback he had picked up back at the airport. When the plane landed in Boston, Ryan accompanied his manager to the baggage area and then outside to pick up a taxi. As D.P. Perryton prepared to climb into one of the cabs, he turned back to Hannegan.

"I don't want you putting any pressure on yourself, Ryno. Moving you up in the lineup and all. I know you can handle it. We're counting on you more than any team has probably counted on you since college. I know you'll do the right thing."

The right thing, just like Dad said. That thought raced through his mind as the cab pulled away and another pulled up to take him back to his condo. *What is the right thing?* he wondered.

It was midsummer in Boston, and it was going to be one of those nights where the high temperatures would be matched by a comparable humidity level. The sticky night was going to be uncomfortable for those who didn't have the benefit of air conditioning. At one of the town's newer condominium complexes, that shouldn't have been a problem, but one of its residents sat in front of his open refrigerator during the wee hours of the morning. He was not seeking relief from the appliance; he was attempting to find an answer for the contents sitting on a shelf inside.

· FIFTEEN ·

THE GAMES AFTER the All-Star break are called the second half of the season, but the reality was the Colonials had only fifty-three games remaining in their one hundred forty games schedule. In the past six weeks, the club had played just break-even baseball. Baltimore's near .700 pace, meanwhile, enabled it to pad its lead. Dallas and St. Louis now had better records than Boston, and the Horsemen gained three games in the standings:

AMERICAN CONFERENCE

NORTHEAST DIVISION			MIDWEST DIVISION		
	W-L	GB		W-L	GB
Baltimore	54-33	—	Dallas	52-35	—
Boston	49-38	5	Saint Louis	50-37	2
New York	48-39	6	Minneapolis	42-45	10
Cleveland	44-43	10	Chicago	41-46	11
Detroit	38-49	16	Kansas City	37-50	15

The Colonials had a six-game homestand against the Lumberjacks and the Ironmen as play resumed. It was an awful time at Patriots' Harbor as the hometown nine lost four of the six games. Keith Lash was able to avoid the Friday the 13th jinx when he won his twelfth game in seventeen decisions, but Raul Gomez was the only other starter to pitch well enough to gain a victory. The offense wasn't bad, despite the absence of Junichi, but it was one of those stretches where the high-scoring games didn't fall the Colonials' way. Ryan Hannegan had settled in nicely as the number three hitter in the lineup, as did Doc Soos batting fifth, yet it wasn't enough. The loss to Cleveland in the finale of the homestand had the Boston fans serenading their struggling warriors with a chorus in Boo-flat.

"You guys suck! Same old Colonials."

"They're probably right, Doc. We do suck right now."

"We just got to keep grinding, Ryno. One day at a time. It'll turn our way. It better."

The road trip began with a return encounter against the Lumberjacks in the Twin Cities. Keith Lash and Kris Fucci completed the club's first doubleheader sweep of the season, but the Lumberjacks got revenge the following evening, knocking off Boston for the third time in the six games over the past week. Now it was on to Baltimore and the first place Crabbers.

Baltimore was on a three-month run of incredible baseball — playing at better than a .600 clip since May first. Baltimore didn't have many high-profile stars outside of Nick Hamilton, but Tom Kiczek, their manager, was considered one of the best in baseball at coaxing the maximum out of a ballclub. The weekend belonged to the Crabbers as they took three of the five games, increasing their advantage over Boston in the Northeast Division to a season-high eight games.

"Nice job, Ryan. You're hitting the ball even better so far here in the second half."

Terry Tate was interviewing Hannegan in the clubhouse following the Monday night loss to Baltimore.

"Nothing nice about it, Terry, if we're not winning."

"I realize that, but you're hitting .370 now," the Boston sportswriter continued, "and, who knows, you might even have a shot at the Triple Crown."

"I'm not trying to be modest, Terry. The results have been . . . well, better than I could ever dream about . . ."

Hannegan tossed his dirty uniform into the laundry basket in the middle of the clubhouse. He gestured toward the rest of the room.

"But, you see these guys? We're getting our ass kicked right now. Nobody gives a shit about what I'm hitting. They just want a way for us to start winning again. Numbers are crap when you're losing."

Back home for their second longest homestand in the remaining games, the C's hoped to get their playoff push going against the two bottom feeders of the Northeast Division, Detroit and Kansas City, after the off-day on Tuesday. Since his All-Star participation meant no real break at all, Ryan was looking forward to recharging his batteries. A phone call at mid-morning, however, changed that thinking.

"Ryan, this is Henry Lamirand from the Players Association . . ."

Hannegan didn't know Lamirand very well, but Henry had done an excellent job as the executive director for the players' group.

"Hey, Henry, how's it going? What's got you interrupting my day off? No problem is there?"

"I hope not, Ryan. Commissioner Hopkins asked me to see if you'd be available for a meeting later this afternoon in New York. I know it's short notice, but you know Hoppy . . . when he asks you for something, it's usually more of a command than a request."

"You're kidding me, right? They've taken enough blood samples over the past few weeks that I think I'm developing needle tracks." Hannegan was trying to keep things light. "What do they want this time?"

"They didn't say specifically. Commissioner Hopkins asked that I be in attendance, and he said you could bring your agent along if you wanted to."

Right, like I'm going to have Curt Paul there. Paul, a college fraternity brother, served as Ryan's lawyer and quasi-agent. Curt checked out the language in the various contracts he had signed through the years, but he was not like one of those hotshot agents who handled the big deals. Big deals; what's that? Besides, Curt was out in California, so he wouldn't be able to make a meeting on such short notice even if Hannegan wanted him there.

"As long as you're there, Henry, that'll be fine. But how am I supposed to get to this meeting?"

"The Commissioner's private aircraft. As we speak, the plane is getting ready to head to Boston. Do you know where Hanscom Field in Bedford is?"

Lamirand proceeded to give Ryan some basic directions to the airfield located about twenty miles northwest of Boston.

"The plane should be there by two o'clock. The meeting's in midtown at four, so you shouldn't have any trouble."

"Okay, Henry, I'll see you there."

Hanging up the phone, Hannegan screamed out an obscenity that reverberated off the walls of his condominium. He was beginning to think this shit would never end. He headed off to shower and dress for his meeting with General Hopkins. When Hannegan arrived at Hanscom Field shortly before two, his transportation was already waiting for him.

"Hey, you're Ryan Hannegan!"

One of the guys at the desk was a big Colonials' fan and had instantly recognized Ryan.

"Is that Lear out there for you? Where you headed?"

"A little business in New York. This is the first chance I've had to catch up because of the All-Star game and then our road trip."

"Oh, right. Hey, congratulations on that all-star thing. Do you think I could get you to sign something for me?"

Hannegan cheerfully obliged him with an autograph.

"What's happening with you guys? Are you going to be able to turn it around?"

"It's been tough with the injuries, but there are enough games left that I still think we're going to make a good run."

Ryan handed back the now autographed piece of paper and moved towards the door. He was grateful he was not taking the train or going through Logan. There'd be way too many people asking questions. The flight to New York City went without a hitch, and upon landing, a waiting limousine was on the tarmac to take him to mid-town. Through the relentless waves of city traffic, the driver expertly picked his way like a broken-field runner in football and pulled up in front of Baseball's offices right on time.

"Ryan, I want to thank you for coming on such short notice," General Hopkins began as he greeted Hannegan in a stylish conference room on the fifth floor.

The retired military leader shook Ryan's hand firmly and gestured for him to take a seat at the table. Hoppy Hopkins went to a seat on the opposite side where he was flanked by Jack McDermott and several other people that Hannegan did not know. Henry Lamirand was also in the room, and after shaking hands with Ryan, he took his place just to the left of the Boston centerfielder.

"It's good to see you again, General. I am sorry that I didn't get a chance to visit with you during the All-Star Game. I spent so much time with my family, I didn't socialize that much."

"That's quite all right, Ryan," Michael Hopkins said with a dismissive wave of his right hand. "Being selected to the All-Star Game is a tremendous accomplishment . . . and to share it with your family is more important."

"It was great, sir. That sort of stuff doesn't happen for me, so it was a big honor to be a part of it."

"An honor well deserved!"

Hannegan was nervous, but he tried to maintain as much composure as he could muster. As he discovered when he met Hoppy Hopkins at the home opener in Boston back in the spring, the General creates an intimidating presence even when he is trying to be friendly. Just try and keep things light, he thought to himself. You don't want to get into anything serious here if you don't have to.

"Incidentally, General Hopkins, I want to thank you for coming to my defense after all those articles by Woody Watson about my blood testing."

Hopkins's fatherly face became stern with Ryan's comment.

"I wasn't coming to your defense, Mr. Hannegan. I was defending baseball. We are America's game, and on my watch, we will conduct ourselves in an appropriate manner. This is the greatest game I know, and I will take the necessary steps to help the rest of this wonderful country to feel the same way, too."

Hopkins's right hand balled up and then slammed into the mahogany table.

"I will punish those who deserve it, but I will not allow people who want to sully this game for their own purposes to step above the law or to damage a reputation without just cause. Do I make myself clear?"

The atmosphere had grown heavy in the room during the commissioner's short lecture. Ryan knew immediately his question was answered: this ain't no social call. Not that he had expected it to be anyway.

The commissioner waited to see if Ryan had any other response than the nodding of his head. When he saw there was none, General Hopkins leaned back into his padded leather chair and assumed a more conciliatory position.

"Let's begin, shall we?"

Michael Hopkins glanced at Henry Lamirand who nodded in approval. With that, baseball's boss turned the proceedings over to Jack McDermott.

"Mr. Hannegan, do you know a man by the name of Vladimir Titov?"

Ryan hesitated briefly before answering.

"Sure, I know Vlad..."

Turning momentarily towards his Players Association boss, Hannegan continued.

"I met him at the fantasy camp that the union runs down in Florida. He was one of the campers."

"Do you know much about his background?"

"I didn't initially. He was one of my players, and I called him Mad Vlad because he was a crazy man when he tried to play in the field.

With a smile, Ryan added: "That big Russian sure could hit, though; he absolutely mashed the ball."

Jack McDermott ignored Ryan's description of Titov's baseball abilities and kept boring ahead.

"I have reports indicating you and Mr. Titov did a fair amount of socializing during the camp. Any comments?"

Ryan's first impulse was to say, "Back off, asshole." Then he thought better of it. Wait a minute, slow down, Ryan. He knew he was only going to get deeper in jeopardy if he challenged this guy. Trying to keep cool, Ryan flashed a bigger smile.

"Sure... Vlad and I got together a few times after the bull sessions. We both like to play cards, and I loved hearing about his life in Russia and his career as an athlete. But I haven't seen him since the camp ended — I take that back — I did see him briefly one night here in New York early in the season at a restaurant. We talked for a few minutes and that was it."

General Hopkins took over the questioning.

"Are you aware, Ryan, that Mr. Titov has been linked to organized crime? He is the nephew of the reputed Russian Mafia boss, Yegor Karpin. Mr. Karpin and his associates are said to be involved in a number of illegal activities, including gambling."

"I didn't find that out, General, until the final night at fantasy camp," Ryan responded, stretching the timeline a little bit. "There was never any discussion about gambling, however, except for what I owed him after our gin games. That guy sure could play cards," Hannegan concluded with a shrug of his shoulders.

"Did you have any concerns?"

"Not really, sir, since the card games weren't any different than the ones we have in the clubhouse. Besides I figured there wasn't a problem since he was at a camp that was sanctioned by the BBL and the union."

"The policy of this sport, as you know, is that we do not want our players having any association with known gamblers." Looking at Henry Lamirand and then Jack McDermott before picking things up again, Hoppy Hopkins added: "It was a failure on our part that this was allowed to happen in the first place. Can I count on your future cooperation in this matter?"

"Without a doubt, sir. Like I said, I haven't had any contact with the man since that night at the restaurant."

The lie came easy.

General Hopkins put both of his elbows on the table and leaned across to Hannegan again with a conciliatory approach.

"I appreciate your help in this matter . . . and for coming here on such short notice. I am not pleased private information out of this office has been exposed to the public, and that's why I wanted this meeting to take place with some secrecy. The confidentiality of this proceeding is paramount."

"No sweat, sir. I've got enough to worry about trying to help my team to get going again; the last thing I need is more publicity about some issue that shouldn't be one anyway."

General Hopkins settled back into the leather chair and smiled for the first time since the early moments of the meeting.

"That's great, Ryan! I am pleased we can bring this situation to a close.

I think we all want to get back to just worrying about the games themselves."

"Absolutely, sir."

Rising from his chair, Hopkins came around the table to shake Hannegan's hand and escort him to the door.

"That's some race we have going in the Northeast . . . what do you think your chances are?"

"Why, General, are you looking to make a bet or something?"

All the other activity and conversation in the room ceased. Shit! You're an idiot, Hannegan. Just get out of here . . . stop trying to be Jay Leno.

"Sorry about that, sir; . . . poor choice on my part. It's going to be tough because of our injuries, but we might get Ellis Nance back this week, and that will really help."

"Ah, yes, the Big E. He could make a difference. As my father always told me, you can never have enough pitching."

Grateful the commissioner made no mention of his bad joke, Hannegan shook hands again with Michael Hopkins and headed for the door. Walking towards the elevator, he glanced back to see General Hopkins in what looked to be a serious discussion with Jack McDermott and Henry Lamirand. The door to the conference room closed, cutting off his view of this huddle, but Ryan saw enough. This baby was far from being put to bed.

Wednesday brought the start of the series with the Detroit T-Birds. D.P. Perryton gathered his players in the clubhouse after batting practice.

"Men, I know we haven't played liked we've wanted to lately, but we still have time to get it together."

The veteran baseball man leaned up against one of the tables in the middle of the clubhouse, aimlessly twirling a fungo bat in his hands.

"It seems to me like we've been playing not to lose rather than being aggressive. Sure, we miss Ellis and Junichi, but hell's bells, you all are big leaguers, you belong here. Play like you know you belong. Come on; have some fun, let it go."

With that, Perryton grabbed an apple from a bowl of fruit on the table, tossed it into the air, and then belted it with the fungo bat into a wall on the far side of the clubhouse. Pieces of the blasted apple dripped down the wall, but nothing else moved. Perryton looked around the room without saying anything more and headed into his office with the rest of the coaching staff.

Ellis Nance, just about ready to return from his ankle injury, stepped into the middle of the room.

"D.P. is right; we've let the pressure get to us. The hell with looking at the scoreboard, worrying about what Baltimore and New York are doing. We just got to take care of our own business."

"I don't know about the rest of you," Doc Soos echoed, "but I am tired of not having fun. Do you know how to have fun in this game? It's by winning, that's how. And do you know how to win? We win by going out there ready to KICK SOME ASS!"

A murmur of assent passed through the players.

"Y'all want someone to show you the way?" Ellis Nance asked. "Just climb on my back because I'll be damned if I am going to sit home and watch the playoffs again when this is gonna be my last year."

Big E hanging it up? Ryan Hannegan was as shocked as the rest of his teammates. He knew the man was almost forty, but he's still as good as anybody in the game.

"That's right; . . . this old man has had enough of being away from his family, and I'm tired. But I love this game — I always have — so I want to go out on top. If that means stepping on some toes . . . getting in someone's face . . . I don't care because I'm going out a WINNER!"

Nance pounded his chest fiercely as he made his last statement and then hobbled into the trainer's room to continue the rehab treatment for his injured ankle. The rest of the clubhouse sat in contemplative silence. Each player knew the reward of making the playoffs, both collectively and individually, but it was not going to be just the notoriety or the financial gain. Making the playoffs meant they didn't have to worry about ending up on the wrong side of Ellis Nance, and that was a situation no one wanted to consider.

With a renewed sense of purpose, Boston went out to lay one on the T-Birds. It helped that Keith Lash was on the hill that night. Detroit could manage only five hits, four of them singles, as they were baffled like so many other teams this season by the off-speed magic of the veteran left-hander. Thursday did not go as well. Detroit, relieved to be away from the junk pitches of Lash, belted four Darren Haddad fastballs over the fence in an eight to two rout. Hannegan had little luck in either game, going just one for eight at the plate.

The last place team in the Midwest Division, the Kansas City Blues, were the visitors for a weekend four-game at Patriots' Harbor. Boston had swept a series in Kansas City right before the All-Star break, and the team with the worst overall mark in baseball was a soft touch in the first two games of this set. Raul Gomez and Nick Ertle, with some late inning help from the bullpen, strolled through the feeble Blues lineup, making it five straight against Kansas City. The victories had added value since Baltimore was dropping two in Saint Louis. The C's deficit was back to six games with thirty-five games to play. Hannegan had bounced back as well, banging out four hits, including his eighteenth homer, and driving in three runs in the two games. Ryan was feeling comfortable again at the plate, and he looked forward to the stretch run.

There had been no repercussions from his meeting with the commissioner, and Ryan was grateful for that. Actually, the baseball media's attention was on George Goodman of the Atlanta Scarlett who failed a recent drug test. Goodman had been suspended for the remainder of the season, a crushing blow for Atlanta who would now have to fight for a playoff spot without their talented catcher and a player short on their roster. It was too bad for Goodman, but as far as Hannegan was concerned, it was the best thing that could happen for him. Just keeping flying under the radar, Ryno, all the way to the playoffs.

THE COMPANY YOU KEEP

Woody Watson, *New York Tribune-World*
www.TheTruth.com

NEW YORK (AP) Growing up, my sainted mother always told me that it was important who my friends were. "People will judge you by the company you keep" was the admonition from Mom anytime I had a connection with someone she thought was unsavory. At times, it might not have seemed like the way to have fun, but her advice was good. The Baseball Big Leagues have had the same philosophy as Mom ever since the betting scandal back in the 1920s. At the entrance to every clubhouse in the Game is a large sign with bold lettering that warns all those associated with baseball must avoid any involvement with gambling, or people who participate in sports betting, legal or otherwise. Seems pretty clear doesn't it? Apparently not to Ryan Hannegan of the Boston Colonials. Sources from within baseball's hierarchy have confidentially informed me that the Boston All-Star met with BBL officials earlier in the week to discuss his connection to a Vladimir Titov. Titov, a former athlete from the Soviet Union, apparently is a relative of Yegor Karpin, the reputed boss of the so-called Russian Mafia. General Hopkins and his staff wanted to know the details of Hannegan's relationship with the Russian due to allegations that Karpin and his associates are involved in a number of illegal activities, including gambling. The Baseball Big Leagues are satisfied that any connection between the Colonials' outfielder and the Russian is not a concern at this time. Insiders have told this reporter, however, that the investigation is not closed. It would be a devastating blow to Boston's hopes for the postseason if Hannegan were to be suspended, particularly with the continued absence of the injured Junichi Nakata. As you know, any suspension of this nature by the Commissioner's office also results in the loss of a spot on a team's twenty-five-man roster. As far as baseball is concerned, the big question this morning is: RYAN HANNEGAN, DO YOU KNOW WHO YOUR FRIENDS ARE?

"Not you, you sunnavabitch," Ryan screamed after reading Watson's syndicated column in the Sunday morning *Boston Journal*. Whether General Hopkins was using Woody Watson as his stalking horse to bring this issue out into the open, or it was just the New York writer finding some informant to fuel his vendetta against Hannegan, this was going to be trouble. Hannegan took his time getting to the ballpark that morning, risking a fine for being late in order to avoid too many questioning eyes in the clubhouse. In fact, the room was deserted when he arrived; the team and coaching staff were already underway with their pre-game rituals. *Hopefully, D.P. will cut me some slack; I'll just go about my business and keep my head down until the storm passes.*

As he was bent over, tying the laces of his shoes, a large shadow came over him. Looking up, Hannegan found the imposing presence — all six feet nine inches and two hundred seventy-five pounds — of one Ellis Nance. The Boston pitching ace was making his first start since his ankle injury, and he had been in the trainer's room getting a quick rubdown from Pete Hudec.

"You wanna tell me what's up, Hannegan? I told y'all earlier in the week that I would get in the face of anybody who messed with my final shot."

Staying seated, Ryan figured a friendly response might help lighten the mood, so he gave his teammate a large smile.

"Relax, big fella; it's just that damn Watson, still trying to get me. Just like I told Hoppy at my meeting, I met this guy at the union's fantasy camp last winter. I figured he was another one of those wannabes who come to those things. I had no clue about who he was."

"I don't give a shit if he was the freakin' Wizard of Oz. The General is checking things out, and I don't like it. With Ju gone, we can't afford to lose your bat or a spot on the roster for the last month of the season. I'm warning you, Hannegan; you don't want to mess with me about this 'cuz I will make your life ... well, you don't want to know!"

With that Nance stormed away before Hannegan could make any further response.

"Not good ... not good at all," Hannegan said softly. With a large sigh he added: "Hoppys, and Watsons, and Big E's ... oh my!"

Ellis Nance took his fury to the mound with him for his first appearance since suffering the high ankle sprain against Cleveland back on the twentieth of June. Kansas City didn't stand a chance. The Big E knocked down their leadoff hitter, Pepe Frias, with the game's first pitch. He then proceeded to blow away the first six hitters, striking out five in a clinic in how to pitch fast, faster, fastest. In all, the veteran fireballer went seven standout innings to win his ninth decision of the season.

Position players tend to leave a teammate alone when he is pitching, and Ryan Hannegan had no problem in giving Ellis Nance a wide berth in the dugout when the Colonials were not in the field. The confrontation in the clubhouse was more than enough incentive to ignore any thoughts of distraction from Woody Watson's latest attack on him, and the Boston center fielder banged out a pair of hits in five at-bats. After just seven hits in the first seven matchups with Kansas City, he had notched six safeties in fourteen at-bats on the weekend.

Hannegan sprinted as hard off the field at game's end as any time during the contest because he did not want to hang around in the clubhouse to be grilled by the local media . . . or to get any more of the third degree from some of his own teammates. It was the old *Tenth Avenue Freeze Out*. Even Doc is giving me a w*hat-the-hell-is-going-on* look. Taking, maybe, his quickest shower since he was a kid, he brushed by the advancing media without comment on his way out of the clubhouse, not more than ten minutes after the game. One member of the media, however, was not going to allow Hannegan off without an explanation.

"RING . . . RING . . . RING . . . Hi, this is Ryan, leave a message after the beep . . . BEEP."

"Pick up, Hannegan . . . I know you're there."

Ryan had sat in introspective silence in his living room since returning from the ballpark. He knew that Jayvee would try to connect with him at some point; he just wasn't certain if he wanted to talk with her right now. *She's probably in her media-mode, and that's not good.* To avoid her, however, would only make the eventual contact even more difficult. He picked up the phone.

"Hey, Jayvee . . . I figured you'd know I would be here."

"Where are you going to go with something like this going down? I knew you would be at home. Now tell me, what's this is all about?"

Hannegan walked around his condo with his portable phone, trying to ease his nervousness.

"I met with General Hopkins and some of his people on Tuesday. Henry Lamirand was there too. I figured it was more about my higher blood count."

"But it wasn't was it?"

"No. They asked me about Vladimir Titov. I told them what I knew and they seemed satisfied. When I didn't hear anything else, I thought the case was closed."

"Remember when Titov and his uncle stopped by the table at the restaurant in New York back in the spring? I asked you then, Ryan, if you knew who Yegor Karpin was."

"Sure I remember — and just like I said to General Hopkins on Tuesday — I told you my only hookup with Vlad was as his coach during fantasy camp. That was the first and only time I have ever met Yegor Karpin."

Jayvee was not mollified.

"If I remember, didn't one of them say they were counting on you? I'm mad at myself for never following up on that. What were they talking about?"

Hannegan grimaced and paused before answering. Damn, I knew she would do this to me. Maybe the pause was too long for Jayvee.

"Remember what I told you, Hannegan! I'm a journalist, and if you slip up, I will be all over you because it's my job. Now tell me, what were the Russians talking about?"

"Honestly, Jayvee, I have no clue."

Hannegan hoped his voice had conviction.

"I had a lot of laughs with the guy at fantasy camp; we played some cards and that was the extent of it."

Jayvee DellVecchio's reporter's antennae were still twitching, but she felt she had to trust Ryan with his explanation . . . for now. The pair's conversation lightened in tone, and they made plans to get together on Friday for lunch when the Colonials came to New York for their next series with the Horsemen. Hannegan wrapped up the call with a final comment.

"Just remember, Ms. DellVecchio, what I have said to people ever since I came under the microscope with all this stuff. Do you think I would honestly get caught doing something that could ruin the best year of my life?"

"And you just remember what I told you, Mr. Hannegan: DON'T MESS IT UP!"

With that, the two professed their love for each other and ended their conversation. After clicking off the portable phone, Hannegan exhaled loudly and sank back down in his couch.

The operative phrase, my love, is DON'T GET CAUGHT. Only a month to go — thirty-four games — and then it will all be over. You can do it, Ryno . . . you have to. Rising from the couch, Hannegan went over and softly began to hit his head against a wall.

Maybe doing a Sandoval wouldn't be the worst thing that could happen, he tried to convince himself without success.

· SIXTEEN ·

Ryan Hannegan's difficulties continued in the final week of the homestand. He went hitless in the Monday night loss to the Blues. Whether it was the result of his confrontation with Ellis Nance, the growing isolation from his teammates, or the Sunday night phone conversation with Jayvee, he didn't know, but he was feeling the pressure.

The situation did not improve on Tuesday when he was called in for a meeting with Paul Simonton and D.P. Perryton. Simonton was seated at his desk in the executive offices of the Colonials. The Boston G-M had an icy stare for Hannegan while D.P. leaned against a nearby wall, head down, pawing aimlessly at the carpet with his right foot.

"I have received the information from your meeting at General Hopkins's offices last week . . . and I am wondering why I ever let Dudley talk me into picking you up last season. You have been nothing but trouble for this organization."

"With all due respect, Mr. Simonton, I don't care what you think. I have given the best I've got for the Colonials ever since I came to Boston. If you don't like it — just like I told you in Detroit — you can kiss my ass!"

Paul Simonton rose angrily from his chair to confront his player. He was as big as Ryan, but Hannegan had never seen Simonton do anything athletic except run.

"I'm tired of all of this. I don't care if you are the boss, if you want some of me, let's go."

D.P. Perryton showed some of his speed from his playing days and got between the pair before things took a bad turn.

"Settle down, both of you. Ryan, you don't want to do anything stupid and Paul, do you really want to find yourself on the wrong end of this?"

Simonton, his face fiery red, made motions like he still wanted to mix it up with Ryan, but it was all for show. He would not have fared very well against the stronger player if they had come to blows. Simonton moved away from Hannegan and Perryton to go back to the desk, but he did not back down verbally.

"I've wondered all season how you have produced the way you have. My statistical evaluations of your career keep telling me that you don't have the ability to do this well — unless, of course, you are getting some help."

"Of course, the infallible numbers system of Paul Simonton. You're telling me the only way I could be doing this is by cheating, that's what you're saying, isn't it?"

"You're batting a hundred points higher than your career average, and your power numbers are far superior to anything you've ever done before. Players don't do these kinds of things at your age unless they find the fountain of youth, or at least the chemical equivalent."

Hannegan raged inside. He strained to keep his anger in check, talking to himself in his mind. *Easy does it, Ryno. No matter how much this son of a bitch deserves it, punching out your general manager's lights is not the way to stay in this league.* He decided to throw some verbal punches of his own.

"I've always suspected you were the one who leaked that information to Woody Watson. Just think how the Boston fans would feel about their general manager if they knew he would be willing to mess up his ballclub just because the spotlight wasn't on him and his boy genius system?"

Simonton leaped from his chair again, but this time remained behind his desk.

"How dare you accuse me of trying to undermine what we are trying to accomplish here. I have had quite enough of your insubordination, Mr. Hannegan. I don't care if you end up being the most valuable player this season, you will not play for my team again next year!"

D.P. Perryton began to protest, but Hannegan jumped in first.

"I wouldn't play for an arrogant son of a bitch like you, no matter what the contract might be . . . and do you want to know why? It's because you don't have the balls to cut me loose right now like you want to. You need me too much, Mr. Baseball Boy Genius, and you know the fans would kill you if you did."

Ryan turned to his manager who had the expression of someone who had just been told his life savings had been wiped out.

"D.P., I'm sorry you've gotten stuck in the middle of this. You're the best skipper I have ever played for, but I won't let this piss-ant jerk me around anymore. You do what you have to do. I'm out of here!"

Hannegan stalked out of the office, not certain what his immediate future would hold, but feeling better about telling off Simonton for the second time this season. He won't to do anything right now; he can't afford to with Ju out. The asshole needs me too much. But you are out of here, Ryno, when the year's done, that's for sure.

The state of things did not change on Wednesday. A curt phone call from Paul Simonton that morning informed him he had been fined for arriving late to the ballpark on Sunday morning. It was only a five hundred dollar fine, so Hannegan didn't see any sense in filing an appeal through the Players Association. He'd let Simonton have his small victory. Woody Watson followed up his Sunday column with another shot at Ryan and the demand for action from General Hopkins. There was nothing new in the report, but the New York writer seemed to take a perverse delight in rehashing the circumstances behind Hannegan's connection with Vladimir Titov. Emboldened by his clash with Paul Simonton, Ryan sloughed off the latest Watson diatribe as no big deal.

Unfortunately, some teammates did not take the same stance. No one openly questioned Ryan — like their general manager, they needed Hannegan's services too much — but an undercurrent of mistrust had definitely grown toward the Boston center fielder. Even Doc expressed his concerns.

"We go back a long way, Ryno — half of our lives when you think about it. I just hope you know what you're doing because right now it sure seems like you're headed into some dangerous shit."

It had been a long time since Hannegan had seen Dennis Soos that serious.

"Doc, you've been like a brother to me, more than just a friend since ... since forever it seems. All I am asking you to do is trust me."

"You know I've got your back; I always have had since we were kids. Why don't you just tell Watson and all the rest of them to fuck off?"

"That's what he wants, don't you see? He wants a battle because he's always going to have the last word. No matter what I say, that pompous S.O.B. is going to twist it around for his benefit. Hoppy and his office haven't found any evidence warranting a suspension, so why should I even bother to answer any of them?"

Hannegan told Soos about his meeting with the Boston general manager the day before, and that brought a smile to Doc's face.

"Boy, when you climb into something, you go all the way, Ryno. I wish that prick would challenge me sometime. It would be the last challenge he would make, that's for sure! I just hope you know what you're doing."

"Don't worry about me, Doc. Like I have told everyone all along: Do you think I would get caught doing something that would jeopardize the best season of my life?"

Soos shook his head, and with a small smile, slapped Hannegan on his knee. Doc then trudged off to the trainer's room for the quick rubdown and nap that has been his pre-game routine for a number of years. Hannegan leaned back on the stool in front of his open locker until his head lay against the back wall, inside. Hidden among the jerseys, pants, and other paraphernalia, he could contemplate his situation without being bothered by the prying eyes of the rest of the people in the clubhouse.

The Wednesday night game with the Wranglers was the first with Dallas since the beanball war that injured Junichi. A few of the players talked about it at the batting cage before the ball game, but that was a month ago and the intensity from that afternoon in Dallas had waned. Not so for the Boston fans; the crowd was a screaming throng, demanding retribution. As a precaution, umpires reminded both teams that any action like that in Dallas could result in a quick thumb. Darren Haddad was the Colonials' starter, and he worked through the first three innings without any real difficulties and looked like he had a good rhythm going.

The Colonials struck quickly in the bottom of the first.

"The Hurricane, Fernando Horrado will lead things off for the C's. Ryan Armijo winds and delivers... swing and a liner into left center, that's heading for the wall... Horrado rounding second... he'll go into third standing... it's a leadoff triple."

One out later, Hannegan lofted a fly to medium-deep right field to drive home Horrado with the game's first tally. It was the eighty-fifth run driven in by Hannegan on the season. The C's added two more runs in the second inning to push their advantage to three.

Darren Haddad didn't have good command in the fourth, giving up three hits and a walk that resulted in a pair of runs for the Wranglers. His pitches were all over the place.

"Two on, two out and a one-two count on Danny Gonzalez; Haddad checks the runners... here's his pitch... UP AND IN and down goes Gonzalez. Gonzalez is screaming at Haddad as Mark Allen steps in front of the Dallas hitter. The Wranglers are on the top step of the dugout... home plate umpire Dave Price is trying to keep things from getting out of hand."

The Boston righty was able to finish off the inning without incident, and Hannegan was the leadoff hitter in the bottom of the frame. Ryan Armijo, the lanky lefthander for Dallas, ran a slider away for a first pitch strike, and stayed outside with a cutter that Ryan was right on, just missing it as he fouled it straight back to the screen.

"Two strikes the count now on Hannegan, who knocked in the C's first run with a sacrifice fly. Armijo winds and delivers... Fastball in on Hannegan and he goes down. That might have caught him on the right shoulder."

As he lay in the dirt, Ryan heard the Boston crowd screaming for blood.

"Dave Price is out in front of the plate, because here come the Colonials. Well, I thought the Colonials would be coming..."

Tom Kingery, the Boston broadcaster, assumed Armijo's plunking of Hannegan would cause a cavalry charge out of the dugout. He was surprised when only Doc Soos and D.P. Perryton made a move towards home plate. In fact, some Colonials didn't get up from their spots in the dugout.

Ryan dusted himself off as he got up, and with a nod toward Armijo that said it was no big deal, he headed to first base while a shower of boos rained down on the Dallas pitcher. Hannegan looked over at the home dugout and not many met his gaze in return. His expression was one of resignation as he thought so that's how it's going to be is it? Screw em ... I'll just keep playing my game.

Price, the veteran umpire that he was, did not eject Armijo since Hannegan's reaction made him believe the pitch had simply gotten away from the southpaw. The Colonials would go on to claim a seven to four win over the Wranglers but continued their up-and-down play by losing the following evening, leaving Boston a game behind second place New York. Hannegan ended up 0-3 with the RBI on Wednesday, and then took the collar the next night. He was pressing big time, and as the team flew to New York for a crucial series with the Horsemen, the crossroads were fast approaching.

The financial world calls it the triple-witching hour when three events take place at the same time — often with catastrophic results. Friday, August third was a triple-witching day for Ryan Hannegan.

A TIME FOR ACTION

Woody Watson, *New York Tribune-World*
www.TheTruth.com

NEW YORK (AP) More light has been shed regarding the investigation of Boston outfielder, Ryan Hannegan by the Baseball Big Leagues. As exclusively reported here on Sunday, Baseball has been looking into the connection between Hannegan and Vladimir Titov, a relative of Yegor Karpin, the reputed head of a Russian organized crime ring in this country. Originally, the inquiry seemed to center on the pair's relationship only as far as the BBL was concerned about Titov's gambling ties. Now a much larger issue may come into play. Vladimir Titov was a rising star in the heavyweight division of freestyle wrestling in the Soviet Union in the late 1970s and early 80s. Titov was successful on the international level, competing in the 1980 Olympic Games. He did not compete in the '84 Games in Los Angeles due to the Soviet boycott, and shortly thereafter, he suddenly disappeared from the sport amid allegations of illegal supplement use. No charges were ever filed against Titov by the International Amateur Wrestling Federation because he retired from competition. Sources have further revealed to this reporter that Titov allegedly became involved, and remains active, in the underworld trafficking of banned substances to Olympic athletes and other competitors. Some investigators believe Titov was a part of the distribution of synthetic EPO, the blood hormone, as well as a new blood-enhancing product, Repoxygen, that has tainted recent bicycle racing competitions around the world. These products are virtually undetectable in blood or urine tests, except for the potential for a higher red blood cell count. Sound familiar? According to reports, Hannegan and Titov met at a fantasy baseball camp last winter. Hannegan reportedly told investigators he has had no further contact with the Russian. In light of blood samples that have shown a higher red cell count, and the fact that he is having an unbelievable season, this reporter wonders if that is all there is to Hannegan's story? Despite earlier criticisms over my dogged pursuit of this investigation, it is clear that Commissioner Hopkins needs to take a stand.

The haughtiness of Woody Watson was not unexpected, but the story still turned Ryan's stomach when he read it. He was already dreading the obvious confrontation sure to come with the New York media this weekend. With Dave Bock back from his sixty-day suspension, this information would make the storm blow that much stronger. Questions were not just being raised by the New York media, however.

WHO'S ON FAUST?

Terry Tate, *Boston Journal*

NEW YORK (AP) With apologies to a classic story of old and the greatest baseball comedy sketch ever written, fear has struck at the very heart of the Colonials' nation. Ryan Hannegan, the star centerfielder for the Colonials, has become embroiled in a controversy that just won't go away. *Why*? According to Abbott and Costello, *Why* is the leftfielder, while the man patrolling the middle of the outfield is *Because*, and that's appropriate *Because* fans want to know *What* is going on? I know, I know, *What*'s on second, but hang with me here. Questions arose earlier this season when Hannegan's blood tests showed a red blood count higher than normal. Despite the protests of some, a logical explanation seemed to have been found. Now that has all come into question with the recent revelations that the Colonials' best hitter this season may have a connection to a gentleman alleged to be heavily involved with gambling and other illegal activities. *Why* (yes, he's in left) would a player hook up with a known gambler when the rules in baseball are clear about avoiding such a relationship? *Why* (don't start with me now) would a player in such a situation not make any public comment about his fate? *Because* (and this is appropriate since that's centerfield where you play) we who love the Colonials have a right to know, Ryan. *Because* your decision to remain silent raises more questions, we cannot help but wonder *What*'s the deal here (at second base or any place else). Give us a reason to understand and an answer to our questions. Legend has long told the story of a man *Who* sold his soul to the devil in order to achieve great things. The tale relates how this bargain ultimately comes to a bad end. The problem here is that it will be the Colonials and their fans, and not just our dealmaker *Who* (stay with me, I am getting to it) will suffer. The devil doesn't always have to be a great-horned serpent breathing fire,or a temptress with dangerous charms. Sometimes, the devil may be a large Russian with questionable connections and the threat of dangerous things. So, our question, Ryan Hannegan, is an important one: *Who*'s on Faust? Say it ain't so, Ryan . . . Say it ain't so!

Shocked would be too strong of a description for Hannegan's reaction to Terry Tate's column because he had an appreciation for Tate's abilities as a journalist. That didn't mean, however, there wasn't some pain. *Damn, Terry, I thought you were on my side?* Hannegan remembered Kevin

Kyle's admonition back in spring training not to cross Terry Tate. Ryan wondered if perhaps he had gone over the line.

The final shot arrived shortly after Hannegan had finished some room service breakfast and the stack of newspapers he had had sent up from the hotel's newsstand. Like a number of players around baseball, he had taken to using an alias for the hotel registry in order to maintain some privacy. Outside of the hotel personnel and Billy Seghi, the Colonials' director of travel, only one other person knew that Hannegan was registered under the name of Jacques DeFarge, in honor of one of the characters from his favorite book, *A Tale of Two Cities*. When the phone rang late that morning, he knew exactly who it was.

"I was hoping you would call. They've got the artillery out and I needed to hear from someone on my side."

"Then let's hope this isn't friendly fire."

"What are you talking about, Jayvee?"

"I mean, I think Terry Tate is right. Ryan, you have to stand up and answer all these questions."

God, doesn't anybody understand? She's just like Doc.

"I can't, don't you see? I'm damned if I do and damned if I don't. There is NO PROOF that I have done anything wrong. If I try to answer the allegations from Watson, or from Tate — or even YOU, for that matter — there is no proof of my innocence either. The media is always going to get in the last word, so why try and fight it. I'm not giving them anything."

That was not what Jayvee DellVecchio expected to hear, and Ryan could almost feel her temperature rising through the phone line.

"You mean you won't even talk to ME about this?"

"It's what I have said all along, Jayvee. Do you think I would get caught doing something that would jeopardize everything I have worked for in my career?"

"That's not answering the question, Hannegan. Yes, you are having a great season ... your best ever. But you do know Vladimir Titov — remember I have been with you when he has been around — and he does have a shady reputation. You'd clear up all of this mystery if you just told people that you have nothing to do with all of this."

"That's what I thought I did at General Hopkins's office! Apparently that's not GOOD ENOUGH FOR ALL OF YOU MEDIA TYPES."

"MEDIA TYPES! So now I'm a MEDIA TYPE?"

"That's not what I meant, Jayvee. I'm just fed up with this constant barrage of questions."

"Then, let's end it all with one question, Hannegan: Are you involved with this guy in doing something wrong?"

Sighing loudly, Ryan answered:

"Jayvee . . . you know I can't . . ."

"You mean if I ask, you won't give me a simple answer?"

"Don't go there, please!"

"All I'm asking, Ryan . . . is YES or NO . . ."

"And all I'm asking, Jayvee, is that you just TRUST me . . ."

"What's it going to be, boy? YES or NO?"

"I can't . . ."

With that, the phone went dead and Hannegan never felt more alone in all his life.

· SEVENTEEN ·

RYAN RODE THE subway to The Hollow for the Friday night opener of the series. He enjoyed his anonymity during the ride, mindful it would end the minute he stepped foot in the clubhouse. The reception was as expected. Many of his teammates avoided Ryan altogether, while Ellis Nance scowled as he brushed by on his way to the bathroom area. Even Dennis Soos avoided eye contact when Hannegan looked his way. If the Colonials were going to give him the silent treatment, that would certainly not be the situation with the media. A cluster of reporters was gathered around his locker with pens, microphones and cameras ready. Fortunately, Bart Danburg, one of the Colonials' media officials, was on hand to referee.

"Anything to say, Hannegan, about today's stories?"

"I have no comment . . ."

"Is it true about you and Titov? What about Yegor Karpin?"

"Again, I have no comment . . ."

"People are saying this Russky taught you how to juice without getting caught?"

Hannegan turned and glared at the reporter who had asked the last question. He continued to stare at him until the reporter turned away, embarrassed. All the while, the questions continued to rain down upon him. Ryan's response was to make no response. He simply sat down on the stool in front of his locker and began to undress, oblivious to the crowd around him. Seeing that Hannegan was done dealing with the whole affair, Danburg cut off the rest of the questioning.

Normally, a player can find sanctuary from the public side of the clubhouse by escaping to the trainer's room, off-limits to the media. No such luck for Hannegan since that day's starting pitcher usually rests in there before the game, and tonight Ellis Nance was taking the hill. Ryan wanted no part of another potential confrontation with the Big E. After pulling on his uniform, he leaned back into his locker, and covered by the clothing that was hanging there, closed his eyes. He didn't move from that position until he had to take the field for pre-game activities.

A murmur rose from the crowd already in the stadium when Hannegan came out to join his teammates for their stretching routine in front of the visitors' dugout. Marty Fergus and Hector Santana turned away from him as Ryan approached, so he found a spot up the third base line, away from the rest of the Colonials. He had an ironic thought: *me, myself, and I . . . not much of a crowd to hang with.*

D.P. Perryton was uncertain how he was going to handle the situation. He leaned up against the top railing of the visitors' dugout with Tommy Gladstone alongside him. Ryan's a good man, he was certain. He couldn't believe he would be cheating. But there was the blowup with Simonton, and those BBL security reports talked about his connection to this Russian.

"Tough spot, D.P. What are you going to do?"

Tommy Gladstone, the skipper's confidante, knew the dilemma for his friend.

"I'd sit him down, Tommy, to avoid all this bullshit, but dammit, we need his bat in the lineup."

"Without Ju, I don't see any other choice, D.P."

"I guess I just have to hope he can handle all this crap through the rest of the season. Or until whatever happens, happens."

Nearly a full house was on hand that evening at The Hollow, looking for the Horsemen to add to their advantage for the final wild card spot in the American Conference. New York had a one game lead on Boston, and with slugger Dave Bock back from his sixty-day suspension, the Horsemen were confident about their postseason chances. Ryan Hannegan's problems with the bat continued with an 0 for 4, and he had now gone hitless in his last seventeen official plate appearances, dropping his batting average to .354.

The news was better for the Colonials with Ellis Nance maintaining the power he displayed in his start against Kansas City. Showing no effects from the month-long absence because of his ankle injury, the Big E simply dominated New York. The giant righthander went the distance, striking out eleven, even though it took him just over one hundred pitches to claim the complete game victory. It was the tenth win of the season for Nance, and the four to one triumph moved Boston back into a tie for second with the Horsemen.

Rummaging around in his hotel room the following morning, Hannegan was surprised by a knock on the door. What the hell? Doesn't a *Do Not Disturb* sign mean anything? He had already eaten breakfast, so it couldn't be room service. Walking over to the door, Ryan peered through the peephole, hoping that it might be Jayvee on the other side. It was a bellman, holding a small package.

"Excuse me, sir," the bellman explained after Hannegan had opened the door for him, "... but I wasn't sure how to handle this. We received this package this morning, addressed to a Ryan Hannegan of the Boston Colonials, but we have no player registered under that name here at the hotel. Someone from your team told our front desk that we should give it to you. Is that okay?"

Ryan didn't appreciate the Colonials' travel director's disclosing his identity and thought with his luck, the package could easily be a bomb. Hannegan glanced at the return address on the package sent through one of those overnight delivery companies. It was from his ex-wife in Florida. What would Deirdre be sending me?

"That's fine ... I'll take it," Hannegan said as he directed the bellman to put the package on a nearby table. "Here's something for your troubles."

Hannegan handed the young man a five-dollar bill and then walked him back out of the room. Checking to make sure the Do Not Disturb sign was indeed hanging on the knob, he returned to the package. Tearing off the seal, Ryan dumped out its contents on the table: a piece of a paper ... and a teddy bear. He recognized the toy; it was the bear he had given Michaela after his divorce with Deirdre had become official. He opened the paper that had been folded in half and read a note from his daughter:

> *To my forever favorite player: I LOVE YOU, DADDY!*
> *Your Daughter, Michaela*

Tears welled in Hannegan's eyes as he picked up the teddy bear. *It's Norm! Michaela sent me Norm.* Ryan had given it to his daughter after his divorce and told her that it meant that nothing was going to change between them. Michaela named him Norm, like normal, to remind her of the promise her father had made. The stuffed animal was a little threadbare in spots — a sure sign that he had been hugged frequently. Ryan ached for a hug from his daughter right now. Hannegan grabbed the phone near the bed and dialed the number for his ex-wife's home in Florida.

"Hello . . ."

"Deirdre, it's Ryan. How are you?"

"Better than you from what Owen and Michaela tell me. I take it Michaela's package must have arrived?"

"I just got it here at the hotel."

"She's pestered me non-stop the last couple days saying she needed to do something to help you. She even took the money to pay for the shipping out of her allowance. I'm not sure I understand what this is all about, but it was really important for her to do something for you. Hold on, let me get her."

After a short pause, Hannegan's daughter got on the phone.

"Hi, Daddy! Did you like it? Was that okay?"

"I sure do, Kiddo. I couldn't figure out who would be sending me something here in New York and then I saw the return address on the label. Good ole' Norm!"

"I've been reading the stories online about you, Daddy, and watching on TV, and it sure sounds like you're in trouble, and I . . ."

"It's not as bad as it sounds, Kiddo."

Hannegan could hear the concern in his daughter's voice.

"Things always have a way of working themselves out. I don't want you worrying about me . . . I'll be fine."

"Anyway," Michaela continued, ignoring her father's last comment, "... whenever things are tough for me, I always give Norm a big hug and that makes me feel better. He makes me think of you, Daddy, and then things don't seem so bad anymore."

A lump caught Ryan in the throat and he had to regain control before answering her.

"And now Norm is going to take care of me, is that it?"

"You just keep Norm with you, Dad, and he'll take care of everything. Just keep an eye on him though; I want him back when you don't need his help anymore."

"I'll take good care of Norm, Michaela... I promise."

Michaela then switched gears and asked her father about Jayvee and whether he had seen her since he was in New York. Hannegan told her he had spoken with Jayvee, and then made up a story about Jayvee having to go out of town on an assignment. *No way, Kiddo, do you need to know what's happening with Jayvee right now.* The conversation shifted to Michaela's summer activities and the upcoming school year until it was time for Hannegan to leave for the ballpark.

"Thanks for sending me Norm, Kiddo. I'm the luckiest father in the world."

"I love you, too, Daddy. Norm will take care of you; you'll see. Call me soon."

Hannegan reluctantly ended the call. *So you're my protection... is that it, Norm?* Ryan picked up the teddy bear once more. *Protection... just like Junichi's mamori.* Hannegan pulled the small charm out of his pocket. With everything that had gone on over the past few days, he knew he could use all the help he could get, Ryan. He put the bear into one of the plastic laundry bags that were hanging in his closet, grabbed his room key on the dresser, and headed downstairs to catch a cab to the ballpark. In the lobby, Hannegan stopped into the gift shop to get something to read on the ride to The Hollow. As the clerk was ringing up the sale at the cash register, Ryan noticed a small gold chain in the glass display case. He asked that the chain be added to his purchase, paid the cashier, and then put the chain in his pocket.

When he arrived at the visitors' clubhouse, the media ambush from Friday was not being repeated. Since it was obvious Hannegan was not going to talk about the circumstances and the accusations surrounding them, the news folks had moved on to other sources and other stories on this day. At his locker, Ryan sat down, took out the gold chain he had purchased, and attached the mamori to it. Then he placed it around Norm, the teddy bear, and placed the bedecked toy on the top shelf of his locker. Hannegan's sentinel was now standing on duty. Screw them if they want to freeze me out, he thought. It's just not worth worrying about it anymore. I've got a little girl who loves me and that's all that really matters.

Invigorated by his daughter's gift, Ryan was on from the get-go in the second game of the series in New York. He laced a two-out double the opposite way in the first inning, and then scored on a Ramon Morientes single, just beating the tag at the plate with a nifty slide that had him barely nipping the back end of the dish when he skidded home. Keith Lash was the afternoon starter for the Colonials, and he was just as effective as Ellis Nance had been the night before. From the Big E's flames to the finesse of the enigmatic Lash, the New York lineup was rendered powerless in the first two games on the weekend. The soft-tosser was now fifteen and six on the year, the best mark in the American Conference.

Hannegan added another double, a walk, and a second run scored as the Colonials cruised to a six to one win over the Horsemen. Boston had regained sole possession of second place in the Northeast Division. They remained seven games behind front-running Baltimore because the Crabbers had taken a pair at home from the Chicago Fire. Twenty-nine games yet to play in the regular season, and eleven of them were against New York and Baltimore. A postseason spot was there for the taking; all the Colonials had to do was work their way down a path filled with land mines.

The atmosphere was considerably more upbeat in the clubhouse following the game; taking two from your archrivals has a way of doing that. Hannegan was just glad he could melt into the background with his teammates getting back to thinking about the games and not all the crap going on off the field. The reporters were gathered around Keith Lash's locker as well as Ramon Morientes who drove in three of Boston's runs. Hannegan was sitting at his locker, slipping on his socks, when Dennis Soos came over.

"What's with the teddy bear?"

"Oh . . . so you're talking to me now?"

"Guilty as charged. I was an asshole about things yesterday, Ryno, and I'm sorry for that. With all the stuff going around, I forgot about what a real friend is supposed to be."

"Forget about it. Everybody around here is waiting for me to screw everything up. I'm not going to blame you if you go with flow on this."

"No, Ryno, we've been friends a lot longer than I have been a teammate with the rest of these guys. I just have to trust that you know what you're doing. You do know what you're doing, don't you?"

Hannegan smiled but offered no response to Soos' last question. Instead he explained about the teddy bear from Michaela and why she sent it to him.

"It might be corny, but it made me feel better."

"Well, that was evident in the way you played today. That's the best you've swung the bat this week."

"You got that right. Hey, I've got the greatest daughter in the world . . . and a friend who told me not too long ago that I needed to just let go with a little W-T-F."

"Amen, brother! Now you're talking! Don't worry about me . . . I've got your back."

"Thanks, Doc, that means a lot to me. I know what I'm doing here. I'm just gonna take things as they come and give it the best I've got."

"Whatever you say, Sundance."

With a big smile, he slapped Hannegan on the back and headed over to his own locker to finish dressing.

On Sunday afternoon Nick Ertle lost for the first time in more than a month. Dave Bock roused the large, sun-baked New York crowd with a three-run homer in the first inning, and that was the start of a big offensive showing for the Horsemen after they had scored just two runs in the first eighteen innings on the weekend. New York scored nine times off Ertle and the Colonials bullpen, plenty of support for their ace, Buddy Pickens who won his twelfth decision of the season.

The Horsemen might have won the war against Boston, but the personal battle between Pickens and Ryan Hannegan still went the way of the C's center fielder. Ryan went two for four including his nineteenth homer and he drove in three. Pickens glared at him as he circled the bases on his dinger, and Hannegan was not surprised when the New York righthander sent him sprawling in the dirt in his next at-bat. *If it makes you feel better, asshole.* Ryan tipped his helmet at the pitcher, infuriating Pickens more. *Just keep bringing it, Pickens. I'm ready for anything you've got.*

The only thing that dampened Ryan's spirits was the lack of any word from Jayvee.

"... Beep. Hi, Jayvee, it's me again. I know I called a couple times earlier, but I thought maybe your answering machine was screwed up and you didn't get my messages. Anyway ... give me a call on my cell or here at the hotel when you can ... I would love to talk to you."

Hannegan had sent flowers to her apartment and to her office at DBC — just like he had right after they first met — but Jayvee had refused to accept them. He knew she was pissed, but how could he make things up with her if she wouldn't even talk to him?

It was back to Boston for a short six-game homestand, including the final four games of the regular season against the Crabbers. Anything less than a sweep would all but snuff out the Colonials' hopes of tracking down Baltimore. Darren Haddad got the nod from D.P. Perryton in the opener on Friday evening. After a tough July, the twenty-five year old righty had knocked off Dallas in his first August start, and this game turned out to be a near carbon copy of his result against the Wranglers as Haddad worked seven strong innings, with a three-run inning in the fourth his only blemish on the night. Hannegan banged out two more hits, including his twentieth round tripper, a three-run shot in the fifth inning that put Boston ahead to stay. Ryan couldn't remember ever hitting twenty homers in a season — even in Little League. *No wonder I've got people all over me,* he thought with chagrin. *Well, screw 'em. I don't give a damn what they think.*

The Crabbers showed why they were the defending American Conference champions in the next two contests. They played little ball on Saturday, using several bunts, a couple of stolen bases, and some timely hitting overall to best Raul Gomez. On Sunday it was a barrage of power: four home runs off Nick Ertle before D.P. could get to his bullpen. The game turned into a slugfest, but it was too much Baltimore in a thirteen to seven triumph.

Hannegan had one of Boston's six hits on Saturday, and then rapped out three singles on Sunday and scored four times overall. He was the final out in the game when he was eliminated in a force play at second in the bottom of the ninth. Hannegan took his time dusting himself off at game's end, and when he finally started off for the clubhouse, he was surprised to see Nick Hamilton waiting for him.

"Hey Ryan, let me see the back of your jersey for a minute."

Hannegan turned away and then turned back to the long-time All Star.

"I thought it was a forty-seven. I wondered if, maybe, it had been replaced by a bull's eye. How you holding up?"

Controversy for Nick Hamilton would be if he was caught putting chocolate in his milk, so Ryan wasn't sure what to make of this. Players on the other teams had not said much to him since the double barrel blasts from Woody Watson and Terry Tate. His Boston teammates had reacted to the controversy because of the potential impact on the team if Hannegan were to be suspended, but it was not the same for the opposition.

"I'm just taking things one pitch at a time, Nick. I did my appearance with the commissioner and that's all I'm going to say the rest of the year. If they catch me doing something wrong, then suspend me like they're supposed to. Otherwise, just leave me alone."

Hannegan wanted to speak his thoughts aloud, but he didn't. *I can't believe I'm having this conversation. I don't think I've ever said boo to this guy since I came into the league.*

"Let me give you a little advice. My father was a lawyer, and you know how those guys are with using Latin phrases. I don't remember most of them, but one has always stuck with me. When I was leaving for the minors for the first time, he told me *Illegitimi non carborundum!*"

Chuckling, Hannegan asked: "What's that supposed to mean?"

"Don't let the bastards wear you down!"

With that, Nick Hamilton gave Hannegan a small salute with two fingers to the bill of his cap and headed off for the field. Ryan stood there watching the Baltimore star until he disappeared down the tunnel that led to the visitors' clubhouse. "I'll be a son of a bitch!" he said aloud and one of the guys on the grounds crew working nearby spun around in surprise. With a laugh and his own salute, Hannegan ran off to the Boston dugout and down the tunnel.

The next night, Nick Hamilton might have thought twice about his advice to Hannegan because the Boston center fielder played his best game of the series. For the third time on the year, Ryan belted out four hits, and he just missed matching Hamilton's feat of hitting for the cycle. Hannegan had two doubles, a triple and a single to push his batting average to a season-high .370. The Colonials had gained a split with the Crabbers — not the sweep they needed — but it sent a message to Baltimore that the C's would be ready if the two teams met in the post-season. New York had won three of four in Minneapolis against the Lumberjacks, so the two bitter foes were tied once again. Twenty-one games to play.

· EIGHTEEN ·

PUSHED TO GREATNESS?

Terry Tate, *Boston Journal*

BOSTON (AP) With just three weeks remaining to the regular season, there are a number of certainties regarding our Colonials: It's time for the final push. The team will need a big push to make it. Can the C's push themselves to the postseason? Will the Colonials have the right stuff when push comes to shove in the pennant chase? What remains uncertain is from where the push will come, at least as far as Boston's offense is concerned. There is no guarantee that Junichi Nakata can return this season as he recovers from the damage done to his face by that Jeff Sibel pitch back on July 8th. Ramon Morientes and Dennis Soos are having solid years again, and Horrado and Kyle are pesky enough at the top of the lineup to bother most pitchers around the conference, but is that enough drive to enable Boston to get back to the playoffs? The certainty — if you want to get right down to it — can come from Ryan Hannegan. The C's centerfielder is having the season of his life despite a whirlwind of controversy around him. His constancy in the middle of the order has kept playoff hopes alive. What pushes Hannegan? Has he been given an unfair boost with some concoction that so far has eluded detection? Or is it simply a matter of an athlete pushing himself to achieve the absolute best he has to give? Back to the uncertainty again, because Ryan Hannegan has chosen to make no comment regarding what has pushed him to greatness this year. I have been a part of the clamor, insisting that an explanation has to be given, but this young man has remained steadfast in his silence: he is not going to be pushed. From wherever his boost has come, baseball has not seen a hitting performance like his since Mike DellVecchio some thirty years ago. It is an absolute certainty to this reporter that if the Colonials are to push their way into the postseason, the main offensive impetus will have to come from Ryan Hannegan, no matter what propellant is driving him to his greatest season.

Thanks for cutting me some slack, Terry, but I'm still not saying anything to anybody about all of this. People are going to think what they want to anyway.

The intriguing element of the Tate column was the reference to Mike DellVecchio. Any baseball fan over the last forty years knew of DellVecchio's impact on the game, and few would not be aware of his magical season in 1971 when he batted over .400 — the last player in the BBL to do so. To be connected to anything that Mike DellVecchio had accomplished on the baseball field left Hannegan humbled. After all, nothing previously in his professional career had warranted any such comparison. If Michaela reads this, she's going to give me a giant *I told you so*. She had made the same connection between her father and DellVecchio back in May. The DellVecchio comparison was another reminder that now it had been nearly two weeks since he had heard from Jayvee. No response to his phone calls, bills from florist shops for flowers that never were accepted upon delivery, he was starting to wonder if their differences were irreconcilable. *She's not killing me on her show, at least. Just let it play out, Hannegan. If she's gonna call . . . she'll call.*

Wednesday brought a twi-night doubleheader with the Detroit T-Birds.

"... swing and a ground ball towards short ... Dermont up with the ball ... fires to first and Hannegan is out number two here in the eighth. Unless Detroit has a huge rally in the ninth, Hannegan's longest hit streak of the year ends at nine ..."

The irony of his phenomenal success this season was the fact that Hannegan did not have any extended batting streaks. The hitless night didn't handicap the Colonials as Keith Lash continued his drive towards The Outstanding Pitcher Award with his sixteenth victory. Detroit, the cellar dwellers of the Northeast Division, was on the short end of a game against the lefty for the fourth time in five decisions.

Darren Haddad won his second straight in the nightcap, giving Boston its second doubleheader sweep, equaling a two-win affair against Kansas City the week before the All-Star break. Hannegan bounced back in the second game with a three for four evening, including a double. Ryan's base hit in a 12-3 loss the next night kept his batting average at .370, and barring a major collapse down the stretch, he was going to win the batting title for the American Conference.

"Ryno, rub some of your mojo on me."

Doc Soos was in a grumbling mood following the game. The Boston third baseman had been in a slump the past two weeks, and his falloff had affected the lineup, especially since Junichi was still not playing.

"So, you're just like the rest of them, Doc? Figuring I must be doing something illegal to hit this good?"

Soos was red-faced until he realized his friend was teasing him.

"You know what I mean ... I'm just trying to find something to get it going again."

"No sweat, Doc ... I know what you meant. I'm not worried about you; you'll come up big when we need it!"

"I sure hope so. We just can't fall short again. By the way, Ryan, do you know what you're hitting?"

"It was a baseball the last time I looked, Doc."

"Bite me, Ryno; I mean you're hitting .370 if the number on the scoreboard during your last at-bat was accurate. Maybe you CAN crack the big 4-0-0 just like back in school?"

"Hold it right there. That was fifteen years ago ... with an aluminum bat ... and with pitching that wasn't anywhere as good as what we're going to see down the stretch. I'm thrilled with how my hitting has gone this year, but I'd be delusional to think that it could get any better than it is right now."

"Yeah, but think of it. Nobody has been as close to four hundred this late in a season since Jayvee's old man did it when we were kids. Hell, I don't even remember when he did it. What were we? About five or six?"

"Something like that. I think Mike DellVecchio's accomplishment is safe from me . . . let's not get crazy here."

"Speaking of the DellVecchio family and crazy . . . how's it going with Jayvee? You'd better not be crazy enough to screw up the best thing you've had going in years."

Ryan related to Soos what had happened with Jayvee when the team had been in New York two weeks ago. He also told him about the calls not being returned and the flowers that were not accepted.

Soos whistled before he responded.

"Boy, you really must have pissed her off. That's a lethal combination there when you're talking about a temper: Italian and Irish. What are you going to do?"

"Keep leaving messages, figuring she'll have to answer them sometime . . . even if it's to tell me to go to hell."

"Hang in, my friend. You two are a good fit; something will work out."

With that, the pair packed their travel bags to get them on the equipment truck for the final road trip of the regular season. The clubhouse boys do much of the packing for a team's trip, but the players still are responsible for the personal items they want to bring from their home clubhouse locker. Hannegan shoved several items into his bag and then reached up for the teddy bear on the shelf of his locker.

"Hey, Doc! You want some of my mojo? Come here a minute . . ."

Dennis Soos had finished packing his travel bag and he was placing it with the pile of other bags that would be loaded onto the equipment truck and eventually the charter flight to Cleveland. The Colonials' captain walked back over to where his friend was sitting, holding the teddy bear.

"When Michaela sent her bear to me, she said I should give him a giant hug whenever I needed some help. It's worked for me, so if that's my mojo, maybe you should do it too?"

Soos was a little embarrassed about the suggestion that he hug a teddy bear to help him with his hitting troubles. Baseball players are a superstitious lot, however, and the Boston third baseman was afraid to pass up a chance on anything that might help him get going again.

"Don't worry. Norm won't tell anyone."

With several nervous glances around the room to make sure no one was paying attention to them, Dennis Soos took the toy from his friend and hugged it tightly.

"What's the little medallion?" he asked as he returned it to Hannegan so that Ryan could place it into his travel bag. "I don't think I have ever seen anything quite like that. Where did Michaela get it?"

"Actually, that's mine; a gift from Junichi earlier in the season."

Placing the bear into his bag, Hannegan placed his arm around the shoulders of Soos.

"Come on, I'll tell you all about it on the way to Cleveland."

With that, the two men — friends for more than twenty years — headed for the team buses that would take the Colonials to the airport to begin their last regular season trip. The Colonials were to play seven away games: five in Cleveland and two with St. Louis. After seven straight on the road, the Colonials would finish the year with eleven games at The Harbor — their longest homestand of the season. If the team was going to make it to the BBL playoffs, it would be because they earned it down the stretch. The way the schedule was playing out, the season could well come down to the final weekend in Boston: five games with the Horsemen!

The city of Cleveland sits on the shores of Lake Erie, where the term *lake effect* can strike terror into the hearts of its residents during the winter. Often, the winds whip down from the north across the water, dropping large quantities of snow on the city and its surrounding area with a chilling force that can cut right through a person. What Clevelanders don't tell visitors to their fair town, however, is that Lake Erie can also have a strong impact during the summer. Thunderstorms rise up suddenly over the lake with some frequency, and the lake can also serve as a giant humidifier when a heat wave comes up from the south.

"Hot" and "sticky" were the adjectives being used by the Cleveland weather people for the Colonials' series with the Ironmen. The temperature on Friday afternoon was in the low nineties, while the humidity was over eighty percent. The forecast was calling for a chance of late thunderstorms throughout the weekend, with no heat relief in sight throughout Boston's visit. It was hot in Dallas when the C's played the Wranglers right before the All-Star break, but they had that steady wind blowing in Texas. In Cleveland, the wind was as limp as the American flag hanging from its pole near centerfield or the clothes that hung on the sweltering populace this mid-August weekend. Then things began to change.

The Ironmen were taking their batting practice before the game when the Colonials came out to stretch.

"Damn. Look at that sky."

Kevin Kyle pointed to some large thunderheads gathering out over Lake Erie just outside the ballpark. The sun had been brilliant in the sky when most of the players had arrived earlier in the afternoon.

"Auntie Em, Auntie Em. It's a twister," Kyle joked.

The wind was no longer a passive participant: dust storms were building on the infield, and the batting cage shuddered from the force of the breeze. No sooner had Boston begun its pre-game hitting when the skies opened. The rain was heavy, falling in thick sheets swirled by the wind. The Cleveland grounds crew fought valiantly to get the tarpaulin over the field, but the infield took a good drenching before it was finally covered.

When the rains come during a team's final trip to a city during the regular season, the problems multiply. The game has to be played — there's no chance to reschedule later — meaning a doubleheader the next day if the game is postponed, or a long wait at the ballpark hoping the rain would end.

"Man, look at it come down! Didya' ever see it like that?"

J.R. Cook was taking swings at imaginary pitches in the visitor's dugout in front of several teammates seated on the bench.

"We had a game once in Atlanta," Boston catcher, Mark Allen responded, "where I swear the rain was horizontal. You couldn't see ten feet in front of you."

Eric Polick joined in the conversation:

"This sucks. Now we'll have to play back-to-back doubleheaders. In this heat, that's going to be a bitch."

"Maybe not," Cook said, "this place drains great. If it ever stops, I bet we could play."

Lehman Field in Cleveland, named after one of the team's most popular owners, boasted one of the best drainage systems in all of professional sports. Reportedly, the field could handle more than five inches of rain per hour without any serious problems, and this Friday night downpour was going to test that reputation.

D.P. Perryton walked over to the group after speaking with the umpires.

"The groundskeeper says, according to the radar, there's a break later on, but that's not going to happen for a couple hours. The umpires want to know what we want to do: sit or play two tomorrow."

"Shit, D.P.," Kevin Kyle piped in, "we'll hang all night if we don't have to double up tomorrow."

"That's what I thought, so I told him for now we were willing to wait it out. Settle in, boys, we're going to be here for awhile."

Eventually, the Boston players drifted from the dugout back to the visitors' clubhouse when it became apparent the storm was not going to let up anytime soon. Several groups began to play cards, others watched a video on the big screen TV in the corner, and more went off to the batting cages to get in some swings to stay sharp. Earlier in the season, Hannegan might have been an active participant in one of the card games, but he had received few invitations to join in the action over the past several weeks. Instead, he returned to his locker to catch up on some correspondence and fan mail.

Hannegan had brought a stack of letters with him from home. Many were from younger fans with baseball cards enclosed for his autograph. When he could, he would add a small note with the cards, encouraging the children who had sent them to stick with whatever they hoped to accomplish, just like he had in his life. Some of the cards were sent by memorabilia dealers, looking to profit from Hannegan's sudden notoriety. Where do these guys find these? I didn't even remember that card from the T-Birds. Depending on his mood, Ryan would either sign the cards and return them, or dump them into the circular file. Tonight was a night for the garbage. Sorry, guys.

Taking care of the correspondence took more than an hour, but the rain showed no signs of stopping. Hannegan grabbed a cup of chicken noodle soup — it might be the middle of a heat wave, but a ballplayer still has to have his soup — and strolled back up the tunnel to the dugout for a closer look at the weather. Sipping his soup, he stood in a corner of the dugout that was protected from the rain. Lehman Field looked like Armageddon with lightning flashing, thunder booming and rain falling in torrents. Baseball in Cleveland didn't appear likely anytime soon.

"Come on, Ryno, let's take some hacks. It's going to be a long time before we get out there."

Doc Soos had walked up the tunnel, toting his bat and one of Hannegan's.

"Not a bad idea. Gotta keep sharp, Doc."

The hitting session also helped break up the growing isolation Hannegan was feeling from his teammates . . . and Jayvee. Part of the beauty of baseball is the opportunity to lose oneself in the simple pleasure of swinging a piece of wood at a small leather ball. Hannegan and Soos took turns working on their swings while the other fed the balls into the pitching machine. They both felt invigorated as they returned to the clubhouse to get a weather update.

The rain had begun a little after six, but the official delay did not begin until the game's scheduled start time at seven. It was now almost nine, and the latest word from the Ironmen's head groundskeeper was the storm was going to last for at least another hour.

"The umpires want to know what we want to do."

Dennis Soos was polling his teammates to determine if they still wanted to wait out the storm or play a doubleheader on Saturday.

"Doc, is it really going to stop tonight, or are they just bullshitting us?"

"They're telling me ten o'clock. Either that or we should start building an ark. How the hell should I know? I'm not a weatherman for chrissakes."

Teammates hooted at their captain but agreed that waiting would still be better than playing two on Saturday and two on Sunday.

Hannegan went back to his locker, grabbed his laptop that he had brought with him from the hotel, and moved into the dining area where there was a phone outlet so he could go online. An e-mail from Michaela was waiting for him. *Kiddo, you are something.*

> *Hi Daddy. How are things in Cleveland? I saw on DBC that your game is being delayed by rain. I hope you get this message. How's Norm? I hope he's helping. Don't lose him because we both need him.*

His daughter was still going full speed with her efforts to boost his spirits. *I wonder what you'd say, Kiddo, if I told you that Mr. Soos has been hugging your bear, too.*

I saw in the newspaper today that you're batting .370. That's great. Just like I said, you and Jayvee's dad hitting .400. Wouldn't that be cool? How's Jayvee? When are you going to see her again?

Who knows? In these moments of isolation, Jayvee's absence in his life was unbearable. *I miss hearing her voice — not the one on TV — but the one that gives me grief, the one that would tell me how much she needs me and I need her.* No matter what the final tally of his accomplishments this season might be, they would be empty without her participation.

Hannegan's ruminations were interrupted when someone in the clubhouse announced that the rain had finally stopped. The grounds crew was beginning to remove the tarp, and without any more precipitation, there would be baseball this evening in Cleveland. *I gotta remember to email Michaela back, he reminded himself.*

Ryan clicked off his laptop, took it back to his locker, and then joined his teammates already out in the dugout. The grounds crew worked in the mud and wet grass, trying to make the diamond playable again. The players waited impatiently, eager to start anew. Even before the grounds work was complete, the players began to drift out in pairs to the edges of the field where they played catch. Others swung their bats at imaginary pitches, and still more raced across the outfield grass to stretch their legs.

A fastball from Cleveland righthander Park Sun Hong pierced the plate at 10:23 p.m. and the game was underway, more than eight hours after many of the players had arrived at Lehman Field. The official length of the delay was three hours and eighteen minutes, and surprisingly, a decent crowd remained when one considers what they had sat through and how long they had waited. The game remained scoreless until Hannegan doubled in the sixth inning with one out, and after a Morientes strikeout, Dennis Soos brought him home with a solid base hit.

"Score one for the mojo of Norm," Hannegan yelled to Soos standing at first base when he returned to the dugout.

"Don't lose that bear!"

Doc Soos was beaming. It was his first timely hit in a number of games. Cleveland would rally in their half of the sixth, scoring two runs on a Jimmy Craddock homer. That was the only blemish on Nick Ertle's performance that night, and when Marty Fergus hit a round-tripper pinch-hitting for Ertle in the top of the seventh, it ensured Old Reliable wouldn't be tagged with a tough-luck loss. As it turned out, the Colonials scored two more times in that seventh inning. The bullpen slammed the door on Cleveland, and Nick Ertle ended up with his ninth win of the campaign.

Deadlines were long gone and the late night local news had already been put to bed by the time the game was over, but there were still a few writers and broadcasters that came to the clubhouse for post-game analysis. On the road, a team bus usually heads back to the hotel forty-five minutes to an hour following the last out. That allows the media to get their information from the manager and players, while giving the team a chance to shower and grab something to eat from the post-game spread. The standard operating procedure meant the Colonials' bus back to the nearby hotel would not be leaving Lehman Field until almost two o'clock in the morning.

"Let's grab a cab, Doc. The bus isn't going to leave for a half hour. I can use the shuteye."

Hannegan and Soos walked out the players' entrance but there wasn't a cab in sight.

"What do you think, Ryno? It's not that far back to the hotel; let's hoof it."

"Works for me. I can't see going back in and waiting for the bus."

The pair began what should be about a ten to fifteen minute walk back to the team's hotel. In no time, the perspiration was flowing thanks to the still humid night. Nevertheless, Soos and Hannegan enjoyed the time on the nearly deserted streets, unwinding from the game and even talking about things that had nothing to do with baseball. As they walked up the sidewalk to the hotel's front entrance, the team bus rolled up to the door. Apparently Billy Seghi had advanced the clocks in the visitors' clubhouse without anyone noticing and he got everyone on the bus in less than thirty-five minutes.

"You guys look great," Nick Ertle teased, "but you're supposed to take a shower after the game."

Their shirts were soaked through with sweat from the walk. Ryan and Doc laughed along with the joking at their expense. Hannegan was the first to get off the crowded elevator, his room was on the seventh floor, and the catcalls to take the stairs rained down on him as he exited. Entering his dark room at the end of the hall, he was surprised by the blinking light on his telephone.

Hannegan flipped on the light switch near the door and set his bag down on the bed. Two-fifteen . . . damn, I've got to hit the rack. Who's calling me anyway? He punched in a few numbers on the phone's keypad to find out. He had again checked in under his alias, so unless it was Jayvee, he had no idea who had called for him, especially since he had asked the hotel to block all incoming calls. If people need to reach me, they know my cell.

"Ryan, this is Clare DellVecchio. The hotel told me you were taking no calls, but being Mike DellVecchio's widow still has some advantages in this town."

"I know you are at the ballpark as I make this call, but I needed to get in touch with you. Jessica has told me all about your recent troubles, but I won't get into that. The last time you were here, I extended a return invitation, and I want to keep my promise to you regardless of whatever difficulties you may be going through with my daughter."

Ryan wondered what Jayvee would say if she knew her mother had called him?

". . . It will be a nice home-cooked meal — I hate cooking for just myself anymore. Plus, it would give me an opportunity to show you some of the scrapbooks I made for Mike that you wanted to see. Indulge an old lady and please come."

Clare DellVecchio concluded the message with her telephone number and one more plea to accept her invitation. Ryan was flabbergasted. He hadn't been able to make any contact with Jayvee for more than two weeks; now here was her mother inviting him back to her home. Hannegan had found Clare to be a remarkable woman — and a gourmet cook — and he had looked forward to a return engagement . . . that is, until he had his big blow-up with Jayvee.

Hannegan looked up at his reflection in the mirror. Jayvee is going to be pissed! It's just a question of who will get the worst from it: me or her mother?

After a fitful night of sleep, and a short one because of the long rain delay, Ryan awoke still uncertain about what he should do. He was meeting Doc in the lobby in about fifteen minutes to catch a cab to the ballpark, so he had to make up his mind quickly. Jayvee is probably going to kill me for doing this behind her back, but I don't want to disappoint her mother. What the hell, things can't be any worse with her anyway.

Hannegan had talked on the phone with Clare DellVecchio several times since that first meeting in the spring, and he had thoroughly enjoyed each conversation. Clare had rekindled some of the memories of the mother he had lost when he was seventeen. Their personalities were a little different, but Clare was the closest thing to Erika Hannegan for Ryan since she had passed away.

"Hi, DellVecchios' residence. No one is here to take your call right now, so please leave a message . . . BEEP."

"Hi, Mrs. D. . . . thanks for the invite. I would love to stop by. If the food is anything like the last time, this will be a treat. I've got your directions, so I'll see you after the game. Thanks."

Hanging up the phone, Ryan found himself feeling better already: at least there was one other female in his life besides his daughter that was still speaking to him. He hurriedly put on some clothes, threw a few things into his bag, and headed for the elevators to meet Dennis Soos in the lobby.

The long rainstorm of the night before had done nothing to improve the weather conditions in Cleveland. The temperature would again hit the nineties for the afternoon tilt with the Ironmen, and the humidity was going to be worse than the day before. The muggy conditions and the short overnight turnaround had both teams moving at less than full speed as the game began under the broiling sun. The lone exception was the Colonials' starting pitcher, Ellis Nance. D.P. Perryton had wisely sent Nance back to the hotel on Friday when it became clear the rain delay would be a long one. The Big E had no complaints, and he certainly looked fresher than any of his teammates that afternoon. Nance would have to change his undershirt and uniform top several times during the course of the game — at two hundred seventy-five pounds, a man does work up a sweat — but he had more energy than anyone else out on the diamond.

Ryan felt sluggish at the start, but the anticipation of the upcoming evening at the DellVecchio house gave him a boost.

"... Hannegan swings and slices a ball down the left side ... FAIR, just inside the line. Horrado rounds third; he will score ... Hannegan digging hard for second. Here's the throw, the slide ... he is SAFE. Ryan Hannegan with an RBI double and the C's lead it three to one."

He collected another hit, Dennis Soos added a home run, and that was more than enough support for Ellis Nance in the four to one Boston triumph. Following the game, an exhausted group of Colonials — grateful for the air-conditioning in the visitors' clubhouse — slowly pulled off their sweat-soaked uniforms.

"I'm getting too old for this," a red-faced, still perspiring Dennis Soos grunted to Hannegan who was sitting next to him in front of their lockers.

Ryan reached over and patted Doc's midsection that had grown more than a little since their younger days together.

"You mean with this body like a god, you're tired? I thought you would be gearing up for another one of your killer post-game workouts?"

"The only workout I'm going to be doing is calling room service when we get back to the hotel and then spending the rest of the evening laying on my bed in my underwear and doing finger exercises with the remote control."

Just vegging did sound nice after what they had gone through over the past eighteen hours — and with a doubleheader in the same conditions less than twenty-four hours away — but dinner with Jayvee's mom was more appealing. Ryan cleaned up with a shower and a shave. The visiting clubhouse manager had arranged a cab and one was waiting outside the players' entrance as he departed Lehman Field. The post-game traffic had thinned out nicely, so the taxi had little trouble getting on the freeway. Less than twenty minutes later, it was pulling into the DellVecchios' driveway. Clare DellVecchio came out of her home to greet Hannegan while he was paying the driver. She hugged him and kissed him on the cheek.

"It's great to see you again, Ryan. I was afraid you might not want to come."

She stepped back from their polite embrace, like she was giving Ryan the once over.

"On the radio, Herb Chandler made it sound like you had a very good game again today. My . . . what a season you are having!"

"It went well, but Ellis was the guy for us. The Ironmen couldn't do much against him."

"He does appear to be all the way back from his injury, doesn't it? But, listen . . . we don't need to talk out here in the heat . . . it's nice and cool inside."

Clare linked her arm with Ryan's and they proceeded up the driveway towards the front door. As they reached the front steps, she pulled away.

"Oh, I almost forgot. I need to get something from the freezer in my garage. Go on in . . . the front door's open . . . I'll be there in a minute."

Hannegan offered to get what she needed from the garage, but she shooed him toward the door. It was still quite bright outside, so it took a moment for Hannegan's vision to adjust to the darker surroundings inside. The air conditioning was most welcome, but that wasn't what froze Ryan in mid-stride as he entered the living room from the front foyer: across the room stood Jayvee.

Hannegan wasn't sure how he should react, but Jayvee took care of that by rushing across the room to wrap her arms around him in an almost desperate hug. Some tears flowed for both of them as they held each other tightly in the middle of her mother's living room.

"When she was in high school, that would have gotten you in trouble, Mr. Hannegan," Clare DellVecchio announced as she re-entered her home, ". . . especially from her father. But now I think it is one of the nicest things I have seen in a long time!"

Jayvee and Ryan pulled away quickly, somewhat embarrassed. It is ironic how often children still get flustered displaying affection when it is observed by a parent — no matter how old the children might be.

"Jessica and I have had some long talks over the past few days, and I told her she shouldn't let that temper of hers ruin things between you."

"Mother!"

Clare DellVecchio walked over and put a hand on a shoulder of each of them.

"It was the same way with her father and me when we first got married. We both had tempers . . . and were MULE STUBBORN! In time we learned nothing should keep us apart if we truly loved each other . . . and I loved that man until the day he died!"

Ryan and Jayvee looked at each other with sheepish smiles and clasped hands. Satisfied, Clare DellVecchio excused herself to finish dinner preparations. The pair stood facing each other; neither one knew who should go first. Finally, Jayvee, wiping away the remnant of a tear, began.

"I'm sorry now I didn't answer any of your calls. And the flowers were quite lovely, but I was so mad at you I couldn't accept them. I was hurt and I was angry because you wouldn't tell me what I wanted to know."

The pair sat down on the nearby couch as Hannegan answered her.

"You're a journalist — the best I know in baseball — and I didn't want you to compromise yourself just because of me."

Jayvee started to protest, but Ryan stopped her with a wave of his hand as he continued.

"If I told you nothing about the accusations and innuendos was true, I was afraid you'd put your credibility in jeopardy by trying to defend me when not many others in your business were. Or worse, that people might think you were supporting me only because of our relationship."

"Ryan, you know I have told you I would not change how I do my job just because of my feelings for you."

"Sure, I do," Hannegan replied, pausing for a moment to give her a brief, tender kiss on her lips. "But how many others would believe that?"

Ryan paused again, took Jayvee's hands into his, and looked for a long time into her eyes before he continued.

"It would be just as bad if I told you I WAS doing something wrong. I'm sure that would have changed things between us. And even if you did try to minimize the whole situation because you wanted our relationship to continue, or because you wanted to shape what people would think about it, it still wasn't going to work. I just decided the best thing to do was simply to ask you to trust me, and then say nothing more."

Jayvee sniffled and wiped another tear from her eye.

"Mom asked me what I felt in my heart, and I told her I wanted to believe you. She said no matter how many disagreements she and my father might have had through the years, it all would somehow work out if she followed her heart. She said if I truly love you, then I should trust you know what you are doing."

"This is hard for me, Ryan. I have always been able to get what I wanted in my life — sports, school, my job . . . even with men — but it wasn't working here. I guess I have to trust you DO know what you're doing because that's what my heart is telling me to do."

Hannegan removed his right hand from Jayvee's and caressed her face. They kissed again, this time with more feeling and for a longer time. When at last they parted, Ryan flashed his smile: one of the things Jayvee liked best about him.

"I told you to trust me; that I would never get caught doing anything to hurt you. Nothing has changed. All I am asking is you trust me — it will be all right."

"Get caught?"

"Can you ever stop being a reporter?"

Jayvee shrugged her shoulders and smiled softly. The subject was now closed between them . . . or at least until Ryan was ready to tell her everything.

"Okay, let's eat; I'm starving!"

"That's the only reason you want me, Ryan Hannegan . . . just for my mother's cooking."

"You're just figuring that out? I thought you were a better reporter than that!"

Jayvee grabbed one of the pillows on the couch and playfully tossed it at Ryan. He blocked it with one arm, and then grabbed her with the other to move into the dining room where Clare DellVecchio was making the last of her dinner preparations. Even with the uncomfortable weather conditions, Clare still made an Italian feast for the evening meal.

"These are great, Mrs. D," Hannegan said with a mouthful of a tomato broiled with cheese and bread crumbs.

"Thank you, Ryan. I'll have you know that those tomatoes come from the back yard. Jessica's father loved to grow tomatoes, and I guess I've kept the tradition going."

The main course was a juicy steak prepared Tuscany style, the area of Italy from which Mike's ancestors came. A salad of zucchini — also from Clare's garden — sweet red peppers and green onions in a seasoned oil and vinegar mix accompanied the steak, with a Chianti classico to finish the meal.

After some Italian ice for dessert, the trio moved into the den where the DellVecchio women pulled out the scrapbooks Clare had made through the seasons of her husband's career. It was fascinating for Hannegan to get such a personal perspective of Mike DellVecchio's exploits, especially with all the photos included with the various newspaper and magazine clippings.

"These are beautiful, Mrs. D. . . ."

"If you don't start calling me Clare, Ryan, I'm going to get mad at you and my temper is much worse than my daughter's."

"Sorry, Mrs. D. . . . I mean, Clare. All these color photographs, where did you get these?"

"Mike took a lot of those himself. He loved the private side of his baseball life . . . his time with his teammates. That was more important to him than all these clippings I saved."

Ryan was particularly taken with the scrapbook from the 1971 season when Mike DellVecchio batted .402. It was a milestone that had not been achieved in baseball for a period of time, and not at all since that season.

"Mrs. DellVecchio, are these all the clippings? I would have thought there would have been more?"

"Actually, that was a lot of coverage for the time. I think Jessica's father was happy he was not playing for the Horsemen or one of the other teams from cities larger than Cleveland because the press interest probably would have been greater."

"Daddy was on The Ed Sullivan Show, I remember that. I thought it was so neat that my father was on the same show as Topo Gigio!"

"Topo Gigio?"

"You know, that little Italian mouse that was on the show all the time."

"Oh yeah, that puppet was so stupid."

Hannegan's needle had found its mark, drawing a punch to his shoulder from Jayvee.

"Mike wasn't bothered by the press when he played," Clare Dell-Vecchio broke in to turn the conversation back to baseball. "He thought it was part of a player's responsibility to use the reporters and others who followed the game as a way to show people what was really happening."

Hannegan pulled away from the scrapbook and turned towards Clare with a questioning look.

"Didn't he worry about guys who had personal agendas? I can think of one who's got one going with me right now."

Clare DellVecchio took hold of Hannegan's arm in that soothing manner that mothers do for their children.

"There were people like Woody Watson when Mike was playing; he just didn't let it bother him too much. He figured if he was straightforward with everybody, then the fans would eventually see someone like a Woody Watson wasn't telling the whole story."

"When I got started in the business," Jayvee added, "Dad told me if I was consistent with everyone, then it wouldn't be the end of the world if I had to be critical from time to time."

"That was good advice. I know some of the people in the game think you're where you are just because you're beautiful and the daughter of a Hall of Famer."

Jayvee blushed and lowered her eyes, but she appreciated his compliment.

"But most of us respect you for the way you go about your job. You're thorough, you don't jump to conclusions too quickly, and most of the guys think you know what you're talking about."

"So some of them think I'm attractive . . . and some of them think I know what I'm talking about . . . and what about you, Mr. Hannegan?"

Now it was Ryan's turn to blush lightly as the DellVecchio women chuckled at his expense. He turned back to the scrapbook and zeroed in on the final weeks of that '71 season and the pressure Mike DellVecchio must have felt about hitting over .400.

"Clare . . . what was it like with your husband in those last days when he was trying to reach .400?"

"I don't know if there was that much pressure about hitting .400 for Mike. I think he was more concerned about the Ironmen winning the pennant. There had been players previously who had batted .400 in a season, and I know Mike didn't think he would be the last one."

"I can appreciate that, but he still had to know that not many have ever done it, and how special it would be."

"Jayvee's father was proud of all he was able to do in his baseball career."

Clare DellVecchio looked at her daughter with a smile.

"Jessica can tell you, however, that nothing meant more to him than winning."

"Mom's right, Ryan. Dad always said personal accomplishments don't mean anything if they don't help the team. He was always preaching that if you did your job to help the team win, that would be the best feeling any athlete could have."

"I truly believe Mike would have given up that milestone in a heartbeat if it meant his team could have won that year."

"Okay, okay. Knowing what I do about your husband's and your father's career, I am sure the Ironmen winning was the most important thing to him. It is for me, too . . . I have never been to the playoffs — much less The Showdown — and I'm going to do all I can to get the Colonials to the postseason. But, I mean, how did he handle it . . . the pressure?"

Hannegan closed the scrapbook and set it on the coffee table. Getting up from the couch, he stretched and several of his joints cracked, drawing a laugh from both women. Looking seriously at Clare DellVecchio, Ryan had to know how her husband did it.

"I've had a hard enough time keeping focused with all this stuff going on around me. I can't imagine what it would be like dealing with trying to hit .400."

"It was easy for Mike. His philosophy was to just let it go. All those distractions didn't matter when he stepped on the field for a game. Baseball was always fun for Mike, and he never let outsiders get in the way of that."

"Just let it go . . . You're not the first person to tell me that."

"It's very good advice, Ryan. Have fun with all of this because it may never come your way again."

Clare DellVecchio reached up and squeezed Hannegan's right hand, while Jayvee stood and lightly kissed him on the cheek. Regardless of what happened for the remainder of this season, he knew he had their support. He and Jayvee sat back down on the couch and the trio continued to look through the scrapbooks, the women recalling at various times facts about different episodes in Mike DellVecchio's career. This quiet evening with just of the three of them was the tonic Hannegan needed after the physical grind of the past few days. Finally, it was time for Ryan to head back to the hotel.

"Jayvee, take my car to drive Ryan back; he doesn't need to get a cab."

"That's okay, Clare. Jayvee doesn't need to be driving me back downtown. The cab will be fine."

He wanted to go slow with this making up process with Jayvee, and she didn't seem to object to his plan. Soon enough a taxi's headlights shone through the front window when it pulled into the driveway. Mother and daughter walked Hannegan to the front door to make their good-byes.

"It was wonderful, Mrs. D. — everything. The food was great, I loved the scrapbooks, and of course, for whatever you did to make this stubborn woman give me another chance."

Clare gave Ryan a big hug while Jayvee stuck her tongue out at him.

"You are always welcome here, with or without my daughter."

"Thank you very much, Mother. I love you, too."

Another quick hug for Hannegan and Clare went off to clean up in the kitchen. Jayvee walked out with Ryan to the taxi waiting in the driveway. Along the way, she slipped her hand into his.

"I'm going to the doubleheader tomorrow, so I'll see you around the dugout before the first game."

"Are you working or just checking things out?"

"Working! The bosses at DBC think I should keep my eye on the pennant races and a certain hitter who is flirting with destiny."

"You're kidding! They really want to follow this .400 thing? I'm not even that close!"

"Closer than you think. You've been hitting nearly .500 over the past couple of weeks, and you're nearer to .400 at this point of a season than any player in a long time. Of course, they want to follow this story . . . and I'm not going to be the only one if you stay hot."

"As long as you're there, I'm not going to worry about the rest of them."

"Just be smart, Ryan. Don't get caught up in all of it and make yourself crazy. Like Dad said: just let it go when you step on the field."

"Thanks for the advice, Ms. DellVecchio . . . and for giving me another chance."

"You're on probation, Hannegan . . . don't mess it up!"

Jayvee reached up and kissed Ryan firmly, but quickly, before running back up the driveway to the house. Hannegan called out to her.

"How about I take you and your Mom out for a pizza or something after the games tomorrow?"

Jayvee gave a *will-see* gesture and then went into the house. Hannegan got into the cab for the ride back downtown. He imagined the driver thought it strange to see his fare sitting in the back seat with a contented smile that didn't leave his face the entire trip. Ryan headed right to bed when he got back to his room — he needed the rest if he was going to play two in the heat tomorrow. For the first time in weeks, sleep came quickly, peacefully. It was a deep sleep minus the crunch of a warning track that was his usual nighttime visitor.

· NINETEEN ·

THE SUNDAY DOUBLEHEADER was no different weather-wise: searing temperatures and high humidity. The conditions, combined with the Ironmen's so-so record, made for a small crowd at what otherwise would have been a standing-room-only event. There were additional members of the media on hand, however, making Jayvee's prediction an accurate one.

"No wonder you've got that shit-eating grin on your face, Hannegan! Your lady's in town," Marty Fergus yelled over to Ryan.

Jayvee had come up from the Cleveland dugout tunnel as the Colonials stretched in front of the visitors' dugout.

"Now I know why he's been walking a little funny this morning," chirped Kevin Kyle.

Kyle didn't see Jayvee coming up behind him. Her full skirt ballooned in an orphan breeze as she leaned down as if she was going to whisper into the Boston infielder's ear, but she spoke loud enough for all the players to hear.

"Is that why your hand is a little sore this morning, Kevin?"

Kyle's face turned bright red from embarrassment while the rest of the Colonials howled. Jayvee went off to talk with D.P. Perryton, giving Hannegan a wink as he grabbed his glove to shag some flies in the outfield.

The Colonials' rule for the media was the players would not be available — unless they wanted to be — until they had finished hitting. When it became obvious the additional members of the press on hand that day were there because of him, Hannegan stayed in the outfield as long as possible. When he took his turn in BP, he was part of the final group of hitters, leaving the waiting media just a few minutes of interview time when he was done. Ryan smiled at the circle of people around him — he was following Mike DellVecchio's advice by way of his widow and daughter — and courteously answered their questions with the stock answers professional athletes are so good at giving.

"Ryan, what's it like to be running away with the batting race?" The reporters were jammed around him, their pencils flying. Flashes popped incessantly and black foam microphones dangled above the heads of the crowd.

"I'm really surprised, but thrilled by it all."

"Did you ever believe you could hit this well as a big-leaguer?"

"I'm seeing the ball really well, and my teammates have been very supportive."

"Do you think you can reach .400?"

"Taking it one game at a time . . . that's all I'm trying to do. The most important thing is to help the ball club make it into the postseason."

"What about all the controversy over your blood tests . . . and the association with Vladimir Titov?"

It was Jayvee asking that last question as she stood alongside her cameraman. The rest of the reporters, recognizing her voice, turned around to face her as she made her inquiry and then turned back to Hannegan.

"As I have stated all along to all of you, to General Hopkins, and to anyone else who might ask the question for that matter, I would never get caught doing something jeopardizing this season for my teammates or myself."

"Get caught?" Jayvee asked with a teasing smile.

Hannegan nodded in her direction while giving a knowing grin in return; it was the same exchange they had had in her mother's living room the night before.

"You can make this to be whatever kind of controversy you want it to be. All I'm going to tell you is the Colonials are trying to get to the playoffs and win The Showdown. I'm going to do whatever I can to make that possible."

"Now, ladies and gentlemen, if you will excuse me, I need to finish getting ready for the game," Hannegan concluded, tipping his hat as he exited from the circle.

Kris Fucci was pitching the first game for Boston, while the Ironmen were countering with their ace, Conor O'Toole. O'Toole was having another fine season for Cleveland, but the Colonials had found good success against him, going all the way back to the home opener in Boston in mid-April. The weekend humidity was at its highest point yet, almost as if the air was deliberately pressing down on the players. There was a spring in Ryan Hannegan's step, however. His reunion with Jayvee had erased the emotional strain he had been experiencing, even if it had not been reflected in his efforts, and he loved hitting against Conor O'Toole. Like Buddy Pickens of the Horsemen, O'Toole's pitch selections and locations just seemed to fit well with the hot zones of Hannegan's swing.

"... two outs, nobody on ... no balls and a strike on Ryan Hannegan. Here's O'Toole's pitch: fastball inside corner at the letters, a called strike two."

The heat and humidity might be slowing down the folks in Cleveland, but the stream of play-by-play from Tom Kingery was flowing smoothly.

"... Hannegan steps out for a moment ... takes a deep breath, and now he digs back in with his usual routine of a tug on his right sleeve and a tap to the top of his helmet ..."

O'Toole, the Cleveland ace, was not going to expend extra energy on this hot, muggy day by wasting pitches against a good hitter. The right-hander fired a split-fingered fastball down and away from Hannegan.

"... swing and liner back up the middle ... down goes O'Toole as Hannegan's ball screams into centerfield for a base hit ..."

Ryan took a big turn rounding first base before scampering back to the bag. Conor O'Toole was stomping around on the mound, wiping off the dirt he accumulated before it turned to mud on his already sweaty uniform. He glared over at Hannegan who responded with a shrug of his shoulders.

The game was still scoreless when Kevin Kyle began the Boston third inning, with a base on balls after an eleven-pitch sequence. Conor O'Toole mopped his brow as he waited for Hannegan to settle in for his second at-bat. The Ironmen hurler's uniform top was soaked through — in fact, he looked as if he had been standing under a shower the way the sweat poured off his body. Fifty pitches thrown already and he hadn't even registered an out in the third inning. D. P. Perryton, figuring Ryan Hannegan would see something in the strike zone, decided to send his base runner, Kyle, on the first pitch.

"... O'Toole comes set ... checks Kyle who is dancing out to a larger lead at first ... O'Toole still holding the pose ... holding, holding ... now he delivers ... there goes Kyle ... Hannegan swings and whacks it ... "

Kyle broke for second base the moment O'Toole began his move to the plate, giving him an outstanding jump. Benito Fernandez, the Cleveland shortstop, raced towards second, to await a throw from his catcher on Kyle's stolen base attempt. Ryan smashed the pitch with solid contact. In an act of self-preservation, Benny Fernandez stuck his glove in front of his chest as the ball rocketed to him. The Cleveland shortstop was, literally, knocked off his feet by Hannegan's shot, but he managed to hang onto the baseball. A stunned Kevin Kyle hit the brakes near second, knowing he had no chance to get back to first base safely. Benny Fernandez scrambled back to his feet and brushed his glove across Kyle's chest to complete the unassisted double play.

Hannegan had stopped about halfway up the first baseline. "Well, I'll be a sunnavabitch," he said in a hoarse whisper. "I couldn't hit it any better."

If D.P. Perryton had not sent Kevin Kyle, there would have been no way for Fernandez to catch the line drive. As Ryan crossed in front of the mound back to the Boston dugout, Conor O'Toole looked at him, not so much with a glare this time, but more in disbelief at how hard that ball had been hit. Ryan gave him another shrug and a *what can I say* look: that's just the way baseball is.

The game remained scoreless into the sixth inning when Hannegan had the chance to start things off for the Colonials. Conor O'Toole had allowed only one base runner since Ryan's line drive double play in the third, but the weather conditions were taking a toll on him. For the first time in Hannegan's at-bats against him, O'Toole fell behind in the count, missing with his first three pitches. Hannegan took the next one for a called strike, but he was still in the advantageous situation. The

Cleveland catcher jogged out to the mound for a quick conversation with his pitcher.

"Tough decision here for the Ironmen. Pitch to the hottest hitter in baseball with a 3-1 count or walk him and put a man on in a scoreless game for the C's cleanup hitter, Ramòn Morientes..."

Cleveland decided to take their chances with Hannegan, and that was a mistake.

"...A swing and a drive...WAY BACK...that ball is going and IT AIN'T COMING BACK!"

The ball didn't have to be seen for fans to know it was going to travel a long way. The magnificent crack made by the ball and bat contact told the story. Conor O'Toole couldn't bear to look. With his hands on his knees, he stared down at the ground while Hannegan circled the bases with his twenty-first homer of the season to give Boston a one to nothing lead. In the ungodly heat and humidity of this August afternoon, the Cleveland pitcher's resolve must have finally melted from the Hannegan blast because he served up an even fatter pitch on his next offering to the plate. Ramòn Morientes crushed it, deep into the seats in the upper deck in right. Back-to-back jacks!

That ended the game for Conor O'Toole...and for the Ironmen for that matter. The Colonials scored four more runs, including one driven home by Hannegan on his third hit of the day. D.P. Perryton turned things over to the bullpen, and they finished it off in the six to two victory. Boston had won its third in a row in Cleveland, and they had now posted victories in six of their last seven games to extend their advantage over New York for the final wild card spot.

D.P. Perryton rested Ryan Hannegan, Kevin Kyle and Mark Allen in the nightcap. Ryan protested he didn't need the break, but he had to admit the playing conditions over the past three days had worn him down. He was used as a pinch hitter in the sixth inning for Hank Cummings and drew a walk. The Ironmen's first baseman, Jimmy Craddock, hit three home runs, two off Cummings, and Cleveland won by a seven to one count. The Horsemen, meanwhile, were sweeping a twin bill in Detroit to again close to within one game of the Colonials.

Even without playing in the second game, Ryan felt sluggish as he dragged himself into the shower room. The water was a little invigorating, and he felt more of his energy come back by the time he met Jayvee and Clare DellVecchio, waiting for him outside the clubhouse.

"Hello, Mrs. DellVecchio — I mean Clare. Thanks for coming. It's my treat tonight," Ryan said to Jayvee's mother as he kissed her and Jayvee.

"I'm just sorry I didn't come down until the second game. I was hoping to see you play in person, and a walk as a pinch hitter didn't give me much of a glimpse."

"You should have seen him in the first game, Mom . . . he stung the ball every time up and had a homer too."

"I know, Jessica. I had Herb on the radio while I did some work around the house before coming downtown."

Hannegan put an arm around the shoulders of each woman and started escorting them towards the exit.

"Like I said, it's my treat tonight. Where should we go, Clare? Ask your daughter. I could do Italian seven days a week, and tonight feels like a good night for some pizza."

"There are some wonderful Italian restaurants up on Murray Hill on the east side, but I know a quiet, little place that's near by, just over the bridge."

"Bruno's! I love that place," exclaimed Jayvee, and off the trio went to Clare's car, which was parked in the player's lot — another one of the perks of being Mike DellVecchio's widow.

Clare's suggested restaurant was, indeed, just a short distance from downtown Cleveland on the near west side of town. It didn't look like much of a place. It was a small building with a take-out window on one side of it, and believe it or not, a dilapidated car wash next to its small parking lot. It might have been a nondescript building in one of the older neighborhoods, but the inside told a different story. Hannegan probably would have paid just to come in for the wonderful aromas permeating the place. The owner-chef greeted Clare and Jayvee warmly as they entered the restaurant.

"Mrs. DellVecchio! So good to see you again . . . and Miss Jessica, too."

"Hello, Bruno, it's nice to be here again. Everything smells wonderful." Jayvee smiled graciously, looking as cool as a spring breeze in a white cotton top that was striking against her bare skin. Every male in the restaurant watched her as Bruno escorted Ryan and the two ladies to a table.

There weren't more than a dozen tables in the dining area, with a small bar area alongside, but it had a feel that told you most evenings every table was occupied. On this early Sunday evening, a smaller crowd was on hand, so they had no trouble being seated. Bruno put them at a table in the far corner, and with a flourish, placed napkins on their laps while the wait staff magically appeared with a plate of foccacia bread and a bottle of the house Chianti. Bruno filled their wine glasses and waited while they toasted each other and had their first sip.

"Bruno, Mr. Hannegan here said he was looking for some pizza, so I knew we had to come here. No one makes pizza like you."

"You make me blush, Mrs. D. You know I would always do anything for you and your late husband, may he rest in peace."

Clare DellVecchio made a small nod in response as Bruno turned to Ryan.

"So what type of pizza does the star player of the Boston Colonials like?"

"I'm not the star, but thanks. I didn't know that you were a baseball fan."

"I became one thanks to Mr. D and his family."

Bruno gestured to Clare and Jayvee.

"He would bring in his family and friends after games . . . and even when they weren't playing. I was honored the stars of the Ironmen wanted to come to my little place."

As if on cue, Herb Chandler, the radio voice of the Ironmen, walked in with his wife, Nancy. Herb Chandler was connected with Mike DellVecchio like Hannegan to Doc Soos, so it was logical he too would enjoy coming to Bruno's. Pleasantries were exchanged while the busboys pushed another table over to the one where Clare, Jayvee and Ryan were seated and added place settings and wine for the Chandlers.

Herb and Mike DellVecchio had come up through the minors as teammates in the Cleveland organization, and the couples were inseparable during the husbands' long careers in the BBL. Herb had been the best man at Mike and Clare's wedding. Jayvee had called them Uncle Herb and Aunt Nancy for as long as she could remember.

"I hope you are treating this young lady well," Herb Chandler asked Hannegan as he lovingly squeezed Jayvee's arm. "I consider her one of my daughters, so you better do things right."

"Yes, sir," Ryan stammered in reply, as Jayvee grinned, her eyes twinkling a dare at his befuddlement. He could imagine how it would be if Mike DellVecchio was still around. He knew he'd probably sink right through the floor.

Jayvee kissed Chandler on the cheek.

"You know I wouldn't let any man push me around, Uncle Herb. He takes good care of me ... most of the time anyway."

She added a poke to Hannegan's ribs and a mischievous grin to her last comment. Herb Chandler gave Ryan a stern look, but then broke into a wide smile and slapped him on the back. Herb Chandler knew very well his late friend's daughter would be in charge in any relationship she had. Jayvee had always been that way.

"We were going to have some pizza, Herb," Clare said. "What would you suggest? It's been a little while since I've been here?"

Chandler leaned back in his chair a moment before answering and then the expression on his face beamed as if he had just discovered gold.

"I don't normally have pizza — Bruno knows I'm a veal guy — but no one makes Pizza Margarita like our friend here."

"Pizza Margarita? Is that some kind of Mexican pizza?"

"This is not a Taco Bell," admonished Herb Chandler. "Bruno, illuminate our young man here about Pizza Margarita."

"Pizza Margarita is not Mexican, and it does not have any liquor in it. It was named in honor of the queen of Italy at the turn of the century. It really is quite good, if I am allowed to say so."

The group decided that Pizza Margarita would be the choice and they ordered two of them. Herb Chandler complimented Hannegan on his fine play during the year, but Ryan was more interested in hearing stories from Herb's playing days with Jayvee's father. Nancy Chandler also added a few tales from Jayvee's past, future ammunition for the teasing matches he planned to enjoy with the love of his life. The time passed rapidly, and soon the Pizza Margarita was ready.

"I don't think I've ever seen a pizza quite like this."

Bruno picked up one of the pies to point out some things to Ryan.

"True Italian pizza is grilled in brick ovens with very high temperatures, and we have one here in the back. You can see there isn't a traditional sauce . . . it's made of chopped tomatoes with a little fresh garlic, sliced fresh mozzarella, and some fresh basil."

"No sauce?"

"Just the toppings which if you notice provide three colors: red, white and green. Those also happen to be the colors in the Italian flag. I think that's why Queen Margarita liked it so much."

The pizza disappeared while the conversation flowed as easily as the wine. Bruno finished off the meal with Italian ices and some Italian almond cookies.

"Nancy, I think it's time for this old man to head home."

"Can you drive me home, Herb?" Clare DellVecchio asked. "That way Jessica can take Ryan back to his hotel in my car."

That presented no problem, so the three of them began to leave. Herb Chandler was going to pay the bill, but Hannegan wouldn't let him, reminding Clare that he had promised tonight was going to be on him.

"You'd better keep him, Jayvee," Herb Chandler instructed. "He's not as cheap as all those other guys you went out with."

"Uncle Herb, stop it."

Ryan got a chuckle out of Chandler's comment and Jayvee gave him another elbow shot. Nancy and Herb hugged Jayvee, and then Chandler shook Ryan's hand and told him he would see him at the ballpark the following evening.

"Thank you for a wonderful night," Clare said as she kissed Hannegan on the cheek and gave him a hug. "I expect to hear from you again soon."

He promised he would stay in touch as he returned the kiss with one of his own. The threesome departed with Clare telling her daughter she would leave open the door to the house through the garage.

"Remember, Jessica, you have an eight o'clock flight in the morning, so don't be out too late."

"Mother, please! I am thirty-five years old."

"Yes, but you will always be my daughter . . ."

An exasperated Jayvee kissed her mother and then returned to the table where Ryan was waiting to pay the bill. They held hands, and although neither said a word, a wonderful conversation was going on with their eyes. As he signed the credit card bill for the meal, a large crashing sound resounded as if every pot and pan in Bruno's kitchen had fallen off their hooks. It was Mother Nature letting loose with another thunderstorm after all the heat of the past several days.

Jayvee and Ryan stood in the doorway waiting for any kind of break in the downpour to make a dash to the DellVecchio car parked in the lot across the street. When it became obvious the storm was not going to end anytime soon, they made a run for it. It couldn't have been more than a hundred and fifty feet to the car, but the pair got drenched anyway.

"Great idea, Hannegan. I'm soaked."

Ryan was trying unsuccessfully to stop the drips rolling down from his wet hair. He could not help but notice how Jayvee looked in her saturated white top.

"That's a great look for you, Jayvee . . . the wet T-shirt."

Hannegan reached over to caress her wet chest, only to have his hand slapped away by Jayvee. They both laughed.

"Slow down, Irishman, or I'll have to send you back out in the rain."

Arriving back at Hannegan's hotel in downtown Cleveland, Ryan suggested that Jayvee come upstairs to dry off before she headed home.

"I know why you want me to come in . . ."

"If you don't want to, that's okay."

"I didn't say that. I just know how you ballplayers operate."

She snickered as she climbed out of her mother's car and handed the keys to the parking valet. They must have looked a sight as they scurried across the lobby to the elevators. It turned out they weren't the only ones caught by the sudden storm. Jayvee and Ryan shared some laughs with an equally drenched older couple as they rode the elevator up to Hannegan's floor. Entering Ryan's room, Jayvee grimaced as she saw herself in the mirror.

"Oh, my God! Look at me!"

"I can't stop looking at you!"

"Cool your jets, Romeo. First, I need to dry off."

Jayvee went into the bathroom and tossed out a large bath towel to Hannegan before closing the door. He could hear her groaning again, but soon the sound of the hair dryer working took over. Ryan took off his wet clothes and draped them on various pieces of furniture around the room. *Hopefully they'll dry out enough by tomorrow so I can pack them for the trip to St. Louis.* He ran the fluffy towel through his hair and dried the rest of his body that was still damp. Hannegan went over to the bed to lie down while he waited for Jayvee to return. He thought about putting on some clothes, but what the hell, a little advertising wouldn't hurt. Ryan closed his eyes and smiled as he mused over his good fortune. Jayvee was back! Nestling into the pillow a little more deeply, he began to dream about once again holding her in his arms.

When he opened his eyes the room was dark. Who turned off the lights? Where the hell was Jayvee? He sat up in bed and looked over at the clock. The red numerals displayed one-thirty on its digital readout... nearly three hours since they had returned from the restaurant. Hannegan turned on the light near his side of the bed and that's when he saw the note on the adjacent pillow.

Talk about making it tough on a girl! I come out of the bathroom and discover quite a sight. Your naked body was very tempting, but when I saw that little boy smile on your face and how soundly you were sleeping, I just didn't have the heart to wake you. This is probably better. I won't have to do much explaining to my mother because I know she will stay up until I get home. The last two days have been wonderful. It made me realize again how important you are to me. I know you will tell me your side of the story when the time is right, and until then, I will TRUST that you know what you are doing. I DO LOVE YOU!! I have an early flight back to the city in the morning, so call me later on my cell. I am sure I will see you later in the week when you get back to Boston. Keep it up and just remember Daddy's advice to Let it Go!

Love, Jayvee

Hannegan reached over and turned off the light before falling back down on the pillow, still clutching Jayvee's note. For the first time, he knew for a fact everything would work out. SHE LOVES ME!

· TWENTY ·

THE STORMS OF Sunday night finally cleared the air in Cleveland, leaving ideal conditions for the last game of the year between the Colonials and the Ironmen. Keith Lash was toeing the rubber that night, and the All-Star's sixteen and seven mark was the best in the American Conference. Boston was looking for its twelfth win against the Ironmen in a streaky season series that had seen the Colonials dominate the action at the beginning and end of the year, while Cleveland had the upper hand during the middle.

Lash was in peak form, tantalizing the Cleveland hitters with his assortment of junk pitches, Lash was as sharp as the night of his perfect game, even with the pair of singles he had allowed in the fourth and sixth innings. One of those baserunners had been eliminated in a slick double play turned by Fernando Horrado and Kevin Kyle. The highlight of his masterpiece came with two outs and nobody on in the bottom of the seventh inning.

"... 0-1 the count on Cleveland's big cleanup hitter, Jimmy Craddock... Lash winds and pitches... big curve ball, SWING AND A MISS by Craddock."

The Cleveland slugger asked for time and stepped out of the box. He looked out at his former Los Angeles teammate and long-time friend.

"Hey, Keith, don't you ever get tired of serving up this CRAP? Just once don't you wish you could throw a pitch like a MAN?"

Craddock had a smile on his face, but he added some finger-pointing, so the fans who couldn't hear his comments, perhaps thought he was threatening Lash. An always-relaxed Keith Lash grinned back.

"Just for you, big guy! Climb back in there, and I'll give you my best shot."

Craddock stepped back into the right-hand batter's box and began his rhythmic swinging routine that had him pointing his heavy-barreled bat directly at the pitcher in a menacing fashion.

"... I don't know what was said in that exchange," Tom Kingery told his radio audience, "but Jimmy Craddock looks like he wants to hit a ball into Lake Erie..."

As promised, Keith Lash delivered his best shot to the slugger.

"... Lash winds and delivers ... OHMIGOD, it's an Eephus pitch, like ole' Rip Sewell used to throw ... the ball must be twenty feet in the air ..."

It's not unusual to see a pitch have a high arc in a slow-pitch softball game, but in baseball, the path of this pitch was ridiculous. The crowd gasped. The ball seemed to move in slow motion, and the Boston players stood frozen at their positions. Momentarily shocked, Jimmy Craddock quickly adjusted at the plate, ready to send the ball into the stratosphere. Even with the incredibly high arc, the pitch looked like it was going to find the strike zone.

"... Craddock SWINGS AND MISSES! He took a mighty cut and he lost his balance and he is now sitting on his backside in the dirt at home plate ..."

The stadium went silent for a moment, uncertain how to react, until Craddock flipped his bat into the air and fell on his back, roaring with laughter. Finally scrambling to his feet, he walked towards Keith Lash who was heading to the Boston dugout.

"You sunnavabitch," Craddock laughed. "Even I hadn't seen that one."

He put Lash in a headlock and gave him a noogie on the top of Lash's head, just like they were two kids on a playground.

Boston finished off the seven to nothing triumph, and it was on to St. Louis for a pair with the leaders of the Midwest Division. After the mandatory Tuesday off, there would be thirteen games remaining for each of the ten teams in the American Conference, and the races in both divisions were far from being decided.

AMERICAN CONFERENCE

Northeast Division			Midwest Division		
	W-L	GB		W-L	GB
Baltimore (7)	78-49	—	Saint Louis	76-51	—
Boston	71-56	7	Dallas	75-52	1
New York	70-57	8	Chicago	60-67	16
Cleveland	62-65	16	Minneapolis	59-68	17
Detroit	8-69	20	Kansas City	53-74	23

(7): Any combination of Baltimore wins or Boston losses that equals 7 will clinch the division title.

St. Louis was all but certain to gain a playoff spot, but they wanted the home field advantage for the postseason. They were not going to go through the motions against the Colonials; momentum was too important in these closing days of the season. The hotel where the Colonials were staying in St. Louis was being besieged with calls from reporters and radio talk show producers seeking Ryan Hannegan. When Ryan went out for lunch with Dennis Soos, several reporters, camped out in the lobby, fired questions at him as he and Soos walked through. The interrogation and pleas for answers continued until the pair climbed into a cab waiting at the front curb.

"Maybe some of them will follow us," Doc Soos teased. "I'll bet one of them has always wanted to say 'Follow that cab!' I know I have."

Hannegan had grown accustomed to the media coverage ever since Woody Watson brought up the blood test issue earlier in the season. That subject had not gone away, but now people were honing in on the possibility he might hit .400. His productivity had increased since the All-Star break, and he had just completed a nine for sixteen effort in the series in Cleveland. With two weeks left to the regular season, his name could be found in the top ten of just about every area:

Batting Average		Home Runs		RBIs	
Hannegan, BOS	.375	Russo, STL	39	Tompkins, DAL	102
Valeron, BAL	.341	Craddock, CLE	30	Hannegan, BOS	99
Hamilton, BAL	.336	Morientes, BOS	29	Hamilton, BAL	98
Tompkins, DAL	.328	Agostino, STL	28	Russo, STL	94
Cuevas, NY	.322	Hegan, NY	24	Flandera, DET	93
Gonzalez, DAL	.319	Jansen, DAL	22	Morientes, BOS	90
Coates, KC	.314	Hannegan, BOS	21	Hegan, NY	89
Kyle, BOS	.311	(3 Tied with)	20	Soos, BOS	86
Otto, CLE	.310			Craddock, CLE	85
Walker, DET	.308			Drabik, BAL	85

At batting practice on Wednesday, there had to be twenty additional reporters and camera people on hand, looking to get some insight from Hannegan. Ryan was cooperative with all of them, although he refused to even acknowledge Woody Watson's presence among the group. He was using the same pre-game routine he did in Cleveland limiting the amount of time he would have to speak with the media before the game. Because of all the requests, however, the Colonials' PR director, Bobby Greene, was scheduling postgame news conferences for as long as they were necessary. The Rivermen won both contests, although Hannegan collected four more hits and a pair of walks in nine plate appearances. His batting average stood at .378 ... just twenty-two points shy of the magical mark of .400. The focus of the postgame news conference following the loss to St. Louis on Wednesday was on Hannegan's individual accomplishments, but he kept trying to push the discussion towards his team's situation instead.

"Ryan, can you tell us when you started believing you might be able to crack the .400 barrier?"

"When I start to believe that, you guys will be the first to know," he said with a chuckle. "Come on, who thinks about hitting .400 when it hasn't been done in thirty years. What I have believed in all year is that the Colonials are a good team, and I want to help my team get to the playoffs any way I can."

"How have your teammates been about this whole thing?"

"This is the best team I have played for, on and off the field! Hey, when you've got guys like Hurricane and Kevin hitting in front of you, and big Ramon covering your back, you're going to get some good opportunities to hit. And that doesn't even include Junichi, when he was in there, and Doc Soos and the rest of my teammates."

"So, how do you explain your success?"

"Like I just said... I have had great people around me all season. Sometimes in this crazy game, you get into a groove where the whole process seems simple. But you also know it doesn't last forever because that's just the way baseball is. Thanks to all the people around me, I have been able to keep my run of good luck going a longer period than I ever expected."

Terry Tate was among the traveling members of the Boston media, covering the Colonials postseason push... and Ryan Hannegan.

"Ryan, I don't want to get into your personal life, but it has been documented that you have some involvement with Jayvee DellVecchio. Since her father was the last person to hit .400 in the Baseball Big Leagues, I wonder if there have been any discussions with her family about your efforts."

"Terry, you're right, I want to keep my personal life out of all of this. It's not fair to me, and it certainly is unfair to Ms. DellVecchio, especially since she has a job to do like the rest of you. I have made it a point not to give Jayvee any unfair edge, nor to put her at a disadvantage in regards to my situation. I will tell you this. I appreciate the support she and her mother have given me... they are great people!"

"What about the reports you have been helped in your efforts this year?" Woody Watson demanded.

"Good to have you with us this evening, Mr. Watson."

Ryan's conscience spoke up. Keep your cool, Ryno; this is not the time to get into it with this asshole.

"I appreciate your efforts to keep alive this story that I might be cheating. Nothing has ever been found to substantiate your claims, so why don't you just move on and find something else to write about."

"Better yet, why don't you go out and find some proof instead making all these insinuations without having anything to back them up."

The award-winning writer was not happy with Hannegan's rebuke. His dark eyes blazed with anger at the daring challenge. Watson sat fuming, plotting his next move, while Ryan answered several more questions until the news conference came to an end.

"Have your moment in the sun, Ryan Hannegan," Woody Watson mumbled softly. "I'm not finished with you."

The consecutive losses to St. Louis combined with New York winning six out of seven at home against Detroit and Dallas dropped the Colonials a game behind their archrivals. Eleven games remained in this dramatic fight for the final spot in the playoffs. The trip from Saint Louis back to Boston takes more than two hours — plus losing an hour with the time change. Hannegan did not get to bed at his condominium until almost three-thirty. The ringing of his telephone jarred him awake less than seven hours later.

"Ryanovich, did I wake you? I am sorry, but it's already the middle of the morning and I did not want to miss you."

A too-cheerful Vladimir Titov was probably the last person Hannegan wanted to hear from at that moment.

"Mad Vlad, we didn't get in from St. Louis until after three . . ."

"Sorry, my friend, but I needed to speak with you about these final games."

"Vlad, we have been over this and over this. I've got everybody watching me like a hawk . . ."

"I know, Ryanovich. A chance to hit .400 . . . and win some money for your friend in the process . . ."

Now it was Hannegan's turn to interrupt.

"That's what I mean, Vlad. If people find out about all those bets you've made, it's going to look real bad for me."

"Relax, my friend. There is no way they can detect any wrongdoing on your part . . . so long as YOU DO what you have to for me."

"And what's that supposed to mean?"

"It's simple, Ryanovich."

The friendly tone was completely gone from his voice.

"The only way that anything would come out about our relationship would be if I tell people about it. If I . . . how do you say it . . . spill the beans about the Soviet science I have given you . . . and the bets I have made."

"Is that a threat?"

An angry Hannegan was now fully awake.

"I never threaten in my business. People do what they're supposed to do, or they suffer for it."

The Russian's level and tone dropped. It wasn't a whisper; it was more like a growl.

"You do what you're supposed to do, Ryanovich. Use the Soviet science to boost you for these final games, and our secret will always remain just that . . . a secret."

With that the phone disconnected. Hannegan rolled onto his back and stared up at the ceiling. The sound of baseball cleats crunching on a gravel track was back echoing through his head.

If the Colonials were looking for a spark following their double-dip in St. Louis, they found it when they arrived at Patriots' Harbor for the first game of the series with the Chicago Fire. Junichi Nakata was back in uniform — maybe not quite ready to play — but with the promise that he might be able to return to the lineup before the season was over. Each of the Colonials greeted their Japanese teammate warmly; the initial wariness about his joining the team had long since disappeared. Ryan Hannegan was particularly pleased to see Junichi again.

"Ju! You're back! Boy, did we miss you."

"And it is good to see you as well, Ryan-san. It is nice to be among my teammates again."

The reminder of what had happened to Boston's baseball import was still evident on his face. Swelling remained in his nose and in the area below his right eye. A welt of ugly purple on that side of his face looked like war paint, but it was hardly the fashion statement some pro football player or heavily made-up television wrestler might make. Jeff Sibel's fastball had broken the orbital bone around Junichi's eye, deviated the septum in his nose, and did some damage to his sinuses. Further surgery ultimately awaited the Japanese star, but the Boston medical personnel — in consultation with specialists from this country and Japan — had given him the green light to resume playing, provided he was adequately protected against any further damage.

"How ya' feeling, Ju? Any problems?"

"The headaches have gone away, although sometimes I still feel pressure here when I am running," the outfielder said as he pointed to the injured area. "And I am not sure I am ready to wear this."

Junichi held up his batting helmet. Since he was a switch hitter, his helmet had protective earflaps on both sides, but his injury would require some additional help. The Colonials' equipment manager had added a clear plastic guard across the front of the helmet. There was enough space between the guard and the bill of the helmet to allow him to see, but it was small enough that a ball — or any other object that size or larger — would not make contact with his face.

"Put it on, Ju... Maybe we can get Teddy to put some Japanese stuff on it. Then you'll look just like a samurai warrior!"

Junichi smiled softly and bowed to Hannegan.

"Thank you, Ryan-san, for trying to brighten my situation. I hope it will work for me."

Junichi bowed again and then turned away from Hannegan to replace the helmet on the shelf of his locker. He headed off to the training room where Pete Hudec was going to put some packing in Junichi's nose to protect against any bleeding that could possibly occur if he exerted himself too much.

Ryan didn't think Ju sounded right... not like the guy from earlier this year. He hoped a few days back with the boys would get him going again. The Colonials had to have these next four games with the Fire. Chicago was below .500 and out of the chase in the Midwest Division. The last seven games with Saint Louis and New York would be difficult for Boston; now was the time to grab an advantage against the Horsemen. A return to action by Junichi Nakata could make the difference.

Before the game that night, as he waited behind the batting cage for his next turn, Hannegan sidled over the Boston manager, D.P. Perryton.

"Hey, Skip... it's going to be great having Ju back in the lineup, isn't it?"

"If he comes back."

The Boston manager's disposition had not been good over the past several weeks as the pressure of the pennant race increased. He was as glum as Hannegan had ever seen him.

"I thought he had gotten clearance from the medical guys to play again?"

"He's been cleared all right, but he's not clear up here." Perryton pointed to his forehead. "A guy gets hit in the face like that, and he's not so eager to climb back into the box."

"You're kidding?"

"I wish I was. Tommy threw him some BP earlier today. He looked pretty gun-shy ... and Tommy doesn't throw it that hard. Now Ju says he won't hit again outside until he says he's ready. That's why he's not out here now. I guess he's just going to work down in the cages."

"Do you want me to say something, D.P.? I've never been hit in the face — not by a pitch anyway — but he and I get along pretty well."

"That would be great, Ryno. I'm looking for all the help I can get. I'd feel a lot better about these last ten days if I could count on Ju, too."

"You got it, Skipper. I'd be happy to see if I can give him a boost."

"Boost?" You'd better watch your choice of words, Ryno."

Apparently the frame of mind for the Colonials' field boss had improved with Hannegan's offer of help.

"And I love you, too, D.P. Kiss my ass!"

His pre-game work complete — including a short session with the media — Hannegan walked along the lower level service way of Patriots' Harbor until he came to the indoor batting cages. He could hear the alternating sounds of swoosh and thwack coming from within. When it became quiet, Hannegan entered the room and found Junichi at the far end of the netted area. He was gathering the baseballs that lay on the ground in order to reload the automatic pitching machine. He was startled by Hannegan's presence.

"Ryan-san, why are you here?"

"Just checking on a friend to see how he's doing."

Junichi had isolated himself from the rest of the team during his recovery period. He remained in Dallas immediately after the injury to let the doctors make the surgical repairs necessary to his face. The surgery was initially postponed to let the swelling around his eye and nose subside, and then again when there was a delay in the arrival of the specialist from Japan who was assisting with the procedures. Junichi did not feel comfortable being with his teammates during his recovery period. Hannegan, Doc Soos, and other players had talked with him on several occasions by phone during his absence, but he did not return to Boston when he was finally released from the hospital. Instead, he chose to recuperate in Seattle with some friends from Japan who had relocated to this country. All the reports the players had received indicated he would not be back this season, so Junichi's presence in the clubhouse caught everyone by surprise.

"I am preparing for my return, Ryan-san, and doing quite well thank you," Junichi answered, but in a voice and with some body language that said otherwise.

"You can level with me, Ju. How are you doing, really?"

Hannegan could sense an internal battle raging for his teammate. Junichi had handled the pressure of going from Japanese baseball to the American brand seamlessly ... or so everyone thought. The sometimes rigid nature of his culture demands a stoic, almost fearless, response to a problem for a Japanese male ... even more than the so-called macho image that an American man is supposed to present. *He wants my help. He just doesn't know how to ask for it.*

"Ryan-san, have you ever been struck in the face with a pitch?"

"No, fortunately, I haven't, Ju, but I've seen it happen to a couple guys besides you. It isn't pretty."

"And how did they return to play?"

"Aw, it takes a little time, but eventually they were fine again. You don't have to worry ... you're going to be all right."

"Do you really believe so? This is a new experience for me. I am not certain how to react. Will the pitchers try to take advantage of my weakness?"

"Weakness? I don't follow you, Ju ..."

"In Japan, players get hit by pitches, but not as some act of aggression or retaliation like here. Such an act would bring dishonor to the team, and a player must avoid that at all costs."

"But, Ju, I've seen guys get dusted off by pitchers in highlights on the tube. What's that all about?"

"Only on rare occasions would that be true, and then it usually involved a *Gaijin*, a foreigner. Would they do the same thing here ... because of who I am?"

Suddenly, Ryan knew his Asian friend was scared. He never thought he'd see that in Ju. To Ryan, it seemed he had had it all together as well as anyone. Ryan wondered if he could shake him out of the doldrums and help him conquer his fear.

"Not a chance, Ju. That might've been true when the African-American guys finally started playing in the big leagues a long time ago, but there aren't too many red-necked assholes around anymore. Nowadays, teams might throw at each other, but it usually isn't personal. You just happened to be the guy who got caught in the middle of it, that's all."

The Japanese player pondered the remarks for a time, feeling a little better, but still not convinced there wasn't more to what happened to him.

"I have seen how some players in Japan have treated the *Gaijins*. Too many resent the Americans having success against them, and they do shameful things ... in the games and away from the field as well. I want to believe such treatment will not happen to me, but I am not sure."

"Listen, Ju ... you can always count on me to have your back — that means I'll be there for you — and there are plenty of other guys who wear Boston across their chest that feel the same way. Now what do you need me to do for you?"

A grateful Junichi bowed to his American friend.

"You are *i tomodachi*, a good friend, Ryan Hannegan. That is what I need right now."

"As they would say in Southern California where I come from: I got you covered, Dude!"

Both men laughed and shook hands warmly. Hannegan headed back to the clubhouse to get ready for that night's game, while Junichi resumed his ball collection duties in preparation for another round with the pitching machine. Nothing had been solved, but perhaps a foundation of hope was being put into place. The game with Chicago went well for the Colonials. Raul Gomez was sharp, scattering seven hits and allowing just two runs in seven innings of work. Hannegan banged out a single in his first at-bat and came around to score on a hit by Dennis Soos. In the fifth, Ryan laced a double down the right field line that just missed going into the lower walkway of the Blue Pier. It was his league-leading forty-second two-bagger of the season and it scored Fernando Horrado easily from first base. It was Ryan's one hundredth run batted in, and the capacity crowd gave him a standing ovation when that information was posted on the scoreboard.

Many players and coaches say they don't look at the scores of other games while they're playing ... and that might be the biggest lie in pro sports, especially in the closing weeks of a baseball season. The Boston crowd, along with everyone in the Colonials' dugout, was keeping close tabs on the game between New York and Dallas, and they roared or groaned with every fluctuation in the action from The Hollow. The only way either team was going to make it to the playoffs now was to win that final wild card spot. No one else was close; so every game from here to the end of the season on Labor Day would draw their undivided attention. A roar from the crowd startled Hwang Sang Hwan, as he was in the middle of his windup for a pitch in the ninth inning: the Wranglers had won in New York! Hwang composed himself and went back to work at extinguishing the Fire. The C's and the Horsemen were back even at seventy-two wins each: ten games to go.

With a day game scheduled for Saturday, Bobby Greene thankfully made Hannegan's postgame conference with the media a brief one. Ryan had an idea germinating, and he wanted to get at it . . . even though it was past eleven p.m. when he left the ballpark. Fortunately, traffic was a breeze back to the condo. He unlocked his front door, tossed his bag towards the living room, and moved to the phone on the wall in his kitchen. Opening one of the drawers below the counter, Hannegan pulled out a Boston phone book as well as an address book that had all of his personal numbers. Picking up the phone, he proceeded to punch out a bunch of numbers. It was almost midnight in Boston, but not yet nine o'clock for his target: his sister, Eileen, in California. If anyone had the information he needed, Eileen would.

The phone rang several times.

Where's your damn answering machine, Eileen?

". . . Hello?"

"Colleen? This is Uncle Ryan. Where were you guys? I thought I would at least get your answering machine."

"Sorry, Uncle Ryan. We've got call waiting and I heard the beep, but I thought it was just one of Cecilia's friends and I ignored it. Do you want to talk with Mom?"

"Please . . ."

A few moments later Hannegan's sister picked up the phone.

"Ryan, is everything all right? Did something happen to Michaela? What time is it? It must be around midnight where you are . . ."

"Eileen, please. I've got no time for twenty questions. Everybody is fine. I just need some information in a hurry and I thought you were my best bet."

Hannegan explained his situation; his sister put down the phone for a minute and then returned with what Ryan needed.

"You're a lifesaver, Eileen. This is perfect . . ."

"So, how's Jayvee? What's the latest . . ."

"Look, Sis, I gotta go — a day game tomorrow and I've got to get some sleep. I promise I will call again soon. Give my love to Tom and the girls."

Hannegan hung up the phone before she could think of something else to ask him. The Boston phone book provided the rest of what he needed. Hey, here's a place that's right on the way to the ballpark. It should only take a few minutes, so I should have time. I hope they have it. Satisfied, Hannegan turned out the lights in his kitchen and headed to bed.

Saturday morning, the timing was right for Ryan. He made his stop and still pulled into the players' lot at Patriots' Harbor on time for batting practice. He had other plans, however, when he went into D.P. Perryton's office.

"Dudley, can I skip BP this morning?"

The Boston manager did not like to be called by his real first name, but he understood this was Ryan's way to get back at him for the shot he gave to Hannegan the previous night. Perryton still managed to get in his own dig.

"Oh, I see. A player leads the league in hitting, and now he doesn't need to practice anymore?"

Hannegan expected his manager to return fire, but he didn't have the time to get into another friendly battle of words with D.P.. Ryan explained to the Boston skipper why he needed to skip batting practice that morning.

"Do you think it will work?"

"Hey, D.P., at this point, what do we have to lose?"

Perryton agreed and gave his blessing to the attempt. Hannegan stopped at his locker, collected a few things, including one of his bats, and headed off to the batting cages. He found a dispirited Junichi, sitting on a folding chair alongside the pitching machine.

"I knew I'd find you in here, Ju. Hannegan the Great is ready to perform his magic!"

"Ryan-san, I do not think making money disappear is going to help my situation. I have spent all my time in this room the past two days, and I fear that I am not ready to face my challenge."

Hannegan set down his bat at one end of the long area that was surrounded by netting, and walked to where Junichi sat some sixty feet away. He placed a bag at his friend's feet, and then covered it with a towel he had brought from the clubhouse.

"Hannegan the Great is now ready to perform his most fantastic magic yet!"

Ryan began rhythmically waving his hands over the covered bag.

"There once was a girl from Nantucket . . . no, that's not right. Hang on . . . oh yeah . . . Hocus-pocus, stay in focus, don't let 'em know it's all lights and smoke-us . . . or something like that."

Ryan pulled the towel off the bag with a flourish and reached in, pulling out Michaela's teddy bear with the mamori medallion around its neck.

"Ju, meet Norm . . . Norm, this is Junichi. Norm belongs to my daughter, Michaela. She sent it to me for good luck awhile back and it has really helped, especially when I added your mamori to it."

"I am pleased, Ryan-san, that my gift has been important for you," a still subdued Junichi responded, "and that you have added it to the love your daughter has sent you through her toy. But I do not see how this can help my situation."

Hannegan dismissed his friend's negative thoughts with a wave of his hand. Striking a pose like the actor Frank Morgan in *The Wizard of Oz*, he continued.

"After consulting and otherwise hobnobbing with my fellow wizards, I have the solution to your troubles. Back where I come from, we have men who we call heroes, and they have no more courage than you have. But they have one thing that you haven't got... a medal."[1]

Reaching back into the bag, Ryan pulled out one of his magic props that with a shake turned into a bouquet of paper flowers. Around the flowers was a chain with two medals attached to it. He placed it around Junichi's neck.

"You are now a member of the Legion of Courage."[2]

Junichi didn't know how to react. He knew his friend had made a gesture of support for him, but he was still confused over the whole process. Realizing that, Ryan got serious.

"As I told you earlier in the season, I'm not much of a religious guy, but my sister, Eileen, is. She goes to Mass practically every day, praying the rosary, all those kinds of things."

"Anyway, I remembered you talking about your uncle — the Shinto priest — when you gave me this mamori."

Hannegan fingered the medallion he had placed around the small stuffed animal.

"You said it is supposed to help heal and protect anyone who possesses it. I guess I'm as superstitious as the next guy in this crazy game, and all I know is whatever this thing is supposed to do, it's working for me."

Ryan picked up the two medals on the chain that he had hung around Junichi's neck.

"This is the medal of Saint Sebastian. My sister says he is the patron saint of athletes." Grabbing the other one, Hannegan told his friend the other medal was for Saint Joseph who is supposed to watch over those who have doubt or hesitation in their lives.

"Wear them, Ju, as a source of strength and as a sign of my faith in you. You'll be fine... all you have to do is what people have been telling me lately: just let it go."

Junichi got up slowly from the chair, gazing at the gift Hannegan had placed around his neck. Straightening, the Japanese star then made a long, deep bow, which in his culture means the highest respect.

"As I said yesterday, Ryan-san, you are *i tomodachi*, a good friend."

---

1. *The Wizard of Oz*, Langley, Ryerson, Woolf, MGM Studios, 1939.
2. *Ibid.*

Then in a surprise for both men, Junichi hugged Hannegan. Stepping back with a big smile on his face, Hannegan said:

"Come on, grab your bat and I'll throw you some BP... it's better than this machine."

Tucking the chain with the medals inside his batting practice jersey, Junichi headed for the other end of the batting cage. Hannegan moved the pitching machine out of the way, and then put a protective screen in front of the pitching mound at his end of the cage. He picked up the bucket of baseballs that Junichi had collected and climbed up on the hill. He was now ready for the second part of his plan. Junichi put on his batting helmet — something a big league hitter normally doesn't do in a batting session in the cages — and dug in at the plate. He still didn't look that comfortable: with the helmet and its protective shield in front, or even with hitting altogether. Hannegan's first pitch didn't help with that comfort level.

The ball was not thrown that hard — Hannegan did have a strong arm when he needed it — it was the location that shocked Junichi. The pitch was several feet over his head, but Ju hit the deck like the ball was headed right for his chin. Silently, he got up, dusted himself off and got set again at the plate. The second pitch had nearly the same location, forcing Junichi to jump away from the plate ... and so did the third. Hannegan shrugged his shoulders.

"Like Doc says, sometimes you've just got to say W-T-F!"

Junichi moved away from the hitting area like he was going to stop. After a momentary pause, he settled back in at the plate and gestured for Hannegan to fire away. Like the first three, Ryan's next offering sailed over the head of the injured star, but this time, Junichi did not move from his spot, other than to gesture for Hannegan to fire another pitch. This time, Hannegan eased back on the speed of his pitch, but the delivery hit Junichi square in the shoulder. Again, there was no reaction from the Japanese hitter other than a signal to throw another pitch. Hannegan's next toss was down the middle of the plate, and Junichi ripped it, sending it right back into the screen in front of Hannegan. Again, the small gesture for another pitch, and again, the same result: a scorcher right back at Hannegan. Five more pitches, five more shots right back up the middle.

Ryan grabbed the white towel he had brought from the clubhouse and began to wave it in surrender. Junichi dropped his bat at the plate and walked to Hannegan's end of the cage. Slowly, he removed his batting helmet to reveal an angry face with clenched teeth which turned into a smile in seconds.

"How's that for a little W-T-F? I am grateful, Ryan-san, grateful for everything you have done these past two days."

Reaching into the bucket for one of the baseballs, he added with a sinister smile, "Now it is my turn to pitch to you, Ryan Hannegan!"

"Not in a million years! I may be dumb, but I'm not stupid. Come on, let's go kick Chicago's ass!"

Junichi did not play on that Saturday afternoon, but he sat in the dugout with his teammates for the first time since he was hit in Dallas. His presence picked up the spirits of the whole team and they rolled for a second straight game against Chicago. Nick Ertle won for the ninth time on the season — his best win total in three years — while Hannegan rapped a pair of hits in four at-bats in the five to two victory. Coupled with another Dallas win in New York, the Colonials had reclaimed sole possession of the final playoff spot. Nine games to go.

· TWENTY-ONE ·

"EIGHT DAYS (TO) A WEEK"

Woody Watson, *New York Tribune-World*
www.TheTruth.com

BOSTON (AP) I may be taking some literary license with the fine works of Messrs. Lennon and McCartney, but the race to the playoffs in the Baseball Big Leagues has come down to "Eight Days (in) A Week": there is that off-day, you know, on Tuesday. The "Long And Winding Road" has brought us to the final steps of what has been a remarkable season. It actually began before the first game was even played, when General Michael Hopkins issued the warning "You Can't Do That" to any player that might consider using supplements to create an unfair advantage for himself. Several times this season, he has given "A Ticket to Ride" to players who have failed the game's drug-testing program. Slip up with Hoppy's program, and it is "Hello, Goodbye." For Ryan Hannegan, this baseball season has been a "Magical Mystery Tour." It has all "Come Together" in a phenomenal campaign that has seen him hit more than one hundred points above his career batting average... to actually threaten a milestone the game has not seen for thirty years. Well, "Help" me if I remain skeptical. Am I to follow Mr.

Hannegan's suggestion that I just "Let It Be" concerning my questions of how he has achieved such success. He has tried to play me lately as "A Fool On A Hill," but he is sadly mistaken if he believes "I'm A Loser." Soon, I plan on revealing some most damaging material regarding the Boston outfielder who has only triumphed this year, in my opinion, "With A Little Help From His Friends." This Tuesday evening will be "A Hard Day's Night" for Ryan Hannegan... and perhaps, for the Boston Colonials and their fans. "I Don't Want To Spoil The Party," but you have to tune in to TWTV that night for *Face-To-Face* if "You Want To Know A Secret." That night I will reveal information that may take us "Back In The USSR." Information that might mean "The End" for Ryan Hannegan.

Woody Watson's syndicated Sunday column was the chief topic of conversation at Patriots' Harbor before that afternoon's game. Members of the media — and players from both teams — added their own Beatles' songs to the ones used in the story. Watson had been an occasional contributor to *Face-To-Face*, the news magazine that was TWTV's most highly rated program, but it was rare for him to make mention of one of his appearances in his newspaper column. The rumors were hot and heavy over his exact plans for the live broadcast Tuesday evening. Ryan Hannegan was a key ingredient in Boston's attempt to hold off Watson's beloved Horsemen for the final playoff spot, so the group speculated about just what ammunition Woody Watson planned to use against him.

The media group, which now numbered more than thirty people, moved towards Hannegan as the Colonials' batting practice session ended. Ryan had become used to the routine, and in fact, he had begun to enjoy the give-and-take with the reporters. Dennis Soos told him he might as well have fun with the process because the media wasn't going away as long as he kept hitting. With four hits in the first two games against Chicago, Hannegan was now batting .381.

"Still going strong, Ryan? How are you feeling?"

"Previous runs at .400 have seen guys fade at the end, but you keep moving up; any comments?"

"Do you think all of this has been a distraction for your teammates?"

Hannegan patiently answered each query thrown his way. No, he did not feel it was affecting the Colonials. If he keeps hitting, then that can only help the team's offense. Yes, he still felt strong. His continued use of some of the techniques he employed during the off-season kept him feeling good. As for the history of other attempts to hit .400, Hannegan said he hadn't even considered that. One pitch, one at-bat at a time; that's all he was thinking about.

"Mr. Hannegan, are you a music lover?'

"And good morning to you, Mr. Watson. I enjoyed your article, though I must confess the Beatles were a little before my time."

"Do you care to comment?"

"I've learned to like Beatles music — they were my mother's favorite group — but I'm more of a blues aficionado, you know, Robert Cray and Stevie Ray Vaughn. As for any comment, well, Robert Cray might say that you've been *Playin' In The Dirt*. Or perhaps, I might ask *Who's Been Talkin* with all these *False Accusations*.

"Mr. Watson, let me tell you this. You do whatever you're going to do on Tuesday evening, but as Stevie might say, if my *House Is A Rockin'*, it won't be the result of anything YOU do that night."

Ryan departed to a smattering of snickers from some of the reporters. The strong front notwithstanding, he was concerned. That *Back in the USSR* stuff has to be about Mad Vlad. What does he think he has that he can be boasting like this? Has Mad Vlad decided to say something? He didn't sound that way the last time he called. For the first time since this whole process got started, Ryan hoped Vlad would call him to explain what was happening.

On the way to the tunnel to go back to the clubhouse, Hannegan noticed D.P.'s lineup card was missing. Normally, a large white card showing the starting lineups and the substitutes for that day's game was posted on a wall at the end of the dugout. Another is hung on the inside of the clubhouse door, and it wasn't there, either. Ryan thought that was weird. D.P. must really be losing it under all this pressure. Ryan dropped his glove into the bottom of his locker, and used the towel on the stool to wipe his face as he sat down. Junichi was absent again from batting practice, so Ryan figured he would grab a cup of soup and then head down to the batting cages to see how Ju was doing. Hannegan walked into the small kitchen area of the Colonials' clubhouse and ladled a cup of steaming clam chowder. Superstition or not, Ryan wasn't going to change his routine of some soup before the game. If it ain't broke, don't fix it.

Returning to the main area of the clubhouse, he saw Junichi sitting cross-legged on the floor in front of his locker, his eyes closed. Ryan hesitated, not wanting to interrupt him, when Junichi opened his eyes and saw Hannegan standing in front of him.

"Ryan-san, you are looking well today."

"Same with you, Ju, but I thought I would see you down in the cages. Is everything all right?"

Junichi pulled the chain out from inside his uniform top to reveal the two medals Hannegan had given him the day before.

"Thanks to you, Ryan-san, I again have musuhi — the power of harmony —back in my life. Here, let me show you something else."

The outfielder scrambled to his feet and reached up to take down the batting helmet from the locker's top shelf. The Plexiglas shield still ran across the front of the helmet, but Junichi had added something to the piece of equipment.

"I took your advice from the other day and had Teddy do a little artwork."

Junichi spun the helmet around so that Ryan could see the small insignia that had been added to the back of it. Players have been known to put initials or numbers on hats or helmets as a sign of respect or a dedication for other players. Rather than numbers or letters, however, on Ju's helmet was painted an elaborate design depicting a flying dragon wearing a red and blue collar as it flew through the clouds.

"It's beautiful, Ju."

"Teddy knew someone who does artwork on motorcycle helmets and recreational vehicles. I asked if they could find something that would have a samurai look to it, and this is what the artist came up with. Musuhi, Ryan-san! The courage from the East . . ." he said as he rubbed his right thumb over the insignia, "and the protection from the West," he concluded as he waved the medals he was wearing around his neck.

"Hey, whatever helps you get back in the lineup, I'm all for it."

Junichi simply smiled at Hannegan's last remark, placed the helmet back on the shelf, and resumed his meditative pose back on the floor.

The reason for the smile became apparent a few moments later. Tom Gladstone was taping one of the lineup cards on the door leading out of the clubhouse. Hannegan knew he would be in the lineup — a team doesn't take the top hitter in baseball out of its offense when it is fighting for the postseason — but he was drawn, by habit, to see the lineup that had just been posted. He was in the lineup as usual, but not in the three hole like he had been for the past seven weeks. There between the names of Kevin Kyle and Ramon Morientes was Junichi Nakata's for the first time since Jeff Sibel hit him in the face in early July.

"I'll be damned!" Ryan said aloud. "It really worked."

It worked for the Boston offense, too. Junichi picked up like he had never left, slapping a pair of hits — one from each side of the plate — scoring each time. He scored a third run when he walked two batters ahead of Hannegan, who belted his twenty-second home run of the season, a monster shot over the Blue Pier in right field in the fifth inning. Hannegan's day was spectacular: four hits in four at-bats — including the homer — and three runs driven home. When he was intentionally walked in the seventh inning, he scored on a Doc Soos blast. The Colonials rolled nine to two, and Keith Lash won his eighteenth game, tops in all of baseball. New York defeated Dallas, however, so the Boston advantage for the final wild card position remained at one game.

The media scrutiny intensified for the last game with Chicago on Monday night. The four for four effort the day before raised Hannegan's batting average to .386. Could he possibly keep up the pace and reach .400? His current hitting streak was at eleven games, and Ryan had managed at least one hit in twenty of his last twenty-one games. His unlikely success the entire season — not to mention this incredible sprint to the finish line — gave even more life in the world of rumors to Woody Watson's claims that Hannegan was cheating. Was Hannegan on the up-and-up? What information was Watson going to reveal on television? If Woody Watson really did have something, then what was General Hopkins going to do about it? Despite the importance of that night's game as far as the race to the playoffs was concerned, it had become almost an unwelcome delay to the big news expected the following night.

Jayvee DellVecchio rejoined the media delegation that evening for the first time since a week ago in Cleveland. To her displeasure, she found herself the subject of too many interview requests rather than being the one asking the questions.

"Yes, it's great that everyone is talking about Dad again . . ."

"No, I don't remember much from that season because I was only five years old . . ."

"I plan on keeping my private life just that: private. I am rooting for Ryan to have success, but that is my only comment on that matter . . ."

The Colonials had the look of a winning thoroughbred that takes charge in the closing stretch of a race. They had won seven of their last ten games, and although they couldn't overtake Baltimore for the Northeast Division crown, they were putting all the pressure on the Horsemen. New York already lost in their afternoon finale with Dallas, so a Boston win tonight would give the C's a two-game advantage for the final play-off spot.

Darren Haddad was masterful for eight innings, surrendering just three runs on six hits. Unfortunately, Tom Downing was even better for the Fire. Boston had mustered only four hits through seven innings, scoring a run in the second on a leadoff homer by Ramon Morientes, his thirtieth of the campaign. With one out in the bottom of the eighth, Junichi was able to finagle a walk off Downing. One out later, it was Hannegan's turn. He had singled in the fifth to extend his hitting streak to twelve, and now the Boston faithful were exhorting him to keep the C's winning magic alive.

". . . Downing delivers . . . fouled back to the screen. Boy, Downing hung a slider there, but Hannegan couldn't put it into play . . ."

Hannegan asked for time and stepped out of the box. He mentally fussed at himself. Dammit, Ryan, that was your pitch. You should have creamed it. Okay, relax.

D.P. Perryton yelled from the dugout.

"Ryno, you know what makes this game so great? You've got a round ball and a round bat, now all you have to do is try to hit it squarely."

The Boston manager watched Hannegan relax; his humor had done its job. Tom Downing worked it to one ball and two strikes, but Ryan had been a good hitter throughout the season when behind in the count, and the Colonials' fans remained hopeful. The Chicago pitcher came to the set position. He took a long look over at first where Junichi danced away to his lead, and then came plateward. His one-two offering was a splitter, maybe to get Ryan with the same pitch that fanned Morientes one batter earlier.

"... swing and Hannegan hits a sinking liner towards left center. Busser is moving toward the alley while Waldheger is racing over from center..."

Andrew Busser, the Chicago leftfielder had not gotten a good jump on the ball and he was not going to reach it. The situation wasn't any better for Ryan Waldheger.

"... Waldheger dives but he can't come up with it ... now Busser has fallen over Waldheger as he tried to avoid a collision ... the ball is rolling towards the Triangle in left center..."

Hannegan was rounding first base and had an excellent view of the play unfolding in left center. The Chicago outfielders scrambled to their feet to chase down the ball headed for the deepest corner of the ballpark. Ryan neatly cut the corner of the bag at second and accelerated towards third.

"... Waldheger finally has the ball on the warning track and he fires it toward the cutoff man..."

You could feel the excitement growing in Tom Kingery's description; if he wasn't standing up with the veins popping out on his neck, it sure felt that way.

"... Junichi has already scored and now Tommy Gladstone is waving Hannegan home ... here comes the relay throw ... it's going to be close!"

"Safe ... Safe!" barked Dave Price, the home plate umpire, as the dust settled from Hannegan's slide across the dish.

Hannegan bounced up and clapped his hands while the Boston crowd roared its approval.

"... Oh, what a slide by Ryan Hannegan! The ball and the runner reached at the same time, but Hannegan went back door and just touched the plate with his left hand while avoiding Klein's tag. An inside the park homer ... the game is tied!"

Mark Allen led off the bottom of the ninth as a pinch-hitter for

Boston's closer, Hwang Sang Hwan. On the first pitch, Allen lifted a fly ball that just kept carrying until it dropped into the seats in the left field bleachers beyond the desperate effort of Andrew Busser. The Colonials had done it again: a walk-off homer to win the game! Boston was up two with seven to play.

Hannegan's inside-the-park home run dominated the postgame media session.

"I wasn't thinking at all about an inside-the-park job until I saw Busser leave his feet. There's a lot of real estate out in left center, so I knew the ball would roll a long way. When Tommy waved me home, I thought I had a chance because you need at least two good relays in that situation. Hey, give Chicago credit . . . they made some great throws and I was lucky to just beat the tag."

More questions followed about his climb towards .400. Two hits had raised his batting average to .387, the highest in baseball since Mike DellVecchio in 1971, and one of the best in the last fifty years. Hannegan continued to dismiss any suggestions of pressure in trying to reach .400; he was more concerned with helping get the C's to the playoffs. Bobby Greene, Boston's PR man, signaled one more question, and it was Jayvee who stepped forward.

"What are your plans for your off-day tomorrow? Are you going to watch any television?"

The obvious reference to Woody Watson's appearance on *Face-To-Face* the following evening brought chuckles from everyone. Hannegan smiled, shook his head, but said nothing. Later that night, as Jayvee snuggled next to him after they had made love together for the first time in weeks, she posed the question again.

"So, Hannegan . . . what are you going to do with your off-day?"

His response was to grab her leg just above her knee and squeeze. Jayvee was extremely ticklish there, and he maintained his grip until she begged for mercy. When he finally relented, Jayvee climbed out of bed to use the bathroom. Ryan rolled onto his back and stared at the ceiling. He knew exactly what he was going to be doing the next night. The crunching noise began to build again in his head.

Hannegan spent Tuesday seeking things to occupy his time. Jayvee left early in the morning to head back to New York, so he puttered around the condo, taking care of some mail and bills, and catching up with an online message to Michaela. In the afternoon, he played golf with Dennis Soos, Kevin Kyle, and Keith Lash. Golf was fine — especially beating Doc and Kevin — but the *Face-To-Face* show that evening was never far from his mind. He watched *Sports Roundup* on DBC as well as Jayvee's pre-game show before the featured contest that night from the National Conference.

It was the top of the first inning of the game between the Denver Mountaineers and the San Francisco Gold Rush when Hannegan's phone rang.

"... Hi, this is Ryan, leave a message after the beep... BEEP."

"Ryan... it's Jayvee... if you're there, please pick up the phone."

"Hey there, I was hoping you would call. Nice show tonight. Who do you think is going to make the playoffs in the N-C?"

"Don't avoid the subject, Hannegan. Are you okay about tonight?"

"Why, is there something going on tonight?"

"Don't do this, Ryan. You know what I mean."

"Jayvee, I appreciate your concern. I'm fine."

"I know you're going to watch the show. I don't know if I could do that alone. I wish I was there with you..."

"It's going to be no big deal. I would love to have you here tonight, but it would have nothing to do with Woody Watson. We've been over this before. It's better if you aren't compromised professionally. Watch his little dog and pony act tonight and then make your own decisions without having me with you."

"I said I was going to trust your judgment on this, Ryan, and I am. But I hate not being able to have any control here. It's not the way I normally do things."

"Don't I know THAT."

Jayvee gave him the raspberries in return.

"Woody Watson has been after me all year. There's nothing to this witch hunt, and I have no worries about anything," he lied.

"It's almost eight; I'll let you go so you can watch the show. I will call you later when I'm done with work. I love you, Ryan."

"I love you, too. Just relax; there's nothing to worry about."

In truth, Hannegan had plenty of worries. Just as Jayvee had complained about a lack of control, this was a situation where he could do nothing but wait and see what would be revealed. It was not a comfortable feeling.

Eight o'clock came and Hannegan hit the buttons on his remote to change his television to TWTV. In typical fashion for these types of shows, *Face-To-Face* previewed the stories to be covered that night, giving particular prominence to Woody Watson's segment. Video clips of Vladimir Titov performing for the Soviet wrestling teams confirmed Mad Vlad would be Watson's information source. The program got underway with a profile of the head of the Senate Foreign Relations Committee. A discussion on business indicators by a panel of economists followed. The waiting was so stressful Hannegan walked outside to release some tension. Finally — about forty minutes into the program — *Face-To-Face* was ready.

The segment began with narration from Woody Watson that chronologically delineated Vladimir Titov's athletic career as the footage showed Titov in action for the Soviet national team. Vlad did not have a beard, and his hair was shorter, but he was easily recognizable. The report then transitioned to street scenes from Brighton Beach, the community near Coney Island in metropolitan New York City. Brighton Beach is often called Little Odessa with more than seventy thousand Russian immigrants living there, and judging from the signs with Cyrillic lettering and the attire worn by many of the people, one might guess the video was shot in the Ukraine rather than on the East Coast of the United States. Titov was shown at his supper club in Brighton Beach, and much was made of his connection to Yegor Karpin, the alleged head of the Russian Mafia in this country.

The scene shifted back to the TWTV studios where Woody Watson sat in an overstuffed leather chair across from Vladimir Titov, who was sitting in a similar chair. Watson briefly re-introduced himself and did the same with Titov. Then the questioning began.

"Mr. Titov, how long have you lived in this country?"

"I came here about ten years ago . . . and as my fellow Russian, Yakov Smirnoff, the comedian, would say, what a country!"

Mad Vlad had a huge grin on his face.

"What is your occupation?"

Still grinning, the giant Russian answered:

"I am the owner of The Cossack, the finest supper club in Brighton Beach. Mr. Watson, you must come; we have Beef Stroganoff like it is meant to be prepared and the best Vareniki outside of the Ukraine."

Woody Watson mumbled a thank you and a promise to visit sometime in the future, but he was clearly put off by Titov's disarming approach. Time to turn up the pressure.

"Are you not a relative of Yegor Karpin, the head of the Russian Mafia in this country?"

"I am the proud nephew of Yegor Karpin. My uncle is in the import-export business."

"Are you telling me he is not the leader of a vicious group that operates in the underworld of drugs, gambling, and prostitution?"

Woody Watson was clearly trying to provoke Titov, and although he adjusted in his seat like he was upset by the questioning, the Russian didn't fall into the trap. Ryan mentally coached the Russian. Come on, Vlad. You love the spotlight. Give old Woody a sample. Hannegan wasn't disappointed.

"He is just an honest businessman," Vlad said, puffing his cheeks and doing his bad Marlon Brando impersonation — just as he had done to Hannegan back in Florida. "Do you want me to say that he makes offers that people can't refuse?" he continued in his Russian-flavored Brando.

The camera caught Watson noticeably wincing at the Russian's last remarks. He had hoped to put Titov on the defensive, but instead, Watson found himself looking foolish.

"Very amusing, Mr. Titov. Let's switch directions for a moment. Tell us about your athletic career. Did your retirement seem premature?"

"Not at all. I had been wrestling on the Soviet national team for nearly ten years. It is quite a challenge to maintain that level of performance. I had grown tired of the sport."

"Your departure from wrestling was not the result of allegations about the use of performance-enhancing materials?"

The Russian leaned forward in his chair; this time Watson had, indeed, hit a nerve.

"The claims that my success — and those of other Soviet athletes — was only the result of chemical help are an insult to our talents and our dedication to our sports."

Sensing his first advantage in the give-and-take, Watson pressed the attack.

"Are you telling me, Mr. Titov, that you and your compatriots did not break the rules of fair athletic competition?"

"Whose rules? Those put in place by the Western world that could not handle the thought we would be better than they are at anything? Our training methods were so superior to what was being done here and elsewhere the West had to crank up its propaganda machine to diminish what we had accomplished."

The Russian slammed back into his chair. Now in command, Woody Watson continued his efforts to keep Titov on the defensive.

"Then tell us about the allegations that you had a role in the blood-doping scandals on the international cycling circuit several years ago. Or, what of the allegations that you were the supplier of human growth hormones and other potentially dangerous body-building supplements that led to the dismissal of several European track and field athletes?"

"No comment," the Russian said, sinking further back into his chair . . . if that was possible for a man of his size.

"And what about the suspicions that you have connections here and in Europe regarding new programs that can illegally aid an athlete, programs that are increasingly difficult to detect?"

"No comment," Titov snapped again.

"I don't want to put you on the defensive, Mr. Titov," said Woody Watson in a more conciliatory tone, although he clearly did. "Let's talk about something else. You're a great fan of the sport of baseball, aren't you?"

"Oh yes, I love the — what do you call it — the grand old game," Titov replied, his disposition brightening. "I learned to play when our sports federation wanted to establish a team to compete in the Olympics. I still go to the batting cages near Coney Island because I love to — as my friend Ryanovich says — take some hacks!"

"Ryanovich? Would that be Ryan Hannegan of the Boston Colonials?"

Now it was Hannegan's turn to wince. Watson was pushing Mad Vlad into a deep hole, and he knew the SOB was trying to shove him down there, too. Hannegan got up from his couch and began to pace around the room, but he couldn't take his eyes off the television screen.

"Yes, Ryan Hannegan is my friend."

"How did you meet?"

"Ryanovich was my coach when I went to a baseball fantasy camp in Florida last winter. We spent much time together, playing the games and with the social activities in the evening back at our hotel."

"But your relationship ended when this fantasy camp came to a close?"

"Oh, no, I have spoken with my friend a number of times since."

Hannegan stopped his pacing in mid-stride. The crunching noise was back in his head like a volcano erupting. *Don't do it, Vlad, don't do it, please!*

"Mr. Titov, do you gamble?" Woody Watson asked in an abrupt change of direction to his line of questioning.

"Of course," Titov replied with a chuckle. "What good Russian doesn't?"

"Are you aware the Baseball Big Leagues has strict guidelines about its players having contacts with gambling and known gamblers?"

"I was not, but then I had no reason to be worried about any such rules."

"And why is that, Mr. Titov?"

The Russian leaned forward in his chair, but he still had a defensive posture.

"Can I ask you a question, Mr. Woody Watson?"

Feeling in total control, Watson was deferential to his interview subject, gesturing with one hand to Titov to ask his question.

"Did you watch The Giant Bowl, the Professional Football Association's championship game, last January?"

"Watch it? I have covered every Giant Bowl since they began more than thirty years ago."

"That's great. By the way, did your newspaper have a Giant Bowl office pool?"

Woody Watson had fallen into the Russian's trap, but there was little he could do about it.

"Yes, the *Tribune-World* has a pool for the game. As a matter of fact, I have won that pool numerous times. What's your point?"

"Then, that makes you a known gambler, Mr. Watson," Titov said with a wry smile. "And since you speak to many baseball players during the season as part of your job, it means you are jeopardizing the careers of many of them."

Hannegan sat back down on his couch in Boston with a thud. *You sly sunnavabitch, Vlad.* The crunching noise was diminishing in his head. Woody Watson had underestimated Vladimir Titov: within that bear-like body and jovial personality lay a cunning mind. Glancing at his wristwatch, Watson realized the segment was almost over. If he was going to make his hit, he had better do it now.

"Very clever, Mr. Titov, but I don't think office pools were what baseball was worried about when they made their regulations. They are concerned about the integrity of the game, and I do believe, if my research is correct, that you enjoy high stakes wagering. Is that true?"

"I certainly do, Mr. Watson, but only at established legal gaming facilities."

"Nevertheless, you have continued to make contact with Ryan Hannegan during this season. Can I ask why?"

"Because Ryanovich has obligations to me."

"Obligations?"

"Yes, obligations. I am prepared to go public with them at this time."

Hannegan couldn't bear to watch, while Watson nearly came out of his seat in anticipation.

"I have it right here," Titov continued, reaching into the breast pocket of his jacket to pull out a piece of paper. With great ceremony, he unfolded the paper and turned it towards the camera which zoomed in for a closer look.

"See it says right here: I, Ryan Hannegan, owe you, Mad Vlad, four dollars and twenty-five cents!"

Woody Watson was speechless; Ryan Hannegan was beside himself with laughter. There was no time left for Watson to extricate himself from Titov's last trap. As the camera began to pull out, signifying the end of the segment, the Russian, looking directly at the camera, crowed:

"Ryanovich, you are a bad card player!" Then he turned to face Watson and added: "Once again I have won at one of your own games . . . the power of Mother Russia is absolute!"

With that, the screen faded to black, followed by a series of commercials.

The phone rang incessantly the rest of the evening at Hannegan's place. Dennis Soos and several other Colonials' teammates checked in, as did his family from California and Michaela from Florida. When Jayvee

DellVecchio called, following her *Totally Baseball* show, her enthusiasm knew no bounds. Hannegan was appreciative of all their support, but cautioned them saying Woody Watson was not the type that would give up, particularly after this public embarrassment. The flood of calls from media across the country seeking his reaction did not stop until he unplugged his phone around midnight. There was the matter of seven crucial games left to make the playoffs, and Ryan needed some sleep.

The following morning when he hooked up the phone again, the symphony of rings resumed at full force. Hannegan had spoken with everyone he wanted to the night before, so he wasn't going to bother with any of today's requests. As he started out the door to pick up that day's edition of the *Boston Journal*, one caller's message made him do a U-turn back to his phone.

"Ryan, this is Henry Lamirand from the Players' Association. I hope you get this message this morning because I..."

"Henry, this is Ryan. Sorry about the machine, but if I don't run my calls through it, I'd be spending all day talking with people I have no interest in speaking to."

"No problem. Hey, quite a show last night, wasn't it? I don't know if I have ever seen Woody Watson like he was at the end. He's an outstanding writer... but it doesn't hurt to see him taken down a peg or two every once in a while."

"He's a pompous asshole, Henry, if I'm allowed to say that, and I don't care how embarrassed he was last night, he deserved everything he got. He's been after me with all this crap since early in the season."

"A man like Woody Watson doesn't take a hard stance frivolously," Lamirand cautioned, "and that's why I am calling you. Watson believes he has solid evidence against you, and I don't think he plans on backing off."

"I don't give a damn what he does. After last night, I don't think anyone is going to take him seriously about it."

"I'm afraid that's not the case. General Hopkins wants to conclude this issue once and for all before the playoffs begin next week."

Henry Lamirand paused before continuing.

"This is an official call, Ryan. The Commissioner is coming up to Boston today, and he asked me to contact you. There will be a meeting in Paul Simonton's office at one o'clock this afternoon, and your presence is requested. I will be there on your behalf, but I am not sure yet who else will be attending. Just keep it cool, Ryan, and we'll get through this. I'll see you this afternoon."

Hannegan mumbled some thanks to Lamirand and then hung up the phone. *Will this thing never end?* The phone rang again, and by force of habit, he automatically answered it.

"Hello?"

"Ryanovich, did I wake you? You do not sound right. Maybe you are trying to be Russian and you toasted me too much last night after my MAGNIFICENT performance?"

"Sorry, Vlad, I didn't know it was you. Yes, you were something last night. I would have loved to have been there at the end. Did he say anything to you?"

"He left without saying a word to me, with his tail between his legs like the dog he is."

Hannegan could feel Titov's pride bursting through the phone line.

"Now I have taken care of that problem for you, Ryanovich."

"It's not that simple, Vlad. I have another meeting with the Commissioner and some other people this afternoon. Apparently they believe there still may be something to all of Watson's complaints about me."

"There is nothing they can prove, my friend . . . unless I let them. You take care of your business like I have told you, and nothing will go wrong."

"Don't threaten me, Vlad. I'm going to do the right thing; you'll see."

"That's all I wanted to hear, Ryanovich," Titov came back in a more cheerful voice. "Soon we will be celebrating the greatness of Ryan Hannegan and the Boston Colonials."

The phone conversation ended a few moments later. Hannegan's good spirits when he awakened had completely disappeared. He walked in a fog to pick up the newspaper on his doorstep, and the cloud hanging over him did not go away as he went through the rest of his activities that morning. He was close enough to reach out and touch the dreams he had made for this season, but once again the possibility was all too real that it could come crashing down upon him. Could he hang on, and could the Colonials?

Hannegan arrived at Patriots' Harbor around twelve-thirty, and fortunately, there wasn't anyone in the Colonials' clubhouse but Pete Hudec and some of the clubhouse boys. He was hoping that word of the meeting upstairs had not leaked out, and the absence of any reporters around told him that was the case. Ryan made some small talk in the trainer's room with Hudec, discussing the golf success he and Keith Lash had against Doc Soos and Kevin Kyle, as well, of course, Woody Watson's piece on TV. A few minutes before one, Hannegan headed for the elevator that would take him to the executive offices. The receptionist smiled in recognition as he stepped out of the car.

"Ryan Hannegan . . . this is a nice surprise. My, what a wonderful season you've been having."

"Thank you, it has been fun. I think they are expecting me in Mr. Simonton's office."

"Yes, they are, but could you do me a favor first? You have become my son's favorite player, and he would be thrilled to have your autograph."

Ryan obligingly autographed a Colonials' cap for her son and then headed down the hallway to the conference room where she had directed him. General Michael Hopkins was in discussion with Jack McDermott, Henry Lamirand, and Paul Simonton when Hannegan walked into the room. The conversation immediately ceased as he entered, with Hopkins, Lamirand, and McDermott walking over to greet Ryan, while Simonton, with a scowl on his face, headed to the other side of room. The pleasantries completed, General Hopkins and Jack McDermott moved to one side of the large table in the conference room, with Lamirand joining Hannegan in some chairs on the opposite side. Paul Simonton maintained his distance by taking a seat at the far end of the table.

"Again, Mr. Hannegan," General Hopkins began, "we meet with little advance notice, and I apologize for that. I appreciate your cooperation in this matter. Baseball wants to put on its best face when the playoffs begin next week, but unfortunately, this issue just won't go away."

"You're the boss, sir. If they tell me you want to see me . . . then that's what I'm supposed to do."

"In any event, I thank you for your understanding here. As we did at our last meeting, I am going to turn things over to Mr. McDermott."

The retired FBI agent unfolded himself from his chair. Jack McDermott was at least six-four, and he looked like he still would have no problem running down a criminal if that was necessary. He walked to the head of the conference table, to the corner nearest to where Hannegan was seated. He put his hands down on the table and leaned forward so that he was right in Ryan's face. It was an intimidating stance, but McDermott spoke with a *good cop* tone to his voice.

"I've got to tell you, Ryan . . . we've got ourselves a chance to have things get real messy. Baseball doesn't want that, and I am sure you don't want that either."

Hannegan nodded in affirmation, adding no other response.

"This is our situation. We have come upon information confirming some of Woody Watson's speculations. The evidence indicates Vladimir Titov has access to some performance-enhancing products that certainly skirt the issue of legality — if not actually violate our rules altogether. More importantly, there is some unsubstantiated evidence he has been involved with certain products which cannot be detected in the standard blood samplings we perform."

"Excuse me for interrupting, Mr. McDermott, but what does that have to do with me, even if it is all true?"

Paul Simonton scoffed, noticeably, from his end of the table, but Ryan was smart enough not to react to it. He wanted to say what was in his mind, however: "Nice support, asshole. I've helped keep your team in playoff contention, and all you want to do is string me up. What are you doing in this business if you hate the people who play it?"

The others in the room also took notice of Simonton's reaction. McDermott continued.

"It does concern you. There is a connection between you and this Russian . . . you have admitted it, and so did Mr. Titov last night on the television."

Hannegan started to respond, but the former lawman stopped him with a wave of his hand.

"There HAVE been irregularities in the blood tests we have performed on you this season. Although nothing has been found that would cause us to take action, we have had our suspicions raised by this recent information."

Jack McDermott walked back to the other side of the table and stood behind General Hopkins. He paused to await a comment from Hannegan. When none was forthcoming, he moved on to his next point.

"The urgency of this meeting was necessary because we are requesting you take a new test this afternoon at Mass General. It is a different procedure from the one we have been using, and it can give us more specific results in approximately forty-eight hours."

Henry Lamirand stepped in.

"This has not been approved by the Association, Ryan. They have no right to make you do this."

"That is true," interrupted General Hopkins, "but if Mr. Hannegan does not agree to our request, he will be suspended until further notice by virtue of the authority granted to me."

Now it was Paul Simonton's turn to join in the protests with Henry Lamirand. The Boston general manager might despise Hannegan for a variety of reasons, but he did not want to see his Colonials play the final seven games of the season a man short, not with a playoff spot on the line. Simonton and Lamirand had come out of their seats and were in a lively exchange with Jack McDermott. Hannegan, meanwhile, remained seated, visibly shaken. General Michael Hopkins sat impassively in his chair, across the table from Hannegan, intently staring at the ballplayer. The trio of standing combatants was quite loud in its discussion, but the leader of baseball brought the clamor to silence when he spoke softly in a voice that, nevertheless, rang like thunder.

"What is it going to be, Ryan? Will you cooperate with us, or will I have to prematurely end the best season of your career? To suspend the leading hitter in the game this year would not be good for baseball, but I WILL do it if that's what I must do to restore integrity to this game."

Hannegan was boxed in a corner. Submit to the test, and if it became public, what reaction would that trigger from Vladimir Titov... or Woody Watson and the other jackals in the media? Refuse to do so, and even with the likely protests of the Players Association, potentially miss the rest of the season.

"I really don't have much of a choice, General Hopkins, do I? I just want all this to be over."

"Ryan, you don't have to do this," Henry Lamirand blurted out. "General Hopkins, the Players Association will file a formal protest over this."

General Michael Hopkins stood for the first time since this meeting began. His commanding presence became even more impressive when he faced you with that ramrod-straight posture. The Commissioner walked over to Henry Lamirand with a stern, but not angry, look.

"Mr. Lamirand, I will be more than willing to take up your protest next Tuesday morning in my offices."

The Commissioner of the Baseball Big Leagues nodded brusquely at the other men in the room, placed his hand briefly on the left shoulder of the still seated Ryan Hannegan, and then left. A hearing on a protest next Tuesday would be meaningless; the season ended on Monday. The General's departure brought the issue to its climax: Ryan Hannegan would submit to the test that afternoon or his season would be over, and likely, the Colonials, too.

Ryan turned down Lamirand's offer to accompany him. He wanted to make the short drive to the hospital and undergo the testing without anyone else around. Even with the hospital prepared for his arrival, the procedure lasted long enough that Hannegan did not arrive back at Patriots' Harbor until five o'clock. Batting practice for that night's game with St. Louis was already underway, so the clubhouse was empty as Hannegan walked in . . . except for one very large man. Ellis Nance was that night's starting pitcher, and his normal pre-game routine for his starting assignments was to remain in the clubhouse during batting practice. However, the giant pitcher wasn't following his pattern of resting on one of the tables in Pete Hudec's training room. The Big E was sitting in the chair next to Ryan Hannegan's cubicle, waiting.

"I happened to see General Hopkins when I came to the ballpark earlier today. When you weren't here with everybody else, I figured something was up. Are you killing this thing for us?"

Ryan gave his teammate a brief recap of the meeting upstairs and the conditions the General had laid down for him. Hannegan said he had no choice but to undergo the new test.

"And what's it going to prove? That you cheated?"

"E, as I have told everyone all season long, I was not going to get caught doing anything that would hurt our chances to win."

"Do you know what it means to win?"

"Of course, I do. Who doesn't?"

"No, I mean to win?"

"I don't follow?"

"Think about it, Ryan; when do you feel better? After you've knocked the shit out of the ball for nine innings, or when we win?"

"Nothing beats winning, Big E!"

"That's my point. If a guy does something to help himself, but it hurts the team, then that guy doesn't really care about winning. There isn't anything that's more important than your team if you truly understand what it means to win.

"Let me tell you something, Ryan. I have been playing organized sports since I was five, and I've won a lot of games. But, you know, in all those years, I've never won a championship; I mean, one where that final gun goes off — that last out is made — and you get to celebrate on the field. I've never had that chance to say I'm a champion, not as an individual, but as part of a team. To celebrate something I know wouldn't have happened without me and my teammates doing it together."

Nance rose from the chair to his full extension: all six-nine of him.

"I want that feeling, Ryan — one time before I hang it up — and I'm not going to let anything interfere with my last chance. Nothing or nobody is bigger than the team . . . MY TEAM!"

His speech over, Ellis Nance looked hard into Hannegan's eyes, poked him in the chest with his index finger. That'll leave a bruise, Ryan thought. Nance turned and trudged to the trainer's room to resume his pre-game routine. Hannegan hung up his street clothes and slowly pulled on his uniform. His teammates would soon be returning from the field. Ryan grabbed his cap off the top shelf of his locker, brushing his hand against Norm, Michaela's teddy bear. He lifted the mamori hanging around the toy's neck and slowly rolled the medallion around in his hand. Releasing it, he rubbed the top of Norm's head, almost like tousling the hair of a child. Superstitious or not, Hannegan was going to take all the luck and protection he could get.

· TWENTY-TWO ·

A RAUCOUS CROWD ASSEMBLED at Patriots' Harbor for the Wednesday night game with St. Louis. The Boston schools had not yet begun, but a number of the students from the many local colleges had already returned to the area, adding even more energy to the ballpark than the pennant race alone would. Seven games left to the regular season, and everybody wanted to be there to see how it would turn out.

Any combination of Baltimore wins and Boston losses that equaled two would give the Crabbers the division title. Simply, Baltimore was a lock to make the postseason. In the Midwest Division, St. Louis had a one game lead on Dallas, but the Rivermen and the Wranglers both had records that all but assured a wild card spot. The options were dwindling for the Colonials. Should the Colonials make the playoffs, they could find themselves playing St. Louis in the first round of the postseason if the Rivermen ended up with a better overall record than Baltimore or Dallas. It added one more element of interest to the series over the next two nights.

AMERICAN CONFERENCE

Northeast Division			Midwest Division		
	W-L	GB		W-L	GB
Baltimore (2)	81-52	—	Saint Louis	80-53	—
Boston	75-58	6	Dallas	79-54	1
New York	73-60	8	Chicago	62-71	18
Cleveland	67-66	14	Minneapolis	61-72	19
Detroit	61-72	20	Kansas City	57-76	23

(2): Any combination of Baltimore wins or Boston losses that equals 2 will clinch the division title.

Ellis Nance lost a hard-luck decision to the Rivermen in Saint Louis six days earlier, and he brought a fury to the mound that evening. Like his performance against Kansas City in late July, the Big E seemed fortified by his clubhouse confrontation with Ryan Hannegan. Nance, in the top five in career strikeouts in the BBL, blazed through the Rivermen with a season-high sixteen strikeouts — the best in baseball this year. Dante Russo, the BBL leader in home runs, was Nance's victim four times.

Ryan Hannegan also was fueled by the little talk before the game. For the fourth time in this long campaign, he whacked out four or more hits in a game. Ryan also drove home his one hundred sixth run when he plated Junichi with a triple to left center as part of a three run first inning for Boston. Junichi was equally impressive, hitting his first home run since his return as part of a three for five night. The eight to nothing stroll — Nance's twelfth win overall — kept alive Boston's faint division title hopes thanks to a Lumberjacks' win in Baltimore.

The postgame conference with the media was pleasantly brief for Hannegan, even though his four hits pushed his batting average above .390. Ellis Nance was with Hannegan on the dais and the assembled reporters were more interested in getting insights to the incredible performance from the veteran pitcher. There were the usual questions that had become a familiar ritual for Ryan, but he was thankful nothing was brought up about his earlier session with General Hopkins.

Such good fortune did not extend to the following day when reports began to air around mid-day that suspicions still remained regarding Hannegan's connection with Vladimir Titov.

"... this building behind me has become the centerpiece of the latest episode in the Ryan Hannegan saga..."

A DBC reporter was standing in front of Massachusetts General Hospital.

"... we have learned that the Colonials outfielder was here yesterday for additional supplement testing at the request of the Baseball Big Leagues. Hannegan, the subject of several previous examinations, has reportedly had unusual blood levels that concern baseball's hierarchy..."

The report next shifted to Woody Watson in New York. Watson was clearly looking to rebuild his image that had been tarnished by his ill-fated television interview with Titov two days earlier.

"Hannegan's activities don't ring true. Why else would the Commissioner and the heads of baseball continue to seek further medical information from him?"

The DBC reporter attempted to ask a question, but Watson never gave him a chance.

"Baseball must take some definitive action immediately to maintain the integrity of the game. I would suggest General Hopkins might consider a search of Ryan Hannegan's home for possible evidence of wrongdoing."

Watson's bluster was expected, but the discovery of Hannegan's latest testing re-ignited the speculation he might be doing something wrong. As the Colonials came out for their stretching exercises before batting practice, more than one hundred members of the press — print and electronic — were ready to ask that question. D.P. Perryton and Bobby Greene felt Hannegan would be better off facing the media, so long as the Colonials controlled the situation tightly. To issue a statement or to avoid the controversy altogether would only increase the speculation. It would be best to do something in person, as difficult as that might be, in order to get Ryan's position out in front of the public.

Hannegan followed his usual pre-game routine: remaining in the outfield until joining the last group for his turn in batting practice. When it was time for the Rivermen to take over, Bobby Greene led Ryan to an area that had been roped off for the many reporters and camera people on hand. Logistically, it might be a little difficult, but D.P. Perryton thought they could control things better this way than to do it in the conference room underneath the stands. Ryan was grateful his manager was standing at his side when the interrogation began.

"Any comments to the latest charges?"

"How distracting is this in the midst of the chase for the playoffs?"

"Does this tarnish your success this year?"

"Are you going to hire an attorney?"

Ryan began to answer some of the queries when D.P. Perryton took control.

"You people kill me. Every move demands immediate action from all of you. How about we let this thing run its course?"

Perryton put his arm around Hannegan's shoulders.

"I will not allow this young man to become the victim of this circus. Ryan Hannegan is having a wonderful year, one that he is quite capable of accomplishing without any illegal help. If baseball finds he did something wrong, then the appropriate action will be taken. In the meantime, I am not going to let this become any more of a distraction for him or my team. Ladies and gentlemen, we have a spot in the playoffs to win. This session is over."

The Boston manager, with his arm still around Hannegan, broke through the circle of reporters and cameras and the pair headed down the tunnel to the Colonials' clubhouse. Groans of protest and requests for just one more answer trailed them, but they ignored them all. D.P. Perryton has long been described as a players' manager, and he has never filled that role any better than on this day.

Even if the new suspicions remained unconfirmed, they did have a numbing effect on the Colonials, much to D.P. Perryton's dismay. Their fans exhorted their heroes throughout the second game of the set with St. Louis, but the Boston nine staggered their way through the contest. The Rivermen scored eleven times against Raul Gomez and Jeff Hennessey in a long night for the C's. Normally, D.P. Perryton would have pulled Hennessey after he had given up four of the runs, but the Boston manager wanted to save the rest of his bullpen for the final series against New York. Hennessey ended up pitching the last five innings of the game, allowing seven runs overall.

It was the worst game for Hannegan in two weeks. Jay Brendan, the St. Louis pitcher, struck him out twice and induced an easy popup in between the strikeouts. In his final trip to the plate, Hannegan had one of those excuse-me hits on a checked swing that enabled him to keep his batting string alive. The consecutive games-with-a-hit streak was now at thirteen, and in light of the happenings earlier in the day, Ryan could not imagine that number being any unluckier.

The postgame news conference generated more requests for Hannegan's response to the latest controversy. D.P. Perryton was on hand at the conference, and he again took offense to what he called the unrelenting harassment against his player.

"I always thought it was 'innocent until proven guilty' in this country. Unless you have something concrete to accuse him of, get off his back. Like I told you before the game, he's told you all he is going to tell you!"

Perryton struck a nerve — all part of his plan. The media turned its wrath on the Boston manager rather than at his player. The tough interrogation now dealt with Perryton's use of his bullpen that night and what that night's loss means if Boston were to face St. Louis in the playoffs next week. Like the session before the game, this gathering eventually ended without Hannegan having to give any real responses.

The Crabbers, meanwhile, had bested the Lumberjacks in Baltimore to clinch at least a tie for the Northeast Division title. The end of Boston's five-game winning streak, coupled with a win by the Horsemen, dropped the C's wild card advantage to only two games. Like it or not, the playoffs were starting five games early for Boston and New York. The Colonials would have to win two games against the Horsemen to get back to the playoffs for the first time in four years.

Terry Tate was Jayvee DellVecchio's guest on *Totally Baseball* Thursday evening. Jayvee was in the DBC studios in New York while Tate was hooked up for a live remote from Patriots' Harbor.

"Terry, how devastating was tonight's loss for the Colonials?"

"Any loss is tough at this time of year, Jayvee, but it's not cataclysmic for Boston. I think the whole idea of the Rivermen or the Colonials sending a message to the other is overrated. I believe the C's still have a good situation going in terms of making the playoffs."

"Boston wraps up the season at home with a five game set against the Horsemen," Jayvee laid out. "They do play well at home, and the number two will play a large role in these final days."

The television screen filled with an ever-enlarging numeral two and then transformed into the current standings in the American Conference.

"The Colonials have a two game lead on the Horsemen. Baltimore is in and the Rivermen and the Wranglers also look good. All Boston has to do is win TWO games in this final series and they become the final team in the American Conference."

The televised image changed again to show highlights of Keith Lash and Ellis Nance.

"And then there is the big two on the mound. D.P. Perryton has his rotation set up perfectly. Keith Lash has been the best pitcher in baseball this season and he goes tomorrow night. If he holds true to form, then New York would have to win the last four and that's going to be really tough at The Harbor, especially since Ellis Nance would work that final game for the C's if it was necessary. The two of them have been a perfect six for six against the Horsemen."

"The Big E has looked great since coming back from his ankle injury. It's like he's been on a mission," Jayvee added.

"You don't realize how true that is. Sources have told me that this will be the final season for Nance and it certainly looks like he wants his finish to be a glorious one."

"Terry, it sounds as though you believe this might be the year for the Colonials to end The Jinx?"

"Don't say that too loud, Jayvee, nobody has to tell me about the power of the Jinx. It would be great for the C's and their fans, but their hearts have been broken too many times. Let's just wait and see how this weekend unfolds, and then we'll deal with the jinx."

Unfortunately, Terry Tate did not realize how prophetic his final thoughts would be. Keith Lash, the American Conference leader in wins, could not get the victory he wanted most of all. Eighteen and seven on the year, seven wins in nine decisions since the All-Star break; those numbers meant nothing in the Friday night opener with New York. The Horsemen took advantage of Lash's lack of command, working deep into counts to coax walks or to hit pitches back up the middle for hits. It was almost as if Peter Beckwith's club had slowed its offensive approach to match Lash's off-speed pitches. The strategy worked as the New Yorkers won the game to grab the early momentum in the series.

The media scrutiny of Ryan Hannegan continued before and after the game, but buoyed by Jayvee DellVecchio's arrival in Boston to cover the series, Hannegan had a good night at the plate. A walk and two more hits were not enough to help produce a Boston victory, but his batting average was still maintaining its unbelievable climb, now standing at .392 with four games to play. For the first time, he began to consider that unreal possibility that he might actually be able to hit .400. The news gathering following the game remained focused on the potential Titov connection until yet another surprise occurred.

"... the most important thing is that we reach the playoffs, not what Vladimir Titov..."

Stirring at the back of the conference area at Patriots' Harbor interrupted Hannegan's reply. General Michael Hopkins came striding vigorously into the conference room. Everything fell silent except for the click of the General's footsteps on the concrete floor... and the whir of the motorized cameras of the news photographers capturing his entrance. Baseball's boss climbed the dais and took a seat alongside Hannegan. He acknowledged the Boston outfielder with a nod and then turned to face the media.

"Ladies and gentlemen, I had hoped to clear up all the discrepancies over this situation with Mr. Hannegan here, but it seems my actions earlier this week only exacerbated the problem. I am here tonight to bring this issue to an end."

Hannegan sat motionless alongside the military hero. General Hopkins placed his hand on Ryan's right forearm and then resumed.

"Forty-eight hours ago, at my request, this young man willingly agreed to undergo some new, more sophisticated testing in hopes of determining, ultimately, whether he had made use of some illegal body-fortifying agents. Much has been made of Mr. Hannegan's relationship with

Vladimir Titov, a man who has allegedly been involved in the distribution of such products."

A low murmur ran through the crowd of reporters, and Hannegan could only hope the involuntary tensing of his body was not being felt in the General's grip on his arm.

"These advanced tests developed by medical personnel associated with the International Olympic Committee were able to give us significant results in a quick turnaround. Those findings indicate some abnormalities in this young man's blood content from what would be considered the norm, but they are consistent with the conclusions reached from the other tests conducted on him this season."

The general paused momentarily to allow the crowd to absorb his points.

"Those conclusions could not determine whether or not any outside stimuli created these abnormalities. That means either Mr. Hannegan has been using a supplement that cannot be detected by the current testing methods available, or his blood differences are the possible result of genetics, as Terry Tate proposed earlier this season."

Hopkins acknowledged the Boston writer, who was sitting in the front row, with a small nod.

"As for Ryan Hannegan's relationship with Vladimir Titov," Hopkins removed his hand from Ryan's arm, "baseball is never happy when there is a connection between one of its players and someone with alleged gambling ties. Mr. Hannegan's contact with this gentleman however, came about through an activity sanctioned by the Baseball Big Leagues. We have no tangible evidence of any other significant contact between this player and Mr. Titov."

Hopkins turned his gaze to Woody Watson, who was sitting at the opposite end of the front row from Terry Tate.

"Mr. Watson, as a member of the press who, I would assume, would fight long and hard to preserve the First Amendment's guidelines for freedom of speech, I am stunned you would want baseball to callously disregard the Fourth Amendment of the Constitution by searching Mr. Hannegan's premises without any reasonable evidence beyond your speculations."

Again a ripple ran through the room. This was not the return to the position of influence Watson had been experiencing earlier in the day.

"For someone who boasts he is The Truth, your position is disappointing."

Mortified by the public dressing-down, Watson arose from his seat and departed the area, causing the ripple to turn into a wave of noise from the assembled. Michael Hopkins waited for Watson to leave the room before resuming.

"My office has concluded no action should be taken in this matter. Unless some new evidence arises, I consider this matter closed."

The media immediately raised their questions to the commissioner, but Michael Hopkins restored the peace by simply raising his hand.

"This is not the forum to continue this discussion at this time. There is another important game that is going to take place in less than fifteen hours, and I would like to turn the focus back to the field where it really belongs. I plan on staying for the duration of this series — I am a fan, ladies and gentlemen — and I will entertain your questions in an appropriate fashion. Right now, I am looking forward to watching some great baseball!"

The General's edict ended the session, and a grateful Ryan Hannegan shook Michael Hopkins's hand and headed back to the Colonials' clubhouse.

"I've never seen anything like that," Jayvee DellVecchio remarked as she lay next to Hannegan in his bed. Ryan was idly tracing one of his fingers along the beautiful curves of her body, almost oblivious to her comment. He was in a state of bliss from their lovemaking... and from hoping maybe the worst was behind him.

"I mean, Hoppy had that whole room in total control. I bet we all would have stood up and clucked like chickens if he had told us to."

"Do you ever give the reporter's side of you a rest?"

"Well, there is one way you can distract me..."

Jayvee rolled onto Hannegan's chest and began to nibble at his neck.

"Come on, DellVecchio... I've got a game in a couple hours."

"What's the problem, Hannegan? Where's that extra boost that everyone says you're supposed to have?" Jayvee needled as her kissing continued down his chest.

Hannegan stroked her hair as he stared up at his ceiling. There was a slight smile on his face, but it was not a smile of contentment.

The final three days of the series — four games with the Sunday doubleheader — were beyond sellouts. There was an almost college football-like atmosphere to the proceedings. Tailgate parties were everywhere in the area around Patriots' Harbor before the Saturday game, and many fans were flying flags with the Colonials logo from their cars, vans, and SUV's. A sidewalk vendor was doing a brisk business painting temporary tattoos of the interlocking letters B and C with the cocked tri-corner hat on the faces of young Colonials fans . . . and even some of the not-so-young.

The thumping on Friday night by the Horsemen saw a subdued Boston contingent leave The Harbor at game's end, but the fans were re-energized by the sunshine on this picture-perfect late summer day. Cries of "Here We Go Boston, Here We Go" and "Let's Go C's" thundered around the ballpark long before Darren Haddad made the first pitch of the game. It wasn't just the perfect day that had Ryan Hannegan pumped. Accounts of General Hopkins's statements from the previous night's news conference got wide play on radio and television Friday night and in the Boston papers Saturday morning. The fans' attitude towards Hannegan was back to positive, and they gave him standing ovations when his name was announced during the introductions of the starting lineup and when he came to bat for the first time in the bottom of the second inning.

". . . A swing and a drive . . . WAY BACK . . . THAT BALL IS GOING AND IT AIN'T COMING BACK!"

Hannegan launched a rocket shot into the bleachers on his first swing to give Boston the early lead. Ryan circled the bases while the tumultuous ovation cascaded down on him.

"Atta, boy, Ryno . . . that gets us cooking!" Dennis Soos exclaimed to Hannegan as they exchanged their six-gun salute at home plate.

"Keep the party going, Doc," Ryan replied, pointing to the Blue Pier in right.

Soos promptly complied with his friend's wishes, mashing a moon shot into Boston Harbor on the first pitch he saw. The delirium started anew, and the fans were aware this day had to belong to the Colonials. Less than fifteen hours removed from a disappointing loss and the fear of another late season collapse, the Colonials and their fans were celebrating a trouncing of their archrivals. The roars grew stronger with each out Darren Haddad registered . . . and every run the Colonials put up on the scoreboard. A six to one victory for Boston pushed their advantage to two games over New York. Three games left: a Colonials' win in just one of them would put them back into the playoffs.

The homer in the second inning was just one of three hits registered by Ryan Hannegan on the afternoon. With three games remaining to a schedule of one hundred forty games, Hannegan's hit total stood at one hundred ninety-five, a remarkable achievement. His .395 batting average was realistically within striking distance of the magical .400 mark, and everyone wanted to talk about Ryan's final push to reach a milestone.

"Ryan, can you tell us when you first started to believe you could reach .400?" a local Boston television sports anchor asked to begin the Saturday postgame news conference.

"You know I keep hearing this same question. This may seem far-fetched to many of you, but I honestly don't think about .400. You really do have to just approach things as one at-bat at a time, one game at a time. I'm happier we won today than I am about anything I did personally."

Hannegan was right; the media did not take his stance very seriously because the line of questioning stayed right on the subject of hitting .400.

"According to my calculations, you will need about seven hits over these last games to do it," Terry Tate pointed out. "Do you worry about having enough opportunities to accomplish that?"

"Terry, there are too many other people in our lineup for any Horsemen pitcher to worry only about me. So much of what I have been able to do this season is because people like Ramon, Ju, and Doc have done great. I just sit in the middle of them and get some great chances to hit."

"Your humility is so refreshing," a New York writer said, "... but let's be real here. This is your moment in the sun in an otherwise ho-hum career. Are we supposed to believe you are not caught up in all of this attention?"

A Ryan Hannegan from earlier in the season would have blown up over that question, but not now ... not after a season of being in the spotlight.

"Am I thrilled to have a season like this one? Of course, I am. Ask anyone who's played this game if they wouldn't want a year like I've had. But it still doesn't beat winning, and that's what I want to do, to win."

The questions continued, and Hannegan responded mechanically, but cheerfully, to each one. In reality, his mind was reflecting on his winning comment and what it really meant. The Big E was right, there is nothing like winning. If what's happened to me this season helps us win, then that's all that really matters. After about ten minutes, the news conference ended and Hannegan headed back to the clubhouse.

Dennis and Lisa Soos joined Ryan and Jayvee for dinner that night at a little neighborhood place not far from the ballpark. There was a buzz in town: the Colonials were on the doorstep of returning to the playoffs. Gratefully, the other diners in the restaurant let the foursome eat their meals in relative peace, although the two players got ovations when they entered and left the restaurant. Enough had been made of the relationship between Jayvee and Ryan that they were now more comfortable being together in public.

"Ryan, I don't think I have ever seen you like this," Lisa Soos began. "If this is what Jayvee's influence does to you, then there is hope for you yet."

"You're talking to the president of the have-pity-on-a-washed-up-ballplayer-club," Jayvee answered. "I've almost got him to understand table manners. Next we may even try a coat and tie!"

"Wait a minute — I draw the line on those neck-chokers. Besides, the only ones I own you've got tied to the bedposts back at my place."

Hannegan's return volley brought a blush to Jayvee's face. She responded by playfully breaking a breadstick over his head. Lisa Soos was right, though; he had never been like this before. He had found someone who fit, someone who understood how a baseball player lives his life. Hannegan was absently playing with Jayvee's hair as she lay sleeping next to him later that night. He chuckled quietly when her gentle snoring had an occasional burst of volume. *Just get through all of this,* he said to himself, *and nothing but Jayvee and Michaela will matter.*

Hannegan's thoughts for the future were interrupted by the sound of his ringing cell phone out on the dining room table where he had left it. Jayvee kept on sleeping, and since she and Michaela were about the only people who had the number, he knew he'd better answer it.

"Michaela, what are doing calling me at this hour? Is everything okay?"

"Certainly, everything is okay, my good friend," came the reply from the other end of the call: Vladimir Titov.

"Vlad, how did you get this number? What do you want?"

"Do not be cross with me, Ryanovich. I did not want to disturb you and your lovely lady, so I waited until I thought the time would be right."

A chill went through Hannegan. The Russian seemed to know every move he made.

"Please ... leave me be, Vlad. I know what you want, and I am doing all I can to make sure your investment pays off. All you're doing is putting more pressure on me; just back off, please."

"There is no pressure, Ryanovich."

The Russian's voice was deceptively soothing.

"I want the same as you do. Just to win."

Titov had used Ryan's exact quote from the news conference earlier in the day. Titov's tone changed, however, with his next comment.

"You do what you are supposed to do, my friend, and those two beautiful women in your life will never know about our arrangement."

"Don't threaten me, you son of a bitch."

Hannegan raised his voice without realizing it could awaken Jayvee. He backed off, but it didn't matter because the phone had gone dead on the other end of the call. Ryan padded back to the bedroom, but sleep would not come easily for him.

"So close," he said aloud softly while Jayvee's peaceful slumber continued. "So close ..."

Hannegan was distracted the following morning, but no one seemed to notice. It was clinching day for the Colonials, and Boston was in a frenzied state of mind. If the beloved C's won either game of the doubleheader, they would accomplish two of their fans' fondest wishes: make the postseason, and do it at the expense of the Horsemen. Patriots' Harbor was packed beyond capacity to watch the finishing blow, and there wasn't a Boston fire marshal anywhere who would dare try to turn away the faithful from their baseball cathedral. It was the warmest day yet on the weekend with temperatures in the high 80s. The soda and beer concessions had endless lines going. The Colonials were as hot as the weather in the early innings of the first game of the doubleheader, and that only added to the party atmosphere.

Nick Ertle was doing a fine job keeping the New York attack at bay. The veteran had allowed a two-run single to Dave Bock, while his teammates had plated five runs against Rick Shoemaker through seven innings. Ryan Hannegan had driven in one of those runs in the fifth with a sacrifice fly, and he also added two more safeties to his hit total during the game. Five more hits — if Terry Tate's numbers were correct — and Hannegan could reach .400.

"Here we go, Colonials' fans; three more outs to the playoffs..."

Tom Kingery was as excited as the capacity crowd and he was on his feet in his radio booth to call the final inning of play by play.

"D.P. has gone to Hwang Sang Hwan to close out the Horsemen..."

The Boston bullpen ace was tied with Matt Lerner of New York for the conference lead in saves, and he had not blown a save situation all year when he had a three-run cushion.

"... Tim Lauer is pinch-hitting for New York... Hwan winds and fires... a fastball and Lauer pops it up... Kyle calling for it on the edge of the outfield grass... he's got it. Two to go for the Colonials..."

The Boston fans were delirious with anticipation.

"Na-na-na-Nah... Na-na-na-Nah... Hey, hey, hey... Goodbye..."

The singing rang throughout the ballpark, growing louder with each pitch, as Wang got ahead in the count, no balls and two strikes, against Nelson Cuevas. Suddenly, everything changed.

"... Unbelievable... Hwan was just trying to push Cuevas off the plate and the pitch hit him on the front shoulder... that puts a runner on first with one down... here's Kareem Lewis... Wang checks Cuevas and delivers... a smash... FAIR, just inside the bag past a diving Morientes at first... it's headed into the corner... Cook fires it back in but Cuevas is now at third and Lewis stops at second with a double..."

When Dave Bock singled them both home to make it a one-run game, the singing had stopped. D.P. Perryton hustled out to the mound to calm down his bullpen ace, and he was joined by the rest of the infield in a huddle atop the mound.

"Nice and easy, Hwang... take a deep breath."

"Skipper's right, Hwang," said Dennis Soos, "forget about it and just focus on getting the last two..."

"Now remember, Hwang," D.P. broke back in, "Hegan likes to extend his arms. Bust him inside and maybe the boys will turn two behind you."

The Korean star nodded to his manager's instructions, and several of the infielders patted him on the back before returning to their positions. The advice and support didn't work.

"... One and one the count on Hegan... Hwang checks on the runner... now he comes to the plate... a swing and a drive towards right center... Hannegan on the move... he's not going to get there... Bock is flying around third with the tying run and Hegan cruises into second with an RBI double. The game is tied..."

Hwan got the next hitter for out number two, but Greg McGregor's flare just out of the reach of Kevin Kyle — who screamed in frustration loud enough for people in the stands to hear — scored Hegan to give New York the lead. The Colonials went down in order in the bottom of the ninth, leaving Patriots' Harbor in stunned silence. The wild-card lead was trimmed to one, with two games to play.

The second game provided more torture. New York, fueled by their improbable ninth inning rally against the C's closer in the opener, jumped all over Kris Fucci in a five-run first inning in the nitecap. The exhale of disappointment from the crowd was palpable, almost tangible, like the air being let out of a giant balloon. In the space of two innings of play, the Horsemen had completely changed the atmosphere in Boston.

Hannegan had one of the nine Boston hits in his four at-bats, and in two of his other plate appearances, the Horsemen' defense took away potential hits with fine plays. It wasn't enough to help the Colonials' cause, and the effort left his batting average at .395. Cracking .400 was now a fading possibility; it would take a near perfect performance in the Labor Day finale the following afternoon. The six to two setback made it only the second double-dip loss of the year by the C's, and a full-blown panic had set in for all of Boston. It would be hard to find anyone who didn't think the Jinx was going to do it to the Colonials again.

Jayvee DellVecchio sat alone at a small desk that had been set up on the top level of the Blue Pier for that night's edition of *Totally Baseball*. The retired players-turned commentators had done their analysis, and all that remained was for Jayvee to set the scene for tomorrow.

"After a mad dash since April fifteenth, it all comes down to one game. Another incredible chapter in this long-running saga of the Colonials and the Horsemen will be played out on the field below me."

Jayvee changed her angle to face another camera and a graphic showing Ellis Nance and Buddy Pickens side-by-side was superimposed on the upper left corner of the television screen.

"Baseball fans couldn't ask for anything better than to have this feud settled by two men who have meant so much for so many years to their teams. Ellis Nance, pitching in, perhaps, his final game in the big leagues, against Buddy Pickens, the number one horse ridden to several Showdown championships by the Horsemen."

The television image changed to a wide shot of the empty ballpark.

"The Harbor is silent for now, but in less than twelve hours, it will be alive with sound. The anticipation is incredible. For the people involved, sleep will not come easy tonight. For *Totally Baseball*, I'm Jayvee DellVecchio . . . we'll see you tomorrow night."

There was one person involved in this drama who missed Jayvee's setup for the final game. Emotionally drained by the disastrous results of the day, all Hannegan wanted to do was collapse in his bed to re-charge for tomorrow. He had given a spare key for the condo to Jayvee so she could let herself back in when she returned from work. It was after midnight — with Hannegan in that state halfway between sleep and consciousness — when Jayvee climbed into bed alongside him.

"What's the matter with you, Ryan? This place is like a freezer in here... aren't you cold?"

They had forgotten to turn on his air-conditioning or open some windows before they had left for the ballpark that morning, so the condo was extremely stuffy and warm when Hannegan got home. He had turned the air conditioning down below sixty degrees to cool things off, and then fell asleep before he could remember to turn it back to a more normal temperature.

"Sorry... I hadn't noticed."

Hannegan raised himself up on an elbow and groggily pointed.

"The thermostat is by that supply closet down the hallway by the other bedroom."

Hannegan slumped back down on the bed, rolling onto his side to fall back asleep while Jayvee went to seek some relief from the cold. Almost lost in dreamland, Ryan was jarred awake by a noise from the hallway. Leaping out of bed, he rushed out of the bedroom only to find Jayvee coming out of the supply closet, pushing a large object: one of Mad Vlad's refrigerated containers.

"What the hell is this?"

She nudged the crate farther down the hallway with her foot.

"I knew I would still be cold, even after turning up the thermostat, so I went looking for a blanket. I get in there," she said pointing back into the closet, "and I come upon this thing... and another one just like it. Talk to me, Hannegan. WHAT'S GOING ON?"

Ryan stared at Jayvee for a few moments without saying a word. The look on her face told him this was not going to end until she got some answers.

· TWENTY-THREE ·

THE WARMTH OF the sun felt good on Hannegan's face. The sound of seagulls squawking out over the harbor was the only disruption to the stillness at Patriots' Harbor. The sky was a cerulean blue and a few puffy white clouds danced across the canvas of the heavens. On top of the wind, there lofted the sweet scent of hope graced by birdsong. At this hour of the morning, Ryan had the place virtually to himself. Soon activity would commence: lawnmowers making a final trim, concession stands being readied, ushers preparing to man their posts. For the moment, however, Ryan Hannegan was safe in his solitude. The Boston outfielder, already dressed in his batting practice gear, sat with his back against the bleachers wall in the Bermuda Triangle corner of left-center field. His eyes were shut as he contemplated his situation, desperately hoping the sunshine on his face would somehow reinvigorate him. He was beyond tired. He was exhausted.

There had not been much sleep the night before, not after Jayvee's discovery of the containers sent by Vladimir Titov. The fatigue, however, came from much more than the lengthy conversation that ended any hopes of going back to bed. His career, on the brink at this time last year, had turned dramatically in the past twelve months. The cost of such success — fateful decisions, internal battles, outside accusations — was a steep one. Hannegan felt totally drained. Could he summon the energy for even one more game?

The crunching noise that had danced through his subconscious ever since the delivery of Mad Vlad's first package before spring training was again clamoring for his attention. God, it's like all I can hear is that damn sound! Ryan opened his eyes, only to be momentarily blinded by the morning sun. When his vision adjusted, he saw Dennis Soos.

"I thought I might find you out in a place like this."

The third baseman looked down at his friend, not exactly certain what to do next.

"Jayvee called Lisa this morning. She said you were already gone when she got up, and she was worried about you."

"I'm tired, Doc; I don't know if I can do this anymore?"

Dennis Soos crouched down and put a hand on Hannegan's knee. He had been in this spot before. Erica Hannegan had passed away, and it was more than her seventeen-year-old son could bear. Soos had found Ryan sitting on the beach near their California homes, sobbing on and off, absently playing at the sand with his feet. Ryan was overwhelmed with grief. Now as Doc watched Hannegan kicking with his cleats at the gravel on the track, he was carried back to that time nearly twenty years ago.

Quietly, Doc sat down alongside Hannegan — occasionally tossing a pebble of gravel towards the outfield grass — and he waited. On that long ago beach he had done the same thing, taking a seat on a piece of driftwood next to his grieving friend. It was not a time for talking, it was a time for just being there. Eventually, the anguish raging inside Ryan was verbalized. Doc just listened — not saying a word — because that was what was needed... then and now.

When, at last, Hannegan finished, Soos again put a hand on his friend's knee.

"I've loved you like a brother, Ryno, for as long as I can remember. We're family. Whatever you need from me, you've got it."

"I've always gotten what I needed from you, Doc, just being my friend."

"That's not going to change, pal. And this team is your family, too — except maybe for a few assholes — we're in this thing together!"

Hannegan returned a small smile to his friend, a glimmer of life that Soos had been seeking.

"Let's go win us a ballgame," Soos barked, slapping Hannegan's leg as he climbed to his feet. Hannegan had to shield his eyes as he looked up at his teammate, appearing larger than life with the morning sunshine haloed around him. Like always, Doc was there: a friend — no, a brother — without compromise. *My life is important, not just to me, but to Doc, Jayvee, Michaela, and all the others who have a stake in what I'm doing.* Hannegan scrambled up to join Soos for the walk back to the clubhouse.

The Boston fans tried to re-discover their courage later that morning as they sought their seats or their standing spots behind the bleachers and across the Blue Pier. Yesterday's festive feel was gone from Patriots' Harbor, replaced by the uneasiness brought on by Sunday's twin losses. The New York fans, meanwhile, appeared to have increased in number with more hats and shirts featuring The Horseman logo found among what would eventually be another standing-room-only crowd. The Colonials and the Horsemen were tied, but the attitude of many in attendance said this race was already over: the Jinx lives!

Neither team took batting practice before the game, not after eighteen innings yesterday. The absence of activity on the field — save for the occasional sighting of players running sprints in the outfield or playing catch in front of the dugouts — gave a surreal feel to the scene. Six months of action, all those games, but still the season would come down to a solitary battle between these bitter rivals. The winners would head to a Wednesday playoff game in Baltimore. The losers would be left with an off-season of contemplation over what might have been.

The Colonials' clubhouse was practically devoid of movement. A few players shuffled into the trainer's room. Some others wandered off to the batting cages to see if a few swings could help cut through the tension. The majority of the Colonials, however, sat by their lockers in stoic meditation or in whispered conversation with nearby teammates. Even the big-screen TV in the corner was conspicuous with its silence. A baseball clubhouse near game time is not like a football locker room. A football pre-game atmosphere has a seething quiet. It is a cauldron of building passion where only an occasional scream of comment pierces the silence. Football demands that kind of build-up, to let the growing emotion steel the body for the physical fury that would soon follow. Ultimately, a fiery speech, by a coach or one of the players, lights the fuse that sends men out to play football's great game of organized mayhem.

Baseball is played passionately, but no player could survive the emotional fever a football game requires when he has to do it one hundred forty times in a season. This baseball campaign was done to one, however, and the feelings for this game bubbled just beneath the surface for each Boston player. With the clock on the wall indicating game time was near, Dudley Perryton walked into the middle of the clubhouse.

"Men, I'm not going to give some rah-rah speech here. That's not my style, and you don't need to be told what this game means to everyone in this room. What I am going to do is ask you to remember why you play this game in the first place. When you were a kid, you played baseball for two reasons, basically: because it was fun and because you were doing it with your friends."

"Look around this room," Perryton requested, pausing to allow the players to do that. "What do you see? I know what I see. I see a group of men who love to play this game. You know there is no better feeling than to be out on that field, playing ball. I know because if I could still do it, I would."

Again, the Boston manager paused. Perryton walked slowly around the room, shaking hands with some players, slapping others on the back or giving them a knowing nod. When he had completed a circuit of the room, he picked up again.

"I also see of roomful of people who appreciate what it means to be a part of a team. We've been through a lot this season — last year, too — and now it all comes down to one game. Go out there and have fun. Do what you love to do with the people who are your family."

Perryton might not consider himself a rah-rah type, but the eyes of every man in the room were fixed on him.

"Screw those people down the hall; they want to take away something that belongs to us, something we have earned! And screw those people up in the stands if they don't believe in us! Let's take that goddamn jinx and stick in somebody's ear!"

There wasn't a huge roar from the players — except for Kevin Kyle's cry of "Let's kick their ass" — but the occasional "You got it, Skip," or just players nodding their heads, showed D.P. Perryton had hit the proper note.

D.P.'s right, thought Ryan . . . The rest of the stuff doesn't really matter. It's all about just playing the game. Ryan smiled and wrapped his right arm around the shoulders of Dennis Soos and they walked toward the brilliant light at the end of the dugout tunnel. When they reached the field, Hannegan stopped, letting Soos continue to the far end of the Colonials' bench area. Ryan wanted to soak in all that lay in front of him. The color of the sky matched the royal blue of their Boston caps, and a light breeze softened a temperature of about eighty degrees. The shirt-sleeved crowd formed a sea of colors, moving in a rhythm that only a baseball setting can provide. The aromas of popcorn, beer, onions and hot dogs mixed with the scent of fresh-cut grass and pine tar as they wafted into the Colonials' dugout. Hannegan took a deep breath and then joyfully exclaimed, "Ain't nothing like that smell, baby!" It was going to be all right; he was home.

The overflow crowd let loose even before the final notes of the national anthem had been completed. With the perfect day as a backdrop, these two bitter rivals took the field for the ultimate game of their series, the ultimate game of their seasons. D.P. Perryton had set his rotation to have Ellis Nance as his man for the final game — if it was necessary — and Peter Palguta had done the same for the Horsemen with his ace, Buddy Pickens. Nance had won all three of his starts against New York, and he had tasted victory in five of his seven decisions since returning from the injured list. The Big E gave up just one hit in the first two innings, and he had the crowd on his feet when he struck out Dave Bock with a fastball that registered ninety-five miles per hour on the radar screen posted on the big scoreboard. Not bad for a pitcher who was in sight of his fortieth birthday.

Buddy Pickens had not been as dominant against the Colonials as he was against the rest of the American Conference this season, but that didn't detract from his reputation. Buddy Pickens had been a big game pitcher throughout his career, and this game was another opportunity to reinforce that claim. The strapping Texan set down the first four Boston hitters, punching the air after striking out Ramon Morientes to begin the Boston half of the second inning. His cocky stance didn't change as Hannegan stepped into the left-hand batter's box for his first at-bat.

"Get your cheatin' ass in there, Hannegan, so I can send you right back to where all you losers belong!"

Hannegan asked for and received time from Bill Wazevich, the home plate umpire. He stepped out of the box and glared out at the New York pitcher.

"You heard me, Hannegan; don't give me any of your macho bullshit. I don't care how many times you've gotten lucky against me; it's not going to happen today. When it matters, you're always going to be a loser!"

The game's leading hitter continued to stare out at the Horsemen's pitcher before stepping back into the batter's box. Hannegan swung badly at Pickens' first offering and then took the next pitch, which was inside for ball one. A slicing foul into the third base grandstands ran the count in Pickens' favor.

"Hannegan steps out of the box and adjusts his batting gloves. Now he climbs back in . . . tugs on the right sleeve of his jersey and taps the top of his helmet . . . Pickens kicks into his motion and fires . . ."

Long-time baseball observers say a certain sound indicates how well a ball is hit. Others contend it is the speed of the ball's departure from home plate or the arc of its flight that is the best barometer. A rare few even believe one can smell the burning friction from leather on wood when the ball has been hit perfectly. Whether it was sight, or sound, or smell, there was no doubt that Hannegan had gotten it all!

"A swing and a drive . . . WAY BACK . . . gone to the bleachers in left!"

The roar of the Boston faithful drowned out the stream of obscenities from Buddy Pickens. Hannegan's twenty-fifth homer of the year continued his improbable string of successes against one of the game's great pitchers. It was Ryan's one hundred ninety-ninth hit for the season, and it gave Boston the early advantage.

The Horsemen came back to tie the score in the fourth inning on an RBI from Casey Hegan. Otherwise, the two veteran hurlers were on their games, limiting the hits allowed or choking off rallies when someone did reach base. The crowd hung on every pitch, reacting emotionally to each ebb and flow of the game. Even in the press box, where veteran reporters usually take an impassive approach, everyone was caught up in the dramatic intensity of this final battle.

Particularly interested was Jayvee DellVecchio. She was still trying to digest what she had learned from Ryan last night. Jayvee had listened patiently as he had revealed his story, and she had fought to keep her emotions in check when she asked him questions. She wasn't sure what she should do, how she should react. Ryan explained to her why he had done what he had done, and he begged her to let the situation play itself out. Reluctantly, she agreed. Hannegan was gone before she had awakened, and she was worried about his frame of mind. The clubhouses had been closed to the media when Jayvee arrived at the ballpark that morning, and that only added to her anxiety. The home run in the second inning was somewhat comforting, but she didn't begin to relax — not that much anyway — until he looked up at her in the press box and smiled following his base hit in the fifth inning.

With two outs in the bottom of the seventh, Hannegan notched his third straight safety with a ringing single to right. The trio of hits kept alive his chance to hit .400, but the thought of making history wasn't on Hannegan's mind as he edged away from first with his lead. The game was running out of opportunities, so if he could get himself into scoring position, perhaps Doc might be able to bring him home. At two balls and one strike on Dennis Soos — a good count for running — Hannegan made his move.

"... there goes Hannegan," Tom Kingery screamed, "... Soos swings and misses ... Jones fires to second and Hannegan is ... OUT. That ends the seventh ... the game remains tied at one here on the Colonials Radio Network ..."

Both teams went up and down in order in the eighth. It didn't seem possible any more tension could be added to the atmosphere in Patriots' Harbor, but somehow, the pressure ratcheted up a little more as the potential final inning got underway. The closers for the Horsemen and the C's were throwing in their respective bullpens, but D.P. Perryton and Peter Beckwith had shown no signs yet of pulling their ace pitchers.

Nelson Cuevas led off the New York ninth, and on a two-two pitch, the Horsemen' speedy center fielder sliced a ball over the head of Doc Soos at third. Junichi hustled in quickly over to foul territory in short left field and made a perfect throw to second base, but Cuevas slid into the bag just before Kevin Kyle could slap a tag on him. Kyle and the Boston crowd screamed in protest, but the television replays seemed to back up the call on the play. New York had the go-ahead run in scoring position with nobody out.

"... Now it's Dave Bock. The New York slugger has been terrific since returning from his suspension and he's one for three this afternoon ... Nance checks Cuevas at second ... here's the pitch ... Bock squares to bunt and he lays one down the third base line... Soos comes charging in... his throw to Morientes... in time... that's out number one..."

Bock's surprising bunt — his first sacrifice of the season — put Cuevas, the go-ahead run at third. The Boston bullpen signaled Hwang Sang Hwan was ready, so Dudley Perryton made a slow walk to the mound.

"Tough call for me here, Big E. What do you think?"

"This might be my last game, D.P. I think I've earned the right to finish this thing."

"I've got Wang nice and fresh out there in the pen... I can make the move."

"Please, D.P! I can finish it."

The Boston manager continued his discussion with his star pitcher, while the rest of the Colonials' infielders, who had gathered around the mound, listened intently. Finally, Perryton departed the diamond without making a pitching change. The crowd cheered with gratitude: they wanted the team's longtime leader to stay in the ball game. Now it was up to Ellis Nance to justify the faith of his manager and his fans by figuring a way to keep Nelson Cuevas from scoring.

Casey Hegan, the power-hitting first baseman for the Horsemen, was the next scheduled hitter, and Boston decided to put him on with an intentional walk. D.P. Perryton didn't like putting another man on base, but he was after a better matchup for Nance and the opportunity for a double play. The next New York batter, Chris Jones, did not have good speed. If the Big E could induce Jones to hit a ground ball at one of the Boston infielders, the C's might be able to turn the twin kill and prevent Cuevas from scoring.

"...Jones has grounded into just five double plays on the season because he always seems to put the ball in the air... Big E has got to find a way to get Jones to put one on the ground..."

With the count two balls and two strikes, Ellis Nance threw a splitfinger, hoping for a strikeout or that double play ground ball.

"...swing and a fly ball to center field... Hannegan is going to have plenty of room... Cuevas is tagging up at third..."

The Boston crowd drew in their collective breath as the ball took flight over the infield; at his position, Ryan Hannegan's heart sank. Damn! I'll never get Cuevas. The ball hung tantalizingly in the air as Hannegan positioned himself to get off as strong and as accurate a throw as he could.

"... Hannegan is lining up to make a throw to the plate ... he makes the catch ... Cuevas tags and here he comes to the plate ..."

As soon as the ball thudded into his glove, Ryan made a quick hop step and launched his throw towards Ramon Morientes, the Boston cutoff man, who was positioned near the mound. Casey Hegan tagged up from first at the same time as Nelson Cuevas did from third. Ramon Morientes recognized that Hannegan's throw would not get Cuevas at the plate, and the yelling from the other Colonials' infielders told him there might be a play at second.

"... Morientes cuts off the throw and fires to Horrado ... the slide and Hegan is out ... but Bill Wazevich is signaling that Cuevas touched home before the out at second, so the run will count. We're going to the bottom of the ninth ... three outs left to the Colonials season ... it's New York two and Boston one ..."

When Bill Wazevich signaled that the run counted, the groan of despair from Patriots' Harbor could probably be heard in Peabody. Ellis Nance hurled his glove off the back wall of the dugout as he came off the field. He had done a yeoman's job of keeping the Colonials in the game, but it might not be enough. In the New York dugout, Peter Beckwith had decided to turn the game over to his closer, Matt Lerner. The Horsemen players not on the field gathered on the top step of the dugout to watch their finisher put the team back into the playoffs once again.

The Boston supporters exhorted their warriors to find some way to rally, but their intensity lost some power when Lerner struck out Eric Polick, who was pinch-hitting for Ellis Nance. Hopes rose when Fernando Horrado dropped a perfect bunt along the first base line and then beat Lerner's throw with a headfirst slide. Two outs left, but now the tying run was on base. The noise level grew louder when Kevin Kyle knocked Lerner's next pitch into left field for a single that moved Fernando Horrado to second. Now the potential playoff securing run was on base, and the C's had the heart of their order coming up.

"... this place is rocking ... two on one out and here comes Junichi ..."

Once again, Tom Kingery was standing in his broadcast booth, but he was just like everyone else in the ballpark except the writers in the press box.

"Junichi had a hit back in the third off Pickens . . . a ball that finds some space here could be the difference for Boston . . . Lerner's ready . . . here's the pitch . . . smashed to left . . . and Bock reaches out and spears the liner . . ."

Bock made the catch about waist high and fired it quickly back in towards second base. Horrado and Kyle scrambled back to their respective bases. The Patriots' Harbor crowd sank back into their seats like they had been collectively hit over the head with a two-by-four. The C's were down to their final out.

". . . that leaves it up to the 'Big Mon' . . . Ramon Morientes . . ."

Kingery's voice tried to stay upbeat but he was as fearful as any of the Boston fans.

". . . the outfield is straight away and deep . . . the Horsemen infield is looking for a force at any base on a ground ball . . ."

Ramon Morientes was an unsung star of the Colonials — even though he had been the team's cleanup hitter for a number of seasons — and it had been that way for much of his career. A quiet man from the Dominican Republic, Morientes' play was solid, if not always spectacular. This at-bat would not go unnoticed, however. The season was on the line.

Casey Hegan held Kevin Kyle on at first, while the New York middle infielders danced towards the bag at second in an attempt to shorten Fernando Horrado's lead.

". . . ball one, high and outside . . . Lerner taps the ball on his chest . . . now puts it into his glove as he leans in for the sign from Jones . . ."

Hannegan was in the on-deck circle, taking practice swings, hoping Ramon could keep the game alive for the Colonials. As he came back to the dugout after his line drive out, Junichi pulled out the medals that Ryan had given him, and nodded in encouragement at Hannegan. Ryan felt for the mamori from Ju hanging around his neck. Doc Soos was standing on the top step of the dugout behind him, yelling words of encouragement. Just one more chance . . . c'mon Big Mon . . . give me one more chance.

". . . here's Lerner's two-two pitch . . . LINED towards short . . . Kesicki leaps . . . it's over his head into left field for a base hit . . ."

Ramon Morientes smacked the ball hard and this time it fell safely in front of Dave Bock. Fernando Horrado quickly put it into high gear . . . he was going to make a run for the plate, no matter what.

". . . Bock comes up throwing . . . Horrado rounds third; he's heading for the plate . . . OHMIGOD, Hurricane has slipped . . . now he's trying to get back to third . . . Kesicki cuts the ball off and fires to third and Horrado is dead . . . NO, wait a minute . . . the Hurricane knocked the ball out on his slide . . . HE'S SAFE! The C's are still alive. The bases are loaded and here comes Ryan Hannegan . . ."

The cheers began as a slow roar, building in intensity as Hannegan knocked the weighted donut off his bat and began to head to home plate.

"Hann-e-gan . . . Hann-e-gan . . . Hann-e-gan!"

It had all come together in, perhaps, this final moment for Ryan Hannegan. He knew what his chances were: make a hit and wonderful things would happen; make an out and his world would crash down around him. The three hits earlier in the game had raised Hannegan's batting average to .39881. If Ryan got another hit here, his average would go over .400, and in all likelihood, the Colonials would be heading to the postseason.

With Hannegan approaching the batter's box, Peter Beckwith popped out of the New York dugout to speak with Matt Lerner. The Horsemen's skipper had no intention of pulling his pitcher — there was no one working in their bullpen — but he knew Lerner needed a chance to regroup. Beckwith also wanted to remind his bullpen star that Hannegan had belted a grand slam homer against Lerner back in May . . . as if Lerner needed a reminder. The conference didn't last long, and as Beckwith departed the field, one could feel the entire ballpark leaning forward, trying to get even closer to the drama, as if that were possible.

When he hit the grand slam off Lerner in the spring, Hannegan had been able to battle back from an 0-2 count. Digging in to await the first pitch, Ryan knew he couldn't afford to follow that script this time. Lerner was a power pitcher's power pitcher, and in this situation, it was unlikely that he would use anything but his best weapon: the heat! Sure enough, his opener to Hannegan was a fastball up and in, that Hannegan fought off, producing a sizzling foul ball into the seats to the left. A second fastball in the same area sailed a little, and Ryan took it to even the count at one ball and one strike.

Hannegan asked for time and stepped out of the batter's box. He turned on his inner guide and tried to pull up the soothing confidence he needed so desperately. *That's it, Ryan. Stay relaxed. Lerner's the guy that has to be worried . . . he's got the bases loaded.* As he touched the pine tar on the upper part of the handle of his bat for a little extra grip, Ryan scanned the stands. The crowd had melted into one solid being, moving and gesturing in frantic fashion, releasing an incredible sound that rose and fell in reaction to each action on the field. If there wasn't so much pressure, the scene would have been almost laughable. He did manage a small grin as he reclaimed his position at the plate.

Lerner's next pitch was a dandy slider, and he caught the Boston hitter by surprise. Ryan took the pitch that was right on the edge of the strike zone.

"... Ball two ... just missed according to Bill Wazevich and is he hearing from the New York dugout. Lerner is stomping around on the mound. This is a guy, folks, who has walked only eight men in more than fifty appearances this season ... I don't think he ever feels he's out of the strike zone ..."

The next four pitches were fastballs in various locations, but all in the strike zone. Hannegan swung through the first one to make the count two balls and two strikes. The next three he managed to foul away, one of which he barely made contact. Both combatants took deep breaths and peered at each other, trying to catch a glimpse of some chink in the other's armor. Four more fastballs followed, and Ryan made contact but couldn't put into play any of the first three. On the fourth, Lerner overthrew it, sending the pitch into the dirt to make the count full.

"... eleven pitches thrown and we're still here ... three balls and two strikes ... bases loaded, two outs ... the Horsemen up two to one in the bottom of the ninth ..."

The madhouse crowd didn't know what to do. The possibility that every pitch could be the last made the fans expend more energy than they thought possible. Now drained by the experience, a momentary stillness enveloped Patriots' Harbor. It was an eerie silence ... like the moment before a tornado or thunderstorm strikes. Matt Lerner stepped off the rubber to take a stroll to the back of the mound in search of the rosin bag and a little mental recharging. Ryan Hannegan took the opportunity to step away from the batter's box.

"W-T-F time, Ryno," Dennis Soos yelled from the on-deck circle. The other Colonials were aligned on the top step of the dugout, showing their support with words and gestures. All the ups and downs in his relationship with some of his teammates during the course of the season were forgotten. Everyone was focused on one thing: win the game and get to the postseason.

His thoughts were loud in his head. All down to this, Ryan. The Big E wants one more shot. Junichi and what he's been through. And of course, Doc. There's never been anyone better, my friend. It's just like you said, Mrs. D. . . . nothing meant more to your husband than his teammates. Mike DellVecchio would have given up hitting four hundred in a heartbeat if his team could have won. Hannegan had never won a title at any level of his baseball career — and .400 or not — he wanted to have that chance to taste the sweetness of victory.

Matt Lerner was back to the pitching rubber, so Hannegan found his toehold in the left side of the batter's box and got himself ready. A quick tug on the right sleeve of his jersey, a tap on the top of his batting helmet, a few practice swings . . . this was it. For all the times with this great game . . . from playing catch with Mom when I was a kid . . . through all those nights banging around in the minors . . . to reach this point with these men wearing Boston across the front of their uniforms . . . for Michaela and Jayvee . . . it was time!

The crowd had caught its breath, and now the sound built to its highest point yet, everyone sensing this was going to be the pitch to decide everything. Lerner agreed to the sign from his catcher and came to a set position on the mound. A quick glance to the baserunners before starting his delivery, the New York fireballer unleashed his pitch with an inhuman grunt. At ninety-nine miles per hour, the ball came tumbling towards home plate at light speed. Ryan Hannegan took his timing step as the four-seamer began its rise towards the upper limits of the strike zone . . .

EPILOGUE

THE CELEBRATION WAS unlike anything ever seen before in Boston. The parade through the downtown streets brought out thousands to salute their heroes, and there was enough ticker tape that children played in piles of it up to their knees. All of New England was rejoicing over the Colonials' first Showdown championship in over seventy-five years: the Jinx was dead!

Following their playoff-clinching win against the Horsemen, the Colonials traveled to Baltimore for the American Conference semifinals. The best-of-five series was difficult since the Colonials had only one game in Boston, and because the Crabbers had the best home record in baseball during the regular season. Baltimore roughed up Raul Gomez and a tired Boston team in the first game, but the C's found life thanks to a shutout from Keith Lash in game two. The hometown crowd at Patriots' Harbor provided a cushion of support for Darren Haddad to give the Colonials a two to one advantage, even though he gave up a pair of solo homers to Nick Hamilton. Back in Baltimore the next day, the Crabbers had no chance against a determined Ellis Nance. Boston had won the first round in four games, and now it was onto the American Conference finals against St. Louis.

Junichi Nakata and Dennis Soos had big offensive series in the elimination of Baltimore, and the pair continued their fine play against the Rivermen. As if there was any doubt, Junichi demonstrated why he was one of the world's top players by driving in seven runs on eleven hits in the six games of the match-up with the Midwest Division champions. The Colonials were like a locomotive gaining speed, with one destination in mind: The Showdown.

The Seattle Stevedores swept the Atlanta Scarlett in the National Conference finals, and they appeared unstoppable, having dominated play in the NC for the last six weeks of the regular season, and by winning the first two rounds of the postseason in just eight games. That opinion grew when Seattle won the first two games of The Showdown, but such belief didn't take into account the will of Ellis Nance. Boston's ace had won the clinching games in the first two series, and the Big E delivered one of the greatest performances in the history of the BBL when he struck out seventeen Stevedores in a game three win for the Colonials. When The Showdown extended, ultimately, to a seventh and deciding game, Nance's presence on the mound made all the difference for the C's!

An interested observer to the DBC's coverage of the victory celebration in Boston was Vladimir Titov. The giant Russian watched his television as he prepared for that night's activities at his supper club in Brighton Beach. The announcers had comments about each of the Colonials players as they were introduced to the packed-to-the-rafters throng inside Patriots' Harbor, and the thousands watching and listening in the area around the ballpark. Titov was a happy man; the triumph by the Colonials had made him a great deal of money, and so had Ryan Hannegan with his remarkable season, thanks to Mad Vlad's Soviet science. Titov glanced up at the television when he heard the master of ceremonies call Ryan Hannegan to the microphone. The crowd screamed in appreciation.

"What a year for Ryan Hannegan," one of the DBC commentators noted, "especially since he had never come close to doing anything like this before in his career."

"What's truly remarkable, however," his partner countered, "was how he could take that pitch in the ninth inning against the Horsemen."

"You're right," the first announcer added. "He gave up the chance to hit .400, but ultimately, he helped his team win The Showdown."

Vladimir Titov shrugged his shoulders as he thought about that fateful ninth inning in Boston. Ryan Hannegan managed to check his swing on Matt Lerner's fastball that rose out of the strike zone, and his walk forced in Fernando Horrado with the tying run. Lerner and the Horsemen were dead at that point, although it took Dennis Soos's single on the very next pitch to actually score Kevin Kyle with the winning tally. Hannegan's base on balls would go down as the most famous in the history of baseball because of what it had meant.

"Ah, Ryanovich," Titov said aloud to the television where the image showed an exuberant Ryan Hannegan in a bear hug with Dennis Soos. "I could have made even more money if you had taken a hack at that pitch. But I am not greedy. We both came out winners, my friend!"

Titov's musings were interrupted by a member of his staff.

"Vladimir, you must come see this."

"What's the matter?"

"There is something that came with today's shipment, and . . . well, just come and take a look."

Vladimir Titov groaned a little as he pulled his large frame out of the chair and followed the cook into the kitchen of his restaurant. Workers were unloading that day's supply of vegetables, meats, and other foodstuffs, but they were giving wide berth to a rather large package in the center of the deliveries. Pulling back the top flap on the box, Titov looked inside, only to step away laughing as he slapped his forehead.

"Ryanovich, my friend," Mad Vlad boomed incredulously. "You must be Russian!"

Inside the box lay six heavy plastic bags filled with a thick, red liquid, all sealed tightly and . . . unopened.